Fierce Fragile Hearts

Praise:

'Barnard has a real talent for honest, flawed characters who you cannot help but fall in love with' *Bookseller*

'This book is exquisite' Holly Bourne, author of *All the Places I've Cried in Public*

'This companion to *Beautiful Broken Things* is a vital, powerful portrayal of the complexities of mental health, friendship and love.' LoveReading4Kids

Books by Sara Barnard

Beautiful Broken Things
A Quiet Kind of Thunder
Goodbye, Perfect
Fierce Fragile Hearts
Destination Anywhere

Floored
A collaborative novel

Fierce Fragile Hearts

SARA BARNARD

MACMILLAN

First published 2019 by Macmillan Children's Books

This edition published 2021 by Macmillan Children's Books
an imprint of Pan Macmillan
The Smithson, 6 Briset Street, London, EC1M 5NR
EU representative: Macmillan Publishers Ireland Limited,
Mallard Lodge, Lansdowne Village, Dublin 4
Associated companies throughout the world
www.panmacmillan.com

ISBN 978-1-5290-3761-6

'There is freedom waiting for you' by Erin Hanson from Reverie:
The Poetic Underground #1 (lulu.com, 2012). Copyright © Erin Hanson.
**Every effort has been made to trace the copyright holders, but if any
have been inadvertently overlooked the publisher will be pleased
to make the necessary arrangement at the first opportunity.**

1 3 5 7 9 8 6 4 2

A CIP catalogue record for this book is available from the British Library.

Printed and bound by CPI Group (UK) Ltd, Croydon CR0 4YY

For Tom, my co-pilot

'There is freedom waiting for you,
On the breezes of the sky,
And you ask, "What if I fall?"
Oh, but my darling,
What if you fly?'

Erin Hanson

1

'Flames'
David Guetta & Sia

I have lost my necklace, and it feels like a sign.

'What are you doing?' Josh asks, voice sleepy and muffled.

'Nothing,' I say. I'm actually crawling around under the covers, my hands sliding over the sheets, searching. I brush his leg and he yelps. 'Sorry. Did you see my necklace earlier? I was wearing it, right?'

'What necklace?'

I shouldn't be offended, but I am. 'You're so observant – Yes!' My fingers close around the thin chain and I sigh with relief. I climb out from under the covers and lean over to switch on the light.

Josh yelps again. 'Christ, Suze, what are you doing now?'

'I have to go,' I say, pulling on my jeans with one hand and shaking out my necklace with the other. 'Oh, shit.' It's *broken*, the chain split a few links down from the clasp. I stare at it for a moment, half into my jeans, half out of them. The dove looks so lonely, set adrift on a broken chain.

'Should I get up?' Josh asks.

I roll my eyes. 'Don't put yourself out or anything. It's not like I'm leaving tomorrow. Or . . .' I pull my phone out of the pocket of my jeans and check the time. 'Today.' It's later than I thought. Or earlier, depending on your point of view. It had felt like a good idea to see Josh rather than spend my last night in Southampton not sleeping in my own bed, but now it's after 4 a.m. and I've got a broken necklace and what might be the beginnings of a headache pressing at the base of my skull. Well done, me. Solid decision-making skills, as usual.

I wrap my necklace around my wrist so it hangs as a loose, tangled bracelet and dress quickly, glancing back at Josh as I open the door to leave.

'I'll see you,' Josh says.

'Sure,' I say.

He grins. 'Take care of yourself, yeah?'

I don't reply, just smile back and lift my hand in a wave goodbye. I head out of the building, taking the steps at a jog. The outside air is cool and I pull up the hood of my jacket, breathing it in. It's going to be a beautiful day in Southampton.

It's about a mile from Josh's to mine and I take it slowly, hands in my pockets. The streets are deserted, which is how I like it best. I take a detour along the harbour and allow myself a few minutes, pulling myself up on to the railing to sit and watch the dawn break in pink streaks across the sky. It's quiet except for the seagulls and the soft, calming swish of the sea against the boats.

I know that when I get home, or what's passed for home for the last eighteen months or so, there'll be boxes in my room and packing to do and goodbyes to say. My foster parents, Christie and Don, will make French toast and we'll go through my transition plan for the thousandth time while we wait for Sarah, my aunt, to arrive to take me back to Brighton.

I close my eyes and listen to the seagulls, which sound exactly the same in Southampton as they ever did in Brighton. Maybe they're even the same seagulls, travelling from one coastal city to another when they get bored or restless. It must be nice not to be tied down like that.

I'm the queen of fresh starts, which is another way of saying I've lived a lot of failures. I've thought *things will be different this time* more than once, but this time it's actually true, for good or bad, whether I want it or not. This time, I'm eighteen. I'm an adult. I'm legally independent.

This time, I'm on my own.

'Good morning, sunshine.' Don greets me when I come through the back door. He's sitting at the kitchen table, paper spread in front of him.

'Hey,' I say. I lock the door behind me and hang the key on its hook. 'You're up early.'

Don smiles. 'Look who's talking.'

I shrug. 'If I don't sleep, does it still count as my last night?'

'That is an interesting question,' Don says, pointing at me. 'Is sleep an essential component of the night? What, in fact, is night? Perhaps it is an illusion?'

I smile. 'I'll nap, OK?' I pause on my way out of the kitchen. 'You weren't waiting for me, were you?'

Don busies himself with the paper. 'They think it might get up to twenty-five degrees today.'

I rest my head against the door frame. 'I'm fine.'

'You should put that on a T-shirt,' Don says, glancing at me to smile. 'Save yourself some time.'

He's worried about me; they all are. All the people who've guided me through the last two years to get me to this place, my shot at independence. Outwardly, they're keeping positive, but I know what they're really thinking. They're thinking that I won't be able to handle this, that I'm going to fall apart.

I'm much more stable than I used to be, which is a lot to do with my medication and also, you know, actual stability, but that's the problem now; the ending of the stability part. Me moving on from Christie and Don – leaving the care system – to live on my own is pretty *un*stable. And I've got previous on falling apart. They've got good reason to worry. But I can't stay in this Southampton limbo forever, and I've waited what feels like such a long time to have some kind of control over my own life. However scary this is, and however badly it might go, I have to believe that it's worth it. Otherwise, what's the point?

Here's where I should explain why they're worried; why I fell apart before, what that even means. This is the bit I hate the most, the bit where I give up any control over how people see me. I want them to look at me and see just that: *me*. If I say that I was abused, that I'm prone to severe depression, that I've tried to kill myself more than once, all of that falls away. When someone knows you've been broken, all they see is the cracks. The knowledge colours everything, an extra filter between me and the world. People look at me differently, and maybe I look out at the world a little differently, too.

That's the thing about trauma, the thing people on the other side of it don't understand. It isn't a bump on the road of your life, a jolt that'll take your breath away, but only for a moment. It's the double yellow lines snaking on either side of everything you do, trapping you on a track down a one-way street. You can't stop. You can't pull over and take a break. You just have to keep going.

I used to think that there must be something so, so wrong with me, that my parents didn't love me enough. Something bad, something they could see, and maybe other people could too. I don't think that anymore – I'm older, I've had therapy. I understand that the wrongness is all on an abusive parent, not the child. I get that. But knowing something and feeling something are two different things. And that feeling of being wrong hasn't ever really gone away. Sometimes someone will say something, just a passing comment really, or look at me in a certain way, and my head will say, they can see it. And I'll smile bigger and dazzle harder and put on the charm until every drop of energy and light from inside of me has poured out on to them. And then when I'm alone again – I'm always alone again – I'm so drained I can't do anything except cry.

There's still so much – too much – I can't deal with. I want it all to just be something that happened, past tense, but it's not. It can't ever be, even though I'm doing so much better now – everyone says so.

Two years ago, when I first started on this track – my last great fresh start – I thought I knew what it meant, getting better. It meant *being* better. No more climbing out of windows, no more sleeping around, no more drugs, no more hoarding pills, no more lies, no more pretending. No more fake smiles. All that crazy just therapied right out of me and nothing to stop my future happiness except . . . what, exactly?

Well, life. Me. My head. My history. Take your pick.

For the record, I managed it with some of the things. I don't lie any more, or at least, not like I used to, not about things that matter. I pretend . . . less. I don't hoard pills. I don't climb out of windows. Everything else . . . well, let's just say I'm a work in progress. And that's OK, right? You can't have everything.

And now I'm moving on again, and this time there's a plan to follow. Me, now officially a care leaver, returning to Brighton to learn how to live independently. I'll be living in a bedsit on the second floor of a converted Victorian terrace, the kind that's ten a penny in Brighton. I'll pay my rent with my wages from my job, housing benefit and my care leaver's allowance. It'll be tight, but doable.

And here's what's waiting for me: my favourite people. My best-in-every-sense-of-the-word friends. Sweet, loyal and goddamn *patient*, Caddy and Rosie. (I mean, I'll have them for about three months, before they both go to university. But still.

I'll be fine by then.) They have this power, my friends, even after all this time, even though I don't deserve it; they're like lamp posts on midnight streets. Lights in the dark.

I would never have believed that I'd want to live in Brighton again, but the truth is it's the only place I've ever come close to feeling like I belonged. That's what I want, more than anything; to feel like I belong, even if that just means in my own life, in my own head.

I have to believe that, finally, that's going to happen now. I'm overdue some goodness.

2

'Home'
Hollow Coves

If I had the choice – and, you know, money – I'd be moving into a gorgeous two-bed flat right by the seafront in Brighton. I'd have a four-poster bed, the kind with those random curtains. A waffle-maker in the kitchen, because why not. A guest bedroom for my friends.

But I don't have the choice (or the money) and that's why I'm walking up the steps behind Sarah to the house on Ventrella Road that is now, officially, where I live. The building has been converted into six flats, one of which is mine. It's a bedsit, which means that it's just one room with a small kitchen on one side and a tiny shower room on the other.

It's small, it's dank, it smells like damp. When I walk in, I want to cry.

'Don't worry too much about how it looks now,' Sarah says, as if she can read my mind. She picked up the keys yesterday on my behalf and had a look around, so she's had time to practise this don't-let-Suzanne-spiral voice. 'Any flat looks a bit depressing when it's as empty as this.'

I nod and try to smile. I'm imagining – and trying not to – eating, sleeping, living here. My stomach turns over. Oh God, what was I thinking, coming here? I need colour and light in my life. I need other people. How can I live in this colourless *room*? By *myself*?

The feeling comes in strong, like a sweeping tide up to my heart. *I have made a terrible mistake.*

'You've already got post,' Sarah says, trying, I can tell, to be upbeat.

I reach for the parcel on the counter, recognizing the handwriting on the label immediately. My brother. My heart lifts with hope and I open it to find that it's full of chocolate. I smile, unfolding the accompanying letter. *New home starter pack*, Brian has written. He's also included a playlist for me; twelve songs all with the same title: 'Home'. I skim the rest of the letter, which is mostly about how far I've come, that this is the next step of my life, that it's going to be fine. My brother is good at saying the right things, and I feel better when I put the letter down on the counter and turn back to Sarah, who's blowing up an airbed in the corner of the room.

'This is just temporary,' she says, seeing my face.

An *airbed*? Me, alone in an empty bedsit, trying to sleep on an *airbed*? My insomnia is bad enough as it is. 'Fine,' I say.

'I know it's not ideal,' she says. 'Honestly, I'd still rather you came back with me. At least until we get you some furniture. I know that you—'

'No,' I interrupt. 'I'm not staying with you. We talked about that.'

'Just for tonight, Suzie—'

'*No.*' I swallow, then carefully soften my voice. 'You promised that you'd let me do this by myself.'

I can tell she doesn't understand, not really. She probably thinks I'm just being stubborn, maybe even a bit petty. But it feels somehow essential to me that I start this new Brighton chapter on my own terms. If I don't, what's the point? Sarah was my legal guardian when I lived in Brighton last time, but this time I'm not her responsibility, just her niece. I don't want to be depending on Sarah. I don't want to be depending on anyone.

When the airbed is fully inflated, Sarah manages to find reasons to fuss around for another hour. She worries about the lack of furniture, wonders if she should pop back to her own flat to pick up some more blankets.

'It's June,' I say. 'I'm not going to get cold.'

'I suppose not,' she says.

'I promise I'll tell you if I need extra blankets,' I say, reaching out an idle hand to open the fridge. 'Oh,' I say out loud, momentarily confused. The fridge, which I'd expected to be empty, is full of food. I glance around to see Sarah smiling a little sheepishly at me. 'Thank you,' I say.

'You know I can't bear an empty fridge,' she says lightly.

It's still another half an hour before she leaves, and even then it's basically because I hustle her out the door, promising to check in tomorrow to prove I survived the night.

As soon as she's gone, I don't give myself time to think about being on my own. Before I've even closed the door behind her, I'm pulling out my phone and sending a **READY!** message to Caddy and Rosie. It takes just ten minutes for them to turn up on the doorstep of the building, God love them. They're falling over each other, breathless and laughing, weighted down by sleeping stuff and a giant cardboard box. As soon as I open the door, Caddy drops her load and launches herself at me for a hug.

'We've been waiting *all day*,' Rosie says from behind her. I look at her over Caddy's shoulder and she rolls her eyes at me, smiling.

'And now you're here!' Caddy releases me and takes a little step back, her eyes shiny but anxious, surveying me. 'Are you happy?'

'*Now* I am,' I say, and she beams.

'Can I say hi now?' Rosie asks.

'HI!' I yell, bubbly with happiness. My girls. My very best friends, here for me, like they always are.

'We brought stuff,' Caddy announces, stepping aside to let me hug Rosie (she lets me, even though she's not much of a hugger) and leaning down to pick up the box. 'Come see!' She bounds off into the building calling, 'Which flat is it?' over her shoulder.

'Five,' I call back. 'Up the stairs.' I turn back to Rosie, who is grinning her trademark smirk-grin.

'Happy to be back?' she asks.

'We'll see,' I say, and she puts her hands on my shoulders to look me square in the eye.

'So long as you're being positive,' she says. She follows me into the building and up the stairs to my flat, where Caddy is standing in the middle of the small room, box at her feet. I catch the look on her face before she paints a smile over it at the sight of me. At best, she's thrown by this place, though who knows what she expected. At worst, she's actively judging it. And me.

There's a short silence as Rosie looks around and ends up standing next to Caddy. She turns to me. 'Is this it?' she asks, and Caddy gives her a shove.

'Uh-huh,' I say. I hear that my voice sounds a little flat so I add, more brightly, 'Bit of a fixer-upper, right?'

'Where's all the furniture?' Caddy asks, a slight, confused frown crinkling her forehead.

'I haven't got it yet,' I say. 'But it'll get sorted.'

They both look at me, dubious expressions on their faces. They just can't *fathom* having to live in a bedsit without any furniture, that no parent is going to come rushing in to save the day, and I almost hate them for it. I take a breath, swallow it down, let a smile fill my face instead.

'Real beds are so overrated.'

'I've heard that,' Rosie says. 'Also, tables.'

'And chairs. I mean, you can just sit on the floor, right?'

'We might have some spare furniture,' Caddy says thoughtfully.

Thought*lessly*. 'I'll ask my parents.'

'No,' I say, with more edge than I'd intended. *I am not your charity case*. 'I'll get it sorted. Can we drop it?'

She looks hurt. 'OK, fine.'

Oh God, this is going well. 'Listen,' I say, because sometimes you just have to say it. 'If this is too weird for you, I'd rather you just left, because it's hard enough as it is.'

'Don't be stupid,' Rosie says lightly. 'We came here to see you. We don't give a shit about how much furniture you have. Ignore Caddy, she can't help being a fixer.'

'I'd rather you didn't ignore me,' Caddy says. 'If that's OK.'

'Actually,' Rosie says, staring straight into my face. 'You know what you need to do?'

When she doesn't answer her own question, I prompt, 'What?'

'Cry.'

Not what I'd expected her to say. 'What?'

'That's what you need. You need to cry, and we need to comfort you, and then we'll all feel better.' She nods, satisfied. 'So can you get right on that?'

I try really hard not to laugh, but it escapes anyway.

'What we all *need*,' Caddy says in a surprisingly firm voice, 'is wine.' She reaches into her rucksack and pulls out a bottle.

'Oh yeah,' I say.

'Oh yeah,' Rosie echoes. 'I forgot we were adults now.'

'Weird, right?' I say.

She nods. 'So weird.'

'Come on,' Caddy says, waving the bottle a little and nudging the box with her foot. 'See what we brought you, Suze.'

'Is it furniture?' I ask, and Rosie laughs.

'No,' Caddy says. 'There are fairy lights in there, though.'

I feel my face break out into a genuine smile, and it's such a relief. 'I love you.'

She throws me a grin; earnest, full of affection. Total Caddy. 'I know.'

We use the blankets and cushions Sarah had left me to make a fort in the middle of the room, just big enough for three, and it's perfect. We're sitting so close our knees are almost touching, the box they'd brought in the middle.

'OK, are you ready?' Caddy's eyes are bright and happy again, her voice light, back on steady ground. 'Cos there's an order to this presentation.'

'So ready,' I say, grinning back.

It takes a long time to go through the contents of my welcome box because they insist on explaining every item, taking longer and longer the more wine they drink. There's a Tupperware carton of crumbly and cracked macarons, garishly pink and stuffed with jam. A 'Welcome Home' playlist that Caddy insists we put on immediately. A fabric doorstop shaped like a bulldog. A recipe book for students. A bag of mint imperials. A box of condoms. A single mango. A thin silver bracelet with a wishbone charm holding it together. The last item Rosie produces is a framed photograph of the three of us, taken at Caddy's eighteenth. It's a candid picture; the three of us caught mid-laughter, Rosie's hand pressing teasingly against my face, Caddy hanging off my back.

Nothing is useful (except the condoms). Everything is perfect.

'This is amazing,' I say, clutching the photo frame and trying not to cry. 'You guys are just . . .'

'We know,' Rosie says cheerfully.

'We are so just,' Caddy agrees. They both laugh.

'So very just,' Rosie says, lifting her glass. 'To being just!'

We order pizza – they insist on paying – and drink the second bottle of wine they'd brought until we're full and happy. All of my doubt and hesitation is gone. Of course I should be here – how could I ever have thought I belonged anywhere else *but* here, with my best friends, these people who love me? This was the right decision. Everything is going to be better now. This is the fresh start that will stick.

Because they are good people and they love me, they don't even complain when they realize that the airbed definitely won't fit three people on it. Rosie refuses to share it with either of us, so she goes to sleep in the fort, leaving enough room on the airbed for Caddy and me. The warmth of Caddy beside me and the sound of the two of them breathing sends me into an immediate, easy sleep.

3

'Flying Solo'
Keri Noble

In the morning, Rosie leaves early to get changed at home before going to work. At 10 a.m., Caddy's boyfriend, Kellan, comes to pick her up.

'Hey, you,' he says to me, beaming, opening his arms for a hug. Because of my self-imposed, almost total exile from Brighton, Kel and I don't know each other that well, but still he greets me like a friend. That's the kind of guy he is. 'Welcome . . .' He hesitates, glancing at Caddy, then back at me. '. . . home?'

'Thanks,' I say, accepting the hug. 'What are you guys doing today?'

'We were just going to chill together,' Kel says, like this is the most natural thing in the world. I assume he means sex, though this is still not something I can quite equate with my friend Caddy, who once asked me, in a tipsy whisper, eyes wide, to tell her what a penis felt like to touch.

Kel is twenty and will be starting his final year of university, where he's studying Engineering, in September. He and Caddy met, improbably enough, on a bus, a few months after I left Brighton. When she first told me this story, I flat-out didn't believe her, because Caddy's not the kind of person to chat with a stranger on a bus, let alone flirt with them. 'Maybe I was channelling my inner you,' she said when I pointed this out, and then she laughed, adding, 'Or maybe it was meant to be.'

'How about you?' Kel asks now. 'Big plans?'

'I'm meeting my personal adviser,' I say, even though I know that by saying this I'm opening up the kind of conversation that I find so enragingly tedious. Usually I'd just lie, but I don't want to start my new, adult, Brighton life by lying to people I like.

'What's that?' Kel asks, on cue.

'Sort of like a social worker,' I say. 'For care leavers.' It's the easiest way to describe what basically amounts to practical help with living when you don't have parents looking out for you. My personal adviser, Miriam, taught me how to budget, explained what funding I'm entitled to, helped me apply for jobs.

'Oh, cool,' he says easily, as if 'cool' is the right word for this. 'It's good they don't just, like, set you adrift.'

My jaw clenches, my teeth grinding down hard, but somehow I still smile and nod, because I've been able to fake a smile since I was about six. It's not Kel's fault he's so clueless. Why should he know what to say?

They stick around for a little longer, which is sweet of them, before I promise that I'm fine and tell them to go and have their day together. I watch them walk off down the street, hand in hand, both of them smiling the thoughtless smiles of the casually happy.

I spend the next couple of hours tacking photos up on to the bare walls and playing with my phone until Miriam arrives with deli sandwiches, two bottles of orange juice and a stack of paperwork.

'Hello, Suzanne,' she says, cheerful.

'Hi,' I say.

'Welcome home,' she says, which is so kind I feel instantly terrible for judging her for wearing Converse even though she's in her forties.

She spends the whole afternoon with me – I'm imagining it written into her work diary: *S. Watts, 1 p.m. to 5 p.m.* – and we go through the moving-in checklist she's brought, talking through what I need, what my home allowance covers. We go into town so I can get boring things like kitchen supplies. She asks me how I'm feeling so many times I lose track of what the real answer is.

We stop off at Madeline's, the coffee shop where I'll be working full time from Friday, so I can pick up my uniform and sign my contract. Miriam buys us both a coffee and sits in the corner to wait for me. Before I follow Tracey, my new manager, round the back, I see Miriam pull out her notebook and start writing. A checklist of her own, probably. One I'm not allowed to see.

I'd found the job at Madeline's by myself, in the end, despite all the options Miriam and I had talked through when we were working on my pathway plan. So much of the conversation about my upcoming post-care life had been focused around my 'future', which meant 'a career'; 'where' I was going, that kind of thing. I could go back to education, she said. I could get my qualifications for . . . something. She expected me to know what that something was, but I didn't. I still don't. As far as I'm concerned, I've got a job, and that's enough.

Miriam comes back to Ventrella Road with me for another cup of tea before she leaves at almost exactly 5 p.m. She says, 'Is there anything else you'd like to talk about?' and I shake my head. She hesitates, her eyes flicking from the airbed in the corner to my face. 'Remember that I'm here if it starts to feel hard,' she says. I'm not sure what she means, really. *Life* is hard, all the time. 'Call or text, or even email, if that's easier for you. OK?'

I nod. I know I won't. I'm not going to contact Miriam outside our mandated eight-weekly meet-ups unless it's completely unavoidable. It's nice to know she's there, I guess, whatever 'there' means, but I'm never going to forget that ultimately I'm just another part of her job, one of many care leavers on her list.

'I'm here to help you, so you don't have to do things by yourself,' she adds when I don't speak.

'I'm meant to be learning to be independent,' I say.

'Being independent doesn't mean not accepting help,' she says. 'Quite the opposite, in fact.' She inclines her head a little to force me to meet her eye, and I shrug, trying to smile. 'I'd really like to hear from you before our next meeting in August,' she says. 'Just to check in.'

Her list is probably alphabetical by surname. I'll be at the bottom – W for Watts – in an inbox divided neatly into folders, one for each of us. When she gets home, her wife, whose name I know is Caroline, will say, 'How was work?' And she'll say, 'Oh, fine. Another one moving in.' And Caroline will smile and say, 'Ah, the checklist?' And Miriam will laugh and nod.

I sound bitter, don't I?

'Good luck,' Miriam says, filling the silence because I haven't spoken. 'Bye, Suzanne.'

When she's gone, I put away the stuff I bought and then sit on the airbed, alone in my four walls for the first real time. I look around, listening to the silence. It's so quiet. *So? This is what you wanted. This is what independence looks like.*

Independence looks lonely.

I pull out my phone to text Caddy or Rosie, then hesitate, my thumb paused over the screen. It's only half past five on my first day on my own in this flat. I don't want to be the kind of person who sees her friends just because she doesn't want to be alone. I don't want to lean on them. They're my friends, not my crutch.

But it's *so quiet*.

I open my laptop and find an old playlist my brother Brian made me – 'Cheerful Songs for Sadful Days', one of my favourites – and turn it up. I dance around until I'm out of breath. I raid the fridge to see what Sarah's left me – lots of vegetables, a carton of soup, toffee yogurts, butter, eggs, cheese – and make a frittata for dinner. It's not satisfying, cooking for one. I sit on the windowsill to eat, the plate on my knees.

When it's dark, I spiral. I pace the length of the floor, back and forth, trying to settle. What do people who live alone *do* in the evenings? I should have asked Sarah. I could still ask Sarah. I could call her. I should call her. I take out my phone, bring her number up on screen, change my mind. I think about breaking into the stash of weed I was saving for when things got tough, but they'll get tougher than this.

I call my brother. We talk for half an hour. He asks how I'm doing and I tell him about Caddy and Rosie, the coffee shop, the frittata. I don't say, 'I am so much better with other people.' I don't say, 'Will I ever be OK?'

At midnight, I try to go to bed, but I just lie there in the dark getting worse and worse until I get back up again, put some clothes on and leave the flat. It's a calm night, cool and quiet. I go to the beach and it helps.

I sit on the pebbles, my arms wrapped around my knees, listening to the sound of the waves. Just over two years ago, I sat on this beach, armed with pills and vodka, ready for the end of everything. It's thanks to Rosie and Caddy that it didn't work, but we've never – *ever* – talked about that. What's there to say, anyway? 'Thank you' is both completely inadequate and also at least half a lie. What I feel is a lot more complicated than that, but they'd never understand. *I* don't even really understand.

It's not that I don't want to live. I just wish I was living a life that . . . isn't this.

By the time I haul myself up and go home it's after 2 a.m. and I'm finally tired enough to sleep. I curl myself up into a ball under the covers and try to think about good things so I might have nice dreams. Sunflowers. Macarons. Puppies. Dresses that fit just right. The way Caddy smiles when she sees me. The look on Rosie's face when I make her laugh. Thunderstorms when you're safe inside.

The playlists my brother makes me. Sunrises. Sunsets. Bus drivers waving at each other. Koala bears. Baymax from *Big Hero 6*.

I dream about dinosaurs.

Over the next few days, I get myself settled into my new Brighton life and home, like a nesting bird. I use Freecycle to find a wardrobe and a table (more of a coffee table than an actual table, but whatever, there's only one of me) and trawl the charity shops and flea markets for small things to make the bedsit seem just a little bit more like mine. By the end of the week, I have basically all the furniture I need, except a bed. It turns out that getting a bed when you're poor is a pain in the neck. I can find bedframes for free – or at least as cheap as I can afford – but I'm not about to take a second-hand mattress. Buying them new is out of my price range for now, so I just sleep on the airbed as the days begin to pass, and it's fine. I hang the fairy lights that Caddy and Rosie gave me, but I get paranoid about my electricity bill, so I only turn them on when they visit.

It surprises me how much I like working at Madeline's. It's not just the fact that the shop itself is cheerful and cosy, with art prints of everything even remotely coffee-related all over the walls, and my workmates are friendly. It's the routine of it all. I love being part of the rota, knowing exactly how my shift works. I like knowing what I have to do and doing it. Some of the customers are annoying, but most of them aren't. I like that I'm already getting to know the regulars, learning their orders and having them ready for when they appear in the mornings. Plus, I get paid. That's pretty great, too.

The evenings and the days when I'm not working I mostly spend with Caddy and Rosie, usually with Kel too, the four of us on the beach or in my flat or Kel's house, drinking, talking, laughing. When I'm with them I feel like a person worth being with. I feel flickers of who I can be.

Still, there are the nights, too many of them, when I have no choice but to curl up on the airbed and try to sleep in the empty silence of my bedsit. Just me, my head and my breath in the dark. Sometimes I lie awake until orange light begins to seep through the blinds and I manage a couple of hours of restless, dozing sleep.

It's enough. It's all enough. If this is my life now, it's liveable. No one is hurting me and I'm not disappointing anyone. And this bit, this crushing loneliness of an empty flat, won't be forever. This is still the transition. In three years, Caddy and Rosie will graduate and, most likely, come back to Brighton permanently. Maybe one of them will want to move out of home by then, and we can live together. Maybe even all three of us, I think, in one of my more hopeful daydreams. But even in that best-case scenario, three years is a long time. When I look around my four walls there's a familiar, sinking hollowness in my chest. Loneliness does funny things to time. It gives it width as well as length; makes it cavernous.

4

'Hoping'
X Ambassadors

It takes me about two weeks to realize that I don't have a washing machine.

By the time the penny finally drops, I've already run out of clothes. I'm standing in the kitchen area in leggings and a ratty old T-shirt, looking around, and that's the moment the blindingly obvious fact hits me. No washing machine. No way to clean all my clothes. Great.

I briefly consider taking everything over to Sarah's and asking to use *her* washing machine, but that seems too much like giving in, so I dismiss the idea. The nearest launderette, Google tells me, is a ten-minute walk away. I've never used a launderette before, and my only point of reference is a vague memory of a really old episode of that TV show *Friends* that I must have watched once, years ago.

The other thing I don't have is a laundry bag, which means there's no way to transport my huge pile of clothes across Brighton to the launderette. 'For God's sake,' I mutter to myself, kicking at a stray sock. I'm already bored by this. It's so tedious. But I still have to go through all the boring motions, because no one else is going to do it for me, and if I ignore it today, I'll still need a clean bra tomorrow. So I throw all the clothes I can fit into my suitcase, shove my feet into my Vans and leave my bedsit.

When I open the main door to the building, I groan out loud. It's raining. And not just drizzle, either; proper sheets of it. I look back at my suitcase and down at my Vans, my bare ankles. Maybe I should wait until tomorrow. I could just go back upstairs, shut the door, crawl into bed and forget the whole stupid world exists.

'Coming or going?' a voice asks.

I jolt, turning to see where the voice has come from. The door to Flat 1, the ground-floor flat, is open, and an old woman is standing there, watching me.

'Er . . .' I say.

'You're letting the rain in,' she says. 'Are you coming or going?'

How did she even know I was here? Was she watching me through the little peephole in her door? Weird.

'Going?' I say, but it comes out like a question.

'Do you want an umbrella?' I genuinely can't tell if she's making fun of me or not. There's a sort-of smile on her face, but it's so dry it might be in judgement rather than reassurance.

That's another thing I don't have, actually. An umbrella.

'I might just leave it,' I say. 'For now.'

The old woman's smile widens, just a little, like she finds me amusing. 'Maybe you should shut the door, then?'

When I do, the hall is suddenly silent. I hadn't even realized how loud the wind and rain was until it was gone. It's just me and this old woman, staring at each other.

'Are you the girl from the bedsit upstairs?' she asks. 'You're new?'

'Ish,' I say. 'A couple of weeks.'

She smiles that smile again. 'Very new, then.'

It doesn't feel new. 'I guess.'

Her eyes travel over my face, and I know what she's thinking. The same thing everyone thinks. *You're too young to be living on your own like this. What happened to you?* I wait for her to ask, but she doesn't. 'Where were you intending to go, before you found yourself thwarted by the rain?'

Her voice is refined – not posh but cultured. The kind of broad English accent that belongs to nowhere specific.

'The launderette,' I say, and then add, unnecessarily, 'I've run out of clothes.'

'I see,' she says. 'Where's your washing powder?'

I look down at myself, as if a box of Persil is just going to appear at my feet. I consider lying and telling her that it's in my suitcase, but what's the point? 'I was going to get some when I got there?'

The woman steps back into her flat, gesturing to me to follow. 'Come on in,' she says, as if this whole conversation has been leading to an invitation.

'Oh, I'm fine . . .'

'Come on,' she says again, more briskly this time. 'Let's get you sorted out.'

Oh God. I open my mouth, trying to think of a way to politely refuse, when a small, scruffy Border terrier appears at the woman's feet and I forget literally everything. 'Hi!' I say brightly, leaning down, feeling a beam stretching across my face. There is a dog in this building! A dog!

'You like dogs?' There's a smile in the woman's voice. 'This is Clarence.'

'Hello, Clarence,' I say. I hold out my hand and he sniffs, then growls. 'I know,' I say. 'That's the appropriate response. Very savvy.'

The woman laughs, low and soft. 'It takes him a while to warm to people. He's not a very friendly dog.'

'That means he's smart,' I say, straightening. I can't wipe the smile from my face. 'I'm Suzanne.'

'Well, it's very nice to meet you, Suzanne,' she says. 'I'm Dilys. Welcome to the building, two weeks ago.'

I follow her and Clarence inside, dragging the suitcase behind me. The flat I walk into is much, much bigger than mine; you could basically fit my entire bedsit into the living room. The ceilings are high and I can see at least three doors leading off into other rooms.

Palatial, I think, ridiculously. There are *two* sofas.

'Would you like some tea?' Dilys asks, already heading towards the kitchen, her movements stiff and slow. Clarence has settled himself into what is obviously his dog bed, his eyes on me.

'I can make it,' I say quickly, following Dilys. 'If you show me where the stuff is. I won't stay long, just until the rain stops.'

'Nonsense,' she says. She opens one of the cupboards and takes out two cups. 'Now, the washing machine is here.' She points. 'Go and get your clothes and I'll show you how to use it.'

I open my mouth to say that I actually know how to use washing machines, but she's already bustling past me, pouring water into the kettle, telling me about washing tabs and fabric softener.

'That's really nice of you,' I say, loudly enough to stop her talking. 'But I really can just take my stuff to the launderette.'

'You could,' she says. 'But there's a perfectly functioning washing machine right here, for free, in this nice, warm, dry flat. And there's tea. And my grumpy dog. Why would anyone say no? That would be very odd behaviour.'

I dither, glancing back towards my suitcase and then at Dilys, who is dropping a tea bag into each cup. Isn't it a bit of a weird imposition to turn up at this woman's flat and just wash my clothes? Who does that?

'It's nice to have some company,' she says then, turning to smile at me as the kettle clicks. I've smiled at people like that before. It's the hopeful smile of the lonely.

I go and get my clothes.

By the time I leave the flat, it's two hours later and the rain has long stopped. Dilys insisted that I 'might as well' use the dryer setting after the washing cycle was done, as there was 'no point' in going upstairs with a suitcase full of wet clothes. We got through three cups of tea each while the machine spun. I tried to ask questions about her but she was more interested in me, wanting to know what had brought me to Ventrella Road, why I was living in 'one of those horrible bedsits'.

I tried to be vague but I ended up telling her, when she'd made her slow way over to the kitchen and back again to get us our second round of teas, that I'd been in care. 'Just a little bit,' I added, which made no sense. 'Like, not for very long.'

'And now you're on your own?' she asked.

'Uh-huh,' I said.

She nodded and we were both quiet for a while, but not in a weird way. I wanted to ask about her family, but I wasn't sure if it would be rude. Instead, I asked about Clarence, who'd climbed up on to her lap and was watching me across the table. I learned that he was six years old, that she'd adopted him from a rescue centre. It had taken over a year for him to settle, she said. 'Something traumatized him. I don't know what, but something did. I tried to put him in a kennel once, when I was going on holiday, but I couldn't leave him behind. He was shaking so much, you'd have thought he was about to be murdered, the poor love. I've never tried since.'

'So you just never leave him?' I asked.

'Oh yes, but I don't institutionalize him. None of this kennel business. He goes to stay with my nephew, whose daughters are only too happy to spoil him in my absence.' She smiled fondly, rubbing her fingers into the top of his head.

Later, when I was loading up my warm, dry clothes into my suitcase, she'd said, 'So what is it you plan to do next time you have clothes to wash?' When I'd looked over at her, she'd been smiling.

'The launderette?'

'That's an option, certainly.' She'd nodded. 'Or . . . you could come here once a week and use my machine and my washing powder, and we can have a chat. We can agree on a time that suits us both. That would be much easier for you, yes? And cheaper?'

'That's really nice of you,' I said, flushing. 'But I can't just use you like a launderette.'

She laughed. 'My dear.' We'd known each other for two hours and I was already 'dear'. 'Let me be frank. I would very much like the company. You seem like you'd be lovely company. And you know, Clarence may even let you stroke him after a few weeks.'

I'd said yes, of course. Spending time with an old woman and her dog seemed like a more than fair trade for all the money I'd save, and anyway I'd take any excuse to spend time outside my miserable flat and with another person. I wasn't sure exactly what we'd talk about, but I figured that she was old, and so she'd probably have lots of stories.

The next day, when I stop in to see Sarah on my way home from work as promised and tell her about this arrangement, she doesn't look thrilled. 'That's very kind of her,' she says. 'But it does sound quite a bit like taking advantage.'

'It honestly felt like it would've been more rude to say no,' I say. 'She's lonely. Plus, did I mention the dog?'

'Maybe you could offer to walk the dog?' Sarah suggests. 'And you could take biscuits or something. I always feel better in that kind of situation if I'm not empty-handed.'

'Feeder,' I tease, and she smiles. 'OK. Shortbread's easy, right?'

'Yes, relatively speaking. You could add some lavender, if you wanted to make them a little less standard. That's nice in shortbread. Or rosewater!' She's getting more animated, like she does when she starts talking about baking, her eyes glazing over slightly as she retreats into the cookbook of her own head. 'I once tried adding amaretto but the consistency was all wrong. They tasted good, though.' She looks at me, her eyes focusing. 'What were we talking about?'

'Shortbread,' I say. 'Specifically, me making shortbread. Me, who has no lavender or rosewater or amaretto to bake with.'

I'm sitting up on the kitchen counter while she cooks dinner, which was my favourite place to sit when I lived here and was in a good enough mood to chat. Today, Sarah is making Normandy chicken, one of my favourites. She once told me that cooking for other people is her very favourite thing. 'Especially you,' she'd added, offhandedly, as if this was so obviously true it didn't need emphasis.

We've come a long, long way from how we used to be when I lived here. We had so many fights then. Tense, snappy arguments, but big, loud, screaming matches too. I'd never been able to fight like that at home before and it must have all been stored up inside me because she got it all. I was awful to her, even as I knew she was trying to help me. I'd wind her up, then cry when she snapped and said something that hurt. I was the queen of emotional manipulation, driving her to the edge and then blaming her when I was the one who went over. I wanted her to say things that hurt, because that was what I knew. More than once, Jill, who lived above us, had to come down and tell us to shut up. That's how bad it was. How bad *I* was.

It all seems so long ago, now I'm sitting here again talking about shortbread. Somehow, Sarah hasn't held any of what happened against me.

'So tell me,' Sarah says, sinking to her knees and peering through the oven door at the casserole dish. 'How's it all going? Shortbread aside.'

'Fine,' I say.

She stands up and looks at me. 'Fine? Oh, Henry, get down.' She pushes a hand towards the cat, who has sneaked up on to the counter beside me, unnoticed, and is trying to get a good look into the saucepan.

'Yeah. Not amazing, but not shit, either. Fine.'

'Down!' Sarah scoops up the cat and drops him on to the floor, where he stays, indignant, swishing his tail at her. Sarah got the cat, a chocolate point Siamese she named Henry Gale, not long after I moved out. 'I'm lonely,' she'd said, when she first told me about him on one of her visits to Gwillim House, the in-patient unit I lived in for five months. 'The flat feels so empty. It never felt empty before.'

'Is he a good substitute?' I'd asked.

'Less entertaining,' she'd said, exaggeratedly thoughtful.

Now, Henry Gale turns his penetrating gaze to me, tail still flicking from side to side. 'Your cat is upset that I'm allowed on the counter and he's not,' I say.

'Human privilege,' Sarah says, smiling. 'How's the job?'

'Also fine.'

'Bit of a placeholder,' she says. 'But OK. I'm glad it's *fine*.' She lifts her fingers in scare quotes and I roll my eyes at her. 'And how's Ventrella Road?'

I bite my tongue to stop myself saying, 'It's fine.' But I actually don't have any other word for it, so I shrug instead.

'You'd tell me if there were any problems?' she asks, raising a hopeful eyebrow at me.

I doubt it. 'Sure,' I say.

'OK, good,' she says. 'You know I'm here if you need me.'

I'd thought, once, that me moving out of her flat would be the excuse Sarah needed to be free of me, but it wasn't, not at all. She came to visit me in Southampton every two weeks without fail, talking comfortably and confidently about my future, entwining herself in it, making sure I knew. She's my family, she's here for me, wherever I'm living. That's a nice thing, even if I'm still not sure I completely trust it. We get along so well now, but in the back of my head, where I try to keep secrets even from myself, I know that this is all going so well because we aren't living together. I'm easier from a distance, even (especially?) for people who love me. This is why I said no when she asked me to come and live with her instead of by myself. *I want to be independent*, I'd said. Half a truth, half a lie.

'I know,' I say. When she smiles at me, I smile back.

I spend the next day with Caddy and Rosie, the three of us sharing a blanket on the beach. I feel happy and free, looking out at the world through the tint of my sunglasses. There's something about Brighton on a summer's day, and I'm not just a visitor; I'm part of it, once again. I belong.

Rosie's talking about the accommodation at the University of East Anglia, which is where she'll be going if she gets her predicted A-level results. She's worried that she might not get her first choice, which is apparently a lot cheaper than the alternatives.

'Most people will want the nice ones,' Caddy says, trying, I'm sure, to be reassuring. 'So I wouldn't worry.'

'I don't know,' Rosie says. 'I think more people worry about money than how nice their room is.'

I let their voices drift over me, mixed in with the usual seagull/waves/tourist cacophony that is the soundtrack of Brighton beach. The first time I ever came to this beach, I'd only just moved here and I didn't know a single person. I'd loved it immediately, even then. I think it might be my favourite place in the world, though I love it best at night, when it's quiet.

'Suze,' Caddy says, 'if you were going to uni, where would you go?'

'I'm not,' I say.

'I said if,' she says patiently. 'Like, where in the country?'

'Right here,' I say.

'Really?'

'I don't want to move anywhere else,' I say. 'No more new postcodes. This is it now.'

Caddy beams at me, as happy as if I'd just complimented her personally, and I think, for the millionth time, how much I don't deserve her. No one's ever believed in me like she does, and she kept on doing it, even when I gave her no reason to. She emailed me every single week for the entire time I lived in Southampton, even when I didn't reply. (And, to be honest, I usually didn't.) I knew every heartbeat of her life. Those first tentative weeks of her relationship with Kel; kissing him, touching him and, later, sex. (These were the emails where I called her immediately, and we stayed on the phone, talking and laughing, and I'd hang up wondering why I was keeping myself so distant from her.) Every now and then a sunflower would turn up on my doorstep addressed to me, with a note – *Sending you sunshine xx* – and I never told her that the sunflowers hurt, that they made me cry, that the bright yellow was too much when I was feeling low, because then she'd stop sending them. And having a friend who sent me surprise sunflowers was the best thing about my entire life.

'But you're not exactly a home-bird, are you?' Rosie says.

I want to be, though. I want to have somewhere that I can return to, that calls me in. I don't *want* to be as rootless as I am. 'I'm a seagull,' I say, making a face at her. 'I return to the sea.'

We all laugh, and Caddy lifts up her arm so I can lean in for a hug. She lifts her other arm for Rosie, who looks appalled, which makes us laugh harder. I think about how we must look from the outside, to anyone who doesn't know us. Best friends, uncomplicated and happy. Everything I'd ever wanted, from those earliest Brighton days.

I'd hoped, then, that I might be able to choose who I wanted to be, that there was some way to escape the parts of myself that scared me. A fresh start, like everyone said. A fresh me. And then there was Rosie, on my first day of school, her wary smile, her sharp eyes. The way her face softened when she told me about her best friend, Caddy-who-goes-to-another-school, a sort of pride in her voice. How she'd said casually, offhandedly, that we couldn't be friends if Caddy and me didn't get along. And then Caddy, her pristine uniform all sharp lines and privilege, her big house, her perfect family. The way Rosie relaxed around her, the two of them fitting together as comfortably and naturally, unthinkingly, as a pair of old socks.

It's not just that I wanted them to be my friends, though I did, desperately. What I really wanted was to be the kind of person who had friends like that. I wanted it more than I'd ever wanted anything.

And now, here we are. If everything else that could go wrong has gone wrong in my life, at least I have them, against all the odds. I was a bad friend when I lived here before. I was an even worse one when I was away. And now I'm back, and they're *happy*. They are so much more than I could ever deserve, and I know that. But this time around, I'm going to be so much better. I'm going to prove to them that it was worth waiting on me.

5

'Berlin Song'
Ludovico Einaudi

Here's something I realize: it's expensive, being poor. I thought I knew, but I didn't. I hadn't realized how much invisible money gets spent in the basic act of living, and how much more it all costs when you've got none spare. I'd expected to spend money on food, but what I didn't think about was how much more it costs to buy food for one person instead of in bulk. (I can't afford to buy in bulk.) The fact that having water coming out of your taps and lights that come on when you flick a switch isn't free.

'Can you really afford to live alone?' Brian had asked, dubious, when we'd first talked about my possible living arrangements. I'd thought he'd meant rent. But it turns out rent is just one part of it. Bills, which had only ever seemed abstract, are the killer.

When I go to Dilys's flat downstairs as planned that week, my laundry in a suitcase and my attempt at shortbread in an old Tupperware container under my arm, I've made a mental list of things I could offer to do in exchange for a bit of money, figuring that she's old and could probably do with a bit of help. Walking Clarence is at the top, cleaning is at the bottom. But when she lets me in – Clarence sniffs cautiously at my Vans and lets me touch his head for a millisecond before running away – she smiles so kindly at me that the idea of asking for money, even if I work for it, seems wrong. Isn't it enough that I get to do my laundry for free?

I load up the washing machine and set it to go before I make tea for us both, taking it over to where she's sitting on the sofa waiting for me.

'Thank you,' she says, smiling. 'Now tell me. How have you been since last week?'

'Fine,' I say. 'I didn't do much. Just work and seeing my friends.'

'Oh?' She takes a sip of tea. 'Where do you work?'

I tell her about Madeline's and she nods, eyes squinting slightly. When I'm done, she says, 'Is that all you do?'

'Should I be doing more?'

'You must be working towards something,' she says. 'What's your goal?'

Staying alive. Not hurting myself or others. You know, the small things. 'I don't have one,' I say.

She frowns a little. 'What about a dream?'

'Dreams are overrated.'

She smiles at this. 'How very cynical from someone so young.' I expect her to push me a little – she seems like the type – but instead she surprises me by getting slowly to her feet. 'Would you like a tour?'

'Oh, that's OK,' I say awkwardly. I don't want to make her move around any more than she needs to. 'Or, you could tell me the rooms, and I'll look?'

Dilys looks at me, her eyebrows moving slowly upward. 'Young lady,' she says. 'Do you imagine me some sort of invalid?'

'No,' I say in a very small voice.

'Ah, then maybe a doddery old woman, one step from falling?'

I stand up. 'I'd love a tour of your flat.'

'Be ready to catch me,' Dilys says. 'In the event of my inevitable collapse.'

I smile. 'Can you give me a warning first? Maybe a shriek? Or a wail?'

She laughs, and I know I'm forgiven.

There's not a huge amount to see, because even though her flat is considerably bigger than mine, it's still just a flat. I nod and smile and make polite noises, and then she opens the door to what I'd assumed would be a guest room. And she says the words, 'This is my music room.'

I actually gasp. The over-the-top, loud gasp that I thought only existed in films. 'You . . . have . . . a music room?'

'I do,' Dilys says, smiling. 'It's something of an indulgence, but I'm seventy-nine and music is my joy. Music and Clarence. And he doesn't need a big room like this.'

The first thing my eye goes to is the baby grand piano, lid open like it's just waiting to be played. There are violins on the walls and one on a stand by a small sofa. One wall is taken up almost entirely by shelving, mostly holding books, but also ornaments and what could be awards. There's art on the walls, too much to take in, and an honest-to-God record player, a proper old-style one, in the corner, next to a record collection in a glass-fronted cabinet. It's like walking into a daydream, this room. Music heaven.

'Wow,' I say.

'Feel free to go in,' Dilys says. 'Do you like music?'

'I love it,' I say. 'It's . . .' What was it she'd said? 'It's my joy, too.'

'Wonderful. What's your instrument?'

'My instrument?'

'What do you play?'

'Oh, I don't. I'm more of a fan. An appreciator. I play the guitar, but just for me. If that makes sense.' I'd learned to play the guitar at Gwillim House, as part of my therapy. I count it as one of the best things that's ever happened to me.

'That's a shame,' she says. 'So much of my appreciation comes from playing. From being immersed in the music. You never played any other instruments?' She sinks on to the piano stool and moves her hands to the keys. 'The piano?'

'I did when I was younger,' I say, going over to one of the frames on the wall to see that it's an old poster for a performance by the Hallé Orchestra. I know the Hallé because we went as a family for my mum's birthday, ages ago, when we lived in Manchester and still acted like a family. 'But not for very long. I never got good or anything.'

'Why did you stop?'

I shrug. 'Not for me, I guess. I love the guitar, though.' I can tell she's going to ask more questions, so I say, 'What do you play, then?'

'The violin was my instrument,' she says. 'But I do love the piano. It's a different kind of magic.'

'What do you mean, was?'

'Professionally,' she says. 'When it was my career.'

I stop, turning back to look at her. 'Wait, what? You were a professional musician?'

She laughs. 'I thought that was clear from this room.'

'You played the violin professionally?'

'I did.' She gives a modest nod. She seems pleased by my reaction. 'I was an orchestral musician for thirty-five years. I toured with the Hallé Orchestra. Do you know what the—'

'You were *in* the Hallé Orchestra?' My voice has risen, because *oh my God I can't believe this.* 'You're from Manchester?'

'No, but I lived in Manchester for a good few years. Wonderful city.'

'Isn't it the best? That's where I was born.'

'How old are you?'

'Eighteen.'

'Oh my,' she says quietly, almost to herself. 'You're so young. I was long gone by then. Gosh, I was already in Brighton.'

I reach out a tentative hand to one of the violins. 'Can I . . . ?'

'Oh yes, please do.' When I touch it and then take my hand away, she says, 'No, no. Don't just touch. Pick it up. Come and sit down, I'll show you how to hold it.'

I have no choice but to obey, even though I'm already regretting asking. I hold the violin by its neck, nervous, and sit beside her on the piano stool.

'Now,' she says. 'Lift it like this, yes . . . Rest it on your collarbone. Hold it out . . . like that, yes. Can you feel your shoulder taking the weight?'

'It feels weird,' I say. 'Like it's growing out of my face.'

She laughs. 'I used to feel like it was a part of me. Like an extension of myself. Here.' She stands and reaches for a bow, then hands it to me. 'Go ahead.'

I can feel my face starting to heat up as I move the bow tentatively across the strings of the violin. Compared to how right and natural my guitar feels when I play, this is so, so weird.

'Hold your elbow more like . . .' Dilys takes a hold of my elbow and adjusts me. Her fingers are cool and dry. 'There.' She takes a small step back, smiling. 'Ah. It suits you. Try again.'

I try again with the bow and produce a hideous, deafening screech for my efforts. Flushing, I take the violin off my shoulder and try to hand it back to Dilys. 'I don't think this is my instrument.'

'Nonsense,' she says, but she looks amused. 'These things take time. Try again.'

'You play,' I say, mostly to distract her. 'Can I hear what it's actually meant to sound like?'

Dilys hesitates, her fingers closing instinctively around the bow. 'I don't play any more,' she says. 'That time of my life is . . . passed.'

'Why?'

She pauses again, her eyes on the graceful arc of the violin. 'Nothing is forever,' she says finally. 'I started to develop joint problems, quite some time ago now. It became impossible for me to play as I once had. Oh, it was painful, leaving that part of my life behind. The heartbreak of my life, I think.' She sighs. 'I focused on the piano for a while after that; I taught for nearly twenty years, right here in this room. It didn't bring me quite the same joy, but at least I still had music in my life. And then, two years ago, I had a stroke.'

'Oh,' I say, alarmed.

'Just a small one,' she says, as if this will reassure me. 'But it affected my mobility and praxis quite a bit for a short while.' She shakes her head. 'These things happen, unfortunately. Perhaps you could bring your guitar next time and you can play me something.'

'I'm not very good.'

She fixes me with a look, as if I'm her student or something. 'I expect not, with that attitude.'

'I just meant it's not something I do as, like, a performance.' Which is funny, I realize, considering everything else I do is. But the guitar is different; it's mine.

We leave the music room when the spin cycle ends so I can set the dryer programme. I make two more cups of tea while Dilys sits on the sofa fussing Clarence, and bring them over with the shortbread. My head is buzzing with violins and record players and music.

'It must have been amazing,' I say. 'Being in the orchestra?'

She smiles. 'Not all the time. It was a difficult life sometimes. But overall, yes, it was wonderful. I miss it very much.'

'Were you married?'

'No, never.'

'Why not?'

'I didn't want to be. It seemed horribly restrictive to me, being tied to a person like that. It still does. And I was never much interested in men, to be perfectly honest. They were so often so terribly dull. I'd meet most of them in some sort of music-related way, and they were patronizing and smug, you can imagine. Always immediately assuming they were better than I was by virtue of them being male, taking it upon themselves to teach me things I already knew.' She shakes her head ruefully. 'I used to think, marry one of those?'

'Did you like women?' I ask.

She laughs. 'Oh yes, it has to be one or the other in this world, doesn't it? Goodness me, no. Not in the way you're implying. There have been women I've loved very dearly, but in friendship. There have been men I've loved like that, too. All very platonic, you see. I never felt like I needed anything more than that.'

'Weren't you lonely?'

'Yes, sometimes, but what you have to understand is, relationships aren't a shield against loneliness. Not romantic ones, that is. One of my dearest friends was unhappy in her marriage for many years; that's a type of loneliness.'

'But you live on your own,' I say.

'I do, but I've had a full life. Full of wonderful people. I get lonely now, yes. That comes with being old.' Seeing my face, she smiles. 'The world is what it is. That's why I'm so enjoying your company.'

I smile back. 'Thanks for showing me your music room.'

'You're so very welcome. It's a pleasure to be able to share it with someone. Perhaps next time we can listen to some of those records I saw you looking at in there.'

'Is it all classical music?'

She looks amused. 'Well, yes.'

I try not to make a face. 'Not really my thing.'

'Then you need a classical education,' she says. 'And that is something I'm more than happy to provide.' The washer-dryer lets out three loud beeps and she smiles. 'Next time.'

6

'Wild Heart'
Bleachers

I've been back in Brighton for about a month when Kel decides
to have a summer party at his house. Kel is actually from Lewes,
which is about twenty minutes from Brighton, but he still lives
in a student house in the city centre rather than stay with his
parents. (I assume this means he has money, but I don't ask either
him or Caddy; they both seem kind of oblivious about money.)
The extra bonus is that it means he can stay in Brighton over the
summer, in a parentless house with his own bedroom. 'You got
lucky,' I say to Caddy.

'Super-lucky,' she agrees happily.

When I get to the house on Saturday evening, it's already full
and loud. Someone I don't recognize lets me in and I find Caddy
in the kitchen, sitting on the counter, eating mini-pretzels out of
a bowl on her lap, talking to Kel as he pours ice into a bucket.
'She's got a lot going on,' she's saying as I walk in, and I wonder
immediately who she's talking about, and can't help but assume
it's me. 'Hey!' she says, holding out the bowl. 'When did you get
here? I came to get these and ended up just eating them, because
I am a terrible host.'

'You're not the host,' Kel reminds her. 'Eat away. Hey, Suze.'

Caddy pats the space on the counter beside her and I hop up,
taking a pretzel and pushing it into my mouth. 'Suze, tell Kel that
people are having a good time,' she says to me.

'People are having a good time,' I say obediently.

'See?' Caddy smiles at her boyfriend, an inside-relationship kind of smile I've never had a chance to see on her face before. 'Told you.' She turns to me, holding out the pretzel bowl again. 'Kel gets paranoid.'

'I'm not paranoid,' Kel says, rolling his eyes with a smile. 'And it's *numbers* I was worried about. I'm used to having parties in term-time, when more people are around. And I thought Matt'd come, but he had to work.'

'There are loads of people here,' I say.

'Thank you,' Caddy says. 'Loads.' She reaches over and gives Kel's shoulder an affectionate push. 'Go and see some of them. I'll see you later.' When he's gone, dropping a kiss on her cheek and waving at me on the way out, Caddy sighs. 'Totally paranoid. But it's a good party, right?'

'Yes!'

'I think it's weird for him, because for most people, they have their uni life and their home life, but for him they're, like, basically the same. He gets a bit angsty during the summer when the lines blur. Maybe he thought having a party would help? I don't know. His best friend lives in London now — Matt — so they don't see each other as much, and I think he was counting on him coming.' She's talking happily, much more freely than she used to when I first knew her. I watch her face, wondering exactly when she got so much more comfortable in her own skin. 'They grew up together and Kel says they're more like brothers. Like me and Roz being like sisters, you know?' She says this so casually, but it stabs. It shouldn't, because I know she's referring to the fact that they've been best friends since they were tiny, but it does.

'Have you met him?'

'Oh yeah, loads.'

'Do you like him?'

'Sure. I mean, we're totally different people. We'd never be friends without Kel, but I guess that's normal. Matt's very cool, you know? He's a good guy and everything, and he's always been really nice to me, but he's still *cool*. He's like this musician living in London working in a bar to get by, shagging his way around the city.'

I laugh. 'Is that actually what he does, or are you making that up?'

'No, he really does. Kel says he's been like that since they were in school. He was in a band then, apparently. All the girls wanted him, Kel says, and he made the most of it.'

'Is he hot?'

She looks at me, finally seeming to remember who she's talking to. 'Oh God, don't even think about it.'

'Just a question,' I say innocently. And then I grin my wickedest grin, and she laughs, and I'm so glad I moved back here.

'Yes,' she says, letting out an exaggeratedly patient sigh. 'He is hot.'

'A hot musician.'

'Suze,' she says, half a whine, half a laugh.

'A hot, cool musician who's also a nice guy.'

'With no sexual integrity.'

'Stop, I'm already sold.'

She chokes on her drink and presses her wrist to her mouth, shaking her head. 'You're such a liability.'

'Thank you. I'm touched.'

'I'm glad he's not here, now,' she says. 'C'mon. I'll give you a tour and we'll find Roz; she should be here somewhere.'

I follow Caddy around the house, which has five bedrooms and a conservatory, and finally out into the garden, where we're stopped by a group of people I assume must be Kel's friends, one of whom sweeps Caddy right off the floor into a fireman's lift. She shrieks and thumps his back until he puts her down.

'You *suck*,' she says to him, eyes bright, her voice a laugh. 'I'm telling Kel.'

'Aw, Cads,' he says. 'Just playing.'

She straightens her top with exaggerated care. 'No more alcohol for you.'

He salutes, and everyone laughs. I just stand there, watching this whole exchange, feeling more like an outsider than I have the whole time I've been back. When Caddy returns her attention to me, steering me towards the patio, I say, 'Remember when you hated parties?' Not because I think she'll actually have forgotten, but because I want to have a moment where we are who I remember; where she is still nervous, shy Caddy and I'm the confident partygoer.

'Barely, thank God. I grew up. Found my inner Suze.' She grins at me. 'Are you proud?'

I grin back, warmth flooding in and dissolving the momentary uneasiness. 'So proud.'

When we find Rosie, we spread over the wicker furniture on the patio, talking, and it's utterly blissful. Rosie pulls me on to her lap like we're still fifteen, hanging out in our form room before registration. We pass a bottle of wine between us, cool and slick with condensation, from the collection Caddy's been keeping hidden in the mini-fridge in Kel's bedroom. When I light a cigarette, they both raise their eyebrows in unison. I tell them I'm going to quit and they don't even try to pretend they believe me.

'I care about your disgusting blackened lungs,' Rosie says, pushing me off her lap on to the spare chair. 'And also how gross that smells.'

'Everyone has a vice,' I say, cupping my hand to keep the smoke I exhale away from them both.

'Yeah, *a* vice,' Rosie says. 'How many are you working with?'

I kick her and she kicks me back, grinning.

Kel comes to join us about half an hour later, a fresh bottle of wine in each hand. He passes one to Rosie and me, keeping the

second for him and Caddy, who's already shifted to make room
for him beside her. We talk about everything, moving from the
fringe festival to the construction work at the seafront to tennis
to university, as the sky gets darker and the wine goes down. I'm
tipsy but not drunk, just warm and cosy.

Caddy and Kel drift away together after a while, curling like
smoke trails around each other at the end of the garden, two
silhouettes framed by tiki torchlight. I watch them as Rosie talks,
her calm voice mingling with The 1975, loud even though the
music is coming from inside the house. The wicker crackles under
my bare shoulders as I shift, resting my head back. The silhouettes
combine and become one. The word comes to my head – 'safe' –
and it's nice, and I'm happy for my friend for a whole thirty
seconds before the opposite word – 'unsafe' – replaces it. I am *not*
safe. There is no one who will make me safe. I have no matching
silhouette, no answering smile in the dark. Just aching, reaching
loneliness. Cold. Inside and out.

I'm not listening to Rosie any more. The words in my head are
louder, more insistent. A steady hum turning into frantic shouting.
I need to be held. I need to be touched. I have to get out of my head.
Is there anyone here? There must be. There's always someone. I
glance around us, the cluster of people dancing, laughing, talking.
I scan the faces, dim as they are in the faded light, waiting for the
inevitable eye contact. I'll smile, just the right kind of hey-I-can-
be-interested-if-you-are smile, and the rest will take care of itself.

'Hey.'

I actually jolt. A spasm of energy shoots up my spine and I turn
to look at Rosie, who has put her hand on my wrist, her fingers
pressing down. 'Hey,' she says again. 'Shall we see if there's any
pizza left?'

The noise has drained from my head at the light touch, her
steady voice. I'm breathing again. I nod and she nods back, eyes

on mine. She stands first and takes my hand, pulling me up beside her. I expect her to let go, because it's Rosie, but she entwines her fingers through mine so we're clasped, close and safe, as we head into the house together.

I'm on my break at work a couple of days later when an email from Darren Watts appears in my inbox. The sight of my dad's name in my alerts makes me jump; physically jump, like he's right there in the room with me. I stare at the name for a while without clicking, looking from it to the subject line, which is the unrevealing 'Bed'. I take a deep breath and click, closing my eyes as I do and then forcing myself to open them. The first thing I see is that the email isn't actually to me, I'm just CC'd in. The email is addressed to Sarah, Brian and Mum. Weird.

I hesitate, still not feeling quite safe enough to read the actual message. I close the email and send Brian a message instead.

Me:

Is that email from Dad safe for me to read?

It takes him a while to reply. I've finished work and I'm back at Ventrella Road when my phone finally beeps.

Brian:

Yeah, it's just Dad being a bit sarky to me and Sarah. Thinks we're not looking after you properly.

Wtf.

I know. Don't worry, it's safe. Go ahead, and let me know what you think about the bed.

I open the email and take it in at a glance before letting myself read it from the top.

All –

What is this utter nonsense I'm hearing about Suzanne not having a proper bed?

If this sort of problem, so easily remedied, has not been fixed in six weeks, I'm really questioning the wisdom of letting Suzanne live by herself and the capacity of the rest of you to supervise. I can only assume you've all lost your minds.

You can say what you like about me being some kind of awful failure as a parent, but at least I always made sure there was a proper bed for my children to sleep in.

Suzanne, I will get you a bed, or if you really can't bear to accept any help from me, I will send you your old bed and you can sleep on that. It's just gathering dust in your old bedroom anyway, and frankly you'll be doing us a favour by taking it off our hands. Deal?

The price of independence is not you having to sleep on an airbed for the rest of your life. Don't be a martyr.

I understand why all of you are reluctant to keep me in the loop when it comes to the goings-on of my apparently estranged daughter (give your mother a call every now and then, won't you?), but if there are actual problems like this, easily fixable problems, please just tell me, for Christ's sake.

D.

*

I read the email three times. It's pure Dad; I can practically hear his confident, sarcastic drawl in my ear. This is the voice I grew up with, the undisputed head of the household, always slightly exasperated with everyone around him. You'd never know *he* was the one causing so much pain. This is the man who once had a go at me – 'Oh, Suzie, look what you did!' – for getting blood on the carpet.

I don't reply. I know he doesn't expect me to, that including me in the email at all was to make some kind of a point. I don't know exactly where on the scale of caring (*I'm concerned you don't have a bed*) to sinister (*I want you to know that I know about your furniture*) he means it to be, but it's probably somewhere in the middle. That's pure Dad, too. And the fact that you never know quite which one it is . . . well, welcome to my life.

I don't see anyone else's replies either, but I assume that's because no one else CC's me in. Which is fine with me, quite frankly.

You want the bed? Brian texts.

Sure, I reply.

Four days later, I have a bed.

7

'Blackbird'
The Beatles

The next time I see Dilys, I bring my laptop. I open it up on the table after I've set the washing machine to go. 'I found you,' I say. 'Look!' I press play on the video. 'That's you, right?'

Dilys squints at the screen, her expression a mix of confusion and pleasure. 'Goodness me,' she says. 'So it is. How did you find this?'

'I searched for Hallé Orchestra clips from, like, the eighties,' I say. 'But that had loads and it was taking ages to look through them, so I tried searching 'Dilys Fairweather', and this came up! See how the names of all the musicians are listed under the video? Cool, right?'

'But . . . why?' she asks, looking from the screen to my face.

'Because I wanted to see you play,' I say. 'You and the orchestra. And there you are! Isn't it cool?'

'You're a sweet girl,' Dilys says, and I look at her in surprise. She pats my hand. 'I'm very glad you don't have a washing machine. Now, it's only fair I get a chance to see you play something. Where's your guitar?'

'Upstairs,' I say. 'I thought you were kidding about that. You don't want me to play the guitar.'

'Of course I do. I want that very much. It's been too long since I had anyone playing music in my company. Indulge an old woman, won't you?' When I hesitate, she says, 'Or . . . I could always teach you to play the piano.'

'I'll go and get my guitar,' I say.

When I get back downstairs, Dilys is pouring out tea from an old-fashioned teapot. I'm just thinking that it looks awkward and unwieldy, too big for her hands, when her wrists seem to give way and she has to fumble to stop herself dropping the entire thing. I leap forward and steady both her and the pot.

'You should have waited for me to come down,' I say. 'I would have poured it.'

The last thing I mean by saying this is to offend her, but I feel her whole body bristle beside me. 'You are not my carer,' she says, in a completely different tone than she usually uses with me. 'I am perfectly capable of pouring out tea.'

This clearly isn't true, judging by the tea spilled all over the table, but it doesn't seem like a good time to say so. 'OK, sorry,' I say. I take a dishcloth from the sink and begin mopping up the liquid, avoiding her gaze.

There's a long, awkward silence. I'm still wiping the now-clean table. Finally, she says, 'This is my favourite teapot.'

'It's lovely,' I say automatically.

'Should I be forced to stop using it because I'm not as dexterous as I once was?'

'No,' I say, mostly because I know that's what I'm meant to say.

'Good. I'm glad we agree. Shall we try again?' She takes a careful hold of the pot and pours out two determined, shaky cups. 'Now, if you could carry these over to the coffee table, I'd be grateful.'

We sip the tea in silence for a few minutes until she puts her cup down and asks, briskly, to see my guitar. I take it from its case and silently hand it over. Her face softens as she takes a hold of it and she smiles a small, inward smile.

'Ah,' she says. 'It's quite worn, isn't it? How long have you had it?'

'A couple of years. It wasn't new.'

'Where did you get it?' Dilys asks, holding it in her lap and looking at it from every angle.

'It was donated,' I say. 'From an arts charity for abuse survivors.' I feel my face flush, my stomach clench.

Her fingers still, just for a moment, on the strings. But, 'I see,' is all she says. 'What are you going to play for me?'

I take the guitar back from her and let the familiar weight rest against my thighs. 'I'm not really that good. I can't play that much. And it's not, like, classical or anything.'

She smiles. 'I wasn't expecting classical guitar from you, my dear. Play anything you like. Something that makes you happy.'

I play 'Blackbird'. It was the first proper song I ever learned to play on the guitar that made me feel proud, like I'd accomplished something. The finger patterns and the chords. The melody, so familiar, created by my own two hands.

I don't sing, because I don't sing in front of people, and I get about halfway through the song before Dilys puts a gentle hand on mine and asks why.

'You asked me to play,' I say, sidestepping the question.

'You're playing beautifully,' she says. 'But won't you sing? The music is half the story.'

'I thought it was the music bit you liked,' I say. 'Isn't that why you like classical music?'

'Classical music is very different from the Beatles,' she says. 'This song has beautiful lyrics to go along with the melody.'

'You know the Beatles? I thought you didn't like pop music.'

'Everybody knows the Beatles,' she says drily. 'Even former classical violinists. Now, won't you sing? Remind me of the lyrics.' She smiles expectantly.

I shake my head, looking down at the strings. My skin feels hot and tingly. 'I don't want to sing.'

'Why not?'

'I just don't.' I strum the opening chords of 'Blackbird' again, trying to distract myself from the whispers in my head. But I can tell this isn't going to be enough, so I add, 'Not when other people are around.'

'I see,' she says. 'What a terrible shame.'

I look up and smile, but it's not a real smile, and I can feel it. It's a Suze smile, the kind I don't do with Dilys. 'You haven't heard me sing.'

She's looking at me like she can see through me, and I suddenly regret ever coming here, playing this guitar, letting her in. 'I'd really love to hear you sing,' she says.

'I could be tone deaf for all you know.'

'That doesn't matter. It would make me happy regardless.'

I can't figure out how to extricate myself from this conversation. The guitar feels heavy against my knees. I hear myself say, 'My dad doesn't like it.'

And she says, 'Your dad isn't here.'

This is an obvious statement of fact, so I have no idea why the words bring on tears. But they do, and I put my hand to my face, instinctively shielding myself.

'Oh dear,' Dilys says, soft. 'I'm very sorry. Of course you don't have to sing.'

I tell her everything, then. It all spills, unstoppable as tears, out of me. I tell her about my family, my first move to Brighton, Gwillim House, being fostered. She listens quietly, her head bent slightly, eyes on the floor. Every now and then, she nods.

'He's why I love music,' I say. 'My dad. I was brought up surrounded by it. But at the same time, he didn't like it if I sang. That's probably why I never played anything, either. Maybe.'

'He was trying to control it?' She says this as part statement, part question.

'Well, probably, yeah. He controlled everything.'

'He gave you this wonderful gift – a joy and appreciation for music – but put boundaries around it for you. Music is about freedom.' She shakes her head. 'How terrible for you, to feel trapped like that. To not be free to share music as well as receive it.'

'It was just about singing, really. He used to say only show-offs and professionals sang in public. That's what he said I was.' I swallow, the memory rising sharp and painful. 'A tedious little show-off.' He'd only said it the once, and it was just a passing comment when he was in a bad mood. He probably wouldn't even remember that he'd said it.

Dilys has taken my hand, which would be weird if I hadn't just spilled my heart out to her. 'It's very easy to be cruel,' she says (which surprises me, because I was just expecting her to say something nice, like 'You're not a show-off'). 'Especially to a child who is vulnerable and seeking approval or love. When you remember these things, and the terrible things that were said or done to you, you must think: *How easy it is to hurt a child*. Do you understand what I'm saying?'

I think of my dad, all six feet of him, solid and strong, sneering at an eight-year-old girl. It's like looking at an old photograph through a new filter.

I nod.

'Good.' She pats my hand. 'Maybe one day you'll feel ready to sing for me. I'd like that very much. But for now, let's have some more tea, shall we?'

August arrives and passes in a haze. Rosie goes on holiday with her friends from sixth form in the first week and returns in time to collect her A-level results. Both she and Caddy get exactly the grades they were predicted and are officially going to university next month. They're thrilled, but the reality of their imminent departure makes me heartsick. I keep it to myself.

After the results, Caddy goes on holiday with Kel — their first couples holiday, which makes her giddy and anxious in seemingly equal measure — and returns tanned, smiling and somehow older. I get the results of the last couple of GCSEs I'd taken in college before I left Southampton — Biology and Chemistry, both passes — to take my overall total to five. It feels good. Not amazing, but good. I still have no idea what I want to actually do with these qualifications, but just having them makes me feel . . . possible. Less useless, anyway. I don't tell Rosie or Caddy because a handful of belated, adequate GCSEs is nothing compared to high A levels, and they'd be too excited anyway and make me even more aware of it. I tell Sarah, who makes me a cake, and beams like I just graduated with honours, and Dilys, who smiles and says, 'Well done.'

On the last weekend in August, I go to Reading Festival with my old friends from my pre-Brighton life. I don't see them much any more, but it's nice when I do. It's basically three days of drunken, musical joy. Friends, music, freedom. My favourite things. I come home on a high, only to find I'd left my window open and the rain's got in, because of course I had, and of course it has.

A couple of days after I get back, Caddy turns nineteen and it feels like the tipping point; the beginning of the end.

'I always used to feel like that,' Rosie says when I mention this to her. 'Caddy's birthday meant school starting again. It's actually weird for me that it *doesn't* mean that any more. Don't worry, we've still got a few weeks before we leave.'

Summer is over, though. That feeling of endlessness and lethargy seems to have been left in August, because everything changes in September. When I visit Caddy and Rosie they have boxes piling up in the corners of their rooms. They talk excitedly and nervously about potential flatmates and seminars and lecture halls. Caddy worries about being in a long-distance relationship.

Rosie worries about being alone. I try to remember how they were when I first met them: Caddy, mousy and self-conscious; Rosie, all snark and bolster. But now they have adulthood and the future in their eyes, and it is brighter than I can bear.

Before, I was new to them, shiny and unpredictable. I was a spark. Now I am the old friend, the one they are leaving behind.

'You'll visit,' Caddy says confidently, as if that's the answer to what I'm really worried about. 'It won't be that different, not really.'

I try to believe her but, one week before she's due to leave to go to Warwick to study Psychology with Linguistics, she mentions casually that she's going to the hairdresser and then meets me in the pub that evening with entirely different hair. 'Holy crap!' I say, hearing how shrill I sound but not quite managing to contain it. Her highlighted hair always fell thick and straight to her shoulders. Now it's a rich, coppery red colour, styled into a long bob with a sweeping side fringe. 'Who are you and what have you done with Caddy?'

She laughs, self-conscious, and slides on to the bench beside me. 'Do you like it? It's my leaving-home present from my sister. Toni & Guy. Cost a bomb.'

'It looks great!' I say, because it does. I don't actually answer her question, though, because the truth is I *don't* like it. She doesn't look like Caddy, and the best thing for me about Caddy is that she is Caddy. 'Has Kel seen it?'

She nods, smiling. 'He likes it.'

I don't know if this is understatement for effect because he likes it a lot, or underplaying that fact that he doesn't like it at all, but I don't ask. I'm not about to start trying to decipher their relationship code. Besides, that's the moment Rosie arrives and lets out a shriek so loud that three other tables turn to look at us.

'God, Roz,' Caddy hisses, face flaming brighter than her

hair. 'Was that actually necessary?'

'Did you know about this?' Rosie demands of me. 'This is you, isn't it? The two of you have been hair-colluding and leaving me out.'

I put my hands up in mock-surrender. 'I'm an innocent bystander. This was Tarin.'

'Can you both stop acting like this even matters?' Caddy says. She's shrunk into herself, shoulders hunched, face still pink. 'It's just hair. God.'

'I'm unconvinced,' Rosie says to me. 'A massive hair-change has your muddy Suze-paws all over it. *And* it actually looks good. This is all you.'

'How are you able to simultaneously compliment and insult both of us?' Caddy asks.

'Years of practice,' Rosie says. 'Should *I* have changed my hair? Is that a before-uni *thing*?'

'No,' she says. 'It's an older-sister-gift *thing*. Can we please talk about something else?'

Rosie grins. 'Hey, Cads? I like your new hair.'

'Thank you.' Caddy attempts a casual hair-toss. 'OK. One drink here and then on to La Choza?'

It's our last Friday together before Rosie leaves for Norwich, and we've had this evening planned for weeks. Cheap wine at a pub, then on to La Choza for burritos and margaritas. After that, it's more cocktails and then shots and then the dizzying crush of a club, the three of us interlinked and close from dance floor to bathroom to bar, sweaty hands clasped, arms around necks, kisses on cheeks. The whole thing is magic. I love them both so much, it fills me up.

We end up on the beach in the early hours, sharing a bag of cheesy chips, huddled together on the cold pebbles. Caddy is loose and giggly, tapping at her phone screen and whispering, 'I just love him. I love him *so much*, guys,' while Rosie takes endless photos of the sea, our feet, our faces.

'Don't leave,' I say to them both, after Caddy has started complaining about her phone screen being all greasy and Rosie is telling her off as she tries to wipe it with the ruffle of her clutch. 'Can't you just stay?'

'Look who's talking,' Rosie says. 'The queen of disappearing.'

'Yeah,' Caddy says. 'At least we'll *visit*.'

'Ooh,' I say. 'Bitter!'

Caddy puts her arm around me and plants a kiss on my cheek. 'I love you.'

'I know you do,' I say.

'But not enough to stay,' she adds. She lets out a happy sigh. 'Rosie loves you too, even if she won't say it.'

I glance at Rosie to see that she's smirking her Rosiest smirk. 'Rosie doesn't feel the need to inflate Suze's ego any further,' she says. 'She *knows* she is beloved.' Only Rosie could get away with saying something like this to me, and we both know it, which makes it perfect. I slide my arm through hers and squeeze, and she wrinkles her nose affectionately at me in response.

'Thanks for making space for me again,' I say. Their shoulders are warm against mine, and I'm so happy.

'Always,' Rosie says lightly.

'Always, always,' Caddy adds.

8

'Hang Loose'
Alabama Shakes

The day before Rosie leaves for Norwich, I go to her house for the afternoon. She's still in the midst of packing, her bedroom floor covered in boxes, and when I walk in I find her on her knees, sorting through a pile of books.

'Hello!' I say. 'Your mum let me in. Has she been crying?'

'Probably,' Rosie replies. 'I think it's just hit her that I'm going. She keeps wailing about empty nests. I was like, I'm not exactly going to the moon.' She leans back on her ankles and sighs. 'Hello, by the way! How are you?'

'Fine. Want some help?'

'No, just company.' She smiles at me. This is a softer Rosie than I'm used to; it feels like maybe she's been crying, too. Or come close to it, at least.

'Here,' I say, opening my bag and pulling out a bottle of Tuaca. 'Your going-away present from me.'

Her smile widens into a grin. 'That's so perfect.'

'Well, I thought so. You could share it with your flatmates as, like, an icebreaker? If you get nervous or something. Not that I think you'll be nervous.'

'I'm *so* nervous,' she says, surprising me.

'Really? Why?'

She laughs. 'Because it's terrifying? Moving to a whole new place and living with a bunch of strangers?'

'Why's that scary?'

She gives me a gentle shove. 'Oh, stop it, Miss Popularity.

You know what I mean.'

I don't, really. I've moved to new places a bunch of times and lived with strangers. At least in this scenario everyone's in the same boat. At least she doesn't have to live by herself in a bedsit. What she's doing seems to me like the most exciting thing in the world. A socially acceptable new beginning. Who wouldn't want that?

'You'll be fine,' I say instead of voicing any of this, because I know it's not fair. 'I liked you straight away when I met you.'

Her face lifts. 'Really?'

'Yeah. I could tell you were a good egg. Plus you were wearing those owl earrings, and who wouldn't like someone wearing owl earrings? Make sure you wear them tomorrow.'

'You know what?' Rosie says, tossing the book she's holding into the box and reaching for the bottle. 'Let's have some of this now.' She casts around for a cup, then shrugs and takes a swig straight from the bottle. 'Ugh,' she says, shaking her head. She hands it to me with a grin. 'Delicious.' She waits until I've taken a sip and replaced the cap before she says, 'Listen, I need to tell you something.'

'OK,' I say cautiously. That kind of sentence is right up there with 'We need to talk' for a signpost of something you don't want to hear.

'I wasn't sure about telling you now, or waiting until, like, later. But then I thought, well, if something happens, I don't want it to be like this great *ta-da!* You know?' She's rambling, which she never does, and I just blink at her in confusion. 'So I figured now would be the best time, when it's not tied to any one person, and you're not going to think, well, of course, she's at uni now—'

'Roz,' I break in. 'I literally have no idea what you're talking about.'

She laughs a breathless kind of laugh that is mostly tension-releasing rather than about actual humour. 'OK. Sorry. God, I thought this would be easy. I mean, it's you! But it feels hard anyway? Like . . . God. I've never had a big reveal moment before. I should probably have planned this better.' She stops talking, rolls her eyes to the ceiling and smiles a resigned, self-deprecating smile. 'So I'm bi.'

'Oh!'

'Yeah. So that's a thing.' She twists the Tuaca bottle in her hands, finding the cap and unscrewing it to take another swig. 'It's not a big deal, like, in any way,' she says. But her face is flaming.

'OK,' I say, trying to follow her lead. 'Thanks for telling me.'

She shrugs, looking away from me, her cheeks still blazing pink. 'Course I've . . . well, I've known for a long time, I think, but it seemed like I should be, like, *sure* . . . and I wasn't sure. But now I figure that's a part of it. Not being sure. Am I making sense?'

I nod quickly.

'I actually think I might . . .' She stops, bites on her lip, then looks at me. 'It might just be girls. I don't know. I'm still figuring it out.'

Apprehension has clouded her face, and it makes me want to tell her that I'm fine with it, but I know better. It's not like she needs or is asking for my permission. I say, 'Does your mum know?'

At this, she smiles. 'Oh yeah, I told her a while back. She got really excited; it was like I'd just told her I had super-powers.'

I laugh. 'That's so nice, though.'

'Yeah, she's all right.' She gives a small shrug, still smiling. 'She was like, "Bringing you up in Brighton, I'd hope for nothing less." And then she got me a rainbow cake.' She tucks her hair behind her ear, her shoulders relaxing, and begins picking up books again. 'Is it crazy to take the entire set of Harry Potter books with me?'

'Yes,' I say. 'Do it anyway.'

'I probably won't even read them.'

'That's not why you want to take them.' I'm guessing, but it's probably true. 'They're comfort books.'

She smiles. 'I like that. Comfort books.' She puts the books into the box and glances at me. 'Listen, are you going to be OK, with us gone?' Her voice is casual and even, like this isn't a heavy question.

'Yeah,' I say.

Her smile quirks. 'Yeah?'

'You know me,' I say. 'I'm always OK.'

There are a lot of things she could say in response to this, and there's a time when she would have said them all, but today she just smiles and shakes her head a little, which is the Rosie equivalent of an affectionate hug. Then she says, 'Can I ask you something?'

'Always.'

'Did you time coming back like this? Like, with us leaving only a few months after you got here?'

I frown. 'What do you mean? Of course not. How would that even work?'

'I don't know, but we just wondered.'

'We?'

'Yeah, Caddy and me. It just seemed . . . like, you were gone for so long. We hardly ever heard from you and you never visited until you had to. And then you tell us you're coming back, which is amazing, but it's not until the summer before we leave? I guess we just worry that maybe . . . it's us. I don't know.'

I bite my tongue and breathe in slowly through my nose, waiting a few seconds before I reply so the sting from her words doesn't show in my voice. 'Roz, come on. You know you're the reasons I came back at all.'

'Well, that's not completely true,' she says, and she's using her matter-of-fact Rosie voice that used to wind me up when we were first friends and she was lecturing me about going off with Dylan Evers. 'Sarah's the main reason, isn't she?'

'Actually, no,' I say, trying to keep my voice steady. 'It's you two.'

'But how can that be true, Suze? We're not even going to be here.'

'It's not my fault you're going to uni!' I snap, then bite my lips together. I don't want to fight with Rosie. And I really don't want to think too hard about them not being here. 'Listen. I know that neither of you understand anything about leaving care—'

'You never tell us any of it, how would we?'

'Roz! For God's sake.'

'Well, it's true. You can't do that thing where you don't tell us something and then get annoyed with us for not knowing it.'

'I don't do that!'

'You do it literally all the time.'

'Some things are hard to talk about, OK? How can you not get that?'

'Sure, I don't get that,' she says, clenching her jaw. 'Me, the one with the dead sister and father who abandoned her. No one else understands bad things except you. Sure.'

'That's not what I meant.'

'Sure,' she says again. 'Sure, Suze.'

There's a long silence, both of us waiting for the other to speak. I pull my knees up to my chest and rest my forehead on them, closing my eyes. After a while, I feel her fingers on my hair. The gentlest tug. I look up.

'We love you,' she says. 'We want to support you. And we worry about you. OK?'

I nod.

'You shut us out more than you should. That's what I'm trying to say. We're on your side.'

'I know.'

She raises her eyebrows slightly, like, *Go on*.

'I couldn't leave Southampton any earlier than I did,' I say, trying not to sigh too obviously. 'I had to wait until the end of the school year. And look, I'd *love* it if you and Caddy were sticking around. But you've got uni, and that's good. It's not like it's forever, anyway. I'll still be here when you get back.'

I see something in her face then, and I finally get it.

'Oh, Roz. I will be.'

'I just worry,' she says.

Everyone worries. That's the role I play in all their lives. The one to worry about.

When I don't say anything, sinking my head back down on to my knees, she speaks again. 'Last time, when you were suicidal –' my entire chest seizes at the word. I close my eyes – 'I didn't know that you were. I didn't even realize. And I was right there with you at school. You don't *say* when you're low, Suze. You don't talk. So of course I—'

'I *do* talk,' I interrupt, lifting my head. My neck feels hot. 'And I'm doing so much better now. I take my medication, OK? I have a crisis plan for if I feel . . . like that again. I've had *therapy*. *Intensive* therapy. That wasn't for nothing.'

Rosie doesn't say anything, her anxious eyes searching mine.

'Roz, I promise. It won't be like it was before. Things are so different now. And, look, we'll talk all the time, OK? You can call me whenever you want.'

'Well, ditto,' she says.

I wait a beat, then attempt a smile that she won't think is fake. 'Can we talk about something else now?'

Rosie leaves Brighton at lunchtime the next day. I don't know exactly when she leaves, but I still feel her absence as if I'd watched her go. Caddy comes bounding over to mine that afternoon, armed with ingredients, and we make a strawberry yogurt cake and listen to an old playlist I made her when we were first becoming close friends. Being with her is safe and comfortable; sometimes just being with Caddy feels like letting the sunshine in.

But she leaves in the evening to see Kel, and that's how the rest of the week unfolds. Rosie's departure has turned me into a third wheel in a way I never was before, and it feels weird to spend time with just the two of them, especially considering it's their last week together before Caddy leaves and their relationship becomes long distance for the first time. *And* Caddy wants to spend time with Tarin and her parents, because it'll be the first time she's lived away from them, too. I'm the extra. A bonus, even. But never an unconditional first choice.

Rosie, for her part, ends up calling me every day that week. The first time is on the Sunday evening of her arrival and she's nervous and breathless, telling me about her flatmates as she dresses for a club night on campus. On Monday she wants to tell me about everyone in so much detail, I worry that she just doesn't want to get off the phone and actually hang out with them. On Tuesday, after midnight, she's drunk and tearful, homesick. Wednesday, she just wants to reassure me that she's fine, totally fine. Thursday, she's drunk again, but excited this time, a bit giddy. She just kissed a girl. 'A girl, Suze!' Friday, she wants a proper chat. She's sitting on the steps in the main square of the university: 'Tell me everything about Brighton. I miss you.' On Saturday it's a pep talk, like she'd been preparing for it, making sure I'll be OK when Caddy leaves.

And then Caddy does leave, and it's fine. For one thing, I'd been so worried I'd fall apart that the fact that I don't feels like a success. And for another, Kel is prepared.

'You want to come to mine tonight?' he asks me. 'We're having a new-semester party. Come and see what a proper student party is like.'

'I'm not a student, though,' I say.

'That's OK,' he says. 'Every student party needs a token civilian.'

So I go, and even though I wasn't sure at first if it was a good idea or not, it's actually great. Kel enthusiastically introduces me to his housemates as 'my friend Suze', which I appreciate, and watches with a proud, brotherly smile as I do what I do best and charm the room. It feels good to be around new people on the exact night I'd been worried about being alone.

I end up spending a while talking to a couple of girls from his course, Maisie and Kat, who work for the music section of the university newspaper and get to go to loads of gigs for free. They're friendly, clearly used to chatting to strangers, and not at all snobby about talking to the 'civilian'; the kind of friends I hope Rosie and Caddy make. The conversation moves on to a guy Kat likes, and somehow I end up doing her make-up in exchange for a future of tip-offs about good upcoming gigs.

I'm telling Kel about this later – I'm smoking a roll-up on his patio with his housemates and he'd greeted us with an obnoxious cough – when his face lights up. 'Hey, did Caddy tell you about Matt?'

'The musician?'

'Yeah! We've been best friends since we were kids. Listen, he's in Brighton next weekend to play a gig at the Third Bridge, this pub down near the seafront. It's just a small one, but I said I'd go, obviously. Want to come? I don't know if you'll like his music, but hey, a free gig is a free gig, right?'

I hesitate, wondering if it's OK for me to hang out one-on-one with Kel like that. I'm pretty certain he's not into me, but it's still potentially dodgy territory, right?

'Feel free to say no,' Kel says easily. He might be the most laid-back guy I've ever met. 'But I thought it might be good. Having a friend to hang out with, you know? With Cads and Rosie gone.'

Ah. I feel a smile spread over my face. 'Caddy told you to look after me, didn't she?'

'Yep,' he says, unfazed.

Caddy. My sweet, kind friend. 'Well, OK, then. Thanks. That sounds great.'

'Great,' he says. 'Listen, I'm not going to forget about you just because uni's started up again and Caddy's gone. What I want is for us to be actual friends, not Caddy-mutuals. You game?'

I grin. 'I'm game.'

He grins back. 'Cool.'

When I see Dilys that week, she's brought out photos from her time at the Royal College of Music and I look through them, smiling as a younger Dilys smiles back at me, violin on her lap. She can't be much older than I am, which is weird and nice at the same time.

'Are these all the photos you have?' I ask.

She's surprised. 'Don't you think it's a lot? I'm quite proud of how many I have.'

'I was just thinking how Caddy and Rosie probably took more photos on their first night at uni than you have in your whole collection.'

She squints at me and I smile so she'll know I'm not trying to be rude. She smiles back. 'It is funny how times change. Are you missing them? Your friends?'

I nod. 'Not as much as I thought I would, though. I speak to them every day.'

'And how are they finding it?'

'Caddy loves it. She's really happy.' I don't have to guess this; when I speak to Caddy, her whole voice is brimming with it. She talks happily about her flatmates, her course, her freedom. 'Rosie's a bit down, I think, though.'

'Homesick?'

'Maybe? I don't think she's made friends with the people she's living with like Caddy has. But the thing with her is that she's not great at talking about it when she's upset, so I don't know like I would if it was Caddy. She's staying in closer contact than she usually does, though. We talk every day. That's not like Rosie.'

'I'm sure she's glad to be able to talk to you,' Dilys says. 'You must be a very good friend to have.'

I try not to laugh, because there's too much history and context to explain in one conversation. 'Well, I try to be. I'm not sure I am, though.'

'Nonsense,' she says. 'Why would you say that? You just told me your friend speaks to you every day. That is the action of someone who appreciates your friendship.'

'I've just made a lot of mistakes that she's had to deal with,' I say. 'She puts up with a lot.'

'So do all friends,' Dilys says. 'And all people who care for one another. Don't be hard on yourself like this. You have such a warm spirit; it's lovely. I'm sure that's what your friends are drawn to. Have you ever heard of Yehudi Menuhin?'

'Er, no.'

'I didn't think so. He was a violinist I admired very much. He once said that the violinist is half tiger, half poet. I thought that was wonderful. So evocative.'

'Is that what you were like?' I ask.

'Were?' Dilys repeats, mock-offended.

'Are,' I correct myself.

'Thank you. My increasing age hasn't changed my personality. I like to think I can still be fierce.'

'And poetic?'

'Quite. But the reason I brought it up is I think it applies to you, too.' She smiles at me. 'Half tiger, half poet.'

'I'm not a poet.'

'He didn't mean a literal poet, my dear. You can have the soul of a poet and never write a verse. It's that mix, you see. The fire and art. It's very special.'

I know she's complimenting me, so I smile even as uncertainty needles my pleasure. It's nice that she thinks of me that way, but I can't help but feel like I've duped her in some way. I've tried to be myself with Dilys, but the person she's describing isn't me at all. Is it?

I keep thinking of it, though, as the days pass and Rosie stays in her uncharacteristic close contact. What the two of us mean to each other. Why I'm the person she wants to talk to, even though she bats away any attempts of mine to check that she really is fine. 'All right, *Mum*,' she says, when I try to ask if she's made friends. 'I can make my own playdates!'

On Thursday, I put together a small care package for her, scouring the boutiques in Brighton's winding lanes for bits and pieces to make her smile. A plasticine owl necklace, a postcard of the old pier at sunset, an ink stamp shaped like a cat. A box of macarons, purple hair clips. Jelly beans, party bunting, a sugar mouse. I handwrite her a letter listing all the things that make her not just my amazing friend but an amazing person, too, which I know will mean a lot to her even if she pretends to be mortified. I send it off with a bow for good measure and feel happy.

She sends me a message two days later: **You made me cry and I hate you xxx**

I smile. Job done.

9

'Celeste'
Ezra Vine

The night before I go to Kel's friend's gig, I have a long Skype conversation with Caddy. She's sitting on her desk, eating spaghetti pesto out of a bowl. I listen as she tells me about her course, going into far too much detail, considering I'm still not sure what linguistics is, and the already-established loyalties in her flat. There's an argument brewing about washing-up, she says.

'You've only been there, like, a week!' I say. 'How can you be arguing about that already?'

'You wouldn't believe how much washing-up a couple of guys can build up when they're washing literally none of it, Suze,' she says, very seriously. 'You should see our kitchen. It's in a total state. I'm on the side of say-nothing-until-it's-done. Sensible, right? But my flatmate, Tess, she's all, *No, you have to establish boundaries early on, say what is and isn't OK*, right? And this isn't OK? So she's out there, right now, piling up all the dirty plates and pans and stuff outside Sam's door.'

'And you're . . . sitting here talking to me?'

'Obviously,' she says, wide-eyed. 'Out of the danger zone.'

I smile. 'The Caddy approach.'

'I don't know why people say "conflict-averse" like it's a bad thing. Who wouldn't want to be averse to conflict? It's so much safer. Anyway. How are you?'

'Fine,' I say. 'I'm very limited on stories to tell you, though. It's very dull here. Same old.'

'You're going to the gig tomorrow though, right?' she says.

'Yeah.' I hesitate. 'That's OK, right?'

'Of course!' She's surprised. 'I told Kel to invite you to stuff! And I think you'll like Matt's music a lot.'

'What kind does he play?'

She looks blankly at me through the screen. 'It involves a guitar?'

'OK, what kind of guitar?'

'Is there more than one kind of guitar?'

I laugh. 'Cads!'

'Well, I don't know. Music is music. I guess he's sort of like Passenger? Maybe. I really don't know. Anyway, you'll like Matt. He's cool.' She frowns suddenly, spinning spaghetti around her fork. 'Don't like him too much, though.'

'What is too much?'

'Suze,' she says warningly. I beam innocently, mostly to wind her up, and she rolls her eyes. 'Look, just don't sleep with him, OK?'

'Why, does he have herpes?'

'Suze! Seriously.'

'Herpes is very serious.' I pause. 'Herpes . . . *are*?'

'You are the worst.' She freezes suddenly, turning her head towards what must be the door to her room. 'Uh-oh.'

'Conflict?'

'Someone's yelling.' She leans away from the screen. 'Something about freedom.'

'The freedom to have dirty plates?'

'I think it's the freedom to be free from other people's dirty plates.'

'University sounds complicated.'

Caddy returns her full attention to the screen, a grin on her face. 'So complicated. I miss you.'

'No, you don't,' I say. 'You're having a ball.'

'Still miss you, though.'

'Mutual,' I say.

'I should go. Let me know how the gig goes, yeah? And remember—'

'Yeah, yeah. No herpes. Good luck with plate-gate. I love you.'

'Love you, too.' She waves at the screen, her face pixelating in the seconds before the connection ends, then disappears from view.

I find Kel at the bar in the Third Bridge the next evening, just before eight. His back is to me as he talks to someone, so I tap his shoulder and smile when he turns. 'Hey.'

'Hey!' He smiles big and steps forward to hug me. 'You made it. Awesome. Want a drink?'

'Sure, but I'll get it. And whatever you want to drink,' I say. It's only fair, considering he's got me into this gig for free. 'Beer?'

His smile gets even bigger, if that's possible. 'I knew it was a good idea to invite you. Hey –' he nudges the guy beside him – 'Matt, this is Suze.'

I look up and take in the person he's talking to properly for the first time. And *Oh. Hello.* This is Matt? I'm not going to waste any words here. The guy is *gorgeous.*

'Hey,' Matt says to me, and as he takes me in I see his casual smile widen with interest. His eyes squint ever so slightly; the corner of his mouth twitches. I swear I see his pupils dilate.

'Hey,' I say.

'I'm Matt,' he says, all charm.

'I know,' I say. 'Kel just told me that.'

I see the look of surprise flash over his face before he smirks and makes some wisecrack about his name being so good it needs to be said twice. But I saw him falter and I know he's breakable. Boys never expect you to make fun of them. Teasing them is the best way to hold their interest.

'So when are you on?' I ask.

'Oh, I'm always on,' he says smoothly.

I just look at him, then turn deliberately to Kel. 'Seriously?'

Kel laughs. 'Mate, you're embarrassing yourself.'

'It's you,' Matt says to me. 'You're throwing me off.'

These same words from just about anyone else would have turned me right off. But Matt is saying all of this with a twist in his voice, a glint in his eye. There's something self-aware about him. He *knows* he's being One Of Those Guys. He knows he's being it to me, The Pretty Girl. If I fell for this act, he'd kiss me, flirt with me, take me to bed, sure. But if I don't, it can be me with the upper hand. I see all of this. He can see it too.

There's a fizz in my chest.

'I'm on at nine,' Matt says, his smile relaxing. 'It's cool you came. Kel said you like music?'

Understatement. 'Yeah,' I say.

'Have you listened to any of my stuff?' His voice is affectedly casual, like he wants me to think my answer doesn't matter to him.

'Not yet,' I answer. 'That's what tonight is for, right?'

When Matt comes onstage an hour later, guitar in hand, the crowd cheers and he grins into the microphone, clearly pleased. He opens his set with an upbeat, folky cover of an old Elvis song, 'Burning Love', which is the last thing I would have expected, but it works.

I'd meant it when I said I hadn't listened to any of his stuff, so it's all new to me. He's got a good voice, smooth but with a slight roughness at the edges that gives it all more depth. He talks between songs, funny but relaxed, a near-constant grin on his face. Caddy had called him cool, and he is, but he's less polished than I'd expected. He's not *trying* to be cool.

At the end of the set, Kel reappears by my side with drinks for us both just as the lights come back up. 'What did you think?' he asks.

'He's good,' I say, meaning 'good' in that understated way that means 'great'. 'Does he have a deal or anything?'

Kel makes a face. 'No. It's a bit of a crappy story, actually. He had one, when he was nineteen. Did Caddy tell you anything about it?' I shake my head. 'He was spotted by a producer at an open-mic night while he was at uni. The guy had all the big talk, you know? I'll make you a star, blah blah blah. And that's what Matt wanted. So he went for it. Dropped out of uni and moved to London.'

'And it didn't go well?'

'It *started* well. He got booked on to loads of festivals and stuff; he was even on one of the small stages at Leeds. He was making an EP and they were talking about the album and long-term plans. But then the EP came out and it didn't get much attention and, well, basically, they dropped him.'

'Why?'

'There wasn't any big reason. Matt says they just lost faith in him, and that happens. Like, a lot. They don't want to put the money into making and promoting a whole album, so they pull out. The thing is, I don't think he was even that upset about it, not really. He wasn't happy the whole time any of it was happening. The producer was a prick and they weren't interested in the kind of music he actually wanted to make, they just wanted him to be the next Harry Styles.'

I smile. '*That* doesn't sound so bad.'

Kel laughs. 'Don't say that to Matt. He'd *love* to be the next Harry Styles. He just knows he's not, you know? And I think that was hard to have shoved into his face all the time.'

'So what does he do now?'

'He's working in a bar and trying to figure out where to go

next. He hasn't put anything on his YouTube channel in ages and he only said he'd do this gig because he knows Ryan, the owner of the pub. I think he's burned out.'

'Isn't he a bit young to be burned out?' I ask.

Kel smiles. 'Yeah, but twenty-one isn't really considered young in the music industry, is it? It's not like there aren't a thousand other wannabes who still *do* want it, ready to take his place at the first opportunity.'

'That's shitty.'

'Yeah.' He gives a resigned shrug. 'But still. There are worse things that can happen to someone than not being the next Harry Styles, right?'

'I don't know,' I say, watching Matt making his way through the crowd towards us, stopping briefly when people talk to him and nodding, smiling for a moment before moving on. 'I think having your dream that close and then it being taken away is a pretty shitty thing to happen.'

When Matt finally reaches us, Kel hands over the almost-full pint he's holding and then leaves to get himself another.

'Nice set,' I say.

'Thanks!' Matt takes a gulp from the pint and smiles at me, touching his hand to his hair as if to sweep it back in place, even though it's not long enough to need it. 'I was going to get you a drink, but it looks like you're sorted.'

'I'm sure there'll be time for more,' I say.

His smile widens, relaxing at the same time. He lifts his glass and touches it to mine. 'Cheers.'

'Cheers,' I say. 'How long have you played the guitar?'

We settle into a conversation about music, which is basically my favourite thing to talk about. He plays the piano and bass as well as the guitar, and has always wanted to be a singer. He draws from a lot of different influences and styles, but has what he calls a 'weakness' for contemporary folk music. 'But the cool kind,' he adds. I point out that he opened his set with a folky Elvis cover, and a spontaneous, genuine grin breaks out over his face. 'What's not cool about that?' he asks.

We're talking so easily, in fact, that Kel has been standing beside us for what must have been a while before he coughs, loudly, and stops Matt mid-sentence. 'Oh, sorry. I was just checking I still existed.'

I laugh. 'Sorry. What do *you* think about the cultural impact of Beatlemania?'

'I think the Beatles are overrated,' Kel replies. 'People talk like they invented music.'

'Oh my God,' I say.

'Right?' Matt says. 'Don't get him started.'

'Kel, I can't believe you just dissed the Beatles,' I say.

'Of course you can't,' he replies. 'You're an eighteen-year-old white girl from Brighton. What you've been missing is exposure to other music.' He grins, full of mischief. 'Less beige music.'

'Oh my God,' I say again. 'Firstly, I'm from Manchester. And secondly, I'm reconsidering our friendship right now.'

Kel laughs. 'Fine, Manchester. My point is the same. You'll thank me one day. Also, "bad" and "overrated" are not the same thing. People make that mistake all the time. The Beatles are great. That doesn't mean they're the greatest ever.'

Matt spreads his hands wide, like, *What can you do?* 'This isn't the first time we've had this conversation,' he says.

'Clearly not,' I say.

It's easier between the three of us after that. We find a free booth near the back of the pub and talk through three rounds. Matt gets his guitar and hands it over so I can try it out. It's a rich teal colour and completely beautiful. 'I want one,' I say, strumming gently. 'How many guitars do you have?'

'Four. Two electric, two acoustic,' he says. 'This is the acoustic I travel with.'

'It's gorgeous,' I say.

At this, Matt's smile widens into a brief, wolfish grin and he all but winks at me. He doesn't need to say anything; it's all in that one grin. My entire body goes *zing*.

I grin back. 'Mine's a bit battered. Plays good, though.' I hand the guitar back to him and he takes it, sliding it carefully back into its case.

I can tell by Kel's face that he thinks we're getting along too well, probably better than we're supposed to. He's glued to his phone and I can guess he's messaging Caddy, telling on us. I angle my head towards Matt's and lower my voice so only he can hear me. 'Caddy told me not to get too close to you.'

He turns his head slightly so our eyes meet. 'Yeah? Kel told me the same thing about you.'

I laugh, and then he laughs, and we're both laughing when Kel leans forward and asks why.

'We were just saying how perfect you and Caddy are together,' Matt says.

'So perfect,' I add.

Kel looks suspicious, but pleased. 'Thanks?' He glances at his phone. 'I'm going to head out, but I'm meeting some friends in town. You want to come?'

I shake my head. 'I've got work tomorrow morning. I can't be out till four.' Usually, I'd *want* to be out until four, but I'm *trying* to be better.

'Matt?'

'I'm wiped out,' Matt replies. 'Sorry.'

Kel shrugs, as easy as ever. 'You two are meant to be the wild ones.'

Matt glances at me. 'Yeah?'

'Yeah,' I say.

We both laugh again. Kel rolls his eyes. 'Right, I'm off. Be good, kids.' He drains his pint and stands, clapping his hands to his pockets to check for his wallet and phone.

When he's gone, I'm suddenly very aware of Matt and me being alone in this small space. The empty glasses on the table. The fact that he looks like he does. Caddy's plea.

'I should probably go, too,' I say. 'I really do have work tomorrow.'

Matt nods. 'Yeah, I need to get back as well. Shall we head out?' He stands, reaching for his jacket, and I follow suit.

It takes us a while to actually make it out of the pub because people keep stopping Matt, like they did earlier, to talk to him. He's polite and friendly, even as he makes his excuses; this is clearly something he's used to doing. When a conversation goes on a bit too long, his eyes find mine and he smiles apologetically. I don't mind. I like being on the inside of this, even for a few minutes.

When we finally make it outside, Matt yelps, 'Watch the step!' an instant before I tumble down it. He doesn't let go of me, so we end up half sprawled against the concrete, both of us laughing. 'Shit,' he says. 'Sorry. I should've said that sooner.'

'Just a few seconds earlier would have helped,' I say. I let him pull me to my feet. 'Which way are you headed?' I hope it's at least part of the way to my flat so I can have his arm around me for a little longer.

'Wherever you're going,' Matt replies immediately. His grin is boyish, full of charm and promise.

'Yeah, no,' I say, laughing.

'Let me walk you home,' Matt insists. 'It's dark. I'm a gentleman.'

'Sure you are.' I am smiling so much it almost hurts. 'I'm sure you'd be a gentleman all night.'

His eyes light up. He bites on his lip momentarily. 'You are something else,' he says.

'I'll take that,' I say casually, as if the words haven't made dragonflies start flitting around in my stomach, poking my insides with jolts of pure *yay*. 'Seriously, though. Where are you staying?'

Matt's lip pouts out dramatically for a second, then he gives in. 'Kemptown way.'

'Damn,' I say. 'We're going in opposite directions.'

Matt puts a hand to his chest. 'You're breaking my heart.'

'Oh, stop it,' I say, but I can't help laughing.

And then he has taken a step closer to me, he is right up against me, right in the middle of the street. His hand is there on the small of my back. His other hand is at my face. He is kissing me.

It is a brief, heart-stopping kiss. His mouth opens mine and our tongues touch before we break apart at the same moment. Sometimes a brief kiss is all you need. Sometimes it's better than more.

I cannot stop myself from smiling a huge, ridiculous smile. His eyes soften and he tilts his head slightly. For a moment I think he's going to kiss me again, but instead he says, simple and sincere, 'You're beautiful.'

'You're not so bad yourself,' I reply.

He smiles, and it's like he knows me. Like he can see me. It's like a light has been switched on inside me.

'Are you doing anything tomorrow?' he asks.

Tomorrow. So soon.

'I'm working till two,' I say, keeping my voice casual. 'Why?'

'I'm not heading back to London till five,' Matt says. 'Want to hang out?'

'Hang out,' I repeat slowly.

He smiles again. 'I'll buy you a coffee. We'll go to the beach.'

I hesitate. 'Like a date?'

He laughs. 'I'm not a dating kind of guy. But I like you. You're fun. And I want to see you again before I go back. You don't have to, though.'

'OK,' I say. Why not? I want to see him again, too.

'Cool. Let me take your number.'

We exchange numbers, the lights of our phones shining in the space between us in the middle of the street. I am thinking: *He likes me. I am fun.*

We separate with a brief touch – he squeezes my fingertips so gently I am left wondering if it really happened – and a smile. No second kiss. He doesn't try to touch me or cajole me back to his place. He doesn't say that he'll see me tomorrow with a leer on his face.

I go home disorientated but with a fizz of happiness that starts in my stomach and bubbles up through my chest. I fall asleep looking forward to tomorrow.

10

'Mess Is Mine'
Vance Joy

I don't hear anything from Matt all the following morning, and there's no way in hell I'm going to message him first. I mean, it's possible I daydreamed about kissing him all the time I was making coffee. So what? That's normal behaviour. It's not like I was imagining him with his shirt off, or anything. Not much, anyway.

My point is I can totally survive without ever seeing him again. It's not like there's a shortage of guys in Brighton for me to—

Buzz.

My heart leaps, the traitor.

Matt:

> Hey! Still on for coffee and the beach?

No kiss. But an exclamation mark. This has potential.

Me:

> Hiya. Sure, where shall I meet you?

Matt:

> Cool. Seafront. Bandstand? 2.30?

> Sounds good. See you then.

I am a cool, collected, in-control girl. My messages give absolutely nothing away, because there's nothing to give away. I'm going to go and chill out with him at the beach. That's what people do in Brighton.

I go straight to the bandstand after work, so my clothes are bog-standard jeans and a T-shirt. Maybe this should bother me, but it doesn't. I've never seen the point in dressing up for guys. If they just want you for what you're wearing then they're not worth dressing up for anyway, and guys who just want sex will take it whatever you're wearing. Meeting a guy in the most relaxed clothes I own makes me feel confident. It's a counter-intuitive way of getting the upper hand.

I did touch up my make-up before I left the cafe, though. I'm not *that* relaxed.

I make it to the bandstand first and sit in the sun, closing my eyes under my sunglasses. There's a couple behind me having a fight, something about an anniversary. I wonder how long they've been together.

'Hey.' The voice is above me. A shoe touches the tip of my Vans. I look up. 'Hey.'

Matt smiles at me. 'Afternoon. Coffee?'

I pull myself to my feet and brush myself off. 'I'm sick of coffee. I've been pouring it all day. But a beverage of some kind would be good.'

He doesn't move in to kiss or touch me, just swings himself so we are side by side and starts walking towards the pier. 'Which coffee shop is it you work in?' he asks.

'Why?'

He grins. 'Suspicious. You don't want me dropping in?'

'No way,' I say. 'I don't want you seeing the apron I have to wear.'

'Now I really want to drop in,' he says, ducking when I take a swipe at him. 'I bet you'd look cute in an apron.'

'Cute?' I repeat, smiling. It's such a daytime word.

'And synonyms thereof.'

I'm about to call him pretentious but he silences me by taking my hand. Just reaches out and takes it, like it's a normal thing to do. He lifts my hand and presses a kiss into my knuckles, his eyes full of something I'm not used to seeing, then lets go.

There's a full-on jazz band playing inside my chest. My heart is a tambourine. I want to step back into the moment, already passed, and stay there. I want to tell him I like his face even more in the daylight.

'How very suave of you,' I say, raising my eyebrows at him, half approving, half teasing. 'Very 1920s.'

'Like I said,' Matt replies. 'I'm a gentleman. Hey –' he gestures ahead of us to the Palace Pier – 'what's your favourite place on the pier?'

I make a face. 'I'm not really a pier kind of girl.'

'Bullshit,' he says cheerfully. 'What's not to love about a pier? Crowds of tourists, obnoxious music on a loop, that oily doughnut smell . . .'

I look at him.

'Come on.' He lets out a laugh. 'It'll be fun. I'll buy you a smoothie. Because, I am . . . wait for it . . .'

'Don't do it.'

'A *smoothie*.'

He looks so pleased with himself that I crack up laughing despite myself.

'If you've never had fun on the pier,' he says, 'it's because you've never been on the pier with *me*.'

'You sound very confident in your fun-making abilities.'

'I know how to show a girl a good time.' He says this with a straight face, then flashes a wicked grin at me. My heart pings.

'Go on then,' I say gamely. 'Prove it.'

*

He does. We spend one of the best hours I've ever spent in Brighton. He buys me a mango smoothie and then drinks most of it himself as he tells me about the Paul-McCartney-is-actually-dead conspiracy. He puts his arm around me as we stand at the edge of the pier, pointing to buildings in the distance and telling me what they are.

We share a bag of chips, and though our fingers touch and collide, even as the salt and the grease and the vinegar coats our fingers and our lips the same way, we don't kiss. He teases me with a chip, holding it out to me, pulling it back, then pushing it into my mouth. But he doesn't kiss me.

Further along the pier, he stops at one of the oversized claw-machine games and promises to win me a giraffe. This is clearly impossible and I lose track of the coins he wastes trying to achieve it anyway. Eventually he turns to look at me with the most adorable mix of embarrassment, guilt and bravado on his face I've ever seen.

We head into the arcade and play air hockey until I'm breathless. After, he parks me at a 2p machine and I realize after a minute or two of feeding in the coins that he's disappeared. I push in a few more coins and cause a cascade to tumble down from the 2p cliff edge. I've never won so many coins in an arcade before and I'm thrilled and annoyed with Matt for missing it, but then I turn and there he is, holding the giraffe so its face is his face. He ducks his head out, grinning.

I give my pot of 2p coins to a girl who'd been trailing after two older siblings and she lights up like I've given her an actual fortune. Matt and I leave the arcade and walk to the end of the pier, where the wind blows my hair around my face so uncontrollably that the world blurs. When I laugh, my hair blows into my mouth and I taste salty air.

Matt uses both his hands to brush the hair from my face, tucking it behind my ears. He's smiling at me, his face is so close, and we kiss because it's inevitable, because that's what you do in moments like this. It is so different from the countless kisses I've had before. He doesn't press his pelvis against mine, doesn't shove his tongue past my own, doesn't push a hand under my clothes. It isn't a question or a demand. It's just a kiss.

He puts his arm around my shoulder and we walk back along the pier. I tell him about how when I was a kid, my family had a Westie named Giles, which is the kind of story I can tell from my childhood that is true, happy and ordinary. I don't have many of those, and I usually ration them, but with Matt it spills out.

And then it's time for him to get the train back to London. I walk with him to the train station and wait as he buys a coffee for the journey. When we part, he takes my hand and kisses my knuckles again. I think *chaste*, and I smile. He tells me he had a great time, and I nod, say I did too. I watch him walk away. We didn't talk about seeing each other again. He hasn't told me he'll message me. Our time together feels bracketed into a day, safe and special and contained. A parenthesis of goodness.

I go home and boil water for noodles, which I eat sitting on my bed, straight out of the pot, watching YouTube videos. Rosie calls and we talk and laugh for a while about things that matter and things that don't. When I go to bed I put Radical Face on Spotify and lie in the dark, listening until I feel sleep coming on.

This is my perfect day.

Matt messages me the next day, and then again the day after, and we fall easily into one of those indefinite WhatsApp conversations you have with the right people. He follows me on Twitter even though I only got an account to follow Taylor Swift when I was about thirteen and never tweet. I scroll through his old tweets – making sure not to accidentally like any from months ago and reveal myself – and see that his Twitter self is a lot like his on-stage self: cool, funny, a bit dry.

I listen to his music, of course. In the privacy of my little bedsit, I go all-in, listening to the songs on Spotify (an EP and a couple of collaborations), SoundCloud (more songs, but rougher) and finally YouTube, where I find a load of videos people have recorded on their phones of him at various festivals and pub gigs like the one at the Third Bridge.

I send a few links to Rosie for her opinion and she sends me back a dry **Is this guy real or am I gatecrashing a daydream you're having?**

Me:

Ha! What do you think, though??

Rosie:

Not my type. Nice voice, though.

Rozzles!! More please.

I see why you're into him. He's very you.

I'm not INTO him.

lol ok. Anyway, I want to meet him properly before I give you the go-ahead.

Why do I need a go-ahead?

Because he's male and you're you.

Rozzzzzzzz.

Rosie:

Just let me protect you goddammit.

Me:

Did Caddy let you vet Kel?

Oh please. As if Caddy needs anyone vetting anyone for her.

So I'm the special case?

Yes. So very special.

I actually just wanted to know what you thought of the music.

SURE YOU DID. Like I said, not my kind of thing.
I could listen to it without dying, though.

Have I mentioned that I love you?

Ew, don't get all emotional now.

Xxxxxxxxxx

I hate you too xx

She messages me the next day – **You liiiiike him** – which makes me laugh because I receive it right in the middle of a WhatsApp conversation with Matt, where we're ranking Elvis songs in order from 'most classic' to least. He knows a lot more Elvis songs than I do – my family was never big on Elvis – so I'm actually googling most of the songs before replying. It's a lot more effort than I'd usually put into a simple WhatsApp conversation with a boy I've kissed.

But I like it. It all feels pressure-free and nice. He lives in London, so it's not like we can see each other and spoil it all by sleeping together. Which we clearly would, let's be honest. And we probably will, at some point. It's basically inevitable. But I like that the physical distance means we get to be properly friendly as well and actually get to know each other. I like him. He likes me. And I like that that's enough.

11

'Bird'
Billie Marten

It's a Monday, and I'm leaning against the counter at Madeline's during a lull in customers, wondering if a basset hound–beagle cross is called a 'baggle', when I hear the word 'abuse', and my whole brain snaps to attention. I glance around at Jamie, who's on shift with me, obliviously washing the coffee machine, and then towards the radio, which spat out that word into my lovely, beagle-y headspace.

'Do you think Tracey would mind if I changed the station?' I ask. He shrugs, but it's too late, anyway. I'm already listening.

The radio, which we're allowed to have on during quiet periods unless a customer complains, is broadcasting the news. *'Colin Ryeland denies murdering his stepdaughter, Kacie-Leigh –'* Oh no. Oh no – *'who was just eight years old when she died of injuries consistent, the prosecution alleges, with being kicked repeatedly in the chest.'* Oh God. Oh God, no. My heart is thundering, which makes no sense at all, and I try to breathe through my nose, slow and steady. *'The trial opened this morning with statements from—'*

I lean over and turn the radio off with one simple click. Silence. *Breathe.* I reach up and tighten my ponytail, feeling the strands of my hair under my fingers. I think: *Blonde.* I touch my bracelet. *Silver.* My apron. *Green.*

Everything's fine.

'Thanks,' Jamie says. 'That shit is so depressing.'

'Mmm,' I say.

'It's a weird story, though, right?' he adds. 'I read about it this morning.'

I try to think quickly of a way to divert him without giving away my secrets, but my brain is working too slow, and 'Mmm' is all I manage.

'It must just've been an accident,' he continues confidently. 'The guy they're blaming says she fell down the stairs, and I believe that. He seems like a decent guy. I know they're saying that he kicked her to death, but how could you kick someone to death?'

Blonde. Silver. Green. Everything's fine. *Blonde. Silver. Green.* But the words have landed heavy in my brain and flipped a switch. I am on the kitchen floor. *Blonde.* There is nothing but noise. *How could you kick someone to death?* Yelling, screaming. *Silver.* My arms around my face, my head. A boot in my chest. *Green.*

My blood is on fire, screaming through my veins, roaring in my ears. I take a step back from the counter, very calmly. I even manage to say, in a completely normal voice, 'Back in a sec.' I head out into the back, through the staff area and into the toilet. I lock the door, and as soon as the bolt slides into place I lose it. That's what happens; it's like losing the part of myself that holds me together. I press my forehead against the door, my hand against my mouth, and give in to it. The roar in my ears that might be my breath, or my panic, or my own thoughts – who even knows? My heart pounding thick and fast and heavy in my chest, like it just wants out of me.

I'm too far into it to do any of the things I'm meant to do. All those tricks and techniques I learned so carefully from the staff at Gwillim. The breathing exercises and the breaking of thought patterns and everything that makes so much sense, they all become pointless little sandbags against a tsunami of panic.

When I find my way back to myself, I'm left shaking all over. My hands have balled into fists so tight, I've cut into my palms with my nails. But I'm breathing, I am me, I am fine. I sit on the toilet lid and breathe deeply in and out for a few minutes, touching my sleeves to my eyes to dab away the wetness so I don't give myself away with big red blotches.

I'm fine.

I spread both hands over my knees, my fingers splaying out and then curling in again. I unclip my badge from my apron and then fasten it back. I stand up and stare at my reflection in the mirror. I smile.

I'm fine.

'Where did you go?' Jamie asks when I take my place next to him at the counter. There aren't any more people in the shop than when I left.

'That is a very weird question to ask a girl who just popped out the back for a couple of minutes,' I say. 'Where do you think I was?'

He laughs. 'Sorry.'

There's no trace in his expression or voice that suggests he can tell I was in such a state only a few minutes ago, so I relax, pleased with myself. If I can do nothing else, at least I know how to put a face on.

For the rest of the day I'm fine, which is a relief. I'm a little wobbly, but only deep, deep inside, and it's easily ignored. What happened was just a blip, a slight but understandable overreaction to a news story, that's all. I serve coffee and cake to strangers, laugh with Jamie, wipe the counters every five minutes. I put one of our staff playlists on over the main speakers instead of the radio. A customer complains about the amount of froth on his cappuccino. The day passes.

By the time I leave work, throwing my hood up over my head as the rain falls in half-hearted sheets, I'm fine. So fine, I decide it's safe to do a quick search for 'Kacie-Leigh Ryeland' when I get home, just to get the facts of the case, that's all. I sit on my bed with my phone and glance through the headlines of the articles that come up, some from today, but a few from a few months back, when she first died and her stepfather was arrested. I read the first one, from BBC News, thinking that I'll choose the most sensible one and then leave it at that. But then I read a *Guardian* article. And then one from the *Sun*. And then the *Daily Mail*. I click, read, scroll. There are pictures of Kacie-Leigh's beaming round face, too full of life to be dead.

When I'm done, it's not by choice. It's because I've run out of articles. I feel sick and sad and hollow all at once. I know more than any one person should know about Kacie-Leigh's catalogue of injuries, especially someone who once had a catalogue of injuries herself. But that's not even the worst thing. The worst thing is the things people say about Colin Ryeland. The various journalists have talked to next-door neighbours, colleagues, friends.

I always thought of him as a decent, hard-working man. Devoted to his family. This is just such a sad story, for everyone involved.

I can't help feeling that there must be some mistake. Anyone who knows Colin would tell you, he loves those kids of his.

This is such a shock. I've always liked Colin and his family. He's so friendly and generous, always willing to help out if we needed it. I'm so shocked this has happened.

I think: *Of course he was friendly and generous. To you.* Why do people think the way someone is outside of the house says anything about how they are inside it? Don't they realize that people *lie*? People would have said exactly the same kinds of things about my dad if there'd ever been news stories like this about our family. I would have, too, if I'd only seen what they saw. But I had to see the other face, the real one. Just like Kacie-Leigh and Colin Ryeland.

I stand up and walk to the kitchen, pouring myself a glass of water just to have something to do. I'm fine, but my throat feels a little tight. Maybe I shouldn't have read all those articles. I pull my phone out again and message my brother. **Did you hear about Kacie-Leigh Ryeland?**

He replies within two minutes. **Yeah. Don't read any of the stories, OK? They'll just upset you.**

Little bit late. I reply, **Why?** just to see what he says.

Brian:

> You know why, that's why you asked me in the first place. Just don't read them. It's a horrible story and I wish people would stop talking about it.

Me:

> Have you talked to Mum or Dad about it?

> What? No, of course not.

> Can you?

> Why??

> I want to know what they say.

> Fuck's sake, Zanne. No. Look, this kind of story upsets me, too. It's not just you.

> Why are you snapping at me?

> I'm not. Jesus. Sorry. I just don't want to talk about this, ever.

> Does it upset you because it could have been me?

> It wouldn't have been you.

The reply is worse than no reply at all, because it's missing the point so completely, I can't help but wonder if he's done it on purpose. I put my phone down and concentrate on my breathing for a while, closing my eyes against the empty room. It works in keeping a panic attack at bay, but that's all. Instead, I have the sudden, overwhelming need to not be by myself. It comes on strong, like it does sometimes, and the room is too small, there's not enough air. The second thought, following on from the brain flare of *See other people!*, is that I don't want to see anyone I know well, or even at all. What I want is to escape myself.

I change out of my work clothes into my favourite black skinny jeans and dark silver cami. I take my time, because it's still early, painting my nails and sipping vodka straight from the bottle while I wait for them to dry. Tiny sips, barely enough to taste.

This is normal. People go out. Sure, it's a Monday, but I live in a student city. There are always people around looking for a good time. All I need is a distraction, just for a night, to drain the weird, churny feeling from inside of me.

A new message comes in. Caddy. She's excited because she's got a job at a juice bar on campus. Eight hours a week. *Good for you*, I think, with a meanness she doesn't deserve. I take another sip of the vodka and don't reply.

I settle myself in front of the mirror, which is propped up against the wall, and lay out all of my make-up in front of me. I build up my face layer by layer, watching myself turn into someone else. Or not someone else, exactly. A different version of me. A better version. Maybe if Kacie-Leigh had had another ten years, she would have been able to do this.

Shit, messed up the eyeliner. Start again. Don't let the hand shake this time.

When I'm done, I feel strong again. I put my hair up in a half-bun, carefully messy, and choose the right gloss for my lips. Perfect.

I head out into the cool air of the night. It's barely past eight, which is just late enough. I'm not sure where I'm going, so I just meander towards town and stop at a pub I went to once with Kel, Caddy and Rosie over the summer. It's a bit of a cross between a pub and a bar, with a couple of pool tables and a dartboard, and I remember Kel saying it was a popular student hang-out during term-time.

It's pretty busy, thankfully, so I take a seat at the bar and order a lime and soda. The barman raises his eyebrows at me, and I smile. 'I'm waiting for someone,' I say. Which is true, in a way.

It takes barely five minutes for that someone to arrive. He's wearing a polo shirt and jeans, and he looks like every other guy wearing a polo shirt and jeans. He could be anyone.

'Same again, please, mate,' he says to the barman. And then he spots me, glances around and looks back. He smiles. 'Hey,' he says.

'Hi,' I say. I smile a brave little half-smile.

'You on your own?' he asks.

'I wasn't supposed to be,' I say. I look towards the door, then back at him, rolling my phone between my fingers like I need it to be close. 'I think I might've been stood up.'

'No *way*,' he says. 'Boyfriend?'

'Tinder,' I say.

He laughs. 'Oh, shit.'

'This doesn't usually happen to me,' I say.

'I bet it doesn't.'

'I kind of . . . don't really know what to do with myself now.' I'm a bit worried I'm not being subtle enough, but one look at his face and I know there's no need. This guy has already fallen way in. 'I should probably go, I guess?'

'No way,' he says again. 'Why waste a night out, right? At least let me get you a drink.'

Success. I'm so proud of myself, I have to bite my lip to stop the grin I can feel trying to spread across my face. 'That's so nice of you. Are you sure?'

'Yeah, course.' He puffs out his chest a little and says to the barman – who has arranged four pints on the bar in front of him and is waiting patiently, if a little pointedly – 'Another one of –' he glances back at me and points at my drink – 'whatever that was.'

Shit. I look at the barman, who catches my eye and smirks. 'Vodka, lime and soda?' he asks.

'Well remembered,' I say, beaming.

'I'm Jake,' the guy says. 'Listen, you want to come hang out with us for a bit? Just so you don't have a wasted night.' He gestures with his head over to one of the pool tables, where two other guys and a girl are clustered, arguing about where to put the cue ball.

I'm careful not to look too keen, swirling my straw in my new drink, nibbling my lip. 'Is that . . . Would that be OK?'

'Yeah, of course!' he says enthusiastically. 'Are you any good at pool?'

'I'm not bad,' I say. I'm actually great at pool. 'I'll be messing up your teams, though.'

'We'll figure something out,' he says. 'C'mon.'

Jake, it turns out, is average at pool in the way of a guy who thinks he's amazing at pool, striking the balls too hard and making loud, meaningless comments about angles. I play down my own ability and miss shots on purpose, letting him give me useless tips for holding the cue, acting surprised when I pot a ball. I make friends with the girl, the girlfriend of one of the guys, who is sweet and shy but cheerful, and doesn't seem to mind that I've gatecrashed her night out.

Everything is going right but I'm finding it harder than usual to play this game. Every now and then, the wobble comes back, catching me off guard, slipping the smile from my face. I push it down and away, willing myself to just be as OK as I want to be. It's all a show, it's just a game. *I am fine.*

I pretend, pretend, pretend until I finally hit the sweet spot of drunk where I no longer care but can still actually function, and then everything really is fine. This is exactly what I wanted.

Jake asks me to come to the club with them, and I don't want to be on my own, so I say yes. We dance, he buys me drinks. He asks if I want to do shots, and I don't want to be on my own, so I say yes. We dance some more. He kisses me, and I let him. I kiss him back. He says, 'Want to come back to ours for an after party?' and I don't want to be on my own, so I say yes. The house is loud and there's beer in big red cups. He takes me upstairs to his room, closes the door, asks me if I want to, and I don't want to be on my own, so I say yes. His hands are gentle until they aren't.

I stumble home when the sky is turning pink, find my way into my shower and sit there under the water until time blurs, the world fades and . . . I jerk awake, pruned and groggy. My head hurts, but a paracetamol or two takes that away. I go to work and the monotony of strangers is blissful until I have to leave. As soon as I'm out the door, everything rushes back, so sharp it takes my breath. I lean against the wall, cool on my shoulders, and close my eyes, concentrating on my heartbeat until it calms down.

I know I'm not in a good place. I can feel myself on the edge of something, but I'm weirdly separate from it. It's hard to care.

So I do the opposite. I ignore all the calls and messages from the people who love me until they drain my battery dead. I go out again, but to a bar this time. The end result is the same. I stay out for as long as I can, long enough that I only have time to shower before I have to go to work. I drink three espressos and shake through my shift until it's time for my break, which I sleep through. 'Are you OK?' Farrah, my favourite workmate, asks.

'Yeah,' I say.

I'm out again that night, sliding effortlessly into a group of strangers. Everything is fine, fine, fine. I'm pulling the same tricks but this time there's a girl, older than me with searching eyes, who pulls me gently off the lap of the guy who'd been reading my palm and puts her arm around me. 'I can see you,' she says, and it makes no sense but I let her hug me and it's the best thing. Somehow, I end up wedged between her and her friends, all girls, clustered around me like shields, and they're telling me about their boyfriends, one story after another. The girl braids my hair absently as they talk and I forget about the palm-reader and it's nice for a while, until one of them asks me what's wrong and part of me breaks and I know they can tell and I say I'll be right back and I leave.

I have to go home but it's still too early, way too early, but there's nowhere I can go, so I go home. I let myself into the building and dawdle there in the entrance. I look at Dilys's closed door, imagine myself knocking on it. She'll let me in. She'll make me tea. She'll tell me everything's OK.

As I stand there, I know I won't. How can I inflict myself on this woman? It's after midnight. She's asleep. And anyway I don't want her to see me this way. The real me, the ugly, worthless real me. *Wasted* me. All the shine stripped away. I can't even smile. Dilys deserves smiles.

I stand in the hallway, staring at the fire alarm, imagining pressing it and forcing everyone else in the building to come out, to be with me, just for a while. There's a whisper from my rational brain, *There are people who will help you*, but I ignore it. I make myself go upstairs and open the door to my shitty, empty flat. I sit on the floor by the window, back against the wall, and smoke the entire bag of weed I'd been saving. Rolling, lighting, smoking, over and over, until it's gone. When I stand up, I feel like I'm underwater and it's disorientating until I pass out on my bed and it all goes away.

When I wake up I go to work, and Tracey's there, and she looks at me, and she says, 'Suze, you're not working today. It's Thursday. And it's almost three in the afternoon. What's the matter, Suze? Suze?'

Somehow, I end up back at Ventrella Road. I'm in Tracey's car. She says, 'I want you to call me tonight, OK? Call my mobile. If you don't, I'll come right back here to check on you. OK?'

I must say something back but I don't know what it is. I walk upstairs, and I'm thinking that I won't make that call.

'Oh, Jesus, Suzie.' And it's Sarah, sitting outside my front door, looking all horrified, getting to her feet, reaching for me.

I say, 'What?'

She's taking my key from me, her hand is cupping my face. She's asking, 'When did you last eat? When did you last sleep?' and I don't know why she looks so worried. We're inside my flat and she's packing a bag for me, talking at me, opening my kitchen cupboards and shaking her head at empty shelves.

I let myself be led out of the flat and down the stairs, across the drive and into her car where I sit, silent, until we get to her street and the place I used to live. Inside the door, the cat, Henry Gale, mews insistently at my feet. Sarah scoops him up with her free hand and takes us both into what was once my room, now a guest room, and I break. I crumble. I cry.

'Oh, Suzie, it's OK,' she says, but her voice sounds helpless and I don't want her to be helpless, I want her to be sure. I want to believe that it's OK, but it's not, it's not, it's not.

The tears are overwhelming and they won't stop. I can't do anything except sit on the bed and cry. At some point I choke out, 'Kacie-Leigh,' and she lets out a kind of sigh-gasp and says something about how she should have known, should have checked, should have thought, but I can't concentrate hard enough to listen.

The photo of Kacie-Leigh from the news reports is all I can think about. Her smiling, happy face. I say, 'She was just a kid.'

Sarah touches my face. 'I know, darling. I know.'

'No one helped her.'

I think she might be crying, too. 'I know.'

What I don't say: *It could have been me. Do you know how easily it could have been me?* Another kid on the news to make people sad, the same people who ignore the kids with bruises and fake smiles, the same people who tut at the girls who grow out of being kids like that and turn into teenagers like me with detentions and suspensions and an attitude problem.

And it's going to keep happening. Over and over and over. Angry men with flying fists and kicking feet and helpless kids like Kacie-Leigh and me.

So I cry because there's nothing else I can do, and I'm so, so, so tired. I cry until I fall asleep.

12

'This Time Tomorrow'
Trent Dabbs

I sleep for the next sixteen hours. What finally wakes me is the softest *whump* by my head, and then the light touch of a nose in my hair. It's Henry Gale, settling himself on the pillow. I just lie there for a while, listening to his gentle purring, trying not to think about anything. I can hear the old familiar sounds of Sarah walking around the kitchen, and the feeling that I never really left this place is somehow both comforting and disconcerting.

After a while, she very quietly puts her head around the door, sees me awake and smiles. 'Tea?' she says simply.

'I have to go to work,' I say. My voice is gravelly.

'It's OK,' she says. 'I spoke to your manager. You're not well and you need to take a few days to get better. She understands. Tea?'

I have tea. Actually, over the next few hours, I have multiple teas. Sarah brings in her laptop and chooses a podcast for me to listen to – *Limetown*, very weird but totally compelling – and I stay there in bed, listening and staring at the ceiling, drinking tea and petting Henry Gale. In the afternoon, I make myself get out of bed and have a long shower, so hot I'm breathing in steam, letting myself cry in the way you can in a shower, punching my knuckles against the tiles hard enough to hurt but gently enough so my skin won't tear and Sarah won't hear. Mini-shower-breakdowns are immensely satisfying, and when I turn the water off and stand for a while in the steam, I feel soothed.

I dress in a pair of pyjamas Sarah's left for me, put on a dressing gown and go into the living room, where she's watching a weather report. I settle myself beside her, tucking my shins underneath me, and lean my head against the back of the sofa. Henry Gale decamps himself from Sarah's lap on to mine, purrs vibrating through his warm little body.

'Are you ready to talk about it?' Sarah asks.

'Not yet,' I say.

I sit in the garden the next day, the cat splayed out in the sunshine beside me. I make my way through all the messages that have accumulated on my phone while I'd cut myself off. There are so many, the increasing worry radiating out of the screen, that they make me feel a bit panicky. Brian, Caddy, Rosie, Kel, Matt, even Farrah from work. I'm replying carefully to each message, making sure I sound as OK as possible, when Sarah comes out with two cups of tea.

'Listen,' she says, and I know what's coming. I put my phone down and pull my knees up to my chest. 'I need to talk to you about what happened. I have to ask you something important, something that's really worrying me.'

'OK,' I say. I wait for her to ask me exactly what I was doing those nights I wasn't sleeping; who I was with.

There's a beat of silence before she speaks, like she's gathering herself. 'Did you speak to Rosie or Caddy when you started to feel low?'

This line is a surprise. 'Um. No?'

'OK. Did you call your brother?'

'No.'

'Anyone?'

My chest has tightened. 'No.'

'Suzie.' My name as a sigh. 'Do you know why that is incredibly frightening for me? Can you see that?'

I let my shoulders lift and then fall.

'Please, I really need to know this. Why not? Why didn't you come to one of us?'

I don't know how to answer this. Why didn't I? Did I even think about doing it? No, not consciously. And when they tried to call me, I ignored them.

'Did you think we wouldn't help?' she presses when I don't reply.

'No,' I say eventually, and my voice sounds all hoarse. I swallow. 'It's more like . . .' I take a breath, slow and even. *Come on, be honest.* 'It's more like I knew you *would.*'

'OK,' she says, and there's a kind of energy in her voice now, like she thinks we're getting somewhere. 'OK. So, on some level, you didn't want help?'

This is what people like Sarah will never understand. What none of them will ever understand. How you can want help and not want it at the same time. It's not even about levels. It's just confusion all the way down.

'We all love you, Suzie. So much.'

'Too much.' I don't mean to say this out loud, but the words spill anyway.

'No,' she says immediately, but firmly. 'Not too much. Why do you think that?'

Because I don't deserve it. Because I'm a burden. Because them loving me just makes those things more true.

'I just . . .' I begin, but there are just too many words and none of them are the right ones, not ones she'll understand.

'Darling,' she says, and I think about my mother using that word, every now and then. Just every now and then. 'You have to let people love you.' When I don't reply, because I don't know how, she says, 'Sometimes that means letting yourself be helped. You don't have to do this on your own. You're not on your own.'

My voice comes out very small. My hands are inside my sleeves. 'It feels like I am.'

'Then I'm sorry. I'm sorry that it feels that way. But you can always come to me. Always. I'm right here. You know I'd have you back here living with me if I could.'

I try to smile. 'Because that worked out so well last time?'

She doesn't smile back. Her face is so serious. 'Things are different now. It won't ever be like it was then. I promise you that.' I look down at my lap so she can't see that I'm crying again. 'Oh, Suzie,' she says, so soft. She hugs me in tight and kisses the side of my head. We've never done this before. I've never let her this close, not ever.

I manage, 'Can I stay another day?'

'You can stay as long as you need,' she says.

13

'Secret for the Mad'
dodie

When I get back to Ventrella Road, the first thing I do is knock for Dilys. Guilt for missing our usual laundry day is eating me up and all I want to do is apologize and see her smile at me. I'll tell her about Kacie-Leigh, I've decided. She won't be over the top with her sympathy, but she'll understand why I got so upset, I'm sure. She'll make me tea. She'll let me cuddle Clarence.

That's what I should have done in the first place, obviously. I realize that, now I've calmed down. I should have just come straight downstairs, knocked for Dilys and asked to play with Clarence. Everyone knows dogs are good for depression.

There's no answer, so I wait for a while, imagining Dilys making her slow way across her large flat, until it occurs to me that there's no barking coming from the other side of the door. If there's no barking, there's no Clarence. And if there's no Clarence, there's no Dilys. She must be out walking him.

Disappointment floods in and I sigh, touching my fingertips to the door. This isn't our usual time to meet, and it was stupid to assume she'd be available to me just because I needed her. It's not like her sole reason for existence is the bedsit girl without a washing machine.

I go upstairs to my flat and let myself in, dropping my bag on the floor and stepping up on to my bed. It's not as comfortable as the bed at Sarah's, and already I miss the sounds of another person in the same space. I settle back against the wall and allow myself a self-pitying sigh, closing my eyes against the empty room.

Maybe more than anything else, I'm frustrated. I feel like I've somehow undone months of progress. It's been three years since I left Reading and my abusive home. Three years. Two since Gwillim and therapy. One since I really started to feel like I had moved past the time in my life when I was prone to panic attacks and the kind of spiral that swallowed my week. But one news story, one passing comment from a colleague, and I'm spun. I'm triggered. I'm *gone*.

I try to think it all through rationally, now I'm actually able to do that again. What made it so bad this time? Would the same thing have happened if I'd still been in Southampton with Christie and Don? *No*, my brain says immediately. OK, but why not? *Because you'd have talked to Christie about it.*

It's not like I'm missing out on people to talk to here, though. Sarah would listen to me. Kel, too, though he probably wouldn't know what to say, and I'd worry about how much would get filtered back to Caddy. And there's Dilys, of course. I could talk to her if I wanted. But the thought of cracking myself open like that in front of her, letting her – letting *anyone* – see how fragile I really am, is unbearable. There's a reason it's easier with professionals.

I chew on my thumbnail for a while, staring at my phone, before I gather every part of me that's mature and sensible and call my personal adviser. It goes to voicemail, so I leave a rambly, probably incoherent message about wanting to get a therapist or a counsellor. Miriam calls me back within the hour and we talk through the options. I obviously can't afford a private therapist and on the NHS it would likely be an eight-week round of CBT sessions, which, after being at Gwillim House, would be like learning the seven-times-table to take a Maths degree. Miriam suggests group counselling, but I did enough of that at Gwillim and I know it's not quite what I need right now.

'Hmm,' Miriam says. 'Let me look into it, OK? We'll find a way.

Is there anything you want to talk about with me? We could meet for coffee?'

'Maybe,' I say. 'I'll see when I'm working.'

We both know I won't.

When I hang up, I see a message from Kel on my phone inviting me to a last-minute Halloween party at his house, and I'm sick of dwelling on my own misery, so I go. I wear a sequinned black skirt and a long-sleeved Superman jumper, which isn't exactly Halloweeny, but I don't care. When I arrive, I decide on a whim that I won't drink, and I spend most of the night on the sofa beside Kel, playing FIFA with him and a bunch of his friends.

Apart from when I first walk through the front door, Kel doesn't ask me endlessly if I'm OK, where I was, what happened. Every now and then I feel him look at me until I turn and catch his eye, and he smiles and I smile back.

'Do you have any sisters?' I ask him, when most people have left and he's brought me a blanket so I can sleep on the sofa.

'Three,' he says. 'Why?'

'It shows,' I say.

In the morning, we go on a McDonalds run together. His car smells of the Jelly Belly air freshener he has hanging from the rear-view mirror, and there are textbooks all over the back seat. We're waiting in the drive-thru queue when he says, 'You can come to mine any time you want, you know. Literally any time.'

I'm not sure what to say, so I don't reply.

'Even if there's not a party or whatever,' he says. 'You can just come and hang out. If you ever need . . .' He trails off. 'There's always someone awake at our place. And even if there isn't, you can play on the Xbox or something. I can get you a spare key, if you want.'

I bite down on the side of my thumb, because I can feel tears coming, the type that come from kindness.

'Caddy told me about how you both used to hang out at night when you lived here before,' he adds.

'Oh God,' I say, finding my voice with a smile. 'I was the *worst*.'

'That's not how she tells it,' he says. We've reached the drive-thru window and he rattles off our order, interrupting himself midway through to tell the server that he likes her Totoro pin. I watch him, wondering what it's like to be so comfortable with the world and everyone in it.

I go home later that afternoon, but there's still no answer when I knock on Dilys's door. No barking, either. I dither nervously in the hallway, wondering whether I should be worried or not. They could be out for a walk together. She might be seeing friends. If there was barking and no answer, that would be reason to worry. She's probably just gone away for a few days and not had a chance to tell me.

The next day, when there's no answer on my way to work and no answer when I get back, I write a note – *Let me know when you're back! Suzanne x* – and slide it under the door. I'm trying not to overreact, but my head keeps leaping to worst-case-scenario mode. I mention her absence to Sarah, hoping for reassurance. 'If she'd died,' she said, 'there'd be a lot of people coming and going into the flat. No news is good news.'

That weekend, Brian drives down from Cardiff to visit for a couple of days. He sleeps in Sarah's guest room but spends the daytime with me. I show him my flat – his face flashes with alarm when he first walks inside, but he tries to hide it – and take him on a Brighton tour, stopping into Madeline's so he can see where I work. He's in full older brother mode, protective and concerned, checking through my rental documents and even my work contract, buying me lunch, borrowing tools from one of the flats downstairs to fix my window frame, which has been loose since I first moved in. We don't talk about Kacie-Leigh, or our parents, or how close I'd come to collapsing. I tell myself there are some things we just don't need to talk about, and he's here, and that's enough.

On Sunday, after a roast dinner at Sarah's, Brian comes back to my flat one last time before he leaves to drive back to Cardiff.

'Listen,' he says, looking around my flat. 'I just want to say, because I don't know if you realize, that you're doing really well.'

I'd been expecting him to give me a lecture about not taking care of myself properly. His words are such a surprise, I just blink at him.

'Honestly, Zannie,' he says. 'Living on your own like this, and having your job and everything. I'm proud of you.'

'You are?' Proud of me. *Proud.* 'But I haven't done anything.' Brian got a first-class degree. My parents went to his graduation. There's a photo of all three of them; I've seen it on Brian's desk. When I think of 'proud', I think of that photo.

'You've survived,' he says. 'And you're still just as brilliant and funny and sweet as you were when you were eight. That's pretty amazing. All things considered.'

'All things considered,' I repeat. The compliments are nice, and they're warming up the parts of me that are still cold after my spiral, but does he have to be so vague at the same time? Can't he just say it?

'You know what I mean,' he says. So, I guess, no. He can't say it.

'Because I was in care?' I ask. 'Or what got me there?'

Brian's face gives a reflexive wince, just a tiny one, like he's bracing himself against me elaborating further. What a weird thing this is, the distance of our adult lives. How strange it must be for him, to have a sister who's a care leaver when he isn't. To have come from the same place but ended up in such completely different circumstances. To have been the lucky one. I wonder how he explains that to his friends, to potential girlfriends. He probably doesn't mention it at all.

I don't push him. 'Thanks. I'm trying.'

'I know,' he says. He pulls me in for a hug. 'And you know you can talk to me any time, right? I'm always here for you.'

I nod, smiling.

'Stay safe, OK?' He's putting on his jacket, glancing at his phone to check the time. He flashes a grin at me. 'Don't make me worry about you.'

The thing is, I know he's kidding. I know this is just a throwaway comment for him, that he doesn't mean it in a bad way. He means to be affectionate and brotherly. But really, what it does is remind me that he *does* worry about me, that I'm a person to be worried about, and that he thinks him worrying about me is something I make him do on purpose. And that all *sucks*, to be honest. That's all the things I hate about myself, all there in a six-word sentence.

But of course I don't say any of that. 'Only on Tuesdays,' I say, and even though it doesn't make any sense, he laughs and we say goodbye and he leaves. I'm on my own again, and everything is quiet.

I take a breath, sit on my bed and pick up my phone. When I scroll, I get to Caddy's name first. I press call. She picks up almost immediately, her happy voice sounding in my ear. 'Suze!'

'Hey,' I say. My eyes have teared over but I blink a few times to clear it, settling back against the wall, imagining Caddy in her little student bedroom, stopping whatever she's doing to talk to me. 'How are you?'

14

'Call It Dreaming'
Iron & Wine

It's not until Tuesday that I get home from work to see Dilys's door open. There's a leap of joyful relief in my chest and I rush forward, leaning my head around it.

'Dil—' I stop. There are two men standing in the living room, but no Dilys, and no Clarence. 'Oh.'

'Can I help you?' one of the men asks. He's middle-aged, with thinning dark hair and a thick, short beard. The second man is holding a clipboard, and he looks bored.

'Who are you?' I ask. Nerves make my voice tense because I know, I just know, that he's going to tell me that Dilys is dead, that she died while I was off getting wasted in some random bar because somehow I still haven't learned how to deal with my own head.

'Who are *you*?' he responds.

'Suzanne,' I say, resisting my usual instinct to be difficult. 'I live upstairs.'

He squints at me. 'You're the one who left the note under the door? Laundry girl from the bedsit?'

I nod. 'Where's Dilys?' I'm thinking about Sarah saying that it would be a bad sign if there were other people in the flat. My heart is pounding.

'In hospital,' the man says. 'I'm her nephew, Graham.'

I take this as an invitation and walk into the flat, trying as I do to control my rising panic. 'In hospital' is bad, but it's not *that* bad. 'In hospital' means 'not dead'. 'Is she OK? What happened?'

Clipboard Man is looking at me with undisguised disdain, probably brought on by the word 'bedsit', so I glare back.

'She had a stroke,' Graham says. 'She's fine, but she needs a lot of assistance in her recovery.'

Oh God. 'Another one? What kind of assistance? What kind of recovery? Where's Clarence?'

Graham's face tightens like I'm annoying him. He glances at Clipboard Man, and they share the kind of look that only middle-aged men being bothered by teenage girls can truly master. 'Yes, another one. The stroke has affected her mobility and communication. Clarence is actually at my house, being spoiled by my daughters.'

I don't know whether it's safe to be relieved or not. 'She's OK?'

'Yes.'

'What are you doing here, then?' The question is probably rude, but I don't care.

Clipboard Man lets out a cough, which is probably meant to be subtle, but isn't. 'Let me give you a moment,' he says, turning away from us and walking towards the window.

Graham bites back a sigh of impatience. 'I'm overseeing the sale of this flat,' he says, lowering his voice. 'After Dilys had her first stroke, we made a plan for if she had another, more serious one. And she has, so here I am.'

'She's not coming back?'

'No.'

'Ever?'

'She'll be moving to a care home,' he says. 'I can see this is a shock for you, but there's no need to worry. We've been preparing for this for some time. Dilys has visited the home in the past and discussed her potential circumstances with them – and me – at length. We're selling the flat to help fund her care.'

There's so much I want to ask before I have to leave and the door to this flat is closed on me forever. What comes out is, 'Is it a nice care home?'

He gives me a funny look, but he answers. 'Yes, it is. You'll be able to visit, if that's something you'd like to do.'

I nod. 'Definitely. When will she go? Can I visit the hospital?'

'Yes,' he says. 'The stroke ward is open to visitors every day from 3 p.m. until the evening. If you call them with any questions, I'm sure they'll be happy to help you.' He gives a definitive nod, a dismissal.

'OK,' I say, dawdling. 'Well, thanks.'

He nods again. I hesitate, take one last look around the room, and leave.

Thanks to work, I don't get to go to the hospital until Thursday. I walk rather than get the bus, using the money I save to buy a tiny bunch of flowers for Dilys. It takes me nearly an hour, and I spend most of the journey thinking – and trying not to – about the last time I walked this route to the hospital. It was dark, then. Past midnight. I had a necklace and a bag of pills in my pocket. Today, flowers.

There's building work going on at the hospital and I end up getting lost trying to follow the diversion signs. By the time I finally make it to the stroke unit, visiting hours are half over. I tell the woman on reception that I'm family, just in case it matters, and she tells me to go on through.

When I get to Dilys's bed at the far end of the unit, by the window, I see that she's asleep. I hesitate, then slide into the seat beside her, settling the flowers on the beside table. There are already a few different types of flowers there, which must mean she's had a few visitors at some point. Good.

I've been sitting there for about five minutes, looking around the ward, trying not to think about how many hours of my life

I've spent in hospitals, when Dilys opens her eyes. For a moment she looks at me, blinking, and I think with a shot of horror that she doesn't know who I am, but then her face breaks into a wide, wonky smile.

'Ah,' she says. Just that.

'Hi,' I say, smiling back.

Her right hand lifts from the bed and flails in my general direction, so I take a hold of it and squeeze. 'Ah,' she says again, elongating it this time.

I swallow, trying to fight off my rising nerves. Graham had said the stroke had affected her communication, hadn't he? Did he mean that she can't talk at all?

'I didn't know where you were,' I say, stupidly. 'I was worried.'

She nods, her eyes on mine. She tries to speak again, but the words don't come out coherently, and I have no idea what she's even trying to say. She shakes her head in distress, closing her eyes.

'It's OK,' I say. It's not OK. 'You don't have to talk. I can talk enough for both of us.'

At this, she laughs. A short, happy bark. 'You?' she asks.

'I'm fine,' I say. 'I mean, like I said, I've been worried. And I missed you and Clarence. And, my God, Dilys, I've got so much washing to do now? It's just piling up in my flat. I tried to get Graham to give me a key to your flat, but he said no. I think he thinks that I'm a chancer or something? Like, maybe I don't even know you at all? So I thought I should come here and take a selfie with you, just to show him. That OK with you?'

Dilys laughs again, more softly this time. She looks so small in the bed. Small and old. She never looked old to me before, not like she does now.

'Hur,' she says. The word is round and breathy, meaningless to me.

'Hair?' I guess. 'Your hair looks fine, considering. But I can put it up for you or something, if you want?'

She sighs, shaking her head.

'Maybe next time,' I say. 'Look, I brought these.' I lean over and lift up the flowers. 'Sorry they're small.'

She smiles. 'Buh,' she says. 'Buh.'

'I thought so!' I say. 'Small, but beautiful.' I look at her. 'Tell me if I'm translating you wrong. Can we agree on a noise that you can make if I'm wrong?'

Dilys gives me a look then, piercing and unmistakable.

'All right, sorry,' I say. 'No special noises. Is Clarence allowed to come and visit? You must miss him.'

She touches her heart, nodding, then makes some kind of gesture with her fingers I can't interpret.

'I don't know what that means, sorry,' I say. 'Graham says he's looking after him?'

Dilys makes the gesture again, nodding insistently.

'Oh, hey,' I say, pulling out my phone. 'You can type it for me, right?' There's a message on screen from Matt, but I click away from it and open the Notes app. 'Here.'

I lean over and hold the phone up in front of her, watching as she squints at the screen, then back at me.

'It's a phone,' I say slowly. She scowls at me and pinches my thumb. 'Ow! OK, fine! I was just saying!'

Dilys jabs at the screen for a few seconds, then stops. I turn the phone so I can see. **Will visit care home.**

'OK, cool,' I say. 'Not long, then. How are you feeling about going there?'

She takes her time over this response, tapping and then pausing, tapping and pausing. When I'm sure she's done, I look. **Sad.**

'I'll visit,' I say. 'Every week, if you want.'

She reaches for the phone, and I hold it up for her. **No washing.**

'No washing,' I confirm. 'Just you and me.'

Music.

'I can bring my guitar?'

She nods insistently.

'And flowers every time.'

Dilys touches my hand, then her heart. 'You,' she says. 'You.'

'No flowers?'

She shakes her head, smiling. 'You.'

'Hello.' A cheery voice comes from above me, and I look up to see a nurse standing there. 'A new visitor for you, Dilys?'

I glance at Dilys in time to see her beam and nod. She's *proud*, I realize, and my chest tightens for a moment.

'Visiting time is over, I'm afraid, my love,' the nurse says.

'OK,' I say, getting to my feet. I smile at Dilys. 'So, I'll come and see you once you're at the care home, yeah?'

She nods. 'You.'

'Me,' I say agreeably. I swing my bag up over my shoulder. 'Bye.'

The nurse seems friendly, so I dawdle behind her on the way out of the ward until she turns to look at me. 'Can I help you?' she asks.

'I was just wondering about Dilys,' I say. 'Can you tell me what's actually wrong? Like, why she can't speak and stuff?'

'The stroke has affected the muscles in her face and throat,' the nurse says. 'It will make communication more difficult for a while, but it won't be forever.'

'It won't?'

'Oh, no.' She smiles kindly at me. 'That's the sort of thing that will get sorted out as part of her rehabilitation.'

'How long will that take?'

'It may be weeks, but more likely a few months.' The nurse looks over at someone on the other side of the hall and nods. 'Just on my way,' she calls. To me, she adds, 'You might like to take some information about stroke and recovery with you?' She points to the desk, which is covered with pamphlets and leaflets. 'Take care, now.'

I gather up a few obediently and make my slow way out of the hospital, taking a longer route to the exit so I don't have to pass A&E and deal with whatever memories it would throw up in me. I wait until I'm outside before I take out my phone to read the message from Matt.

> Hey, I've been booked to do a last-minute gig in Hastings this weekend. Just as a support act, but it sounds cool. Wondered if you wanted to come? If you're free?

I smile down at my phone, leaning against a stone pillar outside the hospital.

Me:
> Congrats! When is it?

Matt:
> Saturday night! Club called the Cliff. I can put you on the list?

> Oh cool! Let me check last train and stuff cos I'm working Sunday morning at 8.

> Sure, just let me know.

> Is Kel going?

> No, he doesn't usually travel for my gig stuff. Is that OK? Would you mind being on your own?

> On my own with you? No ☺

I'm not actually working at 8 a.m. My shift doesn't start until noon, but I don't want him thinking I'm going there to stay over with him. I like the easy flirting thing we have going on over WhatsApp, and I want to tease that out over longer than just jumping into bed with him at the first opportunity.

The last train back to Brighton leaves Hastings not long after eleven, so I'd have enough time to watch his set, talk to him afterwards, maybe kiss a little and then leave to go home. Perfect.

There's a question in my head, just a quiet one, pointing out that Hastings is a long way to go just to see a boy for a couple of hours, that there are plenty of boys in Brighton, and what makes this one so special? But it's easy to ignore, and the feeling in my chest at the thought of seeing him again – and knowing that he wants to see me – is far more persuasive.

I have the day off on Saturday so I head to Hastings early. It's windy and cold and the beach is deserted, which makes me happy. I pull my hood up and hunch myself down on the pebbles, looking out to sea and daydreaming about dark-haired boys and guitars.

When it's almost eight, I take off my comfy, beloved Vans and replace them with heels before I head for the Cliff. I'm wearing a black dress and tights together with a chunky silver necklace and my leather jacket, which was a present from Sarah for my sixteenth birthday and is my favourite piece of clothing ever. I feel good. I know I look good. I can't keep the smile off my face.

The club is bigger than I'd expected, with an upstairs bar and dance floor. The gig is downstairs and the space is already pretty full when I get there. I get a drink and make my way into the crowd, shaking off the attention of a couple of guys who try to get me to stand with them, settling myself a couple of metres back from the stage. I'm close enough for a good view, but with the buffer of other people so I won't look too keen. I've timed it perfectly, because Matt comes onstage only a few minutes after I've found my spot.

He looks good, even allowing for the fact that being onstage makes everyone look instantly hotter. He's all in black – I make a mental note to make a Johnny Cash reference to him later – and he's smiling. The first song in his short set is a cover and I settle into it, but I can't quite lose myself like I usually would. I'm very aware of the audience, which is paying him only the barest amount of cursory attention.

Most people don't care about support acts, me included, but I've never thought anything of it before now, standing amongst a disinterested audience watching Matt, sweet Matt, trying his hardest on an empty stage. I wonder if it's as lonely up there as it looks.

His eyes, wandering over the crowd as he sings, land on me as he launches into the bridge of his second song, and his whole face lights up. That's what happens; an instant transformation from his onstage smile to genuine, delighted recognition. A mix, I think, of being happy to see me specifically and being happy to see a familiar face. I'll take that. I smile back.

After half an hour, he gives a final wave to the crowd – the applause is fairly enthusiastic, considering – and disappears backstage. I dither for a moment on the spot – already the crowd is beginning to grow as people start to claim their territory for the main act – and then head for the bar.

My dithering costs me valuable seconds and I end up in a queue. In the few minutes it takes me to get to the front, three different guys ask me if I'm on my own and offer to get me a drink.

'Are *you* on your own?' I ask the third one, when it's starting to get too irritating to let pass.

He looks surprised. 'No? Of course not.'

'Why do you think I am, then?'

I'm not using a friendly voice, but still he smiles, like he thinks I'm flirting. 'Aw, you know what I mean. You got a boyfriend?'

'Yes,' I say. 'He's the bouncer.' Which gets rid of him.

When I finally get to the bar, I get two drinks. Even if Matt doesn't appear for a while, at least no one will assume I'm 'on my own' if I have a drink in each hand. I sip and wait, watching the crowd, thinking idly about mixers and why it's normal to have Coke with vodka and not Dr Pepper or Fanta. Who makes decisions like that? And how come we all just go along with it?

And then there's Matt suddenly in front of me, a huge smile on his face. 'Hey!' he says. 'You came!'

I smile back – it's probably more of a beam, but I can't quite contain it – and hold his drink out towards him. 'Of course I did! Here.'

'You are a goddess,' he says, taking it. 'I should be buying you the drinks.'

'This is for playing a great set,' I say. 'You can get the next one. Deal?'

He grins. 'Awesome. Was it actually great, though? Be honest. It didn't exactly set the club on fire, did it?'

'Well, *I* thought it was great,' I say. 'And my opinion matters most.'

'Fair,' he says. 'You look gorgeous, by the way.'

Another beam. *God, try and control yourself, Watts.* 'Thanks.' But he looks so good. And the way he smiles is so . . . I take a long, cooling sip of vodka and Coke. 'What's the main act like?'

Matt shrugs. 'They're OK. Do you want to stay and listen?'

'Is there an alternative?'

'We could go upstairs and talk in the bar,' he suggests.

I do want to do that, but I also want to exercise a bit of self-control. 'Maybe stay for one song?' I say. 'Just so I know what they're like?'

He nods. 'Sure. How've you been? It seems like ages since I saw you.'

I end up telling him about Dilys. I don't plan to, but it spills out. I tell him about her being gone after I got back from a few days away — I don't tell him exactly why I was away — and then Graham being in her flat, and eventually seeing her in hospital. I tell him about her music room and how she wants to give me a 'classical education'.

He listens, his head leaning slightly towards mine so he can hear me over the noise of the club, a slight frown of concentration on his face. When I'm done, he says, 'How do you actually know her?'

'She's my neighbour,' I say.

'And like a grandmother?'

'Not really,' I say, meaning to say that she's more like a friend, but I stop myself because it sounds stupid even in my head. Dilys is in her seventies. 'Yeah, I guess so. I don't really know what that's actually like, though, because I never knew my grandparents. And she doesn't have grandchildren, so she wouldn't know either. She's just Dilys.' I correct myself. 'Not just. Forget the just. She's Dilys.'

He smiles. 'Well, she sounds cooler than my grandparents. Mine don't really get the music thing. I think they'd rather I had a proper job.'

'Proper is overrated,' I say. I have to raise my voice because the lights have gone down and the roar from the audience has increased in compensation.

Matt and I look at each other and smile, shrugging. Conversation over. I turn to face the stage and he steps in closer to me as the crowd sways forward, close enough that I can feel the heat coming off him. When the band starts playing and that unique electricity that comes from live music buzzes through the room, tingling my skin, Matt touches his lips to the back of my neck and I feel like

I've come untied. I want to turn and face him, but I know what will happen if I do, and I want to tease it out just a little longer. I wait through the whole song, squeezing his hand as it finds mine, smiling when I take a second to glance back at him.

When the song ends, I turn. He mouths, 'Upstairs?' and I nod.

We drink, we talk, we laugh. I miss my train. I don't care.

We are tangled together in a booth in the corner of the upstairs bar. His hands are in my hair, he is kissing me so deeply it is sending shockwaves through my whole body. I am half on the booth seat, half on his lap.

I'm pretty drunk. So drunk, in fact, that I don't even remember that I'd decided earlier that I would not get carried away, I would not do anything more than kiss Matt Sheffan. I want to do a lot more than kiss him. And there's no question that he wants to do a lot more than that with me.

At some point, we leave the club. I don't think I've even danced. We stumble down the road, pausing every few steps to lock together again. He kisses me against the wet glass of a bus shelter, his whole body hot against mine. We make it to his hotel, tumble into the lift, and stop. We smile at each other. He lifts a hand and runs his fingers so, so gently down my cheek.

The doors ping open and he takes my hand, leading me down the corridor. It occurs to me that at no stage have either of us actually talked about this out loud. Just, somehow, here we are, falling into his hotel room, the door slamming shut behind us. He doesn't even turn the light on. The wall is at my back, his hands are at my waist, his fingers slipping under my dress. I curl my hand into the front pocket of his jeans and he groans into my mouth.

'OK,' he says. 'OK, I need you.'

He steps backwards and pulls me with him towards the bed,

turning us both at the last second so I fall beneath him, the mattress soft and yielding at my back. I pull off his shirt, he does the same with my dress. His hand slides under my back and unclips my bra with a skill I register as a bit too good even through my drunken state of bliss, and then his jeans are off, his hands are on me, I'm arching my back, he's between my legs, his mouth is at my neck, and then we're moving together, his fingers pressing against my skin, his breath in my ear. We're a tangle of sweat and skin and clothes and drunk and sex.

This wasn't what I'd planned. This isn't what I should be doing. I close my eyes and pull his body closer.

I wake up to find I've been sleeping on my bra strap. I don't even need to look into a mirror to know the clasp has left a mark on my face. Trying not to make a sound, I lift my head and glance over to the other side of the bed, where Matt lies asleep under the rumpled covers, sprawled on his back, mouth open.

'God,' I let myself mutter out loud. I feel like hell in every possible way and for every possible reason.

I'm pretty sure Matt is too deep in a post-drunk, post-sex sleep to be anything to worry about, but still I creep around his room in almost total silence, just in case, sliding back into my clothes, locating my phone and bag. It is almost 6 a.m.

I can't stand the thought of making it from Hastings to Brighton in what are clearly last night's clothes, so I pick up one of his hoodies from the floor and put it on. It's far too big for me, but I feel instantly better. Swamped and anonymous. I let the hood flop over my hair, shielding me from the world. And then I open the door and leave.

15

'Liability'
Lorde

I get home, shower, go to work. I deliberately leave my phone uncharged until I let myself back into the flat that evening, at which point I plug it in at the far corner of the room and hide from it on my bed while I use my brother's Netflix account to watch old episodes of *Brooklyn Nine-Nine* on my laptop, eating a stale croissant from Madeline's. At some point I fall asleep.

By the time I jerk awake, it's 3 a.m. and I'm too tired to be lonely, too tired to be scared of what Matt will have said, or if he will have said nothing at all. I get my phone and curl under the covers to unlock it. There are a lot of messages waiting. My heart doesn't exactly leap, but it flickers with hope.

Matt:

Where are you?

Oh shit you left. Fuck.

I'm sorry. Let me know you got back OK yeah?
Let me know if I can call you? Shit.

Also should say, you are amazing.
Please message me back.

Um, sorry for message overload. But am worried 😔

Kel:

> Suze, where you at? Matt asked me to check in on you.
> Are you at work? Just let me know you're OK, chucks.

Caddy:

> You slept with Matt? Seriously?

> I'm not judging you, just kind of surprised.

> I'm judging you a little bit.

> Call me.

Rosie:

> You minx. Turn your phone on so
> I can call you and get the details xxx

Caddy:

> I guess you turned your phone off again.
> I don't know why you do this, Suze. You make
> it really hard to be your friend sometimes.

Hers is the last message and I stare at my phone, my heart seized. Caddy has never said anything like that to me before. She's been disappointed in me, she's hinted at my being hard work. But never like this.

If you push people away enough, they'll go.

Even though it's stupid o'clock and she'll be asleep, I decide to call her and leave a message. I close my eyes against my pillow, the phone to my ear, waiting for the familiar 'Hi, this is Caddy Oliver' message I know so well.

'Hello, stranger.'

My eyes open in surprise. It takes me a second to gather myself. 'Oh. Hi, Cads. I thought you'd be sleeping.'

'I know. You thought you'd get away with not talking to me.' There's alcohol in her voice. Maybe anger, too.

'How come you're awake?'

'I'm a student, remember? This is like the middle of the afternoon.' She laughs as she says this, but it's not for me; it's a laugh I'm not part of.

'I'm sorry about earlier, my phone was out of battery.'

'Yeah, I heard it's hard to charge those things these days.'

I look into the darkness, stunned and stung. My throat has closed. I have no idea what to say. This is not the Caddy I know. I must wait too long because she sighs into the silence, and when she speaks her voice is hard.

'Look, I'm in the middle of something here, OK? I need to go back to my friends. I'll talk to you tomorrow. If you can be bothered.'

She hangs up before I can reply, and I'm so completely shocked, I actually look at my phone to check that it was definitely her I just spoke to. I can feel a choke of panic in my throat. I can't lose Caddy. I cannot lose Caddy.

Me:

> I'm sorry. I'm really sorry. I love you. Please call me back, please xxxxx

God, I sound like a needy girlfriend. And speaking of . . .

> Hey, phone off all day. Sorry I didn't reply. It's fine, don't worry about it. But let's leave it, OK? Was a mistake for both of us.

I feel a bit heartless and mean sending the message to Matt, but to hell with it, I do it anyway. As soon as I've sent the message, my phone buzzes.

Caddy:

Go to sleep, Suze. I'll talk to you tomorrow.

The next time I speak to Caddy, in the early afternoon when I am on my break at work, she has softened. The antagonism from the previous night is gone from her voice, and though she's not exactly contrite, I can tell that she regrets being quite so harsh. Caddy is too nice to hold on to anger. She is good to the core.

'I'm proud of you,' I say, playing with the crusts of my sandwich rather than eating them. 'You told me off.'

She laughs. 'I don't think it counts as telling off. I'd just had a bit to drink. You know I'm a lightweight.'

Affection and relief fills my chest like helium into a balloon. The bouncy, metallic, happy kind of helium balloon. 'I love you,' I say.

'Love you too, Suze,' she replies.

'Do you forgive me?'

'Yes. But, look, don't do the phone-off thing with me, OK? I get if you want to do it with Matt or whatever, but it really kind of got to me that you'd do it to me. I care about you, and when you disappear I *worry*. And then you just reappear like nothing happened and . . . it's like . . . like I'm just incidental to your life. And that makes me feel like you don't give a shit about me.'

The words fly out of me. 'You know I—'

'Yes, I know you do. I'm saying that's how it feels. Just . . . remember that having someone care about you is a two-way street.'

I clutch my fingers around my phone, trying to think of the best thing to say. I want to say, *I miss you so much. I'm so lonely.*

I'm scared that I am no good to anyone. Sometimes I think about dying.

'Can the street have a pub on it?' I say.

'At least one,' she says. 'And a chocolate shop.'

'And a pet shop.'

'A cat cafe!'

'Yes, if it's with dogs. *Puppies.*'

'OK, OK. We can have a cat cafe on one end and a puppy park on the other. And a sandwich shop in the middle, one of the really good ones, when the baguettes are still warm and the butter melts into them.'

'Like you,' I say, without thinking.

There's a pause. 'What?'

Shut up, you moron. 'You. Warm like a baguette. Butter-melty.' Have I ever sounded so idiotic? Being alone so much is clearly getting to me.

But she laughs, because she knows me. 'OK, Suze. I'm warm like a baguette.'

'How's Warwick?' I ask, glancing at the clock on the wall. Seven minutes left of my break.

'Fine, but I want to know about you and Matt.'

'Oh, that.'

'Yeah, that,' she says, but with a warmth still in her voice that stops me tensing up. 'That thing that happened that you said wouldn't happen. With that guy I said you shouldn't let it happen with.'

I'd been trying not to think about Matt. His mouth and his hands. The way he smiled at me when he saw me in the crowd. My heart gives a confusing little *zing*. 'Alcohol was involved.'

'Well, I guessed that bit.'

'How did you know, anyway?'

'Matt told Kel, Kel told me,' she says, like it's obvious.

My heart sinks. 'They talked about it?'

She doesn't say anything for a moment. 'Not in a bad way, to be fair. I think Matt was worried because you bailed and he didn't know where you were. Nice move, by the way. Just running out on him.'

'Wow, you really got the details, didn't you?'

'Kel tells me everything. And Matt tells *him* everything. It's a best-friend thing. You know that.'

Was that a dig? I don't tell Caddy everything. Not even close.

'I had to go to work,' I say. 'That's why I just left.'

'Handy,' she says. 'Have you talked to him?'

'No.'

'Aw, I sort of feel bad for him now.'

'Why? He got what he wanted.'

'Maybe he wanted more, though? At least find out.'

'You were the one who said he wouldn't!' I say, trying not to sound as frustrated as I am. 'You said!'

'That's not quite what I said,' Caddy says, and I can practically hear the shrug in her voice. 'I said don't sleep with him because it could make things messy. But you have, so. Yeah. At least talk to him. He's Kel's best friend.'

'I've got to go back to work.'

'Handy,' she says again, and the warmth is gone now, like I've used up her affection reserves.

'Don't be like that.'

'Like what?'

'You know what.' There's a silence. 'Listen, if you're mad at me, just say so. Don't be all passive-aggressive.'

'I'm not,' she says. 'I just . . .'

I wait. 'You just what?'

She sighs. 'I just don't get you sometimes, that's all. You're like the easiest person to love, and it's what you want, isn't it? But then you make it hard. Like, you actively make it hard.'

My face feels hot. 'OK, great. Thanks.'

'You know you do, Suze.'

'I know that it's hard to love me? Yeah, I actually do know that. I know that really well.'

'I didn't mean—'

'I really have to go back to work now. I'll talk to you later.' I hang up and shove my phone into my apron pocket as I head back out to the front counter. I'm thinking, *Bitch,* but I don't even know if I'm thinking it about myself or her.

So much for us reconciling during that conversation. Nothing's been fixed. That weirdness that spilled out in the phone call last night is clearly still there. Maybe it's got even weirder. But I can't think about it now, because there's a queue stretching towards the door. Total strangers wanting coffee. Perfect.

'Hiya,' I say, plastering a smile on my face. 'What can I get you?'

There's a message from Matt on my phone that's been waiting for me for hours. I saw it when I first went on my break but I didn't open it because talking to Caddy was more important, and then I had to go back to work, and then I had to walk home from work and . . . Anyway, now it's almost nine and I've run out of excuses.

> I didn't think it was a mistake. Sorry that you did.
> I had a really great night, like really great. Can we talk?

I hesitate, reading over the message a couple of times. I think of Caddy saying, 'At least find out.' And then I think of the way she'd said a few weeks ago, an eye-roll in her voice, 'Look, just don't sleep with him, OK?' Something she'd never have said to Rosie. But me, I'm the girl who sleeps around, aren't I? Even my best friends think that way.

When I was younger and first starting to kiss and flirt with boys, it had made me feel stronger. Special, even. The way they'd look at me, a kind of awe, when I'd let their hands slide further up. (And then, later still, down.) It had felt like a kind of magic I could wield. I mean, don't get me wrong. Even then, I'd never mistaken any of it for love. I knew they didn't love me. But they *wanted* me. And that was more than enough.

But something changed at some point, a kind of shift I hadn't anticipated and couldn't control. When they stopped being surprised that I'd let them, and started expecting it instead. And that feeling, the expectation, and the judgements that went along with it, seemed to spread, so it wasn't just in boys I'd done anything with, but other boys too. And not just boys, but girls as well, whispering together, side-eyeing me from across the room. Words like 'slag', 'slut', 'whore'. One day the words aren't there, and then suddenly they are, frightening and permanent, and there's no way to scrub them free from your life.

No more soft, hopeful smiles and gentle touches. No more long kisses and whispers. No more fizz of the maybe. It was smirks. Tugs at my jeans, my skirt. Impatience.

I didn't feel strong or special or magic any more. But I carried on doing it all anyway, and sometimes I don't even know why. I don't know if that's wrong, if that makes me bad in some way. And there's no one to ask, that's the thing. No one who will explain all of this confusion. Guys will do anything, say anything, to get sex, but once they've got it, it's the girl who's made the mistake, the one who's 'given it away'. Why is that? Who decides?

And what does any of that have to do with Matt and me? I stare at my phone, trying to sort through my own confusion before I reply. Is he just another guy who only wants sex? Does it matter if he is? I bite down on the side of my thumb, shaking my head at nothing. What about me? What do *I* want?

I think I'm actually annoyed with myself, not him. It's not like he knew about my resolve not to sleep with him. It's not like he took advantage of me or treated me badly in any way at all. But me, I basically walked out on him. And yet he still wants to talk.

I reply, **Sure.**

I lie back on my bed to wait for his reply, deciding I'll wait and see what he says before ruling him out. If he just wants to make overnight plans, then I'll know he's not worth it. But if he wants to carry on talking like we have over the last few weeks, like actual friends, then I can do that.

My phone lights up, taking me by surprise. He's actually *calling* me. I pick up. 'Hey.'

'Hey,' he says. 'You took your time.'

'I was at work,' I say, instead of what I should say, which is, *Sorry*. And also, *Sometimes I get scared*.

'How was it?'

'Fine, just work. How are you?'

'Not bad,' he says. 'I've kind of been worrying, though.'

'About what?'

He laughs, soft and short. 'About you. You just went silent on me. It felt like you thought I was a right dick, or something. That bit about it being a mistake for both of us. Did you miss your shift? Did you get in trouble at work? I'm really sorry you missed your train. I should've been more of a . . . well, gentleman, I guess, and made sure you left on time.'

For a moment I'm confused, then remember I'd told him my shift started at 8 a.m. instead of noon. 'It's fine, I just started later.'

'Oh, OK, good,' he says. 'So . . . what did you mean about the mistake thing?'

I think about all the messages we've sent over the last few

weeks, the sweet afternoon we'd spent in Brighton. 'I didn't go there for . . . that,' I say.

'I know,' he says quickly. 'And I didn't expect it.'

'Well,' I say, wondering how blunt to be. 'You kind of did, though.'

There's a silence. 'Sorry, what?'

'I know Kel told you stuff about me. Just like Caddy told me stuff about you. That's what you wanted the whole time.'

'Look, I don't know what Caddy told you about me, but Kel hasn't said anything like that about you to me. And even if he did, so what? Him and Caddy are different, they want different things. They're in a relationship, and I don't want that. So maybe they think that just means I want sex? I don't know, and I don't care. I care what *you* think, though. Great to know you just think I'm a fuckboy.'

'I don't think that.' I do think that.

'You basically said you did.'

I don't know what to say, so I stay quiet.

'I like you,' he says. 'I told you that. I like getting to know you, and hanging out with you is even better. Did I want sex? Yeah, of course, at some point, if you wanted it too. You're gorgeous. I haven't hidden the fact that I think that. But that doesn't mean it's all I wanted. It's not why I asked you to come to Hastings.'

'Why did you ask me, then?'

'Because I wanted to see you, and you liked the show last time, so I thought it was a good time. Is that so hard to believe?' There's a pause, and then he gives an incredulous *humph*. 'Did you think I planned it all along? Get you to come to Hastings, get you drunk, get you into bed?'

Yes. That's a lot easier to believe than that he'd really want to spend time with me, just me.

'Look, no offence,' he says, 'and I know this is going to make me sound like a dick, but whatever. If sex is all I wanted, it wouldn't have been hard to find a girl in that crowd, you know? There are always girls after gigs.'

I roll my eyes at the wall. 'That does make you sound like a dick.'

'I'd rather you thought that than think I was trying to take advantage of you or something. I'm really not like that, OK? Is *that* what Caddy told you?'

What was it Caddy had said? 'She says you have no sexual integrity.' I regret it as soon as I've said it, because I know she hadn't meant it quite as badly as it sounds when I hear the words coming out of my mouth.

'Jesus,' he says. 'Well, that's great. Just great.'

'She says that about me, too,' I add, and regret it even more. This is why people don't have telephone conversations.

Silence. 'You're really hard to read, you know that? I don't even know what you want from me right now.' When I don't reply, he says, 'I've tried to be upfront with you. It's not a secret that I don't want a girlfriend.'

'I don't want a boyfriend, either.'

'Exactly,' he says. 'That's what I mean. I thought we were on the same page. That's why it's so easy to talk to you; because we want the same thing. Or rather, don't want the same thing. I thought we could be, like . . .' He trails off, like he's embarrassed, then says it anyway. 'Like mates, or whatever.'

'I thought that, too.'

'Well, great. Can't we be that?'

'Well, not really.'

'Why not?'

'The thing is,' I say, not sure where I'm going even as I'm speaking, 'you can't go back. Once you've slept with someone, that's it. It's like a line you cross.'

'Is it? Does it have to be?'

'How can it not be?' I have a sudden memory of him at the pier arcade, grinning out at me from behind a toy giraffe.

'So you're saying that you don't want a boyfriend, but you don't want me to be a mate, either? You just don't want to see me again?' He sounds hurt, which surprises me.

'I do want to see you again.'

Another silence. 'OK, I'm totally confused about what you want.'

'I don't want labels,' I say. What I mean is that *Kel* is a mate, and there's no part of me that's attracted to him. But I can't deny that there's something between Matt and me. I want more than 'mates', it's true. But I don't want a *boyfriend*.

'Me neither.'

'And I don't want to just be . . .' I hesitate. 'You know. A warm body.' There's a heat in my cheeks, even though there's no one around.

'OK,' he says. 'That's fair. How can I show you that it wouldn't be about that?'

'Maybe we could keep it off the table for a while?' I suggest, surprising myself with the words. 'See how it goes?'

There's a pause. 'OK.'

'Yeah?'

'Sure. If that's what you want, I'm in.'

I feel myself smile. 'I'm in, too.'

16

'Patience'
The Lumineers

It takes a couple of weeks for Dilys to move from the hospital to the care home, which is on the opposite side of Brighton from me, so I have to get the bus to visit. I sit at the back, headphones in, listening to one of Matt's old EPs, watching Brighton through the dusty window. I'm not sure what to expect, but I've brought my guitar anyway, just in case. I'm hoping that Dilys will be a lot better than when I saw her last, maybe even talking and moving around.

She's not, of course. Whatever optimistic recovery schedule I'd had in my head is clearly way out, because Dilys is still bed-bound when I finally make it through reception and the maze of corridors to her room. But she smiles big when she sees me and lifts a hand in a wave.

'Hi,' I say.

'Hi,' she says. It's nothing like her usual voice, but it's a greeting, and it's from Dilys. I'll take it.

'How are you?' I ask, sinking into the chair beside her bed.

She gives me an energetic, slightly sarcastic thumbs up.

'Great,' I say. 'Me too. Look, I brought you dahlias. Sorry they're only small. I don't have much money.' I set the flowers carefully on the bedside table. 'Do you have to stay in bed all the time?'

Marcus, the nurse who'd directed me to the room and has been hovering in the doorway as if he's not sure if he should leave us on our own, speaks at this point. 'Dilys is having plenty of therapy to get her fully mobile again,' he says. He has that cheery, slightly too-loud voice of someone working with the elderly. 'Isn't that right, Dilys?'

She nods, unsmiling.

'You're not in the bed all the time?' I ask her.

'No,' she says. The word is round and weighted. There's a pause, and she tries another, less decipherable sound. A breath, like an *F* noise, and 'Teeg'.

'Fatigue?' I guess, thinking about the pamphlets I'd dutifully read after I'd first visited her at the hospital that had listed fatigue as a common post-stroke symptom.

She nods, pleased. 'Teeg.'

'So you can only do so much at a time,' I say. 'That makes sense. Therapy's hard. I had to take loads of breaks when it was me, and that was just head-therapy.'

Marcus looks at me like I've surprised him, though I don't know why, unless he'd made a snap judgement of me in the tiny amount of time we've been in the same room. I wonder what the surprise is; that I've had therapy, or that I'll talk about it so casually?

'Is there anything I should know?' I ask him pointedly. *Is there a reason you're still here?*

'You seem like you're all set,' Marcus says amiably. 'I'll pop back in later. Just come and find me if you have any problems.'

When he's gone, I lean over and pick up a laminated sheet from beside Dilys's bed. It looks like some kind of communication aid; it's sectioned off with illustrations for things like drinking, eating, reading, sleeping. I glance over it and hold it up for Dilys.

'Anything you want to tell me?'

She gives me a look, a very Dilys look, and pushes the sheet away. 'You,' she says, like a command.

'I'm fine,' I say. 'Not much has happened since I last saw you. Just work and stuff. Oh, I went to the launderette!'

Her eyebrows shoot up.

'I know! It was actually OK. I've just started seeing a counsellor, so I had some stuff to read from them while I was there. It's a good place to do a bit of reading. My clothes came out clean, so I guess that's the important thing. I miss you and Clarence, though.'

She's tapping her fingers at me, so I stop. She makes a backward motion with her hand.

'Go back? To . . . counselling?'

She nods.

'Oh. Well, some stuff happened while you were away that I didn't deal with very well, so I thought I should start seeing a counsellor, because talking helps, right? I thought I wouldn't be able to get one, because I can't pay for private and I don't want to have to go through the whole mental-health assessment thing to get one assigned to me. But my personal adviser, Miriam, found out that I can see a trainee counsellor for free. Sort of helping us both? So that's what I'm doing. Her name is Erin. She's pretty good. She's only been training for about a year and a half, but I think she'll make a good counsellor.'

'You,' she says emphatically.

I hesitate. 'I'd . . . make a good counsellor?'

She nods.

'Really? You think so? I don't know, I think I talk too much to be a professional listener. Anyway, we've only had one session. Other than that, not much to tell. I went to Hastings to see Matt play a show. Remember I told you about Matt? The musician? That was good. Have you ever been to Hastings?' She nods again. 'I liked it. Not as much as Brighton, but it's nice. The beach was really quiet.' I let myself pause to breathe, glancing around the room. 'Do you like it here?'

Dilys makes a motion with her shoulders, which I decide means 'It's OK'.

I say, 'That's good. It seems pretty nice here. Are the staff nice?'

'Mmmm,' she says, nodding.

'Do you need anything? Anything I can bring, I mean.' When she shakes her head, I say, 'I guess Graham is taking care of all of that. I hope you like the flowers, though.' She smiles a smile so full of affection, I have to look away, reaching for my guitar as if the whole move away from her was planned. 'Look, I brought my guitar.'

'Play,' she says.

'Oh, I'm gonna,' I say, unzipping the case and lifting the guitar gently on to my lap. I grin at her. 'Any requests? "Wonderwall"?' She blinks at me. 'Thought not. OK. I've got a surprise for you.' My heart is starting to pound. 'Go easy on me, OK? This is because I'm glad you're still . . . here.'

I swallow, bite my lip, then begin. My fingers find the chords to 'Blackbird' as naturally as breathing. And I start to sing.

This isn't the moment where I reveal that I'm some amazing singer. I'm not. I can hold a tune and my voice isn't terrible, but I don't have much power or range or training or any of the things I'd need if I wanted to do it properly. When I sing, it's quiet, almost to myself. Whisper-singing.

Dilys must like it, though. Because when I reach the end and force myself to look at her, there are tears streaming down her face.

'Oh,' I say, pressing my fingers against the strings and stopping the last note short.

She nods at me, firm and brisk. There's so much emotion in that nod that it loosens something inside me and I start to cry, too.

'Oh God,' I say, wiping at my eyes. 'This was meant to be a good thing.'

She nods again. 'Good.'

I put the guitar back in its case, trying to think of something else to say, something that isn't heavy. 'You need to cheer this room up a bit,' I say, looking around. 'Put more of you in it. Don't you have any photos of Clarence?' When she shakes her head, I say, 'I've got a few on my phone. I could get a couple printed to put up? And maybe some other little bits. Make it a bit more you.' I wipe my eyes again.

This is when her hand, shaky and cool, reaches out and takes a hold of mine. She squeezes, just lightly, and I smile. She smiles back. She mouths, '*Thank you*,' slow and distinct.

'You're welcome,' I say.

17

'Pride and Joy'
Brandi Carlile

I turn nineteen on a blustery Tuesday. My bedsit is just as empty as it was on the last night I was eighteen, but my phone is full of messages and love, which is something. There's a package waiting for me, a joint present from Caddy and Rosie – delicate falling-star earrings – and a card from each of them. I work during the day – Farrah makes me wear a 'Happy Birthday' badge that almost all the customers completely ignore – and then go to Sarah's for dinner. She's made carbonara with garlic bread, followed by chocolate truffle cake. When I get home, I'm full and happy. And then I'm even happier, because Caddy calls.

'Happy birthday!' she says.

'Thanks!'

Caddy and I made up the same evening we'd had our almost-fight – she called me, softened and conciliatory – but I've felt the strain underlying all our conversations ever since. Some tensions can't be undone by wishing them away.

'Did you have a good day?' she asks.

'It was OK,' I say. 'I was at work. Thanks for the earrings! I love them.'

'You're welcome! Listen, what are you doing next week?'

'I don't know . . . Work, I guess? Why?'

'Do you work every day? How does it work with weekends when you're on flexible hours? I'm basically asking you to come and visit. But it doesn't have to be a specific day; whenever suits you.'

I try not to yell too loud down the phone. '*Yes!* I am *there*. Let me check my calendar for when I'm working, but I can get my shifts switched around if I have to. I can come down for a couple of nights, maybe?'

'Perfect. Oh my God, I can't wait, Suze. There's so much I want to show you.'

I'm gripping the phone to my ear. 'Do you want me to bring anything?'

'Thanks, but no. Just you! God, it feels like so long since I last saw you. Do you look the same? Are you still blonde?'

I laugh. 'Shockingly, yes, I am.'

'Good. The world would just be wrong if you weren't blonde. Hey, how come you're not out tonight?'

'I had dinner at Sarah's,' I say. 'And my mum's coming tomorrow, so I don't want to be hungover.'

'Your mum's visiting?'

'Yeah.' My stomach gives a nauseating churn. Part hope, part dread. Last time I saw Mum was about six months ago, not long before I left Southampton, and Brian had been there as a buffer. It's been a long time since the two of us spent one-on-one time together. 'As, like, a birthday thing.'

'OK,' she says, cautious. 'Have a good time. Call me if you need to?'

I smile. 'I will. Thanks.'

The buzzer sounds the next morning as I'm sliding the bracelet Mum gave me for my eighteenth birthday on to my wrist – silver with a topaz stone. I quickly take the stud out of my nose and take one last glance at myself in the mirror. Mum is a birthstone-bracelet kind of person, and she'd hate my nose piercing if she knew about it. I'd love to pretend that I don't care what she thinks of me, but I do, and the thought of her face crinkling with dislike – or worse, disappointment – panics my fragile heart.

I sprint downstairs to let her in at the front door rather than just buzz her up. When she sees me, she smiles.

'Hello, my darling,' she says, stepping forward and touching her lips to the side of my head.

'Hi,' I say. I go to hug her but she's already stepping back, turning from me and closing the door. My arms fall empty to my sides. 'I'm just up the stairs,' I say, leading the way.

When I turn to see her reaction as we walk into my flat, I see an expression on her face I don't quite recognize, and I try to read it as she takes off her coat and glances over to smile at me again. And then I land on it, the word 'hopeful'. She's *hopeful*.

It's instantly contagious. Hope blooms up in my chest and I smile back, properly, reaching out to take her coat even though I don't have anywhere to put it.

'Well,' Mum says, looking around the room. 'It's on the small side, isn't it?'

'I don't need much space,' I say, when what I should say is, *Yes, it's tiny, isn't it? I hate it*. And then maybe she'd say, *Oh, baby, you can't stay here on your own*. And she'd pack up all my stuff, right now, and drive me home, and when we got there she'd make me saffron buns like she used to and we'd—

'Maybe not, but it's a bit drab,' Mum says. 'Still, I suppose you don't have much choice on a coffee-shop wage.'

Some of the hope fades, just a little. The gas turned down on a flame. 'Not really.'

'But you're OK?' She turns to me. 'You're managing?'

'Just about.' I try to smile. I'm still holding her coat.

She smiles. 'Good. That's good. You know, I never lived on my own, not ever.' She looks around the room again, shaking her head a little. 'I'm not sure I'd manage.'

I don't know what to say to this. Whether to agree that, no, she wouldn't, or say that I'm not managing really and can she rescue me? But no. I give my wrist a tiny pinch. I *am* managing. I *am*. I have a job and I pay my bills and I don't stay in bed all day when I'm not working. I'm doing *well*.

'Your dad sends his best,' she says.

'OK,' I say.

We look at each other. 'Well,' she says finally. 'Shall we go?'

She's booked afternoon tea for us both in a hotel near the seafront called The Ogley, the kind of hotel with three varieties of champagne on the wine list and velvet seats set weirdly low so I don't know how to sit properly.

When we sit down at our table, Mum looks around, smiling. 'This is nice,' she says.

'Ladies!' a bright voice chirps from above us. I look up to see a beaming waiter standing beside the table, hands clasped in expectation. 'Welcome to The Ogley. I'm Daniel, your server for today. Afternoon tea for two, is it?'

'Please,' Mum says. She's polite but, compared to his effusive cheer, she seems almost rude.

'You two look so alike!' he says. Mum and I do not look alike. 'Sisters?'

I laugh, and he turns his beam on to me. 'Nice,' I say, but teasing, not meanly, as if we're already friends. 'Smooth. Gunning for that tip already?'

'Damn, you got me,' he says cheerfully. 'That's a solid line, though, right?'

'Nah, it's too obvious,' I say. 'You've got to be more subtle about it. Like –' I put on a voice, that special enthusiasm of paid staff that I know well – 'Is it a special occasion?' I drop the voice, gesturing at Mum. 'And then say –' voice back on – 'Perhaps your fortieth birthday?' Drop the voice. 'And then Mum'll be so flattered, because that was ages ago, but it sounds sincere, right?' I look at Mum for back-up, then remember who she is. I turn quickly back to the waiter before I can trip myself up. 'You've got to put a bit of truth in a good line. *That* makes it solid.'

'I'll bear that in mind,' Daniel says.

'I'll bear your tip in mind,' I say, and he laughs.

'I like you,' he says. 'I'll make sure you get the freshest stuff.' He points to the menu. 'Have you chosen the variety of tea you'd each prefer?'

When he leaves to put in our order, I look over at Mum. She's staring at me with an unreadable half-smile on her face.

I can't help myself. 'What?'

'I always forget what a performer you are,' she says. She doesn't say it like it's an insult, but it's not exactly a compliment either. I hesitate, wondering what to say, because I so desperately want her to love me, but then she smiles warmly and I let it pass. 'So, tell me,' she says. 'How is life in Brighton?'

I give her a highly sanitized version of my life, focusing on the healthy bits and leaving out the occasional breakdowns and insomnia entirely. Caddy and Rosie get the starring roles they deserve, complete with details of their courses and universities. I mean to tell her about Dilys, but I can't find the words to explain the relationship we've somehow formed, because there's part of me that knows she could say something that will lodge in my head and ruin it. So I move straight on to Madeline's, which I describe at length, exaggerating how much I like working there and agreeing that, yes, management could be an option one day, even though it's definitely not.

Around the time I start talking about Kel and his student house, Daniel arrives holding a tea stand aloft, beaming. 'Here we are!' he says, setting it down on the table between Mum and me. He goes through the whole show of describing every item on the stand, like we need egg mayonnaise sandwiches explained to us, and I take the opportunity to look at Mum while she's focused on him, nodding and smiling. She looks older than the image I'd kept in my head. Tired, though she's always looked tired to me. *You look so alike*, Daniel had said. God, I hope not.

I take a picture of the spread and upload it to Instagram almost without thinking about it, tagging the hotel and adding a quick 'Shout-out to Daniel, best waiter ever', before I put my phone down and reach randomly for one of the finger sandwiches.

'Are you back with me?' Mum asks, and I start in surprise.

'Am I what?'

'Do I have your full attention?' She's smiling, so I know she's not actually having a go at me, but I still feel a flicker of irritation. It's not like she's earned the right to be teasing me about being on my phone, is it?

And, excuse me, when have I ever really had *her* full attention?

I nod, though. I even apologize. It's like I don't even know myself when I'm around her; like she turns me into someone else.

'How are Caddy and Kel handling being long-distance?' she asks. It's strange hearing their names from her mouth.

'Pretty good,' I say. 'Or, as good as anyone can, I guess?'

She nods. 'That's good. And how about you?' She says this cautiously, like she's not sure she's allowed. 'Are you seeing anyone?'

I can't help smiling. The question is so ridiculous and she doesn't know me at all. 'Nope.'

'Oh.' She's disappointed. 'You know, I was about your age when I met your dad.'

Which one? I almost say. Almost. 'Yeah, I know.'

'I want happiness for you.' She says it so simply, half her attention on the finger sandwich she's biting into.

I don't say, *Do you?* I don't say, *Maybe you should have*

thought of that earlier. 'I'm doing OK.'

'Good,' she says. 'I'm glad.'

'I've started seeing a counsellor,' I say. 'And that will help a lot, I think.'

I mean this to be a positive thing, but her face falls. 'Oh, Suzie,' she says. 'Do you need a counsellor? Why?'

'Just to . . .' I try to find the right words. 'To help keep me steady.'

'I see,' she says. She finishes the sandwich and brushes her fingers lightly against her skirt. 'So more looking back, not forward?'

I cram a sandwich into my mouth without even looking at what it is, just so I don't have to say anything.

'Suzie,' she says, and she sighs. 'I worry sometimes about how much you've let this affect you.' Her fingers curl around her teacup. 'All of this . . . therapy, and needing counselling and things. It's quite a lot, isn't it?'

My heart stills, like it's bracing itself. 'What do you mean? I've got . . .' I mean to say 'complex-PTSD', but I can't quite form the words, not to her, not out loud. 'Well, I need it. To help me.'

'It's good that it's helping,' she says. 'I didn't mean any of the help is bad. I'm glad for all of it, of course. What I mean is, I wonder if maybe you've . . . built it up a bit, in your head. It all seems quite dramatic, really. I know you had a bit of a hard time with us, sometimes. But it wasn't some great trauma, was it?'

I have no idea what to say. The words are crawling into my head, I can feel them. Nestling in, making themselves comfortable.

I think about all the things I've read about abuse since I left home and felt safe enough to do it. The study that showed how the brains of children who grow up in violent homes actually change. They physically change. The article that used the phrase 'growing up scared'. How the first time I read those three words, I felt like I'd unlocked a shutter over a window I hadn't even known was there.

I want to tell her about these things. I want to tell her so badly, but the words won't come.

'Darling, I'm sorry,' she says, and her hand reaches across the small table to close gently around mine. 'I've upset you. I didn't mean to do that.'

I take my hand back. 'I'm fine.' I shouldn't need to tell her any of these things, should I? She should already know. She should *want* to know.

When I lived with Christie and Don in Southampton, I'd wandered into Don's study once and browsed his bookshelves. He had a whole wall of them; literally an entire wall. I'd been trying to count the books when I saw them. A shelf full of books about kids like me and how to help them. Building self-esteem in young people, understanding complex-PTSD, supporting children in care, attachment theories and adolescence . . . There were so many books. I asked him if he'd read them all and he'd smiled in surprise. 'Of course I have, Suze.' It wasn't just a *yes* for him; it was an *of course*.

'I just want you to be happy,' Mum says. 'And I worry that you're not.'

What am I supposed to say to that? *OK, you're right. I'll just suddenly be happy*. 'You could be a bit more understanding,' I say. 'Just a little bit.'

Her face tightens. She's offended. Great. 'This may come as a surprise to you,' she says quietly. 'But I'm doing the best I can.'

I look at her across the table. My distant, tired mother. I try to summon anger, but I can't feel anything but sad for her.

Time to change the subject. 'How's Reading?' I ask, reaching for a scone and a knife.

'Oh, much the same,' she says, visibly relaxing. 'I've joined a knitting club, did you know?'

'That's cool,' I say. She must be in a social phase; that explains her coming all the way down here to see me, birthday or otherwise. She gets like this every few years, wanting to be more active, seeing more people. Maybe it'll last this time.

'They're a lovely group of people,' she says. 'Mostly women, and I'm not even the youngest one there! I could make you something, Suzie. A blanket, maybe?'

I'm touched, even as I don't want to be so easily softened by her. 'You don't have to do that.'

'Do you remember your Bubba?' she asks.

'My what?' I say, thrown.

'The little elephant toy you used to take everywhere with you. You called him Bubba. You don't remember?' When I shake my head, she says, 'Well, I suppose you were awfully young. Anyway, I knitted him for you while I was pregnant.' She sighs. 'That was such a long time ago.' This story is so at odds with every memory I have of my childhood that I want to ask more about it, but she's already moving on. 'It's nice to be knitting again, and to be getting out of the house more. Actually, speaking of the house, your father and I are thinking of moving.'

I almost drop my knife.

'It's a big old house for just two people. So much space to fill. It seems like a good time to downsize.'

'Are you going to leave Reading?'

'Possibly. It's very early days.' She smiles at me. 'I'll keep you updated, don't worry.'

A thought comes into my mind that it would be pretty cool if they *didn't* keep me updated. If they moved and never told me the new address, and I just didn't know where they lived. How freeing that would be. Wait, that's a weird thought that doesn't even make sense. I shake it off.

We avoid any more sensitive topics as we make our way through the tiers, instead making pointless small talk about Brighton, the weather, the furnishings in the hotel. It makes me wonder what she expected from this outing; what she expected from me. Does she wish I was someone else, as much as I wish *she* was someone else? Do I disappoint her as much as she disappoints me? The thought is painful. I tell her that I like her earrings to compensate, and she smiles as if it's the nicest thing I've ever said to her.

By the time we've reached the top tier and are both clearly sick of eating bite-sized treats, all I want to do is go home and sleep. We've stopped trying to pretend we have anything to say to each other and every second drags.

'Ladies!' It's Daniel the waiter, thank God. 'Are we all done?'

'Yes, thank you,' Mum says, sitting up. I hadn't even noticed that she'd been sinking. 'Would I be able to get a box to take this candyfloss home?' she asks, pointing at the little puffs of candyfloss still in their cups.

'Sure, no problem,' Daniel says cheerfully.

'For your dad,' Mum says to me, smiling an affectionate, genuine smile. 'You know him and his sweet tooth.'

The candyfloss will probably have hardened by the time she gets back to Reading, and even if it hasn't, there's not much of it. Barely a handful of garish blue and pink spun sugar. And yet she'll take it for him without a second thought, because she loves him. The way she points at the candyfloss; that smile on her face. *But he hurt me*, I want to say.

'Oh, and can you pack up anything else that's left into a separate box?' Mum adds. 'For my daughter to take home. And if there are any of those macarons going spare, put them in, too.'

Daniel grins and gives her a cheesy, but nonetheless sweet, wink. 'Absolutely,' he says.

And I just smile and try not to cry, because this is her trying. This is her knowing I like macarons. This is her wanting me to have a box of treats to take home. This is the love she can manage for me.

'Shall I drop you off home?' Mum asks me when we're standing outside. The cool air feels good against my skin.

'No, I'll be OK walking,' I say.

Her face falls a little, which makes no sense. It's not like she can really *want* to spend more alone time with me.

'Have a good trip back,' I say, turning to head towards the beach. I need to see the sea. 'See you . . . um. Soon?'

'Suzie,' Mum says. For one awful second, I think she's going to cry, which throws me so much, I don't know what to do with myself. I turn back towards her, awkward and stilted, waiting for a cue. She lifts a hand and touches my face, just gently. 'Happy birthday, darling.'

'Thanks,' I say softly. *Can I go now? Please let me go.*

'Bye then,' she says.

I wait until she's gone before I let myself cry.

18

'Thunderclouds' (feat. Sia, Diplo & Labrinth)
LSD

It takes me another week before I can sort out my shifts so I can visit Caddy in a three-days/two-nights block. She's there at the station to meet me, wearing a University of Warwick hoodie and a huge beam. When I come through the ticket barriers, she leaps forward and throws her arms around me.

'Oh my God,' she says, voice loud in my ear. 'I'm so happy to see you.' She seems like she really means it, too.

We get the bus to the university and she leads me to her halls, which are by a lake and are much, much nicer than I'd expected them to be. There are eight people in her flat and most of them are in the kitchen when I arrive, right in the middle of a loud argument about . . . I have no idea. Caddy, who'd opened the door with a wide smile, swings it closed again and shakes her head at me.

'Later,' she says.

'What was that about?'

'Cleaning. It's always about cleaning. The guys are such slobs and it makes Tess really mad. Come see my room instead. I figured we could chill tonight, get some food, maybe go to the bar for a bit? There's a club night on campus tomorrow, if you're up for it?' When I nod, she grins. 'I thought so. One sec.' She fiddles with the door handle until it finally gives. 'Come in!'

The room is pretty small and I can take it all in at a glance, but I take my time anyway because I know that's what she wants, looking around with a smile. 'It's nice,' I say. 'Do you like it?'

'Yeah, I love it. It's mine, you know?'

I don't really know, because it's *not* hers, she's just one more in a line of students who'll sleep in that bed and work at that desk, but I nod anyway. 'And what about everything else? You're still loving it?'

'Oh, yeah.' She looks so happy. She's shining with it. 'It's great. Hard sometimes, and the work is tough, but it's all worth it, and I *love* my flatmates. We spend most of our time together. Last week we went to an escape room and Owen – you'll meet Owen – smashed a vase by mistake because he thought it was part of the game, but it was actually decoration.' She laughs and I smile obediently. 'They made him pay for it.'

'Do you have a lot of it?'

'What?'

'Time. What about lectures and seminars and stuff?'

'They're only a few hours overall. But there's reading, too. A lot of it. And essays. That does actually take up a lot of time. And I've got my job, too.' Seeing my face, she adds, 'At the juice bar.'

'You got a job and you didn't tell me?'

Something in her face tightens. When she replies, there's an unCaddy-esque edge to her voice. 'No, Suze. I got a job and I *did* tell you.'

Oh, shit. She did tell me, didn't she? Weeks ago. 'Oh yeah,' I say, trying to think of a way to dig myself out of an awkward hole. 'Um. Sorry.'

Caddy just looks at me, her eyes travelling over my face like she's searching for something.

'You must've told me during all the Kacie-Leigh stuff,' I say. 'Things didn't really stick then. I'm sorry.'

She's blank. 'Kacie who?'

'There was—' I immediately change my mind and stop. 'It doesn't matter. I'm just sorry, OK? I'm crap.'

She closes her eyes for a second, mouth open like she's going to say something, but instead she shakes her head, closes her mouth and turns away from me. 'Fine,' she says.

It's not fine. It's so obviously not fine. 'Yell at me,' I say. 'Be mad.'

'I'm clearly not going to yell at you,' she says, rolling her eyes. 'You know I won't, so don't say that.'

'Maybe you should, though,' I say. 'Here, like . . .' I put on a voice, an exaggerated Caddy. 'Oh my God, Suze, you're the *worst*. I listen to all your crappy problems, *all the time*, and the *one time* I tell you something about my life, you *don't even listen*.'

A small, reluctant smile twitches on her face. 'Is that your attempt at a southern accent? It's terrible.'

'Is that southern? I was just doing you.'

She mimics me. 'I was just doing you.' The accent is so spot on, her version of me so accurate, that I laugh in surprise.

'You should probably have your conversations with that version of me,' I say. 'Much more reliable.'

'True,' she says. 'Maybe I should.'

I lean over and put my arms around her shoulders, squeezing tight. 'Then you couldn't have *this*, though.'

'You can't cute your way into me being OK with you forgetting vital information about my life,' she says, but she's warm again, teasing, the two of us back on safe ground.

That's the only time we're alone together for the rest of the day. She takes me back into the kitchen and introduces me to her flatmates, taking her time over Owen – 'The vase guy,' I say, and he grins, like he's proud – and Tess, a tall, thin drama student who hugs me and says, 'I've heard so much about you!' in a voice that puts my back up, though I'm not sure exactly why.

All eight of them and me hang out in the kitchen for the next couple of hours and I listen to their stories tumbling out over each other with overlaps and crossovers about buildings I don't know and lecturers I've never heard of and people who mean nothing to me. I laugh and smile and make jokes. I go full-on Suze and pretend to myself that I'm not intimidated by this world, even when they ask me normal questions like what A levels I have, where I went to school, what my parents do, and it hurts more than it should. I'm not ashamed of where I am in my life. I might not have the usual trappings of a nineteen-year-old but I've survived things that felt impossible, and that matters a lot more than what's on my CV.

But still. It hurts.

I'm expecting to have dinner with just Caddy, but six of her flatmates come along as well and I have no choice but to go with it. She stays close and affectionate, especially when we all start drinking, but it's still not possible to talk properly with her, not about anything important, not with everyone else around.

The next morning Caddy has a lecture at nine, so I stay in her room until she gets back, looking through her stack of course texts and essays and amusing myself by trying to read them. She has a photo collage up on a cork board and I examine it, this visualization of her life. There I am, sitting on a bench on Brighton Pier with her and Rosie, posing as the no-evils. The two of us on the beach at night, hair blown by the wind. All three of us again at her eighteenth. But that's it. Just three pictures. I look around and try to count the number of her with Rosie, but I can't. There are too many. Them as tiny six-year-olds, beaming ten-year-olds, awkward thirteen-year-olds. They grow up together in the pictures, like they belong together, like they always will.

You were the one who left, I remind myself, and that's when the door opens and Caddy comes in, already smiling, lifting her canvas bag up over her shoulder and dropping it on the bed.

'Hey!' she says. 'God, that was dull. I should've just skipped it. Want to go get some breakfast or something?'

'Sure,' I say. 'Your photos are great.'

She glances at the cork board. 'Yeah? I think it needs more you.' I can't stop my face breaking into a pleased beam and she laughs. 'Come on. We'll take loads of pictures today, OK?'

We get bacon rolls at a cafe on campus and she shows me around, talking happily about why she chose Warwick, how it is and isn't what she expected, how she and Tess are already talking about living together in their second year. I finally admit that I don't know what linguistics is and she explains it in sweet, patient detail.

Later, when we're back at her flat getting ready to go out, I spend an hour on her hair and make-up, talking her through every step of the process. She's giddy and happy, examining her face in the mirror when I'm done, turning to me with her arms open for a hug.

'You're the best,' she says. 'Thank you.'

'Be honest,' I say, screwing the cap on the mascara and pushing it back into her make-up bag. 'This is why you invited me, right? My face-making skills?'

She grins. Her eyes are bigger, sparklier, more striking. 'Also, I love you,' she says. She hugs me again.

The feeling doesn't last, though. When we go into the kitchen for a few drinks before we head out, it's all I can do to stay beside Caddy, let alone talk to her. Somehow, I end up trailing along behind her on the way to the club, which is a sensation so alien to me, I feel like I've forgotten who I am. A crazy part of me wants to turn around and go back to the flat. How long would it even take her to notice?

When we get inside, she turns to me, beaming, and tucks her arm through mine. 'Don't run off,' she says, as if that's the potential problem here.

'Cads,' I say, meaning to remind her that she's the only person

I know here, but we're at the front of the bar and she's turned to the barman, raising her voice to order.

For the next hour, I try to swallow down my anxiety, burying it like I bury every feeling I don't want to deal with, but it keeps bubbling up. Every time I see Tess lean in to say something into Caddy's ear, the two of them laughing. When a guy tries to talk to me by a pillar and Caddy gives me a look. I'm not myself. I don't know how to be myself here.

I shut myself in one of the toilet cubicles to give myself a break for a couple of minutes, and when I come back out again, I can't find Caddy, or even Tess, or anyone I vaguely recognize. I wander around the club for a few minutes, a carefree smile on my face, avoiding making eye contact with anyone, until I finally spot Caddy's head in the crowd near the bar. I head towards her, keeping one hand flat over the top of my cup and feeling the liquid beneath splashing up against my palm. She's standing with Owen, both of their backs to me. Their heads are close together, but their voices are still raised above the music.

'You look good, tonight,' Owen is saying. Or yelling.

I can't see Caddy's face, but I can tell by her voice that she is smiling, bashful and pleased. 'Thanks. But it's all Suze. She's like a miracle worker.'

I lift my hand to touch Caddy's shoulder so she'll know I'm there, but before I can do this, Owen is speaking again. 'Your friend is gorgeous. Like, seriously. Wow.'

Caddy shrugs. 'Yeah.' Now her voice is flat.

My hand hovers in the air between us. It's not really fair to just stand there listening to them talk about me, but something about that 'yeah' has made me stop, nervous.

'Will you put in a good word for me?'

'What? Why?'

'Go on, Cads. Be a pal. Tell her I can be her token student shag.'

He laughs, amiable. 'You can be my way in.'

'You don't need any of that. Just tell her she's gorgeous like you just told me. Get her a drink. She'll be all over you.'

'For real? Awesome.' Owen is grinning as he glances behind him. 'Oh,' he says.

There is a silence that, thanks to the throbbing music, is not at all silent. Caddy turns to him, sees me and freezes.

'Want a drink?' Owen asks me smoothly.

Caddy gives him a shove.

'Yeah,' I say. 'Actually, I do. Rum and Coke. Double.'

He turns away from us, clearly grateful to have a reason to remove himself from the awkwardness, and leaves Caddy and me facing each other. As I look at her tense expression – part guilt, part defiance – the instinctive anger I feel fades. This is Caddy. *Caddy*.

I try and smile. 'What are you drinking?'

'Schnapps and lemonade,' she says. She wants to ask me what I heard, I can tell, but she won't, because she's Caddy.

Owen hands me my drink in a plastic cup and I take a sip without thanking him, tasting the rum against the sweetness of the Coke. I feel better.

'I'm going to have a smoke,' I say. 'I'll see you later.'

'I thought you'd quit,' Caddy says, tentative.

I shrug. 'You know me.'

'Too well,' she replies, almost smiling.

Suddenly, I feel an overwhelming urge to cry. I miss Caddy so much, and she's right here in front of me. This distance we'd both tried to pretend hadn't grown between us during the time I'd been away now feels like something physical. She's so far away from me. I want to tell her I love her, but it won't make any sense. I want to tell her that I can see that she likes Owen, that I wish she would tell me so we could talk about it. I want us to share secrets again, like we used to. I want her to know she can trust me, that it's OK to have crushes, that if she's confused about her feelings, that's what I'm here for. I want to tell her she's my best friend, and it's OK if I'm not hers.

'You really do look good,' I say instead, then turn and head for the exit.

Outside the club, I find a group of guys and flirt my way into a free cigarette and conversation. The anonymity of these people is a relief after the confusion of being with Caddy. Here, drink and cigarette in hand, tossing my hair and smiling at guys who don't know me and never will, I am my best self. I tell them my name is Vanessa. When they ask me what I'm studying, I say Film.

I'm only outside for about ten minutes, but when I try to head back into the noise and crowd, the bouncer refuses to let me in without a ticket, even though I have clearly already been in there. I'm too frustrated and tired to put up much of a fight, so I slope off and find an empty bench in a little courtyard, text Caddy and sit back to wait. There are messages waiting for me, but I decide to read them later because having things to look forward to, even small things, is one way of making life liveable.

I lie back and look up at the stars, trying to shut out the world. I'm starting to wonder why I came here. What had I expected, really? That Caddy would be unchanged by this kind of experience? That she'd still need me to be the fun one?

But what am I if I'm not the fun one?

'Hey, you.'

In the dark, Caddy's silhouette is still familiar. I can see that her head is cocked, can hear a kind of resignation in her voice. She pokes one of my legs and I lift them obediently, turning myself in the same motion so I am sat on the bench as she takes her place beside me. We are both silent for a while. She rests her head on my shoulder.

'I'm sorry,' I say eventually.

She's surprised. 'Why?'

'I don't know. I just am.'

And then she's crying, and I'm so startled and then scared that I start bawling too. She lifts her head from my shoulder and wipes at her eyes, no doubt leaving smears of my carefully applied make-up down her cheeks.

'Just say whatever it is,' I say. I sound surer of this than I actually am. 'Just . . . go on.'

There's another long silence. I've just decided that she's not going to answer me and I should lift the tension with some kind of joke, when she speaks.

'I don't . . .' A slight pause. 'I don't *know* you any more.'

Oh God, my heart.

'I think I've known that for a while, but I just didn't want to. I think I've been clinging on to who I knew when I was sixteen. And I love you so much. But . . . I'm nineteen, and I'm at uni. And I'm meeting all these people that I have so much in common with, and I tell them about you and Rosie, and they don't . . . they don't *get* it. They're like, so you grew up with Rosie, that's cool, and then the other girl is the one who was around for a few months, dropped you through a skylight, then left again? And at first I was like, yeah, shut up, you don't get it, but now . . . well. I don't know. I guess that's pretty accurate.'

My *heart*.

'I don't know what's left of us. Rosie and I have so much history. Even when we fight, and even though we're apart at the moment too, there's so much to keep us together. I know she'll always be around. But I don't . . . *trust* that with you. That you won't just leave. And I try and think about all the things that make us friends, but all I can come up with is that I really love you and being friends with you was like what *made* my life. Before uni, anyway. You made things *happen*, and it was so great, being who I was with you. But then you left – and I get it, I obviously get why you left, I'm not stupid – but you *really* left. You just checked out, like, emotionally. Not just physically. You didn't reply to my emails or tell me anything about your life while you were away, not unless I really pushed you, and it was like, OK, she doesn't actually care about me at all, not really. And that *hurt*, Suze.' She takes a quick breath, shuddery and hitched. 'It honestly felt like that, like you didn't care. Not about me or our friendship, and I'd always thought that mattered to you. And Tess, she said, all of this, it's the kind of thing you say about someone you have good memories of. Not someone who is a lifelong friend. And I think she's right. I'm scared that she's right.'

In the darkness beside her, I am letting my tears fall silent and heavy down my face, keeping my lips clamped together so she won't realize and stop talking out of guilt. I know I need to hear this and that she needs to say it, but it hurts. So. Fucking. Much.

When I don't say anything, she speaks again. 'And, like . . . Suze . . . you do things like leave your phone off. You don't talk to me for days. I feel like I put in so much and you just don't. I think I spend all this time worrying about you and that's not friendship, is it?' She turns to me just as a camera flash goes off somewhere, illuminating our faces for a fraction of a second. 'Oh my God, you're crying. Oh God. I'm sorry, I'm sorry.' She's frantic, patting and then squeezing my wrist and then hand and then fingers. 'That all kind of just came out.'

I try to speak but find I can't. I crush my fingers against my mouth to try and stop the tears and lean forward, my hair brushing my knees. Caddy curls her arms around my shoulders, her face against the side of my head, and I reach up my hands to clutch her wrists. We are tangled together on the bench, both of us in tears. She is saying she's sorry, and I'm trying to reply but I can't.

When I finally manage to speak, it's pathetic. 'I can't lose you.' My voice is thick and hitched. 'Please, I'm sorry. I'll be better.'

'No, it's OK, I'm not . . .' She is pressing her face against my hair, as close as she can get, closer than any boy ever goes, closer than family. Isn't this what friendship is? How could I let myself lose someone like Caddy? 'You're not losing me, I've just been drinking and uni's such a mindfuck.'

I choke a laugh. 'You never used to say things like "mindfuck".'

There's a pause. 'I'm not your mousy friend any more. I haven't been for a while.'

'You were never just my mousy friend,' I say.

'You know what I mean.'

I do.

'There you are!' The voice is cheerful, sudden and above us. It's Owen. 'God, Cads, don't you ever answer your—' He stops abruptly. 'Shit, have I gatecrashed a funeral?'

Something about his arrival jolts me back into myself. I wipe my hair back from my face – it sticks in places – and flash a grin at him. 'This is what happens to girls when they drink.'

Caddy laughs. There's relief in it. 'How can you not know that, Owen?'

'You're usually a happy drunk,' Owen replies, frowning. 'You get all giggly.'

'Suze brings it out of me,' Caddy says. Her arm is still around my neck and she pulls me close, kissing the side of my forehead. 'Any friend can make you laugh. Best friends make you cry.'

I love her so much.

'Girls are weird,' Owen says, definitive. 'You coming back to the flat? Sam's got Calvados.'

'What's Calvados?' I ask.

'Posh alcohol,' Caddy replies. 'It's like a brandy. The guys love it in our flat.'

I smile. 'You're really ruining the student stereotype here. Whatever happened to cider and cheap vodka?'

'We've had that already,' Owen says. 'This is a nightcap.'

Both Caddy and I crack up, and he looks momentarily offended, then laughs too. He reaches out a hand to Caddy and she takes it, beaming at him. I lift myself up and bounce a little on my feet before following them up the path. I watch them, keeping myself an almost imperceptible step behind them, counting seconds. I count nine before they drop hands.

Back in the flat, we gather in the kitchen, stretched out on the seat by the window. My back is against the fridge and I keep drifting out of the conversation and just watching everyone else. Caddy and Tess are playing the totem game, throwing their hands up in strange poses around their heads as Sam, crouching on the seat, takes pictures. The three of them are laughing, and Owen is leaning back against the window, a grin on his face. They all belong here, I think. It's nice to watch, if a little lonely.

The Calvados we're drinking tastes how my head tells me alcohol is *supposed* to taste. Thick, strong and important. Grown-up. I don't really like it but I drink it anyway, slowly, sip by sip.

'Do you have a boyfriend, Suze?' Tess asks me, her voice suddenly loud. It annoys me that she calls me Suze.

I think of Matt.

'No,' I say.

'Don't you get lonely?' There is sympathy in her voice, and it grates.

'No,' I say again. Of course I get lonely, but it's not because I don't have a boyfriend. It's because I don't have a fucking family.

'I would,' Tess continues. 'I mean, even without the love and hugging and stuff, I'd totally miss the sex.'

'You don't have to be in a relationship to have sex,' I say.

'No, but that's not healthy, is it?' She curls her lip in distaste. 'You're, like, *asking* for STIs.'

'Am I?' I ask.

She looks horrified. 'No, not *you*. Obviously not *you*.'

'OK,' I say. I look away, take another sip from my glass.

There's an awkward pause. In my peripheral vision, I see Tess give Caddy a *look*. I know I'm being the bitchy, unfun friend, that I should be friendlier towards someone Caddy cares about, that it's below me to be jealous and even worse to let it show. But, God, I'm so, so tired. I don't belong here and I'm tired.

I force myself to try a little harder, asking Sam about his course – History, which is what Brian studied at uni – and making Owen laugh with a stupid joke about Viagra. It's so much easier with boys. I know I shouldn't admit something like that, but it's true.

Tess goes to bed first and Caddy bounces after her, telling me she's left her moisturizer in Tess's room and will be right back. Sam follows them both, throwing up a lazy, tired hand on his way out of the kitchen.

When they're gone, Owen turns to me. 'So how do you like student life?' His voice and grin say he expects me to love it.

'It's different,' I say. He raises an eyebrow, waiting for more, and I hesitate. 'It looks like it would be a lot of fun, from the inside.'

He shrugs a little, agreeing or disagreeing with me, I can't tell, and drinks the last dregs of Calvados from his cup.

'You and Caddy,' I say, not sure where I'm going with this.

He looks at me, wary. 'Yeah?'

'Is there anything—'

'She's got a boyfriend,' he interrupts. 'So whatever.'

It's not exactly an answer to what I hadn't exactly asked, but I can sense it's the closest I'll get tonight. 'OK,' I say. 'Sorry.'

Owen lifts his cup again, realizes it's empty and puts it down on the windowsill with a grunt of annoyance. 'Look,' he says, turning to me. I wait, ready to tell him that Caddy has Kel and he is everything, that if he hurts her I will kill him. 'Tell me straight. Do I have a shot with you?'

I blink. I make a noise that sounds like, 'Uh?'

'Tonight,' he says. 'I'm single, you know.' His eyes flicker over me. 'You look like you'd be a lot of fun. And I'd—'

'No,' I say. My voice is level. 'You don't have a shot with me.'

He shrugs again, his expression hardly changed. 'Worth a try.'

Like I'm a slot machine at an arcade. A discount on a jacket with a thread hanging loose. Worth a try, nothing more.

Caddy comes leaping across the room and lands on the chair beside me. It's like her whole body is smiling. 'Want another drink?' she asks. 'I've got some Tuaca in the cupboard.'

I shake my head. 'I'm really tired. Sorry, is that OK?'

'Of course!' She smiles at me, then turns to Owen. 'You want a shot, right?'

'At least one,' Owen says, grinning.

The smell of the sweet liqueur makes my head hurt. 'I'm going to go and brush my teeth, OK?'

If she's disappointed, she covers it well. She nods, reaching into her pocket. 'Sure. Here's my door key. Remember to turn the key and lift the handle. And don't lock it behind you, so I can get in later.'

Caddy's room is quiet and still after the constant noise of the night, and it's a relief for about thirty seconds. And then I realize I'm back on my own again, which I hate, and I consider going back to the kitchen. But Caddy is sure to come to bed soon enough and the sooner she does that, the sooner it will be just the two of us, talking like we used to.

I brush my teeth, wash my face, put a long T-shirt on over my leggings and get into Caddy's tiny bed. With the main light off and her lamp shining up into the corner, the room is cosy and dark. I settle against the wall, unlocking my phone to read my messages. There's one from Matt and he's still awake when I reply so we chat for a while as the clock ticks closer to 3 a.m. After half an hour, I tell him I'll talk to him properly tomorrow and slide my phone under the pillow, sinking my head down. Still no Caddy. I let my eyes close, hoping she'll come in before I get too sleepy. We've got so much to talk about, and I can't stay too late tomorrow. It's a long way back to Brighton.

Time passes, the world gets fuzzier. I can't quite tell if I'm awake or not. I have a vague sense that someone is whispering nearby, and then the door closes. The lamp switches off.

I mumble, 'Caddy?'

'Hi,' she whispers. She pulls the covers back and slides down beside me. 'Go to sleep, it's super-late.' Her breathing is faster than normal, and I can feel her heart beating. Her arms close around my back in a quick, tight hug. 'Sorry.'

I am at that almost-drunk point of nearly-asleep, which is why the words come out when her arms release me. 'Don't let go.'

There's a pause, just long enough for sleep to take me over. She says something I don't hear, and then her arms are back around me, secure and safe, as I fall asleep.

19

'All My Days'
Alexi Murdoch

I need to leave Warwick by eleven the next morning so I can get home in time for a session with my counsellor in the evening. All my hopes of having a proper conversation with Caddy have been dashed, so I don't bring up the weirdness from the night before or ask why she'd taken so long to come back to her room. Instead I write her a note telling her that I love her and pin it on her cork board for her to find some time after I've gone, and leave it at that.

I message Matt when I'm on the train and he replies with a phone emoji and a question mark. I curl myself up on my seat, my feet on my bag, and call him.

'Hey,' he says when he answers.

'Hey,' I say. I pull up my coat hood and snuggle into it, phone to my ear, giving myself a small cocoon of privacy. 'How are you?'

'All right,' he says. 'I've got a day off today so I'm trying to write a song.'

'Cool!' I say. 'What kind of song? Can you sing it to me?'

He laughs. 'Right now?'

'Yeah, go on.'

'I've barely got a chorus so far,' he says. 'Try me in a few days and maybe I will.'

'Is it about me?'

He laughs again. 'Do you want it to be?'

'Every girl wants a song written about them,' I say. 'Every *guy* does, come to that. Who wouldn't want a song about them?'

'All the girls in my songs are fictional,' he says. 'Safer that way.'

'Safer?' I repeat, grinning into my hood. He's definitely got in trouble in the past. 'How—' Out of nowhere, there's a hand at my shoulder and I jump, pushing back my hood to see a scowling ticket inspector raising his eyebrows at me. 'You're not allowed to touch me,' I say. This is the kind of thing I've learned after several years of fare-dodging. If you're asleep – or *pretending* to be asleep to avoid a ticket inspector, say – then they can't physically do anything to wake you up. It's literally the law.

'What?' Matt asks, alarmed.

'Feet off the seat,' the ticket inspector says. 'Ticket?'

'My feet aren't on the seat,' I say. 'They're on my bag. And you're not allowed to touch passengers like that.'

'Ticket?' he says again. He looks like he actively despises me. It would probably make his day if I didn't have a ticket.

I just look at him, drawing it out. The other passengers around us are all watching without watching, and it's very British. I can tell that this guy is the kind who enjoys a power trip, and it's wound me up. That and the fact that the no-touching rule is there for a reason, and that reason is to do with things like boundaries and protection, and it's actually not OK for him to just ignore it.

'You've got twenty seconds to produce a ticket,' the man says, his voice louder now, 'or I can fine you and you can get off this train.'

'Great,' I say. I squint at his badge. 'One question, Pete. Do you make a habit of touching teenage girls on trains?'

I hear a distant, 'What the hell?' from my phone, which has fallen down to my lap.

'Ticket,' Pete says. 'Now.'

I pull out my ticket, and the disappointment on his face is obvious. He snatches it from me, reads it far too carefully, then scribbles on it and hands it back, scowling.

'Thank you,' I say. 'For asking so politely.'

He glares at me and I stare back until he turns away and starts taking tickets from the other passengers.

'Sorry,' I say into the phone, lifting it back to my ear and tucking myself under my hood again. 'Ticket inspector.'

'Do you have a ticket?'

'Yeah, but he was just being a dick. Anyway. What were we talking about?'

'Songs, but I want to know about Warwick. You said last night you had a thing with Caddy? What happened?'

I tell him a little about the night and the weirdness, but there's no way to explain the history between Caddy and me in a way he'll understand, at least not over the phone while I'm sitting in a train carriage. I also leave out the bit about Owen, because I don't want it getting back to Kel.

'That sounds shit,' Matt says. 'But, look, uni's a weird time, you know? Don't get too upset about it. Me and Kel had a bit of an off patch when we both went to uni for the first time, and then when I dropped out it got worse. But we're fine now. All this stuff, it's temporary. Being friends is about seeing this stuff through, however hard it is.'

'You think we will?'

'Yeah, of course. Just give it some time.' There's a pause. 'Have I helped? Do you feel better?'

I smile. 'I do, actually. Thanks.'

'You're welcome. Hey, what station are you coming into?'

'Euston,' I say. 'Why?'

'I'm heading into central later,' he says. 'I was just thinking I could head in a little bit earlier and say hi.'

I smile into my hood. Inside my Vans, my toes curl involuntarily with pleased surprise. 'Say hi?'

'If you want to,' he says. 'If you're not in a rush or anything. When does your train get in?'

'In about an hour. I reckon I could spare a few minutes to say hi,' I say. My voice is as casual as his. I'm thinking of the last time I saw him; the two of us falling on to a bed in a hotel in Hastings. 'You could play me the song.'

He laughs. 'Are you going to be disappointed if I don't, now?'

'I'll never get over it.'

'I'll bear that in mind. OK, I better go. I'll see you in a bit?'

When my train pulls into Euston, Matt messages to say he's outside Fat Face. I take my time wandering over there, as if I'm making some kind of a point to myself. When he sees me, he smiles, reaching up to tug the headphones out of his ears. '*Hey*,' he mouths, before I'm close enough to hear him.

'Hey,' I say. 'Fancy seeing you here.'

He grins. 'Right?'

'Where's your guitar?' I ask, leaning back and looking around him. 'How can you serenade me without your guitar?'

'You're funny,' he says. 'So funny.'

'So I'm told.'

'Do you have time for a coffee?' he asks.

'Just one,' I say. 'A quick one.'

'A quick one like . . . an espresso?'

'Not quite that quick.'

We find a Costa and I get us a table, pulling out my phone to check I haven't missed any messages from anyone. Specifically, Caddy, telling me she misses me already, and she's sorry we didn't get a chance to properly talk. The screen is blank.

'One caramel mocha,' Matt says grandly, putting a cup on the table in front of me.

'Thanks,' I say. 'What did you get?'

'A latte. I'm a man of simple tastes. So tell me. What's Warwick actually like? And did it make you want to go to uni?'

I think about it. 'The whole trip felt like having a guest pass to a world I didn't belong in. And everyone knew the code except me.'

'Well, that doesn't sound great. Was it because of the weirdness between you and Caddy?'

'Maybe. I don't know. Anyway, I want to know about you. How's the song actually coming along? I promise I won't make a stupid joke this time.'

'It's fine. I've got half a verse, a chorus and a bridge.'

'I'm really restraining myself from making a stupid joke right now.'

He laughs, shaking his head a little. His eyes slide to mine and it's like being pulled in. 'I know we're in a coffee shop in the middle of a train station,' he says. 'But is it OK if I kiss you?'

No one's ever asked me before. They just go for it, or they do that long, slow lean to give you time to say no. But actually asked me? Never.

I can't stop the smile that breaks across my face. 'Go on, then.'

When we kiss, it's gentle and slow, nothing like the urgent face-eating that was going on in the club in Hastings. It's like we have all the time in the world instead of being in one of London's busiest train stations where the tannoy is a constant reminder of time closing in. God, I like kissing him. I really, really like kissing him. Way more than I should.

We stay in the Costa for a while, alternating between talking and kissing, until I glance at the clock and stand up. 'OK, I really have to go now. Thanks for the coffee.'

'No worries,' he says. 'It was great to see you.'

'You too,' I say. 'And the kissing was good too.'

A smile blooms. 'Just good?'

I smile back. 'Very good.' I hoist my bag up over my shoulder and raise my hand in a wave. 'See you.'

*

The next time I see Dilys, I'm more prepared. As well as my guitar and some flowers, I bring a couple of photos of Clarence, a copy of *The Little Prince* – she once told me it was her favourite book – and a few small bags of dried lavender. Dilys's flat had always smelled like lavender, so I figure she must like it.

She's still in bed but sitting more upright this time, and her movements – though it might just be my wishful thinking – seem more animated.

'I wasn't sure if you wanted something to read,' I say, waving *The Little Prince*. 'Or I could read it *to* you, if you—'

'Yes,' she says.

'You want me to read to you *and* play the guitar?'

She nods.

'OK, well, I'm not a performing monkey, you know. You can't just bleed me dry.' A smile spreads across her face and she shakes her head a little. 'You have to choose,' I say. 'Guitar or book?'

'Book,' she says.

'Was my singing really that bad?'

She laughs, deep and throaty, and then coughs. I reach for her water and hand it to her, watching as drinks, taking it back carefully when I'm sure she's done.

'OK?' I ask softly. When she nods, I open the book to the first page, then frown. 'There's an introduction. Do you want me to read that bit? No? OK.' I skip ahead until I find the first chapter. 'Once, when I was six years old . . .'

The chapter is pretty short, so I barely have time to get into it before I'm done. I glance up to see that Dilys has her eyes closed, and she's smiling. I take a receipt from the bedside table and slide it between the pages.

'More next time,' I say.

I stay for about an hour, telling her about seeing Mum for my birthday, visiting Caddy at Warwick. I try and explain how I'd felt so disconnected from her and she nods like she understands. I wish she could talk to me like she used to in Ventrella Road. I try and imagine what she'd say to me, but it's not the same.

On my way out, Marcus stops me in the hall, a friendly smile on his face. 'Have you had a proper tour?' he asks.

'No,' I say. 'Just Dilys's room.'

'There's not really much to see,' Marcus says cheerfully. 'But as you seem like you're going to be a regular visitor, I thought you might like a look around.'

'OK,' I say. All that's waiting for me at home is a pile of washing-up. 'How long have you worked here?'

'Three years,' he says. 'So, we've got thirty residents. Dilys is among the youngest; our oldest is a hundred and one.'

'Wow!'

'Harold has been here for a long time. He still likes to say that he'll outlive us all.'

'Do you like working here?'

'I do. Here's the kitchen.' He waves me in and pours himself a coffee from the pot waiting in the machine. 'Want one?'

'Sure.'

'I was working in palliative care before I came here,' Marcus says. 'That's end-of-life care. It's what I thought I wanted to do, but it didn't work out. It affected me too much. I couldn't get the balance between life and work, you know? So now I'm here, where it's a bit more like . . .' He hesitates, considering. 'The step before the last step. If that makes any sense at all. What do you do?'

'Oh, I just work in a coffee shop,' I say. When he looks surprised, I add, 'Not what you thought I'd say?'

'I thought you must work in a similar field. Or be studying towards it, perhaps. We don't get many visitors your age that aren't relatives. You're very good with Dilys.'

'I like her,' I say. 'It's not a work thing.'

'I know, sorry. I didn't mean it that way. I was just curious.' He opens the door again. 'If you ever wanted to volunteer here generally, rather than just visit her, you'd be very welcome. We're always on the lookout for good volunteers.'

'OK,' I say, mostly because I'm not sure how to reply.

He looks at me for a moment. 'What kind of area do you want to work in? Long-term, I mean.'

I don't know why he's carrying on with this, but he's giving me free coffee and he's nice to Dilys, so I answer. 'I don't know.'

'Fair enough,' he says. 'If you change your mind, though, think about the care industry? Or even nursing. We need people like you.'

I'm so flattered, and so surprised, that for a second I can't actually speak. 'People like you' is usually such a loaded phrase, and I've had variants of it thrown at me over the years, none of them complimentary. But this . . . he means this in a good way. He sees *me* as someone good, someone who could *do* good.

My impulse is to thank him, but all I say is, 'OK, I'll think about it. Maybe.'

'Great,' he says. 'Sorry to bang on at you. I'll just show you the common area before you go. When Dilys is a bit more mobile, she'll probably spend a lot of her time there.'

'When she's more mobile, will she be able to have Clarence with her?' I ask, following him along the corridor.

'Clarence . . .' His brow wrinkles, then clears. 'Her dog?' When I nod, he says, 'Yes, some residents do have a cat or a dog, if pre-arrangements have been made, depending on the circumstances. That may be some time away for Dilys, though. Now, here we are.'

We've stepped into a wide room full of sofa chairs and tables. There are bookshelves lining one wall and a TV on each side of the room. Old people – residents – are scattered around the room, most either in pairs or with a visitor of their own. I'm looking around, making polite noises, when I spot the piano.

'A piano!' I say, like a child. I head over to it and Marcus follows. 'This is great. When Dilys is better, you should bring her in here so she can play.'

Marcus nods. 'That may take some time,' he cautions. 'If at all. You do know what to expect in terms of her recovery?'

'Yeah,' I say. I don't really, but I don't want to talk about it, either. 'She was a piano teacher, you know.' I lift the fallboard and look down at the keys. 'Is it in tune?'

'It should be,' he says. 'We have a woman come in every couple of weeks to play for the residents. I'll make sure Dilys is here for it, if she's up to it.'

'Great,' I say. 'She'll like that.' I glance over at him. 'Do you play?'

'No, I'm not very musical,' he says. 'Do you?'

I shake my head, touching my fingertips to the white keys. 'I used to, when I was really young.'

'Why did you stop?'

I shrug, pushing gently down on one of the keys, the note sounding clear in the room. 'I don't know. Just one of those things, I guess—' The words die in my throat, because suddenly, out of nowhere, I do remember. The memory surfaces, complete, in my head, like it had never gone away. Me, sitting on the piano stool, playing 'Chopsticks'. Shouting behind me. A hand grabbing a hold of my hair, pulling me off the stool, throwing me against the piano. The explosion in my head. Darkness.

Oh God. Oh my God. I snatch my hand back from the keys, trying to remember how to breathe. How could I have forgotten that? How? I've been in a psychiatric unit. I had therapy. I had *music* therapy. I even talked to the therapist about how I'd played the piano once, but stopped. Nothing had brought the memory back then, in the place where it was safest to bring back horrible memories. But now, standing in the common area of a care home in Brighton, unprompted, there it is. Horrifying and ugly.

'Are you OK?'

I nod. The impact had knocked me out. I must have been seven or eight, because it was in the Manchester house. I remember sitting on a stool in the kitchen, Mum kneeling in front of me, her hands on my face. She'd been crying. *God*. How could I have forgotten this? Maybe 'forgotten' isn't the right word, not when it's trauma. Buried, maybe. Carefully hidden under layers of self-protection. I thought I'd uncovered everything by now. It's frightening to realize that I haven't.

Marcus has disappeared, leaving me alone, staring down at the keys. I can still hear my own breathing but it's levelled out now, steady.

I'd refused to go back to the piano. Just flat-out not gone anywhere near it. Maybe in some families, we'd have dealt with it. Overcome it, even. Mum would have coaxed me back beside her on the piano stool. But this was my family, and so I never played again. Never sat with Mum like that, either. We left the piano behind when we moved to Reading.

Mum. Mum, singing the scales and arpeggios song from that Disney film *The Aristocats* in a soft whisper. Her cool hands over mine, guiding my fingers. A noise escapes from my throat, like a whimper. *Why didn't you fight? Why didn't you fight for me?*

'Here,' a soft voice says from beside me. I look up, blinking past the blur in my eyes. Marcus is holding out a paper cup of water.

'Thanks,' I say, taking it. My voice comes out hoarse.

'Funny the things that get you,' he says. I appreciate how conversational he is, how offhandedly gentle, like this is ordinary behaviour. 'Do you want to sit down?'

'No, I'm fine. I'm just going to go home. Sorry to just . . . randomly freak out on you.'

Marcus smiles. 'You're really not the first person to get emotional here, trust me on that.'

Part of me wants to stop in to Dilys's room again, tell her what I remembered. She'd squeeze my hand and look at me with kind eyes, and that would help. But I came here to be supportive for her, not the other way around. I'll tell her next time, not now. I'll tell her when the memory – and the shock of remembering – has lost its sting.

Instead, I head out of the building, waving at Ines on reception as I go, and pull out my phone. 'Hey,' I say when Sarah picks up. 'Can I come over?'

20

'Keep Breathing'
Ingrid Michaelson

The good thing is that I don't spiral. I take the memory, exploded into my head, and deal with it, talking it through with Sarah and then Erin, my counsellor. This is progress, I decide. I can be blindsided by my own repressed memories and not fall apart. A small victory, but one that matters.

December arrives as the weather turns icy cold, and I learn how bad my flat is at retaining heat. Looking through my clothes for the best layering options, I find Matt's hoodie, the one I'd stolen from his hotel in Hastings. It's big enough that it fits me whatever I'm wearing underneath so I snuggle into it, happily, every evening I'm alone. Rosie and I finally pin down a time for me to come and visit her in Norwich, and her excitement when we talk about it on the phone is enough to chase away my nerves that it'll go the same way as Warwick.

Everything is going pretty great, all things considered, and I'm washing up at the sink, thinking idly about how I need to book the coach to Norwich, when the water from the tap slows to a useless trickle.

'Great,' I mutter, turning the handle ineffectually, trying the hot and then the cold with no success. I stand there for a moment, chewing my lip, then drop to my knees and open the cupboard door under the sink. It's the first time I've opened this particular cupboard since moving in, and I take in the collection of dusty cleaning products, presumably left behind by the previous tenant, before moving them aside.

I have no idea what I'm doing, but I gamely run my hand over the length of the piping, trying to figure out what the problem could be. A blockage somewhere, right? My fingers are suddenly wet. Ah. I lean into the cupboard, trying to find the source. I can see water leaking out from the edge of some kind of gluey gunk, which is spread around what looks like a valve in a pipe. Someone has obviously tried fixing this problem before.

I'm wondering whether I should send a whiny email to my letting agency, fiddling with the site of the leak in a vague attempt to see if I can stop it, when it happens. Something gives under my fingers and a jet stream of water explodes out from under the sink, hitting me full force in the face.

Obviously, I scream. And then I panic.

The thing is, the water *won't stop*. No matter how much I shriek and flail at the pipes with my hands, it just keeps gushing. I'm drenched. The floor is drenched. The bottles of cleaning products are swimming in the growing lake on the kitchen floor.

'Stop – just – fucking—' I manage to get a hold of two pipes and hold them together, which does next to nothing. There's water *everywhere*. And it's *still coming*.

Turn the water off. That's what I should do. I wipe my wet hands on my soaking jeans and run to the boiler. How do you turn water off? Is that even what I'm meant to do? I run back into the kitchen and grab my phone from where I'd left it on the counter. I try Sarah and Brian, but it goes to voicemail both times. Who else can I call? I scroll through my contacts, my heart thundering. There's no one. No one I can call for this kind of panic. This is what parents are for, isn't it? This is when I would call my dad, if I was a normal nineteen-year-old. But I can't call my dad.

The impulse is still there, though. I still want to call him. How crazy is that?

The water is cold against my bare feet. I'm in tears. I try Kel, but he doesn't pick up. For a ridiculous second I seriously consider calling Caddy and asking her if I can call *her* dad, but dismiss it. I have some pride.

I google 'how to turn water off' and find entries about stop valves and turning them clockwise or anticlockwise. I google 'how to find stop valve' and wade through several entries telling me to find it 'before an emergency' before I learn that it's probably under the sink.

It's not under the sink.

The water is splashing up at my ankles. I'm crying and swearing at my phone. Why don't they teach you how to do adult things at school? Why waste all that time on algebra and the periodic table when they don't even teach you basic plumbing?

I finally locate the stop valve behind the boiler, and it's so stiff I blister my hands trying to turn it off, but eventually I do. The water flow in the kitchen slows and then, finally, stops.

And then my phone rings.

'Hey, kid,' Brian says cheerfully. 'What's up?'

'The pipe burst!' I shout, too frazzled to even pretend to be calm. 'There's water everywhere!'

'Oh,' Brian says. There's a pause. 'Shit.'

I wait, but he doesn't elaborate. 'What should I do?' I prompt. I watch as the water begins to seep over the linoleum and on to the carpet.

'Turn the water off?'

'I've done that.'

'Uh . . . call a plumber?'

'It's eight o'clock!'

'Call an emergency plumber?'

'Brian!' My voice is squeaky. 'You're not helping!'

'I'm two hundred miles away, Zanne.' He doesn't sound even the slightest bit sad about this. 'What do you want me to do?'

Be a better brother. 'Oh, forget it,' I snap, and hang up. I know this isn't very fair of me; of all the things I could give him a hard time about, not being able to fix my broken pipe from 200 miles away is a pretty stupid complaint. But still.

I google 'emergency plumbers Brighton' through the blur of more tears and open the first result to load. When I call the number, the very nice woman on the other end of the phone assures me that Gary will be with me in half an hour. I think she can tell I've been crying.

Gary actually arrives in twenty minutes, and it's not until I've opened the door and let him in that I realize what I must look like. I haven't even changed out of the clothes I got drenched in, and my make-up-less face must be blotchy with tears. I almost want to say, *This isn't how I usually look. This isn't how I usually am*, but instead I stutter out an explanation about the pipe and lead him to the sink.

I stand at the edge of the kitchen area, playing with my sleeves and trying not to hiccup too loudly, as he kneels before the sink to investigate. Gary is in his fifties, tall and round, with kind eyes and a reassuring smile. While he works, he tells me about his daughter, Phoebe, who is around my age. She's at university, the first in their family to go. She has a nut allergy, and he worries about her.

Before he leaves, he takes my email address and tells me that they'll send me an invoice tomorrow. 'Isn't it my landlord that pays?' I ask, suddenly panicked.

'In that case, just send the invoice on to them,' he says. 'So long as we get paid, we don't much mind who's doing the paying.' He smiles at me. 'Just give us a call if you have any more trouble.'

When he's gone, I'm left standing alone in the bedsit, looking at the mess. The water has soaked into the carpet, spreading out halfway across the floor. The kitchen floor is still sopping wet. No one is going to come and clean this up for me, and I don't even have a mop. *Don't cry.*

I do anyway.

It's not until the next day that I find out my mistake.

'If you call out a tradesperson without our express approval, we aren't liable for the cost of the repair,' the guy who answers the phone explains. His name is Karl.

'So . . . who pays it?' I ask, stupidly.

'You,' Karl says.

Panic like a punch. My voice comes out shrill. 'It's over a hundred quid!'

'It's company policy,' he says, but he's already distant, like he's not even listening to me. Or, worse, like he is listening to me, but I'm not even registering as an actual person, just a problem he wants to be done with.

'What was I supposed to do?' I try to say. 'There was water everywhere.'

'Contact us first,' Karl says. 'It's in your contract. You should have turned the water off and then called us, so we could send a plumber from our approved list of tradespeople.'

'It was out of hours.'

'That's why we have an emergency number,' he says, overly patiently. 'This is all in the contract you signed.'

'But . . .' I bite down on my lip, forcing myself to not get worked up. 'It's the same amount of money, isn't it? So, OK, it was a mistake, and I'll know next time. But can't you just let it go, this time?'

'It's company policy. I'm sorry.'

'What if it means I can't pay my rent?'

There's a pause. 'Well, then we'll have another problem,' Karl says. When I don't reply, he says, 'Are you telling me you won't be able to pay your rent?'

'No,' I say, and I hear how sulky I sound, even though what I feel is panicky.

'OK. Call us if that changes. Can I help you with anything else?'

I hang up without answering. My throat is so tight. £125. One hundred and twenty-five freaking quid. I feel sick. My hands are actually shaking. How am I going to pay that much money? How?

I've tried to be careful with my money. I've been budgeting, for God's sake, with a spreadsheet and everything. I've actually been proud of myself for being sensible with my money, paying my bills, not getting behind on rent. *See*, I'd even thought. *See how well I cope?*

And now that's all been for nothing, because for all my monitoring of my incomings and outgoings, all my carefully scheduled direct debits, I do not have £125 spare. I just don't. The money simply doesn't exist.

Oh God, life is so hard. It's so hard. Is it this hard for everyone?

But no. *No.* I'm not going to panic about this. What good would that do, anyway? I settle myself down on my bed, open my online banking and start calculating. I have to pay the plumber within two weeks, and my rent is due in three. If I pay the plumber and pay my rent, that will be all the money I have in the world until I next get paid, the following month. That means no money for food. No money for toothpaste or toilet paper or shampoo.

Breathe. I've got stuff in the cupboards to last me if I'm careful, and I'm not a huge eater anyway. I can drop in on Sarah a few more times than usual and she'll feed me. I'll walk everywhere instead of getting the bus. I'll stop buying flowers for Dilys every time I visit; she'll understand. I won't buy any cigarettes, not even roll-ups. I won't go out; Kel won't mind if I hang out at his place instead. So long as I'm not confined to these four walls, I'll be fine.

The thing that hurts the most is the thing I know is unavoidable, even as I go over and over my budget to find a solution. There's just no way around it.

'Hey!' Rosie says. 'An afternoon phone call, wow. What did I do to deserve such an honour?' She laughs, like she does sometimes when she knows she's being obnoxious. 'I love my sober Suze conversations.'

I hadn't expected to smile so wide during this phone call. 'Is it a conversation if I can't get a word in?'

'Yes. An even better one.'

I laugh. 'Roz. This is a bad-news phone call.'

'Shit, really? Well, you're not crying. Or having a panic attack. So it can't be that bad.'

'Roz, shut up for a sec.' Silence. 'OK. So. I had a plumbing nightmare and now I have to pay for it and basically I can't come to Norwich to see you.'

Something in the silence changes. It's like I hear her smile drop. 'Oh,' she says. 'Really?'

'Yeah. I'm sorry. Like . . .' My voice catches, and I swallow. I feel so guilty I want to claw at my own face. 'Really sorry. I want to come.'

'I know. Why do you have to pay for it, though? You're renting. You don't have to pay for stuff like plumbing.'

'I fucked up,' I say bluntly. 'And now I do.'

There's another silence. 'Aw, Suze,' she says. 'That's properly shitty. Which bit can't you afford? Is it travel? Can I help pay for it?'

'It's not just that.' My chest hurts. 'I literally don't have any money. Like, to live on. So even if you helped me with the travel bit, I wouldn't be able to eat. Or go out, or anything.'

'We don't have to spend money to have a good time.'

'I'm not even talking about a good time, Roz. Just basic living.'

'OK, well . . . I guess if you can't come, you can't come.'

'I'm really sorry.'

'Don't be. *I'm* sorry you don't have any money. But I'll be home for Christmas and that's not long away, is it?' She sighs. 'God, I miss you, though. It would've been so cool to have you here.'

I think about Rosie's small face, her curls, the way she smirks at me. I miss her so much. 'Roz, remember when we went to that party when I was still new? The first one we went to together?'

'Yes! My first tequila. Good times.'

'I did your hair.'

'You did! I'd never had it in a bun before.'

We're both quiet for a while, listening to the other's silence. 'I'm sorry,' I say again.

'It's really fine,' she says. 'These things happen. Don't worry. I'll see you soon.'

21

'Tabula Rasa'
Calum Graham

So I guess this is what being sensible is. Eating tasteless tinned beans on thin toast three days in a row until the bread runs out, sitting on the windowsill, watching other people's lives because I can't afford to live my own. I don't turn the heating on because I'm scared of getting hit with a monster bill later, instead wearing three layers and wrapping myself up in blankets and drinking endless cups of black tea. I speak to my manager and message all my colleagues, hoovering up as many extra shifts as I can, not just for the extra cash but also for something to fill up the time.

The rest of the time, I go to Kel's. At first, I'm hesitant, hovering on the doorstep, smiling my very best hopeful, don't-you-just-want-to-take-care-of-me? smile when he answers the door. But each time he's so cheerful and happy to see me that I relax. There's always something going on: drinking Jenga, indoor Tories vs Labour paintball, elaborate baking missions and endless games of Cards Against Humanity. In the quieter moments Kel tells me about his engineering course and makes enough dinner for both of us without waiting for me to ask. We talk about Caddy and how much we miss her. He brings up Matt but I bat him away because I can tell by his voice that he's going to lecture me and I can't be bothered to tell him that he's wasting his brotherly concern on the wrong part of my life.

At home, when I can't sleep, I sit on my bed and play my guitar, trying to teach myself the Calum Graham song 'Tabula Rasa', which is so complicated it takes up my entire headspace.

It feels good to focus my energy somewhere productive instead of just wallowing all the time. At some point I fall asleep, my fingers moving across the fretboard in my dreams, and when I wake up the melody is still in my head.

I message Matt that morning – **Why does anyone bother doing anything else when music exists?** – and he replies with such an overdose of enthusiasm and exclamation marks that it makes me smile. He sends me links to articles about music as therapy, music as its own language, even one about birds and their different songs. **Do you ever get goosebumps when you listen to music?** he asks. I reply, **Of course! When it's special.** He sends me another link to an article about how not everyone does, that it's actually pretty rare, which blows my mind. **We're special**, he says. I smile down at the screen. **So special.**

All of this is to say, it's not all that bad, those weeks when I don't have any cash spare. Not any worse than it was before, anyway. I just have to wait it out, which is easier when I've got the kind of friends I do, the kind who step up.

The buzzer goes while I'm doing the washing-up, which is the fun kind of thing I do on my Friday afternoons now I'm an adult with absolutely no money. I'm not expecting anyone and I consider ignoring it, but the buzzing just gets louder and more insistent, so I wipe my hands on my jeans and press the button.

'Hello?' No reply. I raise my eyebrows at no one. 'Hello?' Still nothing. I release the button and turn to go back to the kitchen.

Buzz.

OK, what the hell? I reach over and press the button. 'Hello?' Silence. 'Seriously?'

This time, when I let go of the button, the buzz is immediate. For God's sake. Swearing, I shove my feet into my Vans, open my door and sprint down the stairs. I reach the front door and wrench it open.

And there's Rosie, grinning, fingers still pressing against my buzzer. She lets go. 'Hi!'

I'm so stunned, I can't do anything but stand there, gaping at her.

'It would've ruined the surprise if I'd said who I was,' she says. 'I wanted you to come down and see me. Hi!' She stretches out her arms. 'Surprise!'

'What . . .'

'Am I doing here?' she supplies helpfully. 'Well, I was counting on seeing you, and then I was all disappointed. And I thought, wait, why do I have to wait for her to come to see me? I can go and see her. *And* go home for a weekend and sleep in my own bed. Win-win. Right?' Her excitement has made her chattier than usual, or maybe it's a new university-Rosie thing. Either way, I like it, and it unlocks me.

I launch myself forward and throw myself at her for a hug. 'Oh my God, Roz!'

She hugs me back. 'Let me in, then. It's cold and I want to see if your depressing flat has got any less depressing since September.'

'Spoiler, it hasn't,' I say, moving aside.

The spoiler doesn't help, because her face still drops when she walks into my flat. She doesn't even try to hide it.

'It's barely bigger than my room at uni,' she says.

'Thanks, that helps.'

'You're aware there's a stain on the carpet, right?' she says, pointing with her foot to the watermark left after the plumbing disaster.

'Pretend it's not there,' I say.

'It feels weird to see you living like this,' she says.

I frown. 'Meaning?'

'Like an actual adult. I've spent the last couple of months feeling like I'm being independent, but now I feel like I've just been playing at it. You're doing it for real.' She looks around. 'Who would've thought you'd be the first one to be responsible, you know? Anyway, listen. I know you don't have money to spare, but we don't have to spend money, right? I have this whole plan. I think we should have a cryfest.'

'A what?'

'A cryfest. It's this idea Mum came up with a few years back. She says it's healthy to have a good cry sometimes, so we'd have a film marathon of guaranteed weepies. That's Mum's word, by the way, not mine. Weepies.'

'Roz, you never cry.'

'I do, actually. Especially when I'm watching . . .' She clears her throat dramatically and pulls up a list on her phone. '*Titanic*. *ET*. *My Girl*. *The Fox and the Hound*.' Her eyes flick to mine. 'You in?'

'Sure!' To be honest, Rosie could have suggested watching paint dry together and I would still have been all in.

'Great! You don't mind coming to my house, right? You don't have a DVD player. Or the films. Or a sofa. Or—'

'All right, point made. I'm in. Let's go.'

We have the best time. We cook frozen pizzas and eat them on her living-room floor. We drink her mother's pink gin and Prosecco until the world gets fuzzy. And we talk. Sometimes we pause the films, but mostly we just talk right over them. I tell her about Matt and she smiles a dry, knowing smile, shaking her head at me. And then she says, so casually she could only have been planning it, 'It's a shame you couldn't come to Norwich, because I wanted you to meet Jade.'

'Who's Jade?' I ask.

She smiles, and I sit bolt upright.

'Roz! *Roz!* Who's Jade?'

And that's how I find out she's got a girlfriend.

'Why didn't you tell me?' I demand, when I've stopped shrieking. I've bounced up on to my knees, grabbing the remote and pausing *ET*.

'Two reasons,' she says. I can tell she's enjoying this. 'One, you kind of never asked. So there's that. And two, it's really early days. I don't want to put pressure on it by making it into a big deal.'

'It *is* a big deal.'

She smiles again. 'Yeah, well.'

'Does Caddy know?'

'Nope. She's never asked, either. The two of you are very self-involved.' She rolls her eyes at me.

'We shouldn't have to ask!' I say. 'I told you about Matt without you asking.' Her eyebrows shoot up and I realize my mistake. 'Not that he's a boyfriend. Not that that's the same at all. Never mind. I'm sorry I didn't ask. Tell me about Jade. I want to know everything.'

She does, her cheeks burning pink even as she smiles. Jade is in her third year and studying Pharmacy, like Rosie. They met at a Pharmacy Socicty social in her first week – Jade's the equality and diversity rep – but didn't start properly talking until later in the semester. Jade is from Somerset and has 'a brilliant accent'. At home she has a parakeet called Dave. She works in the on-campus bar three nights a week. Her mother is Spanish; her father is Iranian. She has a twin sister called Jasmine, but Rosie hasn't met her yet.

'This is all great information,' I say. 'But you're being very coy.'

She grins. 'She's gorgeous, and girl kissing is the best thing in the world. Happy?'

I grin back. 'That'll do for now.'

We stay up until four. By the time Rosie falls asleep during *My Girl*, we've watched five films and cried a *lot*. I manage to make it through *Titanic* with dry eyes – Rosie does not – but lose it during

ET. We both fall apart during *The Fox and the Hound*. So hard, in fact, that at one point Rosie has to pause it and wail, 'Why did we think it was a good idea to watch this?' before FaceTiming a bewildered Caddy so we can share our tearful, slightly drunken commitment to lifelong best friendship.

It's the best night I've had in weeks. I wake up smiling, curled on her familiar sofa, even as the hint of a headache presses against my forehead. I go to work for a double-shift and she spends the day with her mum – when I check Instagram on my break, it's full of beaming pictures of the two of them at the beach in Eastbourne, hair flying around their faces in the wind – but we spend the evening together, eating homemade chilli with her mum in their cosy kitchen, the lights turned down low.

'Why *did* you come back?' I ask before I leave to go home at midnight.

Her nose crinkles as she smiles. 'I thought you needed a friend. And I figured, just this once, that friend should be me.'

22

'Up We Go'
Lights

I've been thinking about the piano ever since my last visit to see Dilys. At first I was focused on the memory itself, how painful it was, how strange it is that I could possibly have forgotten something so horrible. But by now I've moved on from that, and all I can think about is the wasted opportunity. All these years I could have been playing the piano. I could be really good by now. But Dad took that chance from me, and yes, I was a child then, but I'm an adult now. Why am I still letting him control so much of my life? He's not even in it any more. But, no, not even my life. What was the word Dilys had used? Joy. I'm still letting him control my joy.

These thoughts are why, when I go to see Dilys that week, I tell her about what I've remembered, and why I stopped playing the piano. She listens, nodding encouragingly.

'So I think I want to learn,' I say. 'The piano, I mean. I know I'm a bit older now than most people are when they start, but that doesn't matter, does it?'

She smiles and shakes her head.

'And I thought,' I add, 'that you could teach me. Maybe. When you're stronger? I can wait.'

Dilys looks at me for a long moment, her expression difficult to read, and I'm suddenly worried I've offended her somehow. I thought she'd be pleased, but maybe she doesn't like that I just keep taking from her?

'I could—' I begin, meaning to say that I'd pay her back,

somehow, but she puts a hand up and I stop.

She touches her hand to chest and taps. 'On . . . on . . .'

I smile encouragingly, but I'm nervous, and I'm trying not to be patronizing but I'm probably not pulling it off.

'On board?' Marcus suggests, from where he's been writing quietly on a clipboard on the other side of the room. He glances at me and smiles. 'On one condition?'

Dilys taps more determinedly, her eyes on mine. 'Honoured,' she manages, thickly, her voice a hoarse choke.

Somehow, I manage not to burst into tears. 'OK, great! I'll start saving up for a keyboard. It might take a while. What happened to your piano when you sold your flat?'

Dilys points to the iPad on the bedside table and I unlock it obediently, open it to the right app and hold it up for her. **Storage**, she types. **Graham**.

'That's good,' I say. 'So you can have it back one day?'

'Hope,' she says.

'Me too,' I say. 'I hope so, too.'

I play her the Cyndi Lauper song 'Time After Time' on my guitar, which I've been teaching myself over the last few weeks. It's shaky, and I fumble some of the chords, but she smiles all the way through. When I read her a chapter from *The Little Prince*, I glance up near the end to see that she's fallen asleep. I draw a smiley face on a Post-it note and stick it on the iPad with a quick '*See you next week!*' on it before I go, say goodbye to Marcus and head towards the exit.

Christmas begins when Caddy and Rosie come home.

They arrive on the same day; Rosie on the coach with her oversized rucksack, and Caddy, later, in her dad's car. They both take a night in their own homes before staying with me, but when they do they come armed with alcohol, Christmas biscuits and a lot of stories. We stay up for hours, talking. I plait Caddy's hair. Rosie tries to play my guitar.

'How come you're not with Kel?' I ask Caddy when we're halfway through the second bottle of wine she'd brought.

'Because I'm with you,' she says.

We're well into the next bottle when Rosie, who's been glancing around my bedsit looking more and more morose, says, 'I'm so sorry you have to live like this. It's so unfair. You had all that shit before and it means you have to have this shit now and it's so *unfair*. You should have *good* stuff now because of all the bad.'

'*You're* the good stuff,' I say, and she laughs and tells me to fuck off.

'Listen, I had an *idea*,' she says, with the earnest emphasis of someone who's drunk a lot of wine. 'A really great idea that you're going to think is terrible.'

'Oh, good,' I say.

'Seriously!' she says, pointing at me. 'OK, so, listen – are you listening?'

'I'm listening, Roz.'

'You should sue your parents,' she says.

My brain, wine-slowed, can't quite decide in the split second of reaction time whether I should laugh or groan at this, so what I do is choke on my sip instead, doubling over to cough until Caddy pats me uselessly on the back.

'God,' I manage, wiping at my eyes. 'Thanks for that.'

'Hear me out,' Rosie says. 'So, I have this friend at uni – yes, I have friends now – and she's studying law—'

'Roz, no, can we not—'

'And so I was talking to her about you – sorry, but I was – because she wants to go into family law, and she was doing some kind of case study on a trial that just happened, some guy who killed his daughter?'

'Stepdaughter,' I correct, pretty calmly considering my heart has nosedived right into my stomach.

'Oh, you know about it? Kirsty?'

'Kacie. Kacie-Leigh.'

'Right. Her. Anyway, we were talking about it, and I was saying how it's not right that, like, there are only trials when a kid dies?'

'Roz,' Caddy says, suddenly sharp.

'What?' Rosie turns to her, eyes wide.

'Be more sensitive.'

'How was that not sensitive? That's what happened. And, like, if the kid doesn't die, they just grow up, like you —' Caddy puts her hand over her eyes and murmurs something — 'and there's no justice. The abuser gets away with it? That's so wrong. Anyway, Aisha — that's my friend — said that that's not really true, there are things you can do. It's hard to prosecute because of evidence and stuff, but what you *can* do is sue.' She looks at me expectantly.

Slowly, to make sure she actually listens, I say, 'No.'

'Why not?'

'Because I don't want to.'

'Why not?'

I look at Caddy, hoping for help, but she just shrugs sympathetically at me. 'I just want to move on with my life, OK?' This isn't a lie, but it's not the real answer, either. The real answer is to do with things that she would never understand, like the fact that I still, despite everything, haven't given up hope of a relationship with my family, and doing something like this would kill that forever. That just thinking about taking a road like that is painful, let alone actually doing it. That this kind of thing is more complicated than she thinks; in her eyes, I'm a victim who deserves justice. But I'm also a daughter who wants her parents to love her. I can't make that go away, however much simpler it would make my life.

'OK, but, this is the thing, if you sue, you get money. Money you could really use, right? I should have started with that.'

'I guessed, and it's still no.'

'Don't you want to know how much?'

'It doesn't matter.'

'Well, the maximum is five grand,' she says. Her eyes are earnest and hopeful, and I want to be annoyed with her for pushing this, but I can't quite muster it. She so wants to fix this for me. How can I be angry about that?

'Yeah, I'm going to rip out my own heart for a few grand,' I say. 'Put myself through actual hell. Sounds *great*.'

'We'd be there,' Caddy says.

'Every step of the way,' Rosie adds.

'You've gone past cheesy, now,' I say. 'No more alcohol for you.'

They're both home for about three weeks over the holidays; a couple of weeks before New Year and one week after. I see them both almost every day, sometimes one-on-one but usually all three of us together with Kel as an extra bonus. I'm working most days at Madeline's because I'd booked myself in to work pretty much every day of the Christmas season that we'd be open. Extra money and a distraction from my least favourite time of year. Perfect.

I spend Christmas Day with Sarah and a bunch of her chef friends. A foodie Christmas is a just-about-bearable alternative to Christmas alone, and even though I feel the usual churn of sadness somewhere inside me all day, thinking about my friends with their families, the whole world with their families, it's fine. Sarah is clearly, genuinely, happy that I'm there, and her friends are nice. Also, the food is incredible and when I go back to my bedsit that night, I have five Tupperware containers full of leftovers. And that's one more Christmas survived.

On Boxing Day, I get a message from Matt, who's staying in

Brighton with his mum and sister for the holidays, asking if I want to meet up. He comes to Madeline's at the end of my shift to pick me up, and the sight of him makes me smile wider than I'd intended. He's wearing a long black coat like an undertaker, which would look weird if he wasn't both cute and cool enough to pull it off. His cheeks are pink, his eyes warm. When he sees me, he smiles.

We go to the beach together, even though it's cold, and stand stamping our feet on the pebbles for a while before we give up and go to my flat. I'm nervous about him seeing it, but I'm also trying to tell myself I don't care what he thinks about it, so it's all very confusing in my head.

'Small,' is all he says.

'That's what everyone says,' I reply. 'As if I haven't noticed, or something?'

His nose crinkles as he smiles. 'I just mean it doesn't really suit you, that's all.'

'Who *would* it suit?'

'You know what I mean,' he says. I kind of like how easily he bats off the traps I set for him. His face changes as his eyes fall on something behind me and I glance around to see what he's looking at. 'Is that *my* hoodie?' he asks.

His Hastings hoodie is still lying on my bed where I'd left it. 'Er . . .' I say, trying to think of a lie, feeling my face start to burn. 'Maybe?'

He laughs, reaching for it. 'God, I wondered where it went.'

'You can have it back,' I say with a shrug, trying to style this out and failing. 'I was just . . . looking after it.'

He tosses it to me. 'Put it on, then.' When I do, pulling up the hood so it falls over my eyes for maximum cute effect, he grins. 'Nah, it looks better on you. Keep it, I've got loads.'

I drop the hood back and smooth down my fluffed-up hair,

smiling as I go to the kitchen to make us tea. When we're sitting on the bed together, him leaning against the wall and me cross-legged, I take a deep breath and say, 'Do you know why I live here? Has Kel told you . . . stuff?'

Matt nods, cautious. 'Yeah, some. I said he shouldn't have, but he can be a bit blabby. Plus, he's protective.'

'Of you?' I try not to show how hurt I am. What does Kel think, that I'm the kind of damaged goods with sharp edges, the sort that cut people? He wouldn't be the first, but it's *Kel*.

Matt half smiles. 'No, of *you*. He wanted to make sure I knew I couldn't "fuck you over". His words. Not that I *would* have fucked you over, obviously. But you know how Kel is, he thinks monogamy is the only proper way to have a relationship, and anything else must be bad. I've never led a girl on or lied to her or anything. And you and me, we're both on the same page, right?'

I nod. 'One hundred per cent. No labels, no bullshit. And I'm not going to be your manic pixie dream Suze.'

He cracks up. 'Oh my God.'

'Seriously!'

'What does that even mean?'

'You know,' I say. 'The mysterious sad girl who comes in and teaches you all about life and you think you're going to *save* her, but you don't and you actually end up learning all about yourself – ooooooh.' I wave my hands around a little, wiggling my fingers, and tea sloshes out from my cup on to my sheets. 'Whoops.'

He starts to laugh even harder. 'You're not mysterious, for a start.'

I have to be honest. That is not what I was expecting him to say. 'Well, *I* know I'm not,' I say. 'But don't guys always think a pretty girl is mysterious?'

He grins. 'You think you're pretty?' His voice is warm, teasing but in a sweet way.

'Oh, shut up.' I sock his upper arm. 'You see? Manic pixie dream Suze. I'm supposed to be all beautiful-but-not-knowing-it and only you see me, blah blah blah bullshit.'

'You've given this a lot of thought.'

'You have to promise you won't do that. That you won't put a filter on me. A lot of stuff has happened that I don't always deal with that well, and it's not, like, a cute kind of breakdown. It's messy and crap. I want you to know that now so you're not disappointed when you get to know me.'

I expect him to make another joke but he's nodding instead, eyes on me. 'No manic pixie dreams,' he says. 'And no manic pixie dream boy-ing me, either. I've had my own shit, you know.'

'The music stuff?'

'Well, I was thinking more my dad being a cheating dickhead. Seeing as we're sharing.'

'Oh,' I say. Kel didn't tell me that.

'Yeah.'

'That's why you don't want to get into a relationship?'

His jaw tightens. 'Hey, I didn't psychoanalyse *you*, did I?'

'Sorry.' I hesitate. 'Do you want to talk about it?'

His eyes slide from mine, a distancing, self-protective quirk of a smile passing over his face. 'Ah, it's just a load of bullshit.'

'Isn't everything?' I say. There's a pause, so I reach out my foot and nudge him. 'Hey. I'll tell you mine if you tell me yours.'

He looks back at me and I smile as casually as I can, as if the two of us sharing our worst stories is no big deal. When he does tell me, he does it in a rush. He tells me about his dad – 'not a bad guy, not really; just a good guy who can't help himself' – and his multiple affairs, the woman he got pregnant while Matt was at uni, how Matt's never met his half-sister, how his mum kept forgiving his dad, over and over, how their decision to split up the previous summer was mutual, even though it shouldn't have been, and that still makes Matt angry. I keep my questions to a minimum; I just nod along and let him talk until he runs out of steam, turns to me and says, 'Your turn.'

Not that it's a competition, but my stuff is so much worse than his, and I can tell by his face that Kel must have left out a lot but he's trying not to react too obviously. I keep my voice light as I run through my story as quickly as I can – violent stepdad, left home at fifteen, lived in Brighton with Sarah, it went badly, tried to kill myself (again), got professional help, foster care – and when I finish he's looking at me like I'm a glass vase that just smashed on the floor.

'I'm really fine,' I say. This was a mistake. I should not have started any of this.

Matt opens his mouth to say something and then changes his mind, shaking his head. When he tries again, he says, 'That was intense.'

'I tried to make it non-intense,' I say. My skin feels prickly.

'I could tell,' he says. 'How many times have you told that story?'

'Not as often as you'd think, actually,' I say. 'I don't usually . . .' I mean to say 'let people in', but I stop myself, because that's a whole other level of intense that I don't want to open either of us up to. 'I don't like talking about it. Sorry. I shouldn't have—'

'Shit, don't apologize,' he says. '*I'm* sorry. I'm reacting like a twat. I don't even know what to say, and I keep thinking of questions but—'

'Go ahead,' I interrupt. 'Ask me whatever. I can take it.'

He hesitates, eyebrows crinkling. 'OK . . . your mum. Didn't—'

'No, she never did anything.'

'Never?'

'When I was really young, sometimes she'd wake me up before he could get to me and then lock us both in the bathroom until he'd calmed down. And sometimes she'd cry for him to stop if it was really bad. Oh, and he used to do this thing where he'd lock me out of the house, like, just in the garden? Overnight, I mean, when I was in my pyjamas. She usually came and got me once he was asleep.' The look on his face makes me laugh a completely humourless laugh. 'Too intense again?'

'Why the fuck didn't she leave him?'

'Because she loves him. You're hearing all the bad stuff from me. She'd tell you the good stuff. Also, she feels guilty, because she cheated on him and had another guy's baby. There's that, too.'

'She feels guilty about *that*?!'

'My real dad was best man at their wedding,' I say, which is a detail I've never told a single person outside of Gwillim House. 'Yeah, she feels guilty about that. So she should. What a dick move. Cheating on your husband with his best friend? It's just tragic. I'm embarrassed for her.'

'What's he like?'

'Who? Oh, my "real" dad. No idea. He's not interested. He fucked off when my dad – stepdad – found out that I wasn't his, which, by the way, was about nine years before *I* found out my stepdad wasn't really my dad. My brilliant family, right? Actually –' I realize as I speak that I'm overdoing the casual act, trying too hard to pretend that this is OK, and I try to dial it back – 'I'm being harsh on my stepdad. He *did* raise me. And it wasn't all bad all the time.'

'You're *being harsh* on your abusive stepdad?' Matt's voice is higher than usual, pitched with incredulity. 'I'd throw that fucker off a bridge. Jesus.'

How to explain feeling defensive of the parents who destroyed you? You can't. 'My emotions are complex,' I say, hoping to make him laugh with dry understatement, and it works because his eyes crinkle as he smiles. 'So, now you know about my tragic life.'

He's freaked out a bit. I can see it in his eyes. People always think they want to know, but they don't, not really. I haven't even told him any of the details, none of the hospital admissions, none of the things Dad used to say when he really wanted to hurt me. What I've said is so sanitized, and still it's too much. Is it any wonder I don't like to talk about it? Can anyone really blame me?

God, he clearly came here because he wanted to kiss me. At the very least. And instead we've both over-shared and now it's awkward. Damn. Fucking *damn*. Haven't I learned anything? It's *Boxing Day*, for God's sake.

'Hey, I've heard worse,' he says. His eyes meet mine and he smiles.

I smile back, trying to keep the relief out of it. 'Have you actually?'

'Well, no.' We both laugh, and the awkwardness lifts.

'Have you got any more gigs coming up?' I ask. I already know he doesn't, because Kel and I had talked about it, but the question does what I meant it to do and steers our conversation back on to safe ground. I make us more tea and he tunes my guitar, talking happily about songwriting and his favourite chord progressions, his callused fingers deft on the strings.

I end up seeing him almost every day over the next week before New Year, often with Kel, Caddy and Rosie as well. It feels good to hang out as a group, and that's how we spend New Year's Eve: together. We go to one of the clubs near the seafront for a 'Nineties New Year' and it's cheesy as hell but perfect. I might hate Christmas, but I love New Year's Eve. I love how hopeful it is, all that optimism. The baseless belief that things will be better just because the calendar changes. It's so endearing, and it's impossible not to get swept up along with it.

When the countdown starts, my heart races, like it always does, with hope. I want what I always want, which is for the next year to be better than this one. And, to be fair, it has been. This year was better than last year, and that was better than the one before. The bar's pretty low, it's true. But still, I'm getting there.

The clock hits midnight and the whole club screeches out in drunken unison, confetti raining from the ceiling. I turn to Rosie and we hug, tight and sweaty. She laughs in my ear and kisses my cheek. 'Happy New Year!' When we disentangle, I wait the couple of seconds it takes before Caddy stops kissing Kel and opens her arms to Rosie before I let myself look at Matt. He's waiting, sparkling eyes only on me, a quirk of a smile on his face. When we kiss, I forget the room.

I'm cat-sitting for Sarah while she's in Dublin with a couple of her friends, which is why I suggest on a whim that everyone comes back with me for after-party drinks. Kel looks a little put out when Caddy squeals an enthusiastic 'Yes!', which must be because he was expecting us all to go back to his instead, but he doesn't say no.

When I let us into the flat, Henry Gale winds himself around my legs, mewing, and I lean down to pick him up. 'Hey, you. Come in, guys. I'm just going to feed him.'

I head towards the kitchen, listening to Caddy's breathless 'I'm so excited to be back here. Is it weird that I'm so excited to be back here?' behind me, and measure out the food for Henry, who immediately begins to wolf it down.

'Suze?' Rosie's voice sounds behind me and I jump. I hadn't realized she'd followed me. 'Am I the fifth wheel, here?'

'Oh my God, no,' I say. I open Sarah's alcohol cupboard and begin sorting through the bottles, trying to figure out what I can get away with stealing. 'It wasn't like that tonight, was it? Why would it be now?'

'Because beds,' she says.

I laugh. 'We're just going to hang out all together,' I say. 'It'll be fun. Promise. What do you want to drink?'

'Nothing,' she says.

I glance at her. 'Everything OK?'

Before she can reply, Caddy comes bounding into the kitchen, beaming, followed by Kel. 'It all looks just the same,' she announces. Kel slides an arm around her, dropping a kiss on the top of her head. She leans back against him, smiling.

'It's only been a couple of years,' I say, watching as Henry Gale, clearly bothered by all the strangers, stalks out of the room. 'What did you think would be different?'

'Three years,' Caddy corrects. 'I'm really happy that we're all back here. I thought we never would be again.'

'OK, dramatic,' I say. 'What do you want to drink?'

'Do you have any lemons? And triple sec?' Kel asks. 'I could make lemon drops with the vodka.'

'Suze meant, like, vodka and a mixer,' Caddy says. 'Something simple.'

'I wasn't asking her to make them,' Kel says, brow furrowing. 'Lemon drops are nice. You like them.'

'Sure, but not now,' she says.

Rosie and I look at each other. Her eyebrows lift slightly and I shrug back, making a face. 'I'll see what Matt wants to drink,' I say. 'There are probably lemons in the fridge. Make whatever you want, OK?'

When I walk back into the living room, Matt is holding Henry Gale like a baby. They both have matching looks of euphoria on their faces.

'Are you a cat person?' I ask.

Matt turns to me, beaming. 'Hell, yeah,' he says. 'Bloody love cats, me.' Seeing my face, his beam drops. 'You're not?'

I put a hand to my chest. 'Dog person.'

'Ah, shit,' he says. 'Guess we're incompatible then.'

'Shame,' I say. 'We could have had it all.'

He grins at me, giving Henry Gale a little twirl, and I tell him to hold the pose so I can take a picture. He obeys, lifting Henry higher so he can nuzzle his head. It's adorable, even though Henry is a cat.

'How come you're looking after this one if you don't like cats?' he asks.

'Henry Gale is the exception,' I say, leaning forward to touch my nose to Henry's. 'Everyone's allowed an exception.'

He smiles. 'Are they, now?' He leans down to let Henry jump out of his arms and on to the floor. 'So this is where you used to live?'

'Briefly,' I say, trying to remember why I'd come in here. I was meant to ask him something.

'It's nice.' Matt sinks down on to the sofa and holds out a hand to me, pulling me down on top of him when I take it, reaching up and tugging the blanket down over us. He's warm and cosy and I curl into him, his arms closing around me. We adjust instinctively; both of us stretching out across the length of the sofa, me mostly on my back, him on his side. Our foreheads touch.

He whispers, 'Happy New Year.'

'Happy New Year,' I whisper back. We're too close, and I think we both know it. This is more than friends, more than benefits. I lift my chin just a little closer and we're kissing, snuggled together on a sofa, under a blanket, in the earliest hours of New Year's Day.

'Oh God.' Rosie's voice, getting louder as she comes into the room. 'Seriously? You promised me fun, not couples hell.'

I twist myself so I can see her. 'If Jade was here, you'd—'

'Jade *isn't* here,' Rosie interrupts, and there's a snap in her voice that makes me disentangle myself from Matt and roll away from him, out from under the blanket and off the sofa.

'Sorry,' I say. 'I am definitely here for fun.'

Rosie looks past me, towards Matt. 'On a scale of one to ten, how much do you hate me right now?'

He laughs. 'Where are Caddy and Kel?'

'Kitchen,' she says. 'As a couple. Look, I think I'm going to go.'

'No!' I say immediately, flushing with guilt. 'I'm sorry. No coupling. Let's get some drinks and . . .' My mind has suddenly gone blank. What could we do that's fun? All I can think about is the feeling of Matt's body against mine under the blanket and how much I wish I was still there. 'We can play a game or something.'

Rosie's eyebrow quirks. 'Monopoly?' Her sarcasm bites.

'I was thinking more like "I Have Never",' I say. 'But we can play Monopoly if you want.'

'Well,' Rosie begins, but there's a noise from the other side of the flat and we both pause just in time to hear Kel's raised voice saying 'For fuck's sake!' and then quietening off. Rosie and I look at each other, then at Matt. He's sat up, frowning.

'Should I check everything's OK?' I ask uncertainly. Caddy and Kel are the golden ones out of all of us. The fact that they don't need anyone to check on them – either of them, ever – is like their *thing*. But Caddy's my best friend, and it sounded an awful lot like Kel just shouted at her. Plus, it's Sarah's flat, which means right now it's *my* flat.

So I head out of the living room and down the hall to the kitchen, pausing in the doorway until they both look over at me. 'Hey,' I say. 'Everything OK?'

'Yeah,' Caddy says.

I don't move.

'It's fine,' she says. Her voice has that tinge of impatience that comes with *not* being fine, but not wanting to have to acknowledge it. I know it very well.

I look at Kel and raise my eyebrows a little. *I heard you raise your voice at my friend, and I will kill you if you hurt her, and you shouldn't raise your voice in my house anyway, OK?* I can tell he gets it without me saying it out loud because he looks away from me.

'This is kind of private, Suze,' Caddy says, and the tinge of impatience is thicker now. 'Can we just have a minute?'

I put up my hands and leave them to it. When I get back to the living room, Matt is lying on the sofa with Henry Gale on his stomach kneading his chest. I can hear him purring – the cat, not Matt – from across the room.

'Where's Roz?' I ask.

'She left,' Matt says, craning his neck but not moving enough to dislodge Henry. 'She said she was taking the opportunity to slip out.'

'For God's sake!' I say, pulling out my phone and calling her. 'She can't just walk home on her— Roz! Where did you go?'

'Home,' Rosie says. 'I'm tired, and you guys have your own thing. It's fine, honestly. I'm in an Uber.'

Guilt feels heavy in my chest. I turn instinctively away from Matt and lower my voice. 'I'm sorry.'

'Don't be. Seriously, it's OK. I miss Jade and it's just a thing.'

'But you were going to stay here.'

'Right now I just want my own bed.'

I don't know how to say what I want to say, which is that with her gone, it really is a couples thing, and I don't know how to feel about that.

'Hey, Suze?' she says.

'Yeah?'

'I like Matt.'

I'm suddenly glad my back is to him, because a smile has burst on to my face at the words, wide and obvious. 'Do you?'

'Yeah.' I can tell there's more she wants to say, but instead she says, 'I'm nearly home. I'll talk to you tomorrow. Or, later today, I guess? Love you.'

She doesn't usually say things like that out loud. 'I love you, too.'

I turn back around to face Matt, who pushes Henry Gale gently off his lap as he sits upright to ask, 'Are Kel and Caddy OK?'

'I think so,' I say, glancing towards the open living-room door. 'Sorry. This isn't how I thought it'd go when I said you should all come back here.'

He smiles and holds a hand out to me. When I take it, he squeezes my palm and then my knuckles, the tips of my fingers, sending tingles up my arms and through my whole body. 'I don't mind,' he says.

'Guys?'

I break away from Matt like I've been pulled backwards, leaping away from him, turning to face Kel, who's standing in the living-room doorway next to Caddy. Neither of them is looking particularly cheerful.

'We're going to go,' he says.

'Oh,' I say.

'Yeah,' Caddy says. 'Sorry.'

'You coming?' Kel asks, directing the question at Matt, who's stood up beside me. 'You're staying at mine, right?'

'What, so it's OK when it's Matt?' Caddy snaps at him, which makes no sense at all.

'Cads,' Kel says, his face creasing. 'You know—'

'Let's just go,' she says. She reaches out her arms to me and I let her hug me. 'Sorry,' she says again, into my ear. She squeezes tight.

When we separate, I realize Matt and Kel are having one of those silent conversations you can only have if you've known each other for a long time. Kel notices me watching first and pastes on a smile. 'See you later, Suze. Happy New Year, yeah?' He gives me a brief hug, then turns to go.

I look at Matt. Matt looks at me.

'See you later, I guess,' I say.

His face falls, but only for a moment. He smiles and shrugs. 'Sure, OK.' He glances towards the door, sees that Caddy and Kel have already disappeared through it, then grins at me. 'Busted by the chaperones.'

I feel my face break into a mirroring grin. 'God damn.'

Matt takes my hand, eyes on mine, then lifts it to his mouth and drops a kiss on my knuckles. Sweet and soft, like that first time at the pier. My heart is as unprepared for it now as it was then. I don't say anything, just smile and watch him leave, closing the door behind the three of them.

I call Henry's name and he comes flying out of Sarah's bedroom to see me, winding himself around my ankles until I pick him up. 'Just you and me, then.' I wait to feel the horrible, churning ache of loneliness, but it doesn't come. Maybe I'm too tired, but what I'm feeling is closer to happiness.

Holding Henry Gale close to my chest, I head along the hall to bed.

23

In the morning, I sleep in until eleven and then head into town to meet Rosie and Caddy for a New Year's Day brunch. Rosie's in a good mood but Caddy is quieter than usual, stabbing at the pancakes she ordered harder than necessary and leaving little fork dents.

'Everything OK?' I ask.

She shrugs. 'Bit hungover.'

I glance at Rosie, who raises her eyebrows at me.

'What was that thing about last night?' I ask. 'You and Kel.'

Caddy frowns. 'Oh, it was nothing.'

'Tell me, then.'

There's a long silence. In the seconds she doesn't speak, my skin starts to tickle with nerves. If she doesn't want to talk to me about this kind of thing, if I'm not someone she can be honest with, then are we even friends any more? We could always talk to each other, that's what made us friends in the first place.

'He thinks we haven't spent enough time together,' she says finally. 'In the time I've been back from Warwick.'

'Oh,' I say. 'Haven't you been together, like, basically every day?'

'Yeah . . .' She sighs. 'He means just the two of us.'

'Oh,' I say again, getting it this time. 'Because it was always all of us together?'

'Pretty much, yeah. He thinks . . .' She hesitates, then glances at me. I smile, not my big Suze smile, but my smaller, real smile.

'He thinks I've been, like, avoiding him. By wanting you and Roz around. But I was like, I don't *see* them any more. And Christmas is hard for you. I'm not going to not see you guys because of my *boyfriend*. So us all hanging out together is the solution, right?'

I nod. 'You'd think.'

'Well, yeah. But it bothered him, and we'd sort of talked about it, but then at New Year when I wanted to go back to yours with you, it all kind of came out. Plus there's the whole Matt-and-you thing. That's stressing him out.'

'Why?'

Caddy glances at Rosie, and they exchange a look that makes my stomach twist. They've talked about this. 'Because he thinks it's going to blow up and then we won't all be able to be friends any more.'

'I think you can give us a bit more credit than that,' I say. 'If we were in an actual relationship or something, then yeah, maybe. But we're not.'

'Suze, that's literally the exact problem,' she says. 'How can you not see that that's the exact problem?'

'Cads,' I say. 'We're different from the two of you, OK? We know what we're doing. Honestly, me and Matt are just having fun together. There's no pressure, and that's a good thing. It's not a big deal at all. We don't even see each other that much, just if we happen to be in the same place.'

'If you happen to be in the same place?' Rosie repeats.

'Yeah. Like, at the moment, he's hanging out with us because of Kel.'

Rosie snorts. 'No, he's not, you muppet. It's you.'

'Definitely you,' Caddy says.

'He's Kel's best friend,' I say. 'They hang out when they're both in Brighton.'

'Your wilful blindness is very endearing,' Rosie says, rolling her eyes. 'Stupid, but endearing.'

I feel my face starting to burn. 'I just meant that Kel is the main reason, and I'm like a bonus.'

Caddy laughs, sudden and genuine. 'Oh my God. This is adorable.'

'If you need it spelled out,' Rosie says, 'Matt never spent time with all of us until you were around. *Last* New Year, for example. No Matt.'

'Well, he had all the music stuff going on,' I say. 'So he didn't have much free time.'

'What is wrong with you?' Rosie asks.

'Ouch,' I say, pouting for effect.

'Seriously,' Caddy says. 'Why are you having such a problem with this?'

'Stop ganging up on me!' I protest. My face is flaming now. 'You're making it sound like a "thing", that's all. And it's not a thing.'

'It's definitely a thing,' Rosie says flatly.

'It's not!'

'Suze, what is it you think people in relationships do that you and Matt aren't doing?' Caddy asks. 'Seriously. What is it?'

'Use the word "relationship"?' I suggest. 'Use pet names?'

'Is that it?'

'No, obviously,' I say. 'People in relationships *want* to be in relationships. And we don't. Relationships are, like, exclusive.'

'So you're sleeping with someone else as well?' Rosie asks.

The obvious thing to do at this moment is tell them that we're not actually sleeping together, but I don't. They'll be even more convinced that it's 'a thing' if they find out. So I roll my eyes and sigh. 'Don't be so literal. No. But I could, if I wanted to. And so could he. He probably is, I don't know.'

They both gawp at me. Caddy's eyebrows have gone right up to her hairline. 'You think he's still sleeping with other girls?'

'I don't know – that's the point. It doesn't matter.'

'How can it not matter?'

'Why do you even care?' I demand, trying not to get annoyed. 'What's it got to do with you what kind of relationship we have?'

'Quite a lot? Like, the fact that his best friend is my boyfriend? And even if he wasn't, I think you deserve better.'

'Than Matt?' I'm instantly defensive on his behalf, surprising myself with it. 'What's wrong with him?'

'No,' she says, overly patient. 'Not him specifically. You deserve better than benefits. Or being someone's benefits.'

'Do you hear how judgemental you sound right now?'

There was a time when me saying this would have been more than enough to make Caddy's eyes go Bambi-wide and her to back off. But today she just rolls them and says, 'I care about you and I worry that Matt – who Kel and I introduced you to, so I feel responsible – could hurt you. Girls fall for him all the time. They say they won't, but they do.'

'You and Kel are *both* judgemental,' I say. 'Maybe you should work on that before worrying about me.'

'Yeah, well, you and Matt are deluded,' she says. 'We all saw you together. We saw it. You know what Rosie said when the two of you "went to get drinks"?' She lifts her fingers in scare quotes.

Rosie lets out a bark of a laugh. 'Oh God, don't tell her what I said.'

'What did you say?' I demand, spinning a little in my seat to stare at her.

'She said she shipped it,' Caddy says.

'Oh my God.' Rosie starts laughing harder. 'I was drunk. I wasn't myself.'

I'm not laughing. 'Make up your mind. Are you shipping us or are you saying he's a fuckboy who's going to hurt me? Or that *I'm* the problem?'

'Suze—' Caddy begins, face creasing.

'Listen,' Rosie interrupts, her voice calm. 'We like you. We want you to be happy. And Matt makes you happy, that's obvious. We don't get why that's so hard for you, that's all.'

'Don't you *want* love?' Caddy asks, and my head, previously tense, starts screeching *Alarm! Retreat! Shutdown!* at me. 'Isn't that what you want? I don't get why you don't want this.'

'I know you don't,' I say.

'Are you scared of it?' Rosie asks.

Of course I'm scared of it. How can anyone not be? That's what I don't understand. Giving yourself to someone that way, exposing all the vulnerable parts of you. How could you ever trust anyone that much? How could you ever trust *yourself* that much? Letting someone love you like that is giving them ammunition to destroy you. The more you care, the more it hurts.

'This is all irrelevant,' I say. 'Matt doesn't want any of it either. We're on the same page. We want the same thing. Which is to not want a thing.' I smile, pleased with myself. 'It's a thing.'

Rosie rolls her eyes. 'Kind of not the point.'

'How is it not the point?'

'Because this is bigger than you and Matt,' Caddy says, as if she and Rosie are one person, sharing one mind. 'Fine, you and Matt don't want a relationship – weird, but OK. What about the next guy? What about the next ten years, or twenty? You're just going to be on your own forever?'

I'm starting to feel suffocated. My throat is tightening. The first tug of panic somewhere inside me. 'Why is it that you can have loads of great people in your life, but if you're not in a traditional relationship, you're "on your own"?'

'You know what I mean.'

'I don't,' I say. 'And I don't know why you think you can say something like this to me, when you've got every traditional relationship going and I'm the exact opposite. Let me deal with that in my own way, OK?'

Caddy and Rosie look at each other, and I want to get up and leave. 'We just want you to be happy, Suze,' Rosie says again. 'You know that, so don't get all stressed. You know we love you and that you can trust us. This is all coming from a good place. Chill.'

My food's gone cold, but I stab a piece of bacon and shove it in my mouth, just so I don't have to look at them. My happy, normal friends in their happy, normal relationships. I do know they love me, and I do know I can trust them. But that doesn't mean I can't find their judgemental concern annoying. Why do I always have to be the one everyone worries about? Why can't I be on the other side of this for once?

It's not until I'm home later that day that it occurs to me that Caddy never finished explaining what was going on with her and Kel, and that she'd done a me in how deftly she'd moved the conversation away from something she didn't want to talk about. It was almost impressive. I pick up my phone and shoot Rosie a quick message, because part of being a trio is separating off into twosomes to talk about the other one.

Me:

> Should we be worried about Caddy and Kel?

Rosie:

> Hmmm . . . depends what you mean by worried.

> !!! Roz!! It's that bad?

Rosie:

No, it's fine. But long-distance relationships are against the odds anyway, right? And it's not great right now.

Me:

Who's in the wrong?

Neither/both? Sounds to me like Kel's being a bit possessive, but if she's always been super-close and then starts drifting off, it makes sense that he'd worry? Plus we both know she fancies that guy.

You know about Owen?!

Suze. Of course I know about Owen.

She's told you that she fancies him?

No, but I'm not an idiot. You met him, right? What's he like?

Basic.

That bad?

Not even bad, just blah. Just your basic guy. You know he came on to me?

Every guy comes on to you.

Still, bit of a dick move if she fancies him, right?

'Roz, don't be silly, not every guy comes on to me. I'm not that beautiful. Or big-headed.'

Me:

🙂

Rosie:

It's fine, I understand. You can't help the face you were born with. Or your massive ego.

Are you done?

Don't worry about Cads and Kel. They'll be fine.

Promise?

Yes, I obviously promise something so completely out of my control.

OK, good, so long as you promise xx

24

'Tonight'
Secret Nation

It hurts when they go back to uni. They leave on the same afternoon, Rosie on the coach up to Norwich and Caddy driving up with her sister. Having them back in my life for three weeks has made me realize how much I miss them when they're away, which I guess is stupid, considering how much time we'd spent apart while I lived in Southampton, which was entirely my decision and my fault.

In their absence, January rolls forward, grey and dull. I meet Miriam and we talk about my progress ('You really are doing so well'), the whole plumbing thing ('But why didn't you call me?') and how my pathway plan is playing out. She wants to talk about careers, whether I've started thinking more long-term, and I tell her no even as I think about Marcus giving me a tour of Dilys's care home, and what he'd said about nursing needing people like me.

The truth is I've been thinking about it a lot, but the only person I've told is Dilys. In her own silent way, she's been pushing me to talk about it each time I see her. She does this thing where she puts her index finger up in the air whenever I shake my head and say I couldn't do it. It means 'But!'. So I'll say, 'It's a stupid idea, I couldn't even get into university,' and she'll put her finger in the air and raise her eyebrows: *But! What if you could?*

Matt, who went back to London the day after New Year, has been doing some session guitar work for a studio and has dropped back his bar hours to part-time. He's excited, he tells me on WhatsApp, that this could be the way forward for him. A couple of weeks into January, he suggests that I come up to London for the day and play tourist. When I do, he meets me at Victoria station with two cups of coffee and a smile. 'Caramel mocha, right?'

'Well remembered,' I say. 'Thanks. So what's on the itinerary, tour guide?'

We go to Spitalfields market for lunch and to spend some time browsing the stalls, lingering the longest over one with a huge vinyl record collection. Matt tells me that he wants to own a real record player one day, and I say of course he does. I buy a teal scarf with silver stars, even though I probably shouldn't, because I want something I can keep from today. Matt buys two pastéis de nata on the way out and we eat them as we walk back towards the tube. From there, we go, in his words, 'full-on tourist'. We walk to Leicester Square and through to Piccadilly Circus, stopping at the National Portrait Gallery on the way to Trafalgar Square. We sit on the walls of the fountain for a while, talking, his hand curled comfortably around my knee, and then head off again towards the South Bank.

Matt leads me across one of the Golden Jubilee Bridges, pausing in the middle and pointing at the London Eye. 'That,' he says, 'is my favourite tourist attraction in London.'

'Really?'

'Yeah. I just love it. Is that weird?'

'Yes,' I say, smiling. 'But in a good way.'

'Do you want to go on it?' he asks hopefully. 'We can do something else, if you want.'

I reach out and take his hand. 'Definitely want to,' I say.

We join the queue, which seems long considering it's an ordinary Thursday evening and the London Eye isn't exactly a new tourist attraction. But still, I don't mind. Matt happily tells me a load of London Eye trivia until he spots the look on my face and flushes pink.

'Don't stop!' I say.

'You're laughing at me.'

'I'm not! It's sweet. You don't seem the type to store tourist trivia.'

'Hey, I contain multitudes,' he says.

'Clearly,' I say.

When we finally get on, I head to the side of our pod and look out, touching my fingers to the rail as we make our slow progress up and round. Matt stands behind me, one hand light on my waist, the other pointing out landmarks in the darkening skyline.

I turn, my back to the view, so I can smile at him. 'You know your stuff.'

'My dad is a trivia nerd about stuff like this,' he says. 'I guess I picked it up from him. I mean, he's a dick, and I don't want to be like him, but . . .' He trails off, then shrugs uncertainly. 'I don't know. I like knowing this stuff.'

'That's not a bad thing,' I say.

'Confusing, though.'

'I had a therapist who says it's good to recognize what good came with the bad,' I say. 'She says it's a way to remember that people are human, not monsters. Like, it's OK to love music and be glad I grew up with a dad who made me love music, but still feel legitimate anger about the bad stuff. They don't cancel each other out, you know?'

Oh, God, what the hell did you say that for? My face has heated up. I open my mouth to try and take it back, ready to make a joke, but he's reached for my hand and squeezed it, just gently. 'That's a good point,' he says, nodding. 'I might tell Mum. She's actually thinking about getting a therapist, but she's not sure if it'll help.'

'She should,' I say. 'Therapy's great.'

'Is it?'

'Well, maybe "great" isn't the word. But it's helpful, yeah.

Maybe if more people had it, the world would be better.'

He smiles. 'State-sponsored therapy.'

'Yeah! Even better. Sometimes I think people feel like they need permission to have it. If it was state-sponsored they wouldn't need an excuse. I wish *my* mum would have it; she actually needs it. I said that to her once, but it didn't go down well.'

'How come?'

'Oh, she said something about how only dramatic people have therapy.'

'Did she say that before or after *you* had it?'

'After.' I see a flash of appalled confusion on his face, which he tries to cover, bless him. 'My mum doesn't like me very much,' I say. 'Which is another thing that sounds dramatic but is actually true.'

'Why not?' he asks, but he asks it like it's a normal question, with an actual answer, instead of brushing me off and telling me that of course she likes me, she's my mother.

So I answer. 'I'm just not what she wanted, really. I think sometimes that she'd *like* to like me more than she does, if that makes sense. But some things just are.'

'Do you like her?' he asks. No one's ever asked me this before, not ever, and the question surprises me.

'No,' I say, surprising myself further. 'I actually don't.' It feels like a revelation and a betrayal all at once. Too much to examine right now, so I fold up the feeling and store it for later, sighing out the tension that's formed in my chest in one long breath. 'Anyway. Sorry. That got heavy.'

'Don't apologize,' he says. 'You don't need to do that. Don't they teach you that in therapy?'

I give his shoulder a flick. 'Fuck off.'

He laughs and hugs me, spontaneous and warm, his arms closing lightly around my shoulders. I let my head rest against his collarbone for the seconds we're together. He feels so solid and I think, *I could stay here.*

When we disembark half an hour later, it's dark and we're both hungry. He hoists me up on to his back and gives me a piggyback along the South Bank, my arms looped around his neck, jogging us both up some steps to get to the food market. He buys us both burgers and fries and we sit on the wall by the Thames to eat. The air is cool against my face and the burger is so good. I'm happy.

'Do you need to get back any time soon?' Matt asks me when we're done.

I shake my head.

'OK, great. Then . . . do you want to see my flat?' he asks.

I feel a smile stretch across my face. 'To see your etchings?'

He laughs. 'Can't say I've got any etchings, but I'll show you my guitars, if you want.'

'Cool,' I say. Super-casual. 'Lead the way.'

Matt lives in a room in a house on a residential street in Putney. He tells me, as we walk up the stairs, that he doesn't really see his four other housemates much and they're not the kind of house that socializes together.

'They're all nine-to-fivers,' he says. 'And I do shifts at the bar at all hours, so we don't really run into each other. Here, this is me.' He pushes open the door and smiles my favourite of his smiles. Soft, a little self-mocking. 'After you.'

His room is pretty small, about the size of my bedsit without the kitchen area. His bed takes up most of the space, with a wardrobe and a desk filling the rest of it. There are two guitars in view – one on the desk chair, one leaning against the wall – and a couple of amps piled by the door. There's not much on the walls; some gig posters, a minimalist mosaic of album covers too small to differentiate from where I'm standing, a cartoon map of Brighton that makes me smile.

'There's not much to see,' he says. 'But it'll do for now. Do you want a drink or anything?'

I turn, smiling, and shake my head. He takes a tentative step towards me and I tilt my chin up, just slightly, so he knows it's OK. When he kisses me, it's gentle. One hand starting on my hip and making its way to my neck, my face. After a minute – or five, or ten, who knows? – we realize the door is still open and he shifts back, still attached to me, to close it with his foot. This would probably be a cool move, but he stumbles slightly and messes it up, his teeth knocking against mine as the door slams and he starts to fall. I grab hold of his shirt to stop myself losing my balance but it's too late. We collapse against his bed, hard, me already laughing and him with a mortified yelp.

'Shit,' he says, rolling on to his back. 'Smooth move, Sheffan.'

'So smooth,' I say, still laughing, pushing my hair out of my eyes and sitting up. 'You can't be super-cool all the time.'

He grins at me. 'Hey,' he says. He reaches out to take my hand, tugging me down so I'm lying next to him. I let my body curl against his, my head resting against chest. It's a move I've seen in countless film and TV scenes, but not one I've ever done myself. I want to say it feels natural and perfect, but it doesn't. I'm too aware of what I'm doing, too self-conscious of the cliché. I wait for a couple of minutes, then sit back up. He glances up at me, forehead crinkling. 'OK?' he asks.

I nod. I can tell he's waiting for more, so I say, 'Just a bit . . . coupley, that's all.'

He laughs. 'Don't worry. I'm not going to go all boyfriend on you.'

'Better not,' I say, trying not to show how relieved I am. 'I'd be right out the door.'

'We're still on the same page,' he says. 'Right?'

'Right,' I say emphatically. 'No labels, no bullshit.' I let out a breath. 'Sorry, I got paranoid. And Caddy and Roz don't get it, and—'

'Oh, that's what this is,' he says, smiling, shaking his head a little. 'Kel had a "talk" with me, too. After New Year's. He doesn't get why anyone wouldn't want what he wants.'

'Yeah, they don't either.'

'I mean, it's not crazy,' he says. 'I get the whole wanting-a-relationship thing, if you're that kind of person. If you don't have the sort of hang-ups we have.'

Something stabs at my chest, a quick, defensive tug. 'Hang-ups?'

'Yeah. You've got your stuff and I've got mine. I think Kel just thinks it's about not wanting to commit, and having freedom and stuff.'

I frown. 'That *is* what it's about.'

'Is it?' He's still lying down, looking up at me. 'It's more than that for me. I mean, that's good, obviously. I *don't* want to commit, and I *do* like being free. But it's more about . . .' He stops himself, his eyes sliding from mine for the first time, then back again. I see a brief flash of the kind of fear I recognize on his face, a vulnerability he usually hides.

'Tell me,' I say, softening my voice. 'You're right; I've got my stuff. Tell me yours.'

'Honestly?' he says, and I nod. 'I don't want to hurt anyone. I watched my dad do it, to my mum, over and over. And the crazy thing about it was that he did love her, and he did it anyway. Like he couldn't stop himself. I couldn't handle loving someone and hurting them like that. And I'm scared that . . .' He closes his eyes for a moment too long, then opens them again. 'I'm scared that I would. I think I would.'

'I know what you mean,' I say, and his face lifts.

'You do?'

'Yeah. I'd be a terrible girlfriend.'

'I'd be a terrible boyfriend,' he says. We look at each other, both of us breaking into a smile at the same time. He laughs. 'Look at us. What a pair of fuck-ups.'

'A pair of fuck-ups on the same page,' I say. 'That counts for something.'

He reaches for my hand and I let him take it. When he pulls me gently down towards him I'm the one who kisses first, my hand on his chest, eyes closed. We'd kissed in the club in Brighton, in Sarah's flat, on the London Eye, but there's nothing like kissing on a bed in a room with the door closed and nothing but the night stretching on ahead of us. This is different. The heady inevitability of it is irresistible.

He does something to me, there's no question about that. I want him. I want every single inch of him. And he feels the same, I feel that too. It's not just because he's hard underneath his jeans, pressed against me, though that helps. It's the way his hands cup my face. How he looks at me between kisses.

I don't want a boyfriend, it's true. But I want him. I want him in a way that feels simple and horribly complicated. Sweet and dangerous.

I breathe him in, pushing my body up against his. Our kissing gets harder, his hands slide down over my back, pulling me closer. We move without words, one, two three movements, and then we are tangled together, my legs around him, he is gripping my hip with one hand, his other arm curled around the back of my head. My arms are around him, my fingers in his hair. We are kissing, kissing, and then his hand is at the zip of my jeans, he's easing denim down, just far enough, his fingers find me and begin to move.

He uses the ridge of his palm and the tips of his fingers in motion, rolling his wrist, pushing with his fingertips until I'm gone, loose underneath him, all of me untied. He is over me and on me and I just want more. He is telling me I am beautiful, so beautiful. He's saying my name. He wants me.

He has me, and it feels like every pill I've ever taken, every shot of tequila, every joint, all at once. At some point I pretty much lose my lucidity, but the last thing I remember thinking is that I didn't know it could feel like this. I did not know it could feel like this.

We don't sleep.

The hours pass, a perfect blur of togetherness. Scrolling through his Spotify account while he plays with my hair. Sitting in his lap with his guitar against my chest, his arms around us both, strumming soft chords. Leaning out of his window, smoking a cigarette down to a nub. Dancing to Secret Nation in the tiny space between his bed and the wall, him trying to twirl me. Kissing him, long and slow. Lying on my side with his arm around me as he strokes my bare back with his free hand, tingles running down my whole body. Lying facing each other, noses almost touching, so close we only need whispers.

Morning comes as I'm beginning to doze off. I seriously consider calling in sick to work so I can stay, but the paranoid part of me doesn't want to risk the perfection of the night by dragging it into day. It is almost 6 a.m. when the two of us walk to the nearest tube, fingers entwined, the air cool and damp. He buys me a coffee and a croissant at the Costa by the station. By the ticket barriers he kisses me one last time, the sweetest, softest smile on his face.

'I wish you could stay,' he says.

'You'd get bored of me,' I say. I press my Oyster card against the reader and the barriers snap open.

'Never,' he says.

When I get on the train at Victoria to take me home, I am too sleepy despite the coffee to do anything but rest my head against the window and pass out. I wake up as the train pulls into Brighton, groggy and with the beginnings of a headache. The worst part of staying up all night is when it's not night any more, but it was worth it. It was worth every single second.

25

'Happiness is Not a Place'
The Wind and The Wave

At the end of January, I take a few days off work and go to Cardiff to see Brian. He pays for my train tickets, like he always does, and meets me at the station on Thursday evening with a smile.

'Hey,' he says, hugging me. '*Croeso.*'

I hug him back. 'You're not *actually* Welsh, remember. You just live here.'

He grins. '*Rwy'n dy garu di.*'

'What?!'

'Come on,' he says, slinging an arm around my neck. 'I'll get us Thai food on the way home.'

Brian lives in a flatshare with another teacher, Ben, and a school librarian, Bets. I've met them both a few times, which is good because it means we did the whole awkward introductions bit ages ago. Bets steals one of my spring rolls and talks enthusiastically at me about books I should read. Ben marks a stack of essays in silence, glancing up every now and then to check we're all still there.

On Friday, I sleep through them all leaving for work and wake up to an empty house. I go into the kitchen to find the ingredients for pancakes – each measured to exactly the right quantity – waiting on the table beside a frying pan and spatula. There's a note held down by a spare key beside it. *Morning!* Brian's handwriting. *Promise I'll make these myself tomorrow, but today here's everything you need! Have a great day. Call me if you need anything x*

He can be pretty great, my brother.

I spend the day wandering around the city centre until it's time to meet Brian outside his school. We go to Cardiff Bay and the Millennium Centre, which is what we've done every time since I first visited him in Cardiff when I was fourteen and he was a fresher. Before my first suicide attempt, before I left Reading, before Sarah and Brighton and everything that went wrong. There's a peace to how it all looks the same every time, even as the exhibitions and shows and tour posters change.

The next day is all blue skies and sunshine, so Brian drives us across South Wales to the Gower Peninsula, where we spent a family holiday once when we were much younger. He takes me on a walking trail that ends up on a long sandy beach so beautiful it doesn't feel like it belongs in the UK.

'Do you remember it?' he asks me. 'The holiday, I mean.'

I shake my head. 'Not really. Probably for the best.'

'It was a good holiday,' he says. 'We rented bikes. And we got a kite that day it was really windy, here on this beach. You don't remember?'

I shake my head again.

'Well, it was great, anyway,' he says. 'That holiday was part of the reason I wanted to come to Wales to go to uni, you know. It's why I love it here.'

I'm not sure why he's telling me this, what it is he expects me to say. 'Is that why you stayed in Cardiff after you graduated, instead of going home?'

'Cardiff *is* home,' he says. 'I made my home here, just like you're doing in Brighton.' A spaniel has come bounding over to us and Brian squats, beaming, to stroke his head. 'Hello, mate.'

We both fuss over the dog for a few minutes before he turns and bolts off towards his owners. It's a relief to focus my attention somewhere else, even for a tiny slice of time, and Brian must feel the same way because when I look back at him he's smiling, just like I am. When he sees my face, his smile widens. 'Damn, I really do miss you,' he says. 'I'm glad you're here.'

I let him hug me, and it's nice. 'Me too.'

But then he says, 'It really was a great holiday. We did have some good times, didn't we? Like, remember when Dad was in a good mood, sometimes he'd stop in at McDonalds on the way home from work and bring us both a McFlurry?'

I look away, because I do remember. Smarties for me, Crunchie for Brian.

'And when he used to build us those forts in the living room and we'd play pirates? You were Captain Zanne? Remember you used to wear that bandana? He got you that little telescope?'

Oh, God. My heart gives a painful lurch. Captain Zanne. I'd forgotten all about that. 'Shiver me timbers!' Dad used to yell, lifting me up on to his shoulders. 'There be treasure, Cap'n Zanne!'

'Why are you doing this?' I ask quietly.

He's surprised. 'Because that stuff shouldn't be forgotten, don't you think? Sometimes I worry that you think it was all bad. And it wasn't, you know?'

'So what?'

He blinks. 'So what, what?'

'So what if it wasn't "all bad"? What point are you trying to make?' My throat is tightening, because I'm thinking about therapy, about everything I'd learned about emotional manipulation, how it goes hand in hand with abuse. How this is my brother, who I adore, manipulating me, and he doesn't even realize. 'A few good times don't make up for long-term physical and emotional abuse.' The words land hard. I see him flinch. 'And I shouldn't feel guilted into feeling that way, especially not by you.'

'I didn't mean that. You know I didn't mean that. I just . . . God, I'm your brother. This is my family too. I want to be able to have some memories that aren't tainted.'

'Tainted by . . . my trauma?'

He throws up his hands in frustration. 'Forget it. Just forget it, OK? I'm obviously not explaining myself well enough.'

'You can have whatever memories you want,' I say. 'I'll have different ones. That's all.'

'But so many of them are the same,' he says. 'Like, remember that time we went to see the Counting Crows? It was your first ever concert, and Dad took us both? Remember how great that was?' His face is light with hope. 'That's what I mean. That kind of thing. Fun that we had together, despite all the other shit.'

I bite my tongue, hard. *Remember how great that was?* I must have been about ten when we went to that gig. Dad's favourite band, and music that formed the soundtrack to my childhood. Dad had been excited – genuinely excited – to be able to take us both, and for it to be my first gig. He'd taken us for dinner first, bought us tour merchandise – a T-shirt for Brian, a hat for me – and given me a piggyback during the show so I could see better. Of course Brian has good memories of that show. It went so smoothly. Dad didn't even get angry, not once.

But here's what I remember: terror. A constant, churning terror in my stomach, from the moment we left the house to the moment we got back in it. I'd been so scared I'd do something wrong and make Dad mad. He was in such a good mood, which meant he'd be even angrier if I somehow spoiled it. I was so on alert it was physically painful. And all at the same time, I knew I had to be happy, excited, grateful.

If I tell Brian this, it will crush him. So I don't. Instead, I say, 'You know, everything you say is basically the opposite of what everyone else says.'

'What do you mean?'

'Like, you're all, *Think about the good things. Give them another chance. Stop being so hard on them.* Everyone else tells me I'm trying *too* hard. That they don't deserve . . .' I hesitate, my throat tightening. 'Me.'

When I say this, something happens to his face. Just for the briefest of seconds, but it happens, and it's like I'm looking at Dad. He looks *just* like Dad. The moment passes and he's Brian again.

'Who is "everyone else"?' he asks.

'My friends. You know Rosie thinks I should sue them? Like, actually sue them?'

At this, he laughs. 'Well, that's ridiculous.'

'Is it?'

'Of course it is. Look, you're right, they don't deserve you. It's right that you're angry. But suing them? That's crazy. Rosie's great, but she doesn't understand.'

Considering this is almost exactly what I'd said to Rosie, my annoyance at Brian saying the same makes no sense. But I'm annoyed anyway. 'She cares about me. And would it be that crazy? Don't you think I'm owed?'

'Owed what? Money?'

'Yeah. Like, if I wanted to study, I'm at least a year behind everyone else because I don't have A levels. And I don't have A levels because my education got fucked up because I was abused. It'd cost me money to make that time up. So doesn't that mean I *am* owed?'

There's a long silence. Eventually, he says, 'You want to study?'

My instinct is to say no, but I force myself to lift my chin and say, 'Maybe.'

'That's *great*, Zanne.' The sincerity hurts. I don't want him to be nice and sincere right now. I want him to carry on being unreasonable, so I can be mad at him, and this will stop being so complicated. 'That's amazing. What do you want to study?'

'Nothing, it was just an example.' I wait for him to push me on it, say something like, *But you could, if you wanted. You could do anything if you wanted*. But he doesn't, and something inside me sinks a little. I clench my hands into tight fists and make myself say, 'Maybe nursing.'

He's surprised, and he doesn't even try to hide it, which makes me sink still lower. 'Nursing?'

I wish I hadn't said anything. Not a single word of this entire conversation. I wish I'd never come here at all. I swallow, hard. 'Can we talk about something else now?'

'Maybe that's a good idea,' he says.

26

'I Wanna Get Better'
Bleachers

Kel:

Suze! Party at mine this Friday. Housemate's birthday. It's fancy dress and there's a THEME. You in?

Me:

OBVS. What is the theme, please?

SPACE EXCELLENCE.

????

Basically Star Wars or Star Trek. Space-related TV/film stuff.

OK cool! I'm in.

Need help with a costume?

How insulting.

Ha! Sorry. See you Friday!

'Holy hell,' Matt says, a grin breaking out across his face. 'Look at you.'

I pose, arms spread. He'd messaged me when he started walking to Kel's from his mum's, where he's staying for the weekend, so I'd met him at the door. 'You like?'

'You look stunning,' he says. He's good at giving compliments; casual but firm, like it's a fact. Nothing about him is try-hard.

'Do you know who I am?' I ask, closing the door behind him. I'm dressed as Han Solo; an outfit I know from past experience is a guaranteed crowd-pleaser.

He laughs. 'I'm offended you'd even ask.'

'What's *your* costume?' I ask, looking him up and down. He just looks like Matt.

He glances down at himself. 'Oh, I'm just me.'

'But there's a theme.'

He shrugs. 'I'm not really a dress-up kind of guy.'

I'm surprised by how disappointed I am. 'Why not?'

'Just not my kind of thing. You look incredible, though.'

I don't know why I assumed he'd be into this, except that maybe I'd been thinking of him being a lot like me, and I *love* dressing up. This is probably a good reminder to stop assuming I know him, when I clearly don't. Besides, he doesn't have to like fancy dress. It's hardly a crime.

'Well, thanks,' I say. 'And hey, you should know, I shoot first.'

His whole face lights up into a wide grin. 'Are you trying to make me fall in love with you?' he asks.

I laugh, and he smells so good, and his face is so close to mine. I love that we can joke about this, that we can be so easy together. I step into him and he puts an arm around me, pulling me in close. I drop my voice low. 'Why? Is it working?'

He kisses me in reply, and it feels so good. Electricity and fire, all at once. Sparks and flame. I'd happily stay there all night, to be honest, but it's a party and it's still early, so we break apart eventually and go to find Kel, who's Jedi-robed and, as usual, playing bartender. When he sees Matt, he smiles. When he sees me behind him, our hands entwined, it dims a little. 'You two found each other, then,' he says.

'Yeah, just on my way in,' Matt says casually, as if we hadn't been locked together just a couple of minutes before. He glances at me and flashes a wolfish, conspiratorial grin, eyes alight.

Kel rolls his eyes a little and mutters something I don't catch, but neither of us pushes him on it. 'What do you want to drink?' he asks Matt. 'Beer?'

'Sure,' Matt says. 'Have you got enough? I can run out and get some more.'

'No, we're good,' Kel says. He uncaps a bottle and hands it to Matt. The three of us hang out for a while in the kitchen, me swinging myself up on to the counter beside Kel as he and Matt talk. I like watching them together; the ease of their years of friendship showing in their body language, the way they talk to each other. It makes me think of Caddy and Rosie, how being with them feels effortless.

After a while, Kel's housemate Aziz – dressed like a redshirt – comes over to recruit us on to his beer-pong team. Matt and I go with him but Kel shakes his head, claiming bartender status. I want to tell him he doesn't have to be such a giver all the time but Matt's already followed Aziz out of the kitchen so I decide it can wait and bound after them instead.

The game of beer-pong is a mess – no one seems to know or care what the rules are – and so Matt and I duck out after ten minutes, heading out on to the patio together instead. It's cold but there are enough people to make it bearable, and someone's docked iPhone is blasting Bleachers across the garden.

Matt and I are sharing a cigarette, his arm around me, alternating between smoking, talking and kissing while we move unconsciously to the beat, when someone calls, 'Matt!' from behind us.

Matt's arm uncurls from around my waist and I glance over to see a pretty, dark-haired girl wearing a blue uniform dress that I think might have something to do with *Star Trek*. She's smiling at us. No, not at us. Just at Matt.

'Oh, hey,' Matt says. 'Didn't know you'd be here.'

'You didn't ask,' the girl says. Her eyes flick towards me, up and down my body in an instant, then back to Matt, dismissing me. 'How've you been?'

Matt reaches his hand up to touch the back of his head, the way guys do when they're nervous or awkward and trying to hide it. 'Not bad. You?'

I can't believe he's letting this go on with me just standing here. Even the best guys are utter wimps. So I shrug and stub out our cigarette before I walk away, because like hell am I putting up with it. I head into the kitchen, winding my way through the chatting, laughing people, and find Kel at the table pouring shots.

'Hey!' he says, smiling at me. 'Tequila?'

'Tequila!' I sing, taking one, and he laughs.

I close my eyes when I take the shot, feeling the spirit burn down my throat, warming me up from the inside. When I open my eyes again, Matt's standing there, looking sheepish, like a little boy.

'That was just Tegan,' he says.

'Great,' I say. 'So what?'

'Sorry.'

'For what?' I reach for the bottle of tequila but Kel swipes it away, raising his eyebrows at me.

'I didn't want you to leave,' Matt says.

'I haven't left anywhere. I'm right here.'

'Come back out with me?' he asks.

Kel thunks a bottle down on the table harder than is necessary and we both look over at him. 'Oh, don't mind me,' he says. 'I'm just the mutual.'

There's an awkward silence. Kel starts rearranging beer bottles. Behind us, someone yells, 'Stacey! You goddess!'

Searching for a solution to all of the weirdness that seems to have erupted between Kel and Matt and me, I say, as brightly as possible, 'Hey, did you know I can open beer bottles with my teeth?'

Kel glances down at the bottles, then back at me. 'That sounds dangerous.'

I flash a mischievous grin at him, holding out my hand for a bottle. 'All the best things do.'

His laugh is dry. 'Go on then, you show-off.'

It's a party trick I've been able to pull off since I was fifteen, a sure-fire way to impress people, if that's what I'm going for. The ultimate cool-girl trick. But tonight, for the first time ever, I fail. And I fail hard. The first bottle cap lifts between my teeth as normal, but the second wrenches, the bottleneck jerks in my mouth, and suddenly there's glass and blood and— *Ow!* Shit. *Ow!*

'Fucking hell, Suze!' Kel pushes someone aside, already reaching a tea towel up to my face. I lean past him, spitting glass and blood into the sink.

'Oh my *God*,' I hear a girl say, her whole voice a shudder. In my head, it's Tegan. 'Gross.'

'What did you even do?' Kel demands, trying to get a proper look.

'Kel, chill,' Matt says, his hand on my back. 'Give it a minute, yeah?'

The taste of blood in my mouth is so horribly, painfully familiar that it's making tears sting in my eyes. I rinse my mouth out, once, twice, three times, but still blood rises fresh against my tongue. 'Fuck's sake,' I mutter, taking the tea towel from Kel and winding it into a small enough wad to fit into my mouth.

'Do you have to go to A&E?' Kel asks.

I shake my head. 'It'll be fine.' Through the tea towel, my voice is muffled.

'You didn't swallow any glass?'

I shake my head again, running my tongue over my gums and teeth, checking the damage. A shard of glass must have cut into my gum, but my teeth are still intact and the wound, currently pulsing blood, will heal. Mostly, I feel ridiculous. And a little shaky.

'OK, good, but you're dripping blood on to the floor, so . . .'

I glare at Kel. He glares right back.

'We'll go to the bathroom,' Matt says. 'Come on, Suze.' He takes a light hold of my elbow and steers me out of the kitchen. 'Don't mind him,' he says. We step over the NOT UPSTAIRS sign and head towards the off-limits bathroom on the first floor. 'He's not good with blood. Or accidents in general. Or basically anything not going to plan.'

In the bathroom I rinse my face, wash my mouth out another couple of times, and then press the tea towel back in because there's not much else I can do. I roll my eyes at Matt, aiming for cool self-deprecation, and he smiles in that way he does, like he's seeing me.

We sit together on the floor, backs against the wall. When the flow of blood seems to have stemmed enough for me to take the tea towel out of my mouth, I say, 'Sorry.'

'Don't be. It's cool.'

'This wasn't how this was supposed to go.'

'How was it supposed to go?'

I think about how we'd kissed in the hallway, the feeling of his hand at my neck. I'd imagined an evening of that, and more. Us together, punctuated by drinking and laughing and talking.

'Well, there was meant to be less blood,' I say, trying to smile. 'Less Kel being grumpy. Less glaring from random girls.'

'Who? Tegan?'

I roll my eyes at him.

'God, don't even think about her. She's not worth thinking about. You don't have to be jealous.'

'Get over yourself,' I say, a little more sharply than I'd meant. 'I'm not jealous.'

His eyebrows go up.

'I'm not,' I say. 'I'm annoyed that you just totally ignored me when she turned up. And that you sound like a fuckboy.'

'How am I sounding like a fuckboy?'

'Think about it. Am I going to go to a party one day and see you there with another girl, and then after you'll talk to her about me like you're talking about Tegan right now?'

'That's not the same,' he says. 'Tegan was one night. Once was enough.'

Irritation makes my voice harsh. 'Are you being this much of a dick on purpose?'

'I'm just saying it was a one-night thing. She knew that.'

'You *literally* just said, *How am I sounding like a fuckboy?* Do you still need me to tell you?' I shake my head. 'No costume *and* you're being a dick about a random girl. You're very disappointing tonight.'

'All right, no need to be a bitch about it,' he says.

'Kind of not OK to call me a bitch, but OK,' I say.

'You literally just called me a dick. Twice. And you called me disappointing.' He turns away from me, resting his elbow on the edge of the bath. I hear him mutter, 'Fuck's sake.'

'Fine, just go if you're pissed off,' I say.

He looks back at me. 'Do you *want* me to go?'

'I don't care either way.'

I don't mean it, and I regret it as soon as the words are out of my mouth. Mostly because of how his face drops, how hurt he looks, in the seconds before he covers himself. 'Whatever,' he says, standing.

'The whole point is we don't mean anything to each other,' I say.

'The whole point is we *do*,' he says. He pauses, and I know he's giving me a chance to make this better, but I just shake my head and look away, like he's nothing but a temporary annoyance. 'Fine,' he says, mostly to himself. 'Forget it. I'm out.'

He leaves and I'm alone, sitting on the bathroom floor, bloody tea towel in my hand, dressed as Han Solo. What a total failure of a night. I'm annoyed with myself and Matt and everything. Why can't things just go right for once? Why does something always have to go wrong?

I lean my head back against the wall and take out my phone, scrolling through Instagram for a while to pass the time. I'll wait until my mouth stops hurting so much, and then I'll go and find Kel. Maybe I can at least smooth things over with him before I go home. If I wait long enough, maybe everyone will have forgotten about the whole broken bottle thing by the time I go downstairs.

After about half an hour, when I've started counting the tiles over the bath, the door opens a little and I look up, expecting to see Kel, but it's Matt.

'Oh,' I say.

Matt rests his head against the door frame and eases his hand through the gap in the door. He's holding two beer bottles that clink between his fingers. 'Peace offering?'

I swallow, trying not to smile. 'I should probably be the one with a peace offering.'

'Is that a Suze version of an apology?'

I point at the beers. 'Is that a *Matt* version of an apology?'

He smiles. 'Touché. How are the gums?'

'Bit better.'

'Can I . . . come in?' When I nod, he eases through the gap in the door and closes it behind him, sitting down on the floor beside me. He hands me one of the bottles, already uncapped, and I take a sip. 'Feeling better?'

I make some weird motion somewhere between a nod and a shrug. 'How's everything downstairs?'

'Dramatic,' he says. 'You missed a fight. Some drunk guy spilled his drink on a girl, and her boyfriend wasn't happy. It got violent.'

I'm suddenly, weirdly, grateful for the glass that cut my mouth and sent me upstairs for long enough that I'd miss a fight that would probably have triggered me. Being around violence – even the kind that isn't directed at me – makes me panic. The thick, paralysing kind of panic I can't disguise. If it had been a choice, I would definitely have gone for Matt seeing the bitchy side of me rather than the weak one. *Thank you, beer bottle.*

'Is it still going on?' I ask.

'It was over pretty quickly,' he says. 'Kel got between them. But they're both still around, so it could kick off again, who knows.'

'OK,' I say. I hesitate, not wanting to reveal myself. 'Maybe we could stay up here a bit longer?'

'Sure,' he says, easy. 'Hey. I'm sorry tonight went south.'

'Me too.' I touch my head to his shoulder and he drops a light kiss on my hair. It's nice.

'What are you doing tomorrow?' he asks. 'We could try again.'

I smile and lift my head to face him. 'Yeah? I'm working, though.'

'We could hang out after? I could take you out,' he says.

'Intriguing,' I say. 'Are you going to try and charm me?'

He laughs. 'I wouldn't dare.' His eyes meet mine. 'I'll be positively charmless.'

I raise my bottle to his and he clinks it obediently. 'OK,' I say. 'I'm in. Let's try take two.'

27

'Everywhere I Go'
Lissie

The first half of my shift the next day drags long and slow. After the morning rush there are barely any customers and it's just me and Tracey, my manager, sharing the space behind the counter, making small talk. I spend my break on my phone chatting with Rosie on WhatsApp, talking about one of our old friends from school who's just got pregnant and is having to drop out of their university course. It feels good to be talking about someone else's problems for once. Matt messages, suggesting we meet in town to find food at six. I smile as I reply, reminding him to leave the charm at home, and he responds with a selfie of his deadpan face.

At the end of my break, I push my phone deep into my apron pocket and head back out to the front counter, glancing at the clock as I go. Four more hours of shift and then I can go home. Madeline's is quiet and there's no queue, just Tracey talking to a man who—

Oh fuck.

Oh fuck.

It's Dad. It's fucking *Dad*. Standing there at the counter, talking to my manager. He's all smiles, his face cheerful and open. There are two versions of my dad, that's something you should know. The version the world sees, and then the version behind the closed door of my childhood home. The public Dad is warm and friendly. Charming. 'Oh, your dad, he's great.' A lie in the shape of a person.

I'm frozen in place. As I watch, Tracey laughs at something he's said, nodding. I've never told my manager anything about my childhood; why *would* I? So she has no idea who she's really talking to, what it will mean for me that he's here.

'Ah, there she is,' Dad says. He's spotted me. He's smiling.

'Suze,' Tracey says. She's smiling too. 'I was just about to come and get you.'

'Suze,' Dad repeats. Is he mocking me? I am not 'Suze' to him. 'Suze' was invented post-Reading. Post-Dad. I am *not* 'Suze' to him. 'Can you spare some time for your dad?'

'I'm on shift,' I say. Thank God for employment and shift patterns and being behind this counter. 'Sorry. You should've said you were coming.' *So I could have been far, far away.* 'I would've timed my break or something.'

'Oh, it's fine for you to take a bit of an extra break,' Tracey says. She thinks she's being kind. 'It's quiet. If it gets busy, you can just jump up and come back, OK?' I look at her, trying to keep everything that is inside me off my face. She blinks, the first hint of confusion in her expression. 'Your dad was just telling me how you don't see much of each other since you moved to Brighton.'

Dad looks at me, still smiling warmly, in just the way any father would if his nineteen-year-old daughter had moved away to a different city and didn't keep in touch as much as he'd like. 'Spare a few minutes for your old man?'

Everything I ever knew about putting on a face in public I learned from my dad. Both me and Brian are charmers, just like him. And now he's here, the reality of that makes me feel sick. So much of me is him, but he is not good. So how can I ever be? When I was a kid, I played along. Willingly. I went to his work functions and had whole conversations with him in front of his colleagues like the two of us were best mates. A double act, like he was Father-of-the-fucking-Year. 'You're lucky,' one said to him once. 'My daughter will barely talk to me in public these days.'

'Ah, Suzie's well-trained,' Dad said, and everyone laughed. Ha, ha, ha. He put his arm around me. 'Aren't you, Suzie?'

'Yes, sir,' I said. 'I mean, Dad.' And everyone laughed again – and see how I was complicit in my own nightmare? Do you see? My therapist said surviving is not the same as being complicit, but it feels like it is. I think that's exactly what it is.

And you know what I do right now? I smile. I roll my eyes. I say, 'Go on, then.' And I make him a goddamn cappuccino. I don't know what's wrong with me, why I can't just tell him to leave. I try to conjure up Rosie in my mind, her straight-talking, blunt self. 'God, Suze, just tell Tracey he's literally your abuser and go and sit in the back until he leaves.' That's what she'd say, right?

My hands are shaking. Why is he here? What does he want? *Why am I walking over to him?*

Dad is sitting at a table in the centre of the cafe, which is something, at least. It's in full view of everyone, so he's obviously not planning on hurting me. I put the tray on the table and he takes the cappuccino, glancing up at me to smile. 'Thanks, Suzie.' Genuine. Unexpected.

I sit opposite him and put my fingers on my own cup, then change my mind and slide my hands on to my lap, out of his view. I don't want him to notice if they start to shake again.

'You look well,' Dad says.

'What are you doing here?' I ask.

'Seeing you,' Dad says, his forehead crinkling. 'Is that so strange? Relax.'

I don't smile. 'Why?'

'Because it seemed like a good time. I've got a conference at the Amex this weekend, so I thought I'd stop by.'

'Here?' I say. 'Where I work?'

Dad frowns, then nods. 'It seemed like a better option than turning up at your flat,' he says. 'I thought you'd think I was . . . Well, trying to scare you or something. If I did that.'

I would definitely have thought he was trying to scare me if he'd turned up at my flat. Because he would have been. 'Why didn't you ask first?'

'What is this, an interrogation?' he asks, an edge of irritation in his voice. 'Why is it so awful to want to see you for ten minutes? Have you taken out a restraining order I don't know about?'

Should I? I think, but I'm not brave enough to say it. I don't say anything, just look down into my coffee, concentrating on keeping my breathing slow and normal. Sometimes I go off into little daydreams about all the things I'd say to my stepdad if I had the chance, and now he's here in front of me, I know I will never, not ever, say any of them out loud.

'Listen,' he says. His voice has softened. 'I just wanted to see you. That's all. I'm not trying to upset you.'

Does he mean it? I really can't tell.

'This is a nice place,' he says, looking around Madeline's. 'Cosy.'

I feel some of the tension in my shoulders ease. I can handle a slightly stilted conversation. I'd take awkward over scary any day of the week. 'Yeah, it's not bad,' I say.

'It doesn't pay well, though, does it?'

'It's OK,' I say carefully, looking for traps. 'I can pay rent, so . . . that's good.'

'But you need money,' he says.

I look at him, confused, trying not to show it. Dad's a master manipulator, and he's probably just trying to throw me. I mean, of course I need money. Doesn't everyone? 'Well . . . yeah? I guess?'

'You guess,' he says, deadpan.

What is he getting at? Anxiety is starting to tingle at the base of my neck, crawling down my spine.

'Suzie,' he says, and he's smiling. No, not smiling. Smirking. 'Don't be obtuse, now. I know you want money from us.'

All of the heat leaves my body in one sickening instant of

realization. I'm cold all over. Because, oh fuck. No. He can't . . . How can he . . . ?

'What?'

'You want money,' he repeats. 'That's right, isn't it? You want to take us to court?'

I can't speak. I can't breathe.

'Sue me?' he adds, and he doesn't look angry or annoyed or even worried. He just looks amused. 'Say something, then.'

I can't believe he's come all the way here to blindside me like this. Except I can. 'Who told you that?'

'Your brother.'

No.

'Decent of him to give us a heads-up.' And then he actually chuckles.

He can't have. He wouldn't do that to me. He *wouldn't*.

'Now, listen,' Dad says, all friendly, resting his elbows on the table and leaning slightly towards me. 'That all seems like an awful lot of fuss, doesn't it, Suzie? Imagine how traumatic it would be for you, getting up in court, telling them all about your sad little life. Why should you have to go through that? If it's money you want, we can give you money.'

My head, which has been one long scream for the last thirty seconds, suddenly goes quiet. What?

'What is it you want, five grand?' Dad continues. And somewhere inside me, buried underneath the fog of shock, a small voice says: *He looked it up.* 'We can give you five grand, if you need it.'

He looked it up. He found out how much I'd get if I successfully sued them. He *researched*.

'You don't want to sue us,' Dad says. 'Do you?'

He's scared. He came here to scare me, because he's scared.

'Say something,' he says.

I could say, *I was never going to sue you. That was just something Rosie said.* But I'm thinking about him looking it up, figuring out how public it would be, who'd find out. His colleagues, his friends. Deciding to come here out of the blue when my guard was down, in a place that's always been safe. Offering me the money like he's doing me a favour. 'I'll think about it,' I say.

His casual smile disappears, just for a moment, before returning with an edge. 'Suzanne,' he says. 'Don't be ridiculous. Do you want the money or not?' I let the silence build, my eyes on my coffee, until he breaks it. 'You'll need it, if you want to study.'

For God's sake, Brian. My heart hurts. I say, quietly, 'He really told you?'

The question is a mistake, and I know it immediately, just by the look on his face. The slight smirk, his eyes sharp. He is about to skewer me.

And he does.

'Oh yes,' he says. 'It was a bit of a surprise at first, but we had quite a laugh about it in the end.' And then he smiles, like I'm in on it.

He's lying; Brian wouldn't laugh at me. I know that. And he knows I know that, too. But it doesn't matter. The fact that Brian has told our parents something I clearly wouldn't want them to know, that he's aligned himself with them, compromised the loyalty I'd always thought he had to me – all of that has created an opening for Dad to say those words and make me doubt everything. *Brian* has created this.

'Don't be upset with him,' Dad adds. 'Of course he had to tell us.'

'Was that all you wanted?' I ask, getting to my feet and reaching for his cup. *He's just a customer and I am just doing cup collection.* He's just a customer. 'I should get back to work.'

'Suzie,' Dad says.

'I'll have a think about the money,' I say. All I want is to turn and walk away from him, but I force myself to look him in the eye, just for a moment. I want to say something dramatic like, *Come here again and I'll call the police.* Or, *By the way, I hate you.* I manage, 'Bye then.'

'Thanks for the cappuccino,' he says.

I carry our cups across the coffee-shop floor, behind the counter and through the door to the kitchen. There's no one else round the back so I throw them, hard, into the industrial sink, watching as they smash into large, jagged pieces. I want to rage. I want to smash everything. I want to cry and scream and break.

I pick up the shards, wrap them in paper and put them in the bin. I pull my hair out of its ponytail and shake it out over my face. I wind the hair-tie around my fingers, down over my wrist. I twist it until my skin turns white, then red. I breathe in. I breathe out. I tie my hair back up, pulling it back from my face, tight and steady and safe.

I message Brian. **I will never forgive you for this.**

And then I turn off my phone.

'i can't breathe'
Bea Miller

By the time I get home, I'm caught in a spiral I don't have the strength to fight. Seeing Dad for the first time in three years. Watching Tracey laughing with him. Listening to him use that voice with me, like I'm still a kid he can destroy at will. The fact that I couldn't even say one thing, just one thing, to stand up for myself.

Being in my flat should make me feel better, but it doesn't. It makes it worse. My head, which had managed to keep a lid on the panic while I was at work, starts to talk to me the moment I walk through the door. *You think this is safe? Ha!* It is safe. I'm home. He's far away. *What if he comes here? He knows the address.* Of course he won't come here, why would he? Don't be stupid. *But what if he does?* He came to Madeline's. He's not going to come here as well. *But what if that was just a false-sense-of-security thing? He could come here, if he wanted. There's no one around. He could . . .*

Stop it. That's obviously not going to happen.

But it *could*.

I put my headphones in and try to listen to music, but I can't settle into anything. The lyrics are putting me even more on edge because I can't focus on them, but I can't shut them out, either. I click from song to song, but the panic keeps rising in my chest. I'm working myself up into even more of a state and it's really, really not helping.

I leave the safety of my flat to go to the corner shop. One bottle of vodka, one bottle of Coke. I drink one glass and give up on the

Coke; it's just slowing me down. Then I give up on the glass, too, and stick with the bottle. *Look at me*, I think. *Cliché of the year. Drinking straight vodka on my own in a bedsit. Look how well I deal with my problems.*

I've drunk about half of the bottle when there's a knock at my door and I freeze, choking a little on the sip I'd just taken. My head immediately goes: *Dad. He's come to hurt me.* But no, that can't be. Dad would have to buzz to get in. How many people know the front door code? Dilys and Sarah. That's it, isn't it?

No, wait. It's not. There's one more person it could be. I hear a muffled, 'Zannie?'

I open the door and there's my brother. He looks at me for a moment, taking me in. He looks stunned. Brian has seen me at my absolute lowest. Pre-, mid- and post-breakdown. He's seen me flip out at the side of a motorway. He's seen me drugged up to my eyeballs on morphine. He's seen me crying like my heart is broken.

But he has never seen me drunk.

'Ah,' I say. I put the bottle behind my back.

'Jesus,' he says, but in a worried way, not an angry way. 'Zanne. Are you OK?'

I block his way when he tries to walk in. 'Nope,' I say. 'Nope. No entry for you.'

'Zannie,' he says. 'Let me in so I can talk to you, OK?'

'OK?' I repeat, mocking. 'Maybe you should just go, OK?'

He shakes his head and comes into the flat, pushing me gently out of the way. Even though I said no. Three times.

'If you stay here,' I say, turning to face him and swaying slightly on my feet, 'we are going to have a *huge* fight.'

'I'm not here for a fight,' he says.

'Oh no, of course not,' I say. 'You're just here to *explain*, right?'

'Well, yeah. Shut the door, Zannie.'

I clench my fist around the neck of the bottle. 'I said I don't want you here.'

'I came straight here,' he says. 'I got straight in the car and drove here, Zanne.'

I hate how he keeps saying my name. No, not just my name. My childhood nickname, the one only he still uses.

'So?'

'So I have to talk to you.' When I still don't move, he leans past me and closes the door, because who cares what I want, right? 'Are you . . . drunk?'

'Yes,' I say, swinging the bottle around and hugging it to my chest. 'Yes, I am.' I lift my chin and hold his gaze until he caves and looks away. Ha. Who's the weak one now?

Brian looks around, like he's hoping someone else is going to materialize and help him deal with me. 'By yourself?'

'Clearly.'

'Shit, Zannie. That's really bad.'

'What is?'

'Getting drunk by yourself. You're nineteen. Jesus. Alcoholics get drunk by themselves.'

'So do abuse victims,' I say, because like hell am I above using my own trauma as a weapon in an argument with my pious, perfect, un-abused brother.

He rolls his eyes. Just quick, like he can't help it. And then he leans over and tries to take the bottle from me.

'Uh, no, thank you,' I say, spinning away. 'This is mine. I paid for it, and it's mine.' He just stands there, and he suddenly seems too tall to me, all awkward in my tiny little bedsit. 'Hey,' I say. 'Remember when I said I didn't want you here? That's still true.'

'Where the hell is Sarah?' he mutters, almost to himself.

'Er, at home?'

'Why isn't she here looking after you?' he asks. 'Why has she left you to get drunk on your own?'

Which is a real dick thing to say.

'Sarah has done more for me than you or anyone else ever has, so don't you fucking *dare* put this on her.'

There's this weird thing that happens when you get drunk, which is that certain things become clear, and you realize things that you didn't even know you thought. I've never consciously thought that about Sarah before, but it suddenly feels like the truest thing in the world. I feel *fierce* with the truth of it.

He says, 'I'm going to make us both some tea.'

I watch him walk into my kitchen and begin busying himself with the kettle. I lift the bottle to my lips and take a quick, burning gulp. Ugh.

'You told them,' I say, and he freezes. Which makes no sense, because isn't that why he's here?

I see him swallow. He doesn't say anything.

'How could you tell them?'

'I didn't . . .' he tries, then stops. 'It wasn't like whatever he said to you, however he made it sound. It wasn't like that.'

'Then what was it like?'

The kettle clicks as it comes to the boil and he reaches for it. 'I saw them last weekend. Just a normal visit, you know?'

'No,' I say. 'I don't know.' A normal visit. What's that like?

He winces. 'Sorry, I just meant . . . I just meant it wasn't unusual. I didn't go there to tell on you, or anything. We were talking, I was telling them about how you were thinking about going back to studying, and how great it is.'

I have a sudden image of the three of them, my family, sitting around our old kitchen table, cosily talking about me and – what was it Dad had said? – my *sad little life*. Oh, bless little Suzie, thinking about trying to earn an actual qualification! Isn't it nice that she has goals?

I lift the bottle to my lips again.

'And I said I wasn't sure how you would pay for it.' At this point he hesitates, and I *know* that he's wording this *so* carefully, that he's presenting it in the best way he can. It's still lying that way, even if it's dressed up a bit nicer. 'And I . . .' He trails off, and I wait. 'I said that someone had told you that you should try and get the money from them. In court.'

He stops, like that's the end of the story, and I can't stand it. 'And?'

'And . . .' He opens my fridge and takes out my carton of milk, pouring it into my cups on top of my tea bags. 'And they were a bit . . . surprised. And, look, OK, I wanted to know if that was a thing that could actually happen. If it was even a possibility.'

There is a burning, burning rage in my chest, and every sip of vodka is like fuel.

'But I wasn't telling them to . . . I don't know, warn them, or whatever it is you think. And I had no idea Dad was going to turn up at your work and bring it up, Zanne. Honestly. I would never have told him if I'd known. You know that, right? I could kill him for this.'

'Why do you care?'

Brian looks up at me, rabbit-in-headlights. 'What?'

'Why do you care if it's a possibility? What's it got to do with you?'

Clearly, this is not what he was expecting me to say. 'Zannie, if you sued our parents, that would be a lot to do with me.'

'Why?'

He stares at me for a long moment. 'Zanne—'

'Stop saying my fucking name like that.'

'Put the bottle down, OK? Put it down and we can talk about this properly.'

I don't move. 'What would change? You think things could get worse than they already are? You think I could have even less of a relationship with them? You think they'll love me any *less*?'

He hesitates and sets his hands on the counter, leaning his weight on them. 'It's about more than just that.'

'*Just that?* Me making them stand up and admit what they did to me is about more than me and them?'

He releases his grip on the counter and turns away slightly to toss the used tea bags into the bin. 'Yes, because it's not just you. They're my parents too.'

That's the breaking point. This moment.

Without thinking about what I'm doing, I hurl the bottle across the room towards him. It spins as it flies, spraying vodka all over the carpet, before it collides with the wall near his head in one immensely satisfying crash. Glass and vodka rain on to the floor.

'Get. *Out.*' My voice doesn't even sound like me. It's so full of rage.

The bottle missed him completely, but still he jerks to look at me with the poleaxed expression of someone who's never had a bottle thrown at them before and had never even thought it could happen. It's not like I was actually aiming for him or anything, but still. He didn't even *duck*. Amateur.

The silence stretches out between us. I can hear my own breathing, loud and harsh.

'OK,' he says.

And for a second I'm terrified that he really is going to leave, that this is the horrible, defining moment we're going to end in, that he's going to go and never come back.

But, 'I'm sorry,' he says. 'That was a shit thing to say. I'm sorry.'

My brother. If nothing else, he really knows how to nail a quiet, sincere apology. God knows he's had enough practice with me.

'You don't really want me to go, do you?' he asks. Gentle.

I shake my head, and that's when the tears really come. Because

I do want him to leave, but I don't. I hate him and I love him. How can two opposite things be true at the same time?

'Oh, Zannie,' he says, and I hear the helpless, frustrated worry in his voice. *So* familiar. I've been hearing it from him my whole life. He comes over to me. 'Please let me hug you?'

'No,' I say, stepping away from him, even though all I want in the world right now is for someone to hug me. I cross my arms in front of me, but it's not enough of a shield, so I push my hands further until I'm clutching my shoulder blades, trying to hold myself in.

'I'm *sorry*,' he says. 'I made a mistake and I'm sorry. That's why I came here – to say that. Not to start a fight. It's OK that you're angry with me.'

I know it is! I want to say, but before I can voice the words, the buzzer goes. We both look at each other automatically, startled.

'Who's that?' he asks.

I lift my shoulders, trying to think through the vodka and residual rage-fog who it could be.

'Sarah?' Brian suggests as I spring into life and move to answer the buzzer.

'She knows the code,' I say. I press the button. 'Hello?'

'Hiya.' It's Matt. Shit. 'It's me. Can I come up?'

'Er . . .' I say.

'Who's that?' Brian asks again from behind me.

I'm so confused I press the button that unlocks the front door, so I have no choice than to say, 'Come up.'

'Who's that?' Brian asks again.

'It's Matt,' I say, unhelpfully. I try to think about how to explain Matt, but he's already knocking at the door and I'm opening it on autopilot. 'Hey.'

Matt's face, which was presumably wearing a smile a second before, drops in undisguised shock at the sight of me.

'All right, I don't look *that* bad,' I say, glancing down at myself. 'Do I?'

'What's wrong?' he asks, taking a step towards me and into the flat. His concern is so genuine, and so intense, that it's too much. He reaches for me, his hand on its way to my face. The gesture is way too intimate to happen in front of my older brother, which is why I rear away from him and his touch. He doesn't know that, though. He looks hurt.

'I'm actually in the middle of something,' I say, trying to brighten my voice. 'So . . . could you come back later?'

'What's *wrong*?' he asks again, more intensely this time. His focus is so completely on me that he hasn't even noticed there's someone else in the room.

'Me,' Brian says, and Matt jerks in surprise.

'This is my brother,' I say. 'We're fighting. It's kind of a thing.'

Matt, who'd relaxed slightly at the word 'brother', tenses again. 'Fighting about what?' His forehead crinkles slightly and he glances around me. 'Did you spill vodka in here?'

'She threw it, actually,' Brian says. 'The bottle, that is. At me.'

'I didn't throw it *at you*,' I say. The viciousness in my voice surprises me. 'It didn't even touch you.'

'Will you just calm down?' Brian's starting to lose his composure, I can tell. Matt's appearance has completely thrown him, and it's like he doesn't know how to deal with me any more.

'Why does she need to calm down?' Matt asks. 'What did you do?'

'No,' I say, loud enough to stop Brian responding. 'Don't turn this into a two-of-you thing. *Please.*' I look at Matt and soften my voice so it's just for him. 'This isn't anything to do with you.'

He hesitates, glancing at Brian and then back at me. 'Do you want me to go?' he asks, giving me the choice my own brother didn't.

'No,' I say, the answer coming so easily I don't even think

about it. 'Stay? But give me a second to . . .' I point at Brian, who clenches his jaw in poorly concealed frustration. I go over to him. 'You have to leave.'

'Zanne . . .' Brian begins.

'Go,' I say again. It's all I can manage, because my mind is stuck on this: Brian, aged twelve, scooping up my battered seven-year-old self off the floor and carrying me away, hugging me safe and close. Brian, thirteen, coaxing me out from under his bed, where I'd gone to hide. *He's gone*, he'd said. *I promise*. Brian, fifteen, carefully counting out the coins of his allowance, sharing it with me. Brian, seventeen, standing in front of me like a shield. *Fuck off, Dad*, he'd said. He actually said those words. *Can't you just leave her alone?* Brian, eighteen, driving me around Reading while the Kinks played over the stereo until I fell asleep and we returned to a silent, calm house.

I'm waiting for another rush of rage to take over me, but it doesn't come. I just feel . . . heartbroken. That's what it is. For him and me and the lives our parents gave us both and what it's turned us into.

He does leave, finally; a hollow victory. The cups of tea that he poured are still waiting on the kitchen counter.

'Do you want tea?' I say to Matt, who's stayed quiet, waiting for his cue.

'Sure,' he says, cautious.

'I don't want tea,' I say. 'I would've told him that, if he'd asked.'

'Suze,' Matt says. 'What happened?'

'Did I drink all my vodka?'

'No, Suze. You smashed the vodka, remember?'

'Oh,' I say.

'Come on,' he says. 'Let's get you some water.' I watch him hunt around my cupboards until he finds a glass. 'So . . . that was your brother, huh?'

'I don't want to talk about it.'

'Hey,' he says. He puts the glass down and reaches for me, folding me in for a soft, light hug. It's a very nice hug. I want to give in to it, let myself be comforted. It would be so easy. But I can't take it back if I let him see me like this; if I give away the only cards I have; if he sees what a state I'm actually in, a state I'm never truly that far away from.

I want him to stay, though. So I kiss him, because then he'll stay, and he won't be looking at me like he can actually see me, and I won't have to talk or think or feel.

I kiss him, and he pushes me away. Very gently, but still.

'Not tonight,' he says, just as gently.

'Why not?'

'Because you are very, very drunk,' Matt says. His face is slightly fuzzy. He reaches forward and moves a wayward strand of hair from my face. 'And very, very sad.'

I shove his hand away. 'I'm not sad.'

'OK,' he says, meaning, *You are*. 'But you are drunk.'

'So?'

He laughs a little. 'Come on, Suze. Let's just chill until you sober up a bit, OK?'

I put my hands to the zip of his jeans. 'It's OK,' I say. 'You can have me. I don't mind.'

He reaches down and takes hold of my wrists, lifting my hands up and away from him. 'Hey,' he says, soft. 'It's OK. Stop.'

'Why are you here?' I demand, pushing him away harder than I should and stepping back. 'Why did you even come if you don't want me?'

'I do want you,' he says. 'But not right now. Not like this. I came here because you didn't turn up in town, and then my replies weren't going through and my calls wouldn't connect. I was worried; I wanted to check you were OK.' He hesitates.

'Which you're not. So I'm going to stay because of that, not for . . . anything else.'

I move my hands behind my back and latch them together so hard my wrists rub and burn. 'If you stay,' I say, trying to keep my voice steady but no longer sure exactly what steady even means, 'I will cry on you.'

'You're already crying.'

Am I? '*On* you.'

'That's fine.'

I shake my head. 'Why aren't you leaving?'

'I know you're drunk, but do you really think for a second I would leave you like this?'

'Like what?'

Matt looks at me like he doesn't even know where to start. 'Want me to be honest?'

'Yes.'

'Like a total mess.' He says this simply, no malice or sneer in his voice. If anything, he seems sad. 'Like someone who needs to have another person with them until they sober up.'

I hear, *Like someone who needs*. 'I'm not some charity case.'

'That's not what I said.'

'*Is* what you said.'

Matt shakes his head, his eyes moving over my face. 'What can I do? Do you want to eat something? That might help. We could order a pizza or something?'

'What time is it?'

'About nine.'

Oh God, it's so early. He takes a gentle hold of my arm and begins leading me towards my bed. He's bunching up my sheets, piling up pillows, coaxing me to lie down, pulling one of the blankets over me. 'Not a child,' I mutter.

'Sleep it off for a bit, OK? I'm right here.'

'Don't care if you're here.'

He doesn't speak for a while, but I can hear him rustling around as I try to fight off sleep. He settles at the end of the bed, squeezing my foot but not coming any closer to me. A moment later, the strumming of a guitar fills the room.

'Don't fucking serenade me,' I say, but it comes out like a growl, ridiculous and sulky, and he laughs but doesn't stop strumming. It's actually quite nice. I let myself ask, but just quietly, 'What is it?'

'"Time in a Bottle",' he says. 'Jim Croce. Don't worry. It's not serenading if I'm not singing.'

I listen for a little longer. My head feels foggy. 'Will you teach me how to play it?'

'Sure,' he says. 'In the morning.'

'You'll still be here in the morning?'

'I'll still be here in the morning.'

29

'Like Gold'
Vance Joy

He is.

When I wake up in the morning he's asleep beside me, on top of the covers, still fully dressed. I lie there for a while, half dozing, listening to him breathing. Most of last night is a blur, but I have vague memories of being awake with him, crying on to his shoulder. The uncontrollable, raspy kind of heartbroken crying. The kind I don't do in front of people. I'm not sure how much sleep either of us actually got. I feel hungover in a way that is more to do with the crying and shouting than the vodka I drank. Drained, like all the light in me has gone, leaving me empty and cold. After a while, I slide out from under the covers and go to the kitchen to pour myself some water. It occurs to me that this is the first time I've ever slept with anyone in this flat, and that's all we did. Sleep.

I make tea and toast, eating mine over the sink and leaving a plate and mug for Matt on the floor by the bed. It feels a bit weird to shower while he's in the flat, but I feel so rubbish, I do it anyway. I close my eyes under the water and it helps. When I come out of the shower area, Matt's awake, sitting cross-legged on the bed, tapping into his phone. He looks up and smiles.

'Hey,' he says.

'Hey,' I say. I'm wearing leggings and a T-shirt, my face scrubbed clean, my hair still wet, combed through with my fingers. I feel raw. 'Thanks for . . . um. Staying.'

'Course,' he says. He puts a hand out to me. 'C'mere.'

I sit next to him on the bed, leaning against his side while he drinks his tea, and find my phone under my pillow. There are messages from Brian, asking me to call him when I've 'calmed down', apologizing again, telling me he loves me. I scroll through them, clenching my jaw so tight it hurts, until I get to the one where he tells me he's staying with Sarah. Damn. I should have seen that coming. I have a missed call from her and a message saying **Give me a call when you can. I've spoken to your mother.** And then, maybe because she can read my mind or maybe because she knows me, she's added, **I'm on your side, every time.**

'You're not working today, are you?' Matt asks. When I shake my head, he says, 'Want to go for a drive or something? It might be good for you to get out for a bit?'

'OK,' I say. I know there'll be no getting around seeing Sarah today so I do the adult thing and reply to her message instead of ignoring it. **Thank you. I'll call later – promise. Spending today with a friend. I'm fine xx**

I'm in the passenger seat of Matt's car when my phone lights up with 'Mum' onscreen and my stomach turns over. Mum hardly ever calls me, because we don't have that kind of relationship, and every learned instinct is yelling at me to answer it, quick, before she goes back to pretending I don't exist.

But I don't want to talk to her. I don't want to hear her defend Dad or Brian or apologize for them. I don't even want to see her name on my phone screen. I reject the call, and it feels like smashing a hammer down on one of those Test-Your-Strength games at a carnival. I feel strong. And then I follow the thought through, and I take it one step further. I pull up her contact card on my phone and block her number. And then Brian's.

It'll just be for a couple of days, but doing it makes me feel calmer. A couple of days to steady myself, to debrief, maybe. To feel safe.

'OK?' Matt asks.

'OK,' I say.

We spend the day driving around the south coast from Brighton, through Eastbourne, past Hastings, all the way to Camber Sands. 'See?' he says when we walk over the dunes. 'Genuine sandy beaches, right here in East Sussex.' It's bright and sunny but cold, the two of us buried deep in our coats. He tells me to race him to the sea and I do, even though the tide's out and it looks miles away. After a few seconds of feeling stupid, weighted down by my coat and boots, I feel this impossible kind of freedom take over me, lifting me up, carrying me along. When I get to the sea, just behind him, I'm laughing. I take off my boots and socks, roll up my jeans and let the icy cold waves sweep over my feet.

'You're crazy,' Matt says. 'It's February!'

'It's great,' I reply, teeth chattering. 'Bracing.'

'*Brrr*-acing,' he replies, and the joke is terrible but I laugh so hard my eyes tear over.

On the drive back we listen to Vance Joy and when Matt sings along, I do too, because why the fuck not. We play a version of 'I packed my bag' with album titles. When we get back to Brighton and it's time for him to leave I almost say, 'Stay?'

I wait until later in the evening before I go to see Sarah, because I'm hoping if I leave it late enough Brian will have left. This turns out to be unnecessary, as she'd sent him home hours ago.

'I told him it would be best,' she says. 'I thought you'd need time. Was that the right thing to do?'

I nod. 'Thanks. What did he tell you?'

Everything, it seems, from what she says. It actually sounds like he was honest about it. I guess that's something.

'If your dad ever pulls anything like that again, you don't have to talk to him,' she says. 'You don't owe him anything. Call me, or call the police if you want to. But don't put yourself through that.'

'Did Mum know?' I ask. It's the only thing I care about right now. 'Did she know he was going to do that?'

Sarah shakes her head. 'She was very upset.'

'*I* was very upset.'

'From what she said to me, it seems like they'd discussed coming down here together to talk to you, with me. All of us sitting down together to talk about the money. But Darren jumped the gun a bit.'

Something in my chest tightens. Even Sarah, who's on my side, can't help but minimize it. *Jumped the gun.* Seriously?

'I wish you'd told me about the suing idea,' she continues. 'We could have talked about it.'

I bite down on my tongue to stop myself snapping at her. 'That was never a thing. I just mentioned it to Brian. I'd obviously never do it. This is all so stupid.'

'You'd be within your rights,' she says. 'It's not stupid at all to want some kind of justice.'

'I just want to live a life that they're not constantly stomping all over,' I snap. 'That's all. Why can't they just leave me the fuck alone if they're . . .' I mean to say '*if they're not going to love me*', but the words don't make it out. I try again. 'I don't even want any money from them.'

She's calm. 'Suzie, think about how far that money could go in your life. How useful it would be. Don't turn it down without thinking about it.'

'What I'm thinking about is the fact that I've been living on no money in a bedsit and they've just got five grand lying around,' I say, trying to keep my voice at a normal level but not quite succeeding. 'Seriously? They can just throw around that kind of money like it's nothing? While I'm . . .' I swallow, bite down on my lip and turn away.

After a few moments, she touches my chin, nudging me gently

to look back at her. 'I'm sorry,' she says, quiet. 'I'm sorry this is the life you have to live. If I could make it better for you, I would.'

'I know,' I say, and I hear the defeat in my voice, how helpless I sound.

'Think about the money,' she says. 'Take the time to be angry, that's fine. But think about it. OK?'

Me:

So. My parents want to give me some money.

Rosie:

??

Me:

Long story, but they found out that suing might be an option, even though it's not, and they want to skip that bit and just give me the money.

Rosie:

GOOD!!

Caddy:

Eugh!

Rosie:

What?

Caddy:

What?

Me:

This is really helpful so far.

Caddy:

You're not going to take money from them, are you?

Rosie:

CADDY.

Caddy:

What?

Rosie:

Suze, of COURSE you are going to take the money from them. RIGHT?

Caddy:

???? Roz, wtf?

Me:

Er.

Caddy:

It's the principle.

Rosie:

What is?!

Caddy:

Not taking money from terrible people.

Rosie:

CADDY, SHUT THE FUCK UP.

Caddy:

?!?!

Me:

This time, there's no response, and the ticks that would tell me they'd read my last message don't appear. I know this means that Rosie has called Caddy, or vice versa, to straighten their own mini-argument out before letting me back into the conversation. I wish they'd carried it on in front of my eyes. It feels weird knowing they're out there in their separate university bedrooms, talking about me and my shitty life dilemma. I wait for a few minutes.

Me:

Still nothing. I curl myself up on my bed and rest my head on my crooked arm, eyes on my phone, trying to fight off a rising resentment. It's not fair that they get to talk about me like this. It's not fair that my awful is their discussion topic.

It's early evening and I'd decided to ask Caddy and Rosie what they thought about the money – leaving out the details of yesterday's breakdown entirely – because I'm trying to be better at including them instead of just shutting them out. But this is reminding me why I don't do that, because they inevitably turn to each other to talk about it. Which feels *rubbish*.

I message Matt. **Did you know that corgi means 'dwarf dog'?**

He replies immediately: **Did you know that in Istanbul there are stray cats everywhere? In a good way** ☺

Rosie:

Sorry!

Caddy:

Sorry! Back now!

Me:

🙁 You were talking about me.

Caddy:

Rosie needed to yell at me.

Rosie:

It's true, I did.

Me:

🙁🙁

Rosie:

Caddy was being sheltered and privileged.

Caddy:

All right! God, once was enough.

Me:

Cads, your opinion is totally valid. I want to hear it.

Caddy:

My principles are a luxury.

Rosie:

Well, they are.

Caddy:

Go on, then. Say your bit.

Me:

I want to hear more about what you think, C.

Rosie:

Grahhhh.

Me:

Roz, shush. You can talk after.
Cads, please? You think
I shouldn't take it?

Caddy:

☹

Me:

Be honest.

Caddy:

I wouldn't take it if it were me.

Rosie:

IT IS NOT YOU.

Caddy:

OK, BROKEN RECORD.

Me:

I feel like I shouldn't.

Rosie:

Why? Because people like Caddy say they wouldn't?

Me:

It feels wrong.

Rosie:

Why?

Me:

Taking anything from them.

Rosie:

Taking it wouldn't mean you forgave them.
It wouldn't make anything that happened OK.

Me:

I don't want to owe them.

Rosie:

You won't owe them. THEY owe YOU, that's the point.

Caddy:

That's true.

Me:

But they can't ever pay it back, right?
So isn't it a bit . . . like . . . I don't know,
cheap, to take money from them?

Rosie:

Maybe if you just wanted it for manicures or whatever.

Me:

Manicures. Really? That's where your head went?

Rosie:

You know what I mean. But you're going
to use it for rent and stuff, right?

Me:

It's more of a long-term thing. Like . . . for studying.
To get my A levels, or do an Access course or something.

Caddy:

Me:

Just an idea.

Caddy:

Amazing! OK, I've changed my mind. Take the money.

Me:

What I use it for doesn't change whether
it's right to take it or not, though?

Rosie:

I still don't think 'right' or not is relevant
for this. But if that's really bothering you,
think of it this way: if it wasn't for them,
you'd already HAVE these qualifications.

Me:

I can't ever know that.

Rosie:

I do. You would.

Caddy:

I think so, too.

Me:

You guys. ♥

Rosie:

THEY are the reason you don't have that stuff.
OK? You were literally abused.

Me:

My dad thinks I would've
been a trainwreck anyway.

Caddy:

wtf

Rosie:

Your dad is a c***
Censored for Caddy's sensitive eyes

Caddy:

HEY!

Me:

☺

Caddy:

I'm 19. I know the word cock.

Rosie:
OH MY GOD.

Me:
OH MY GOD.

Caddy:
That was a joke. You know I'm joking.

Rosie:
Dying.

Me:
ACTUALLY DYING.

Caddy:
I hate you both.
Why can't you let me be funny? ☹

Rosie:
ANYWAY. Seriously, Suze. You know that, right?

Me:
Yeah . . .

Rosie:
Do you actually?

Me:
He might be right though.

Rosie:
Nope.

Caddy:
Nope.

Me:
You guys have to say that.

Rosie:
Er, no I don't. Caddy, maybe.

Caddy:
HEY

Rosie:
But you KNOW I'd tell you straight.
You are not innately a trainwreck.

Me:
No?

Rosie:
Nope. You're a bit trainwrecky, yeah.

Caddy:
ROZ

Rosie:
But there's CONTEXT. A train can't
help the tracks it's on, right?

Me:
oh my god.

Rosie:

Blame your parents for poor track-
laying. Think of the money like
National Rail fixing the track so the
trains can start running properly again.

Me:

Have you been waiting to use that analogy?

Rosie:

No, I just thought of it! It's great though,
isn't it? I should proper be a therapist.

Caddy:

Oh my God.

Me:

I'm crying, Roz.

Rosie:

Oh shit.
Like . . . laughing crying?

Me:

I can't tell!

Caddy:

Can I just say that I miss you guys so much.

Me:

I MISS YOU TOO

Rosie:
Me toooooo.

Me:
COME HOME AND VISIT. I NEED YOU.

Rosie:
Funny you should say that . . .

Me:
What?

Caddy:

Me:
WHAT?!?!

30

'Wrecking Ball'
Mother Mother

They've been planning it since Christmas, ever since they figured out they both had reading week – like half-term, but for students – at the same time. They're both coming to Brighton for a few days and they're bringing Owen, Sam and Tess (Caddy) and Jade (Rosie).

'Can you believe none of them have been to Brighton?' Caddy says to me when we Skype a couple of days before they all come down. 'Ever?'

'I'd never been before I moved here,' I say. 'It's not *quite* the centre of the world.'

She grins. 'It's close enough.'

I'm working the day they arrive, so I miss them checking off all the usual tourist stops from their list: the beach, the pier, the Pavilion. By the time I meet them all at the Airbnb Owen, Sam and Tess are sharing, everyone's already two drinks down.

'I better catch up,' I say, hugging Rosie, who's sitting on one of the beds next to a dark-haired girl who must be Jade, looking a little awkward. 'Hi! I'm Suzanne.'

'Hey,' Jade says, smiling. I'd intended to hug her but she doesn't stand up, so I restrain myself.

'Welcome to Brighton,' I say. 'How was today? Sorry I missed it.'

'Me too,' Rosie says. She raises her eyebrows at me, then lowers her voice so I have to lean in slightly to hear. 'You missed some drama.'

'Oh my God! What? Stupid job. Tell me.'

'Haven't you noticed who's missing?' Rosie asks, just as Caddy, who'd greeted me at the door with foundation blobs all over her face, then run off to fix it, comes bounding into the room.

'Why haven't you got a drink yet, Suze?' she demands. She's hyped up, which I'd thought was down to alcohol, but now I notice something in her eyes I'd missed before. The kind of manic edge of someone pretending everything's OK when it's not.

Where's Kel?

'I only just got here and I was saying hi to Roz,' I say. 'And Jade.' I smile at Jade again, who grins back like I'm amusing her. 'What are we drinking?'

'Sam's making mojitos,' Caddy says. 'Want one? I'll get you one.' She disappears before I can even reply.

'Where's Kel?' I ask, swinging back to Rosie.

'Well,' Rosie says. 'That's the thing.'

It takes her the rest of the next hour to tell me what happened, because she has to do it in the snippets between Caddy, much more flighty than usual, coming into the room and then leaving again almost as quickly. It had started when they all met at Brighton station, Rosie says. Kel was there to greet them, but things were obviously already off between him and Caddy, 'even though neither of them was acknowledging it. Suze, it was so awkward. I was like, "Cads, want to talk about it?" And she goes, "Talk about what?"' They'd got fish and chips at the beach and Caddy got her own portion instead of sharing with Kel like normal, and he was obviously annoyed but let it go. Then they'd gone on some of the rides on the pier, and something had happened – Rosie wasn't sure exactly what, but it seemed to have something to do with not going on the same log flume – and everything had blown up. 'They were yelling at each other, right there on the pier,' Rosie says. 'Can you believe it? The least yell-y people ever. And he stormed off, said that if she wanted space so badly, she could have it. And she *didn't go after him.* She just let him leave. And she's been in this I'm-so-fine state ever since. I think she learned it from you.'

'Is it serious?' I ask. 'Or just a fight?'

Rosie shrugs. 'Who even knows? Ask Cads. You might have more luck getting an answer out of her than I did.'

I don't. Caddy is generally pretty easy to read, and tonight she's radiating *Don't ask.* When I go to find her to offer to do her make-up for her, she's already fully made-up, sitting in the bathroom with Tess.

'Did you do that yourself?' I ask. 'It looks great.'

'I did it,' Tess says from the sink. She glances at me, and I swear she smirks. 'Thanks.'

I decide the best thing to do is ignore this, so I put my arm around Caddy and give her a squeeze. For a moment I feel her lean into me, her fingers squeezing down on my arm, but then she stiffens and I let go. 'Can I do anything?' I ask.

'We're good,' Tess says. 'We should go soon, don't you think, Cads?'

I tell myself, *It's nice that Caddy has a friend who is protective over her.* I tell myself, *She doesn't know me.* I tell myself, *I come out of any story Caddy would tell about me really badly. Of course Tess thinks she hates me.*

I think, *Bitch.*

I smile my biggest, warmest, most charming Suze smile and Tess falters, confused. 'You're right,' I say. 'We should go. Your hair looks really nice like that, by the way.'

It takes us another hour to actually get out of the Airbnb, across Brighton and into the club. I have this nagging feeling that this night is going to end badly, and that I should go home, but I ignore it. This is my best friends and me, regardless of arguments and boyfriends and new girlfriends and whatever else happens. We'll be fine once we start dancing and drinking.

But we're not. If anything, things actually get worse once we've put our coats in the cloakroom, got our drinks and found a space on the dance floor. Caddy seems to be actively avoiding me – I'd think I was being paranoid, but I can tell by Rosie's face that she's noticed too – which would be bad enough, but the worst thing is who she's giving most of her attention to instead.

Owen.

Caddy's not what you'd call a natural flirt; she's too self-conscious and shy to really pull it off. But tonight, everything that she's kept down, that's been simmering under the surface – anger, resentment, attraction – mixes with the alcohol she's knocking back and spills out of her in brazen, shameless flirting. At Owen. Who laps it up.

It's a weird thing, watching someone self-destruct. I'd known it must be upsetting – people had told me as much over the years – but I'd never realized how frustrating it was before. I want to shake her. *What are you doing?* I want to say. *You don't want to do this.*

I try. I follow her to the toilets and lean against the sink when she washes her hands, trying to force her eyes to meet mine. 'Kel loves you,' I say. 'You'll figure it out.'

She doesn't look at me. She snaps a sheet of paper out of the dispenser and dries her hands, shaking her head. 'Relationship advice?' she says. 'Really?'

This is probably the first time Caddy has ever felt like this, that dizzying thrill of standing on the edge of sensible, but I know it well. I'd talk to her about it if she'd let me. If she wanted, I'd leave right now, sit with her in the cold until she found her way back to herself. I'd do anything for Caddy. And Kel, for that matter.

But tonight, she won't let me. She'll barely even look at me, and I know why. Because I'm too close, because I know the real her too well. What she wants right now is to not be herself. And don't I know *that* feeling as well? I should leave her to it, dance with

Rosie and Jade until the night ends, let things run their course.

But I can't not do something. She is my best friend, and I love Kel. He doesn't deserve this, whatever he said on the pier, and Owen just isn't worth it anyway.

We're all back on the dance floor, Caddy and Tess dancing with their arms around each other, Sam and Jade trying to out-robot each other while Rosie doubles over laughing, when I catch Owen's eye, hold it for longer than necessary, then smile. He smiles back. Two seconds later, he is by my side. We dance for about half a song before he makes a drinking gesture with his hand, pointing at me, one eyebrow up. I nod, and we head to the bar together.

He puts his hand on the small of my back as we join the large, confusing queue, leaning his head closer to mine so I can hear him when he says, 'You look great tonight.'

I let a wide, flirty grin flash over my face, just for a second. 'Thanks.'

'What are you drinking?'

I suggest shots and his face lights up. God, it's *too* easy. He gets us both Jägerbombs and we move off slightly to the side of the bar to down them in one. Owen is beaming when we put the glasses back down on the bar, his eyes bright. I know from that look that he's seconds from leaning down to try to kiss me so I spin quickly on the spot and head back towards the dance floor, holding my hand back for him to take.

We find the others, all of them still dancing where we'd left them. Owen, his sweaty hand still in mine, pulls me in a slow spin towards him. He's a better dancer than I'd expected, moving in time with me. When the next song starts he steps closer and I move into him, my face near his collarbone, his mouth against my ear. His hands slide down my back, his thumbs touching my bare skin. I turn so my back is to him and he presses himself against me. I feel his face against my hair, hear him murmur something.

I close my eyes, smiling as he puts his arms around me, then open them to see Caddy staring directly at me. There's a look on her face I've never seen before. Owen's hand slides up the light fabric of my top, his fingers grazing my stomach. I hear his voice in my ear: 'Turn back around.'

Caddy is still looking at me. I turn, keeping my body close to him, my hips turned into his, both of us still in motion. His mouth finds mine, as I knew it would, as I'd wanted. We kiss as we dance. His hand rests on the small of my back and moves me in. It is the full-on, sweaty kind of kiss you can only have in the middle of a dance floor. Part performance, part warm-up.

He kisses the corner of my mouth, my jaw, my neck. 'Want to go outside?'

I let him take my hand again and lead me through the crowd to the edges of the club where I can suddenly breathe properly again. Neither one of us looks back. I follow him outside where it's colder than I'd expected. Goosebumps prickle up over my skin, and to my surprise, he notices immediately.

'Whoa, hey,' he says, smiling. He runs his hands up and down my arms with an innocent kind of sweetness I'd never have expected from him. 'Too cold?'

'It's fine,' I say. 'Do you have any cigarettes? I just want a smoke.'

His brow furrows a little. 'You just want to smoke?'

I nod.

'You don't want to . . .' He looks so baffled, I almost feel guilty. Almost. 'I thought you were coming out for . . .'

How is it not blindingly obvious that the show in there was just that, a show? Is he really that dense? He can't really think that I, who turned him down once before and is best friends with the girl he's been flirting with, could want to actually be with him?

He gets it eventually, though. And I know the exact moment

he does, because he grabs a hold of my arm and says, almost incredulously, '*Bitch*.'

I'm not sure exactly what would have happened next if it had been left up to us, but it's taken out of our hands when Caddy appears. A Caddy so angry she's actually shaking.

'We're going,' she says. 'Just thought you should know.'

'Going?' I repeat. My voice is a bit of a squeak.

'Yeah.' I've never seen her like this. Behind her, I spot Rosie, making a you've-done-it-now face at me, and Jade, hanging slightly off to the side, arms crossed. 'I thought I should say bye. Because I never want to see you again.'

'Caddy!'

'Hey, Cads,' Owen begins.

'Fuck you, Owen,' she snaps, and I can see tears brimming in her eyes. 'Just . . . fuck you, OK?' Her voice cracks, and it stabs my heart.

'Caddy,' I try again. 'Look, this was just—'

'This was just you being you,' she interrupts. She turns suddenly. 'Owen, get lost.'

He scarpers without another word, like the weasel he is, leaving the two of us staring at each other. Rosie hovers, anxious.

'You—' Caddy begins. Slowly, with purpose.

'Um,' Rosie pipes up. 'Cads?'

'Go ahead,' I say. 'Say it.'

'No, don't say it,' Rosie says, stepping forward and taking a hold of Caddy's wrist. 'Come on, Cads. You're drunk and upset. Let's go. We can talk it over tomorrow.'

'You think I got with him because I like him?' I ask, trying to keep my voice steady. 'You think I'd want that waste of space?'

'He's *not* a waste of space.'

'Yes, he is, Caddy! He's so below you. And you're risking everything you have with Kel, who *loves* you, for him?!'

'You don't know anything.'

'I have eyes,' I snap. 'You were making it so obvious tonight, Caddy. It was pathetic.'

'*I'm* pathetic?' Her voice is three times its normal volume. Rosie's eyes widen in alarm. 'Says you? *Really?*'

'I'd know, right?'

She's so furious she can barely speak. It would probably be funny if it wasn't so devastating. But, hell, I'm pretty mad, too. Devastated and mad is not a good mix.

'You,' she manages. She actually points at me. 'You need to sort your fucking life out.'

I do the worst thing. I laugh.

'Suze,' Rosie hisses, looking anguished.

Caddy's tears have spilled down her face, streaking mascara, and out of nowhere I think about the first time we met. Caddy, sixteen and awkward, staring at me from the front door of her house, naked dismay all over her face. It's kind of like how she's looking at me now. Like I'm the most disappointing thing she's ever seen. The last thing she'd ever want in her life.

I turn and walk away, back into the noise of the club. I ignore Owen, who is hovering by the bar, and head for the cloakroom. I just want to get my coat and escape home.

'Hey,' a voice calls, and I groan. 'Um, Suzanne?'

I turn because I have to, even though it's Tess's voice and she's the last person I want to speak to.

'Did it work?' she asks.

I look at her, trying to figure out if she's being sarcastic. But her face is anxious, as if she's really asking me.

'I don't know yet,' I say.

'Well, good work, anyway,' she says. 'You're a hell of a lot braver than me.'

Brave. Well, that's one way of putting it.

31

'Pyro'
Kings of Leon

I'm woken the next morning by my phone buzzing by my head. I reach for it, groggy, pushing my hair out of my eyes. Matt. Why is Matt calling me? At 8.06 a.m.?

'Er, hello?'

'Hey,' he says. 'Listen, I'm coming to Brighton.'

'What? Why?' I sit up, blinking. Did we make plans? Did I call him while I was drunk and ask him to come down?

'I'm on my way to Kel's,' he says, and I realize why before he even says it, the knowledge landing solid as a punch. 'It's him and Caddy. They've broken up.'

I'm waiting on the front steps of my building when Matt pulls up. Caddy hasn't answered any of my messages and she's ignoring my calls, so I'm guessing she's still furious with me. Rosie, being Rosie, had anticipated my stream of messages before I'd even sent a single one with the line: **Keep me out of this.** She'd followed it up with a softer, **Love you, obvs. But seriously. Keep me out of it.** I'd hesitated over how to reply, tempted to make my case anyway and pester until she promised that we're still friends, but I'd restrained myself. Instead, I'd replied, **I love you. Have fun with Jade? Go to the Pavilion. Sorry for being the worst.** She sent an eye-rolling emoji and nothing else.

'So,' Matt says, when I slide into the passenger seat beside him. 'Last night.'

'What do you know?'

'Just that they've broken up.' He changes gear, glancing into the rear-view mirror. 'Kel called me at, like, 4 a.m. He's gutted.'

'Who broke up with who?'

'It kind of sounds like it was a mutual thing. Not in a good way, but mutual.'

'Oh.'

'He said they had a fight earlier in the day and she went out without him? And then she called him crying so he picked her up.'

'And that turned into them breaking up?'

'Sounds like it. Haven't you spoken to Caddy?'

I mumble something deliberately unintelligible and shrug, which makes him shake his head and smile a little. 'Bad night, huh?'

'It wasn't the best.'

It had seemed like a good idea to go to Kel's with Matt, but when we arrive Kel just rolls his eyes, like he's annoyed.

'Mate,' Matt says, opening his arms and bringing Kel in for a brief, backslapping man-hug. Why don't men just hug properly? Hugs are so nice. They're missing out. 'How are you doing?'

'Shit,' Kel says. 'Totally shit. Hey, Suze.' I make sure to give him a proper hug and he squeezes me back tight. 'Didn't think I'd see you.'

'Why not?'

We follow him into the house and through to the conservatory. Matt and I both sit on the sofa but Kel stays standing, rubbing the back of his neck.

'I thought you might have enough going on with Caddy?' He raises his eyebrows at me and I flush. 'She told me everything. She's pretty mad at you. Have fun being the scapegoat.'

'Scapegoat?' Matt asks.

Kel lets out a humourless laugh. 'Suze didn't tell you about Owen?'

'Who?'

'This isn't about me,' I say. 'Why are we talking about me?'

'Good question,' Kel says. 'But seeing as we are, you want to fill me in on what's actually been going on with this guy? Did you know about him and Cads?'

Oh shit. Matt looks at me.

'Um . . .'

'Did you?' Kel repeats. 'Look, I get that you're loyal to Caddy, but seriously, Suze. Fucking hell. You're meant to be my friend, too.'

My face feels incriminatingly hot, even though I'm more confused than guilty. Should I have told Kel? I hadn't even thought about it. Besides, it wasn't like she'd even done anything with him, was it? What was there to tell?

'And if you knew she liked him,' Kel continues, his voice picking up, 'why did *you* get off with him?'

Oh God, this is all too confusing. And Matt is sitting right there, staring at me. If I say the truth – I was trying to make a point and, hey, it obviously worked, right? – will that make things better or worse? I swallow and sink a little into the sofa, shrugging.

'Wait,' Matt says. I look at him beseechingly, but he says it anyway. 'Who did you get off with?'

'Owen,' Kel says impatiently.

'I'm still not clear on who Owen is.'

'The guy Caddy—' Kel's voice breaks and he stops, waves his hand in frustration and walks out of the room.

'OK,' Matt says to me. 'You're going to have to fill me in.'

'Caddy has a crush on a guy from her flat,' I say. 'And he was there last night, and they were being flirty. So I . . .' God, it made so much sense last night. 'Well, I kind of kissed him.'

'The guy she has a crush on?'

'Yeah.'

'Why?'

'I wanted to show that he wasn't worth it,' I say. 'Like, he's obviously not good enough for her if he'd get off with me, right?'

His whole face scrunches, incredulous. '*What?*'

'You know what I mean.'

'Do you know how completely fucked that reasoning is? Why would you even get involved?'

'Because I love Kel, and she was going to do something stupid. Seriously. I was worried *she* was going to kiss Owen, and that would have been even worse.'

'But now they've broken up over it.'

'They haven't broken up over that,' I say, the words coming out like a snap. 'They've broken up because they've been having issues for months. You must know that. Owen is a symptom, not the problem. Besides, are you even surprised? Isn't this always inevitable, anyway? This is why we don't want relationships, right? Because of bullshit like this.'

Matt's eyebrows have risen as I spoke. 'Oh, you want to have that conversation?'

'What does *that* mean?'

Kel comes back into the room then, saving both of us from having to hear the answer. 'I'm going to get drunk,' he announces.

'Mate, it's not even eleven,' Matt says.

'Fuck time,' Kel says. 'Fuck fucking everything.'

'Wow,' I say. 'This is a whole new side of you, Kel.'

'And fuck you, too,' Kel adds, and he's kind of joking and kind of not. 'You'll drink with me, right, Suze? There's tequila in the kitchen.'

'Kel, even I draw the line at tequila in the morning.'

He rolls his eyes at me and leaves the room again. I glance at Matt, who's pinching the top of his nose, face scrunched.

'Maybe I shouldn't have come?' I ask, lowering my voice.

'Maybe you should just have guy time?'

'Maybe,' Matt says, shaking his head. 'He's not usually like this. I thought he'd be happy to see you, otherwise I would've said don't come.' He breathes out a sigh. 'Plus, I didn't know about all the shit that apparently went down last night. Kinda wish I'd been there now.'

'Me too,' I say. I can hear Kel clattering around in the kitchen, the sound of a kettle being poured.

Matt smirks. 'Oh yeah? Sounds like I would've been competing for your attention.'

'Oh, please,' I say. 'As if.'

I love how he can light a spark in me with just one smirk. I really do wish he'd been there last night; maybe I could have talked to him about Caddy and Owen instead of just reacting, and we could have fixed it somehow, together. Or, more likely, we could have just been kissing. Either would have been better than what actually happened.

He raises his eyebrows at me and I can't resist leaning over to kiss him, just once. Kel's still in the kitchen, it's fine. But then Matt kisses me back, and it suddenly feels like a really long time since we kissed, and I'm sliding across the sofa, on to his lap, his arm is around my waist, everything is *great*—

'Guys, seriously.' Kel's voice is sharp as glass. '*Seriously.*'

I duck my head away from Matt's, hand over my mouth, and move sheepishly back from him, as casually as I can, up on to the arm of the sofa instead, like I was meant to be sitting there all along.

'Sorry,' Matt says.

'Sorry,' I say.

'Sure,' Kel says. He's holding three mugs of something steaming, and the sight of them balanced so carefully in his hands, the fact that he was in there making drinks for all three of us, makes me feel suddenly sick with guilt.

'Kel, want me to make breakfast?' I offer. 'If you don't have bacon, I can go out and get some, make bacon sandwiches?'

He shakes his head, leaning to put the mugs on the table. 'Don't bother.'

'What can I do? Just say.'

'Nothing. Just . . . It would be really great if you could stop using me as your excuse to make fucking doe eyes at each other.'

I feel my eyebrows lift as Matt glances at me, then back at Kel. 'That's not what we're doing,' he says.

Kel rolls his eyes. 'Whatever. I just can't deal with this today, OK? Suze, why are you even here?'

'For you,' I say, stung.

'Yeah? It's not my lap you're dancing on.'

'Mate,' Matt says, sharp. 'Chill the fuck out.'

My skin is tingling with the shock of not just what Kel said, but the way he said it. He's never talked like that to me before. I didn't even know he could. So cold, so sarcastic. Part of me knows I should get up and leave, because that's probably the safest thing for our long-term friendship, but another part of me, the part I have trouble controlling and the part I don't understand, wants to snap, *Do you want it to be?* To see what he'd say, to push him, to light the fuse and watch it blow.

But I force myself to wait three seconds before I speak, and that's long enough for Kel's face to crumple, his fist to go to his forehead, his head to shake. 'Suze, I'm sorry. Fuck. It's not you I'm mad at.' He closes his eyes and sighs a long, jagged sigh.

'I should go,' I say, sliding off the arm of the sofa.

'You don't have to . . .' Kel begins, but I shake my head at him.

'It's OK. This should be your guy time. No doe eyes.' I chance a smile, and he sighs again, a reluctant, answering smile flickering on his face.

He hugs me, his arms pulling in tight around my shoulders. 'You're all right, Suze,' he says, quiet.

'I really did come here for you,' I reply. 'Honest.'

'Ish,' he replies. 'I'll talk to you later.'

Matt has got to his feet. 'I'll drive you back, Suze,' he says, as if I haven't walked the twenty minutes from Kel's house to mine a dozen times or more.

'OK,' I say.

We're both quiet as we walk to the car, and still neither of us speaks as Matt starts the engine and eases out of the space. Finally, he says, 'Don't mind him. He's just upset.'

'I know,' I say. 'It was a bit of a dick move for us to kiss like that, though. I feel bad.'

'Well, yeah, maybe.' He gives a sheepish shrug. 'We probably could've saved it for later.'

I smile. 'Later? There's a later?'

'I'd like there to be a later, if you would.' He's not looking at me, his eyes on the road, but he's smiling.

'Can later be right now?' I say, only half joking.

He laughs. 'Don't tempt me.' We're already at Ventrella Road. 'I have to get back to Kel, though. He's got to come first right now.'

I sigh as if I'm disappointed, when actually what I'm thinking is how much I like that Kel is his priority. How decent he is. 'Let me know about later, then,' I say.

'Are you working today?'

'No, tomorrow.'

'OK. I'll call or message later. Listen . . .' It's so weird when people ask you to listen in the middle of a conversation, as if up until that point you were doing something else. Especially when they don't follow it with anything.

'Yeah . . . ?' I prompt.

Matt looks at me, then out at the parked car in front of us. He grimaces, rubbing the side of his forehead with the palm of his hand. 'It bothers me that you kissed that guy.'

'Why?'

He lifts his hand slightly to look at me. 'You know why.'

'Well, no, I don't. Because we talked about this, and I thought the whole freedom thing was a part of it. Which means you're free to kiss other people, and so am I.'

'I know that.'

'So why are you bothered? It's OK for you to kiss other girls but I can't kiss other guys?'

He lets out a quiet yet audible groan. 'I haven't.'

'Haven't?'

'Been kissing other girls. Or anything else.'

'Since when?'

'Since . . . Christmas?'

Oh. *Oh*. 'Why not?'

'Because I just . . . haven't wanted to.' He shrugs a little. 'It's all you, in my head. All the time. I know you're free to do whatever you want, but I guess it's just not that great to hear that you don't feel that way about me.'

The honest truth is I do feel that way about him, but that's the last thing I'm going to admit out loud. Saying that would open a door I don't want to walk through.

There's a silence. 'This is the bit when you say something,' he says.

'I like this song,' I say.

He closes his eyes briefly, jaw clenching, like he's trying to control himself. 'Yeah.'

'Who is it?'

'Kings of Leon.'

'What's it called?'

'Suze . . .' His jaw clenches tighter. He glances at me, sighs, and says, '"Pyro".'

'OK. I like it.'

He waits a little longer, then shakes his head. 'I should get back to Kel.'

'Yeah.' I open the car door and get out, all in one natural movement. 'See you later, then, maybe.'

He mutters, 'Great.'

I take a second to lean down before I close the door to smile at him, properly, so he doesn't drive away and forget why he likes me, then head up the steps to my building without looking back.

32

'Need the Sun to Break'
James Bay

Matt arrives at Ventrella Road early that evening with a paper bag in one hand and a plastic bag in the other. 'Burritos,' he says, lifting the first. 'And beers!' He lifts the other, and I smile at the familiar *clink* from within.

'Hi,' I say.

'Hi!' he replies, beaming. He steps through the door I'm holding open, leaning to kiss me on the cheek on the way past. He's never done that before, and it's so coupley it makes me laugh.

'Are you stoned?'

'Only very slightly,' Matt says. He laughs.

'You didn't drive, did you?'

'Nope! Walked. Now, I wasn't sure what kind of burrito you liked, so I got five, all different meats and salsa types.'

'You got *five* burritos?'

'I panicked,' he says. 'Didn't want to turn up with the wrong burrito like a dick.'

'You could've just called and asked,' I say.

'I could,' he says. 'But then I wouldn't get to be the guy who turned up with five burritos. And we wouldn't get to laugh about this in three years' time. You'll go, "Hey, Matt, remember when you bought all those burritos?"'

'Three years' time?' I repeat, smiling.

'A conservative estimate,' he says, and he smiles back. 'Come choose a burrito.'

We sit on the floor together, leaning against my bed, to eat. I'm tempted to offer to open the beers with my teeth, but I restrain myself and he uses his keys instead.

'So how's Kel?' I ask. I've taken the beef with habanero salsa and it's hot and spicy and so good.

'Better,' Matt says. 'He's mellowed out a lot since earlier. The weed helped, obviously. He says it's not actually a surprise; it's been coming for a while. Long-distance, you know? He hoped they'd beat the odds, but they haven't. It happens. Have you spoken to Caddy?'

I shake my head. 'She's super-mad at me. It might take her a while to cool off.' I don't add that she might never cool off, not this time. That I might have blown it. 'I hope she's OK.'

'Do you think she'll get with that guy? The one Kel says she liked?'

'I doubt it,' I say. 'It wasn't about him, anyway. Not really. Besides . . .' I mean to say that I've probably ruined him for her, but change my mind. 'He's not worth her time.'

Matt raises his eyebrows at me, and I shoot him a grin, all innocence and mischief, and he laughs. Thank God, he's not going to be weird about that whole thing again.

'Was Kel all right with you leaving?' I ask. 'To come here, I mean?'

'He said I should,' Matt says, surprising me. He smiles. 'We talked about you.'

'Oh God.'

'All good things,' he says. As he speaks he lifts his hand and trails his fingers along my wrist, sending tingles up my skin, to my neck, tracing down my spine.

'Can I hear some of them?' I ask, teasing. 'I could do with an ego boost.'

He kisses me instead, which is just as good, if not better. I sink into him, the two of us unfolding together the way we do, and I think *all good things*. Every single tiny good thing, and this. Out of nowhere, I laugh, and I don't even know why. He could be offended but he's not, because he laughs too, his nose brushing mine, tongue against teeth.

'Sorry,' I say. It's hard to kiss when you're smiling so wide.

'Suze,' he says, his mouth moving from my lips to my cheek to my neck. His hand, still at my wrist, slides down and entwines in mine. His voice is a breath, he's still half laughing. 'I'm so completely in love with you.'

And everything stops. My laughter, the breath in my throat, my heart.

He doesn't notice, not straight away. Not until he pulls back from my neck to see my face, which is rigid. Definitely not smiling any more. I'm trying to keep the panic down, to stop myself running for the door.

There's a moment when we just look at each other, like we both want to put off what's going to happen next. When the grenade that he's thrown with these words explodes.

'What's wrong?' he asks.

'Are you joking?' I'm giving him an out. *Take it back*, I think. *Please*.

He squeezes my hand, which he's still holding. 'Nope.'

There is so much wrong, so much I want to say, that I don't even know where to start. What comes out is, 'You think it's a good time to tell a girl you love her after your best friend just broke up with her best friend?'

For some reason, Matt smiles. 'Firstly, we don't really know who broke up with who. Kel says it was mutual. And second, if your objection to me saying I love you is the timing, then I'm pretty happy about that.'

'You know it's not.' I try very, very hard to keep the panic out of my voice. 'You *know* it's not. What do you even want from me?'

'Well, you saying it back would've been good,' he says. 'But that's OK.' He smiles at me, so genuine and sweet I have to turn away, snatching my hand back too hard, getting up and walking away from him. 'Hey,' he says. 'I'm sorry. I didn't mean to freak you out. I thought it was a good thing.'

'What do you *want*?' I say again. I cross my arms over my chest, tight and safe. 'Can you just spell it out, because I can't—'

'You,' Matt says, standing. 'Isn't that obvious?'

Oh God, I don't know how to deal with this. 'What, you want to be my boyfriend or something?' The word 'boyfriend' makes my stomach turn over, the heat rising from my chest up to my face. Boyfriend. Commitment. Pressure. Dependence. Love. I feel sick.

'Well, yeah.' He's more cautious now, his head tilted just slightly as he looks at me, his voice more gentle, like I'm a hissing cat he's trying to soothe. 'If that's what you wanted, too.'

'It's not. You *know* it's not.'

'OK, but—'

'I'm not ready for a relationship. I don't even want one. You know that.'

'I thought . . .' He trails off, his forehead creasing. 'I thought maybe you'd change your mind, like I have.'

'Why?' It comes out like an assault, and I try to get a hold of myself. 'Because you're just so great?'

Matt's eyes widen a little, like I've really surprised him. Which just proves my point, really. Because he clearly doesn't know me very well if he's surprised that I get mean when I'm blindsided like this. And how can he want to be with me if he doesn't know me? (*That's probably why*, my head says. *Because he doesn't know you at all.*) 'Hey,' he says, gentle. I don't want him to be gentle. 'I meant the way we are together. It's like . . . like we fit. Don't you feel it too?'

'No,' I say, a total lie. 'And even if I did, I don't want to be your girlfriend. I don't want to be *anyone's* girlfriend. You *know that*. I *told you that*. We . . .' I know the words are going to sound stupid, but I say them anyway. 'We had an agreement.'

'Things can change, though,' he says. He's still so calm, and it's winding me up, making me feel both cornered and exposed. 'I didn't think I wanted any of that stuff. But with you it's just . . . it makes sense. All of it – it makes sense.'

'How nice for you,' I say.

'Suze, come on,' he says. 'Tone down the bitch attack, yeah?'

God, I hate this. I *hate* this. I hate that he calls me Suze and he says 'come on' like he knows me, that his voice is so warm. I hate that he still thinks this is a romantic scene that hasn't reached the kissing bit yet, instead of realizing that I'm fucking serious about being unloving and unlovable. *I do not want this.*

I must say it out loud because he says, 'But why don't you want it?'

'Because I'm fucked up!' The words burst out of me, much louder than I'd intended. 'OK? Don't you get that? It's not about you. It's about me. If you think I'm just waiting around for the right guy to love me, that's *not it*. I'm not waiting to be saved. That isn't what this is.'

'You're not fucked up.'

'Yes, I am.' My hands are shaking, so I ball them into fists. 'I don't need you to tell me that I'm not. I'm dealing with it.'

'Well, fine,' he says. 'That doesn't have to mean you're on your own. Do you think only stable people have relationships?'

The words feel like a trap, so I sidestep them. 'You're ruining everything. This isn't even about me. You spent too much time with Kel, you had a bit of weed, you're jealous that I kissed some other guy, and you want me to be *yours*.'

'I want us to be each other's,' he says, and even though my head is a mess of confusion I still manage to think what a shame it is that he's wasted this great line on me.

'Today,' I say. '*Today* you do.'

He shakes his head. 'I lied about not writing songs about you,' he says. 'I've written five. Five since I met you. One of them is called . . .'

'Don't.'

'. . . "Manic Pixie Dream Blues".'

I can't help it; I laugh, even though it's the last thing I thought I'd do in this middle of this hellish conversation that's only going to get worse.

He grins, hopeful but still cautious. 'I'll sing it for you.'

'Don't you dare.' I cross my arms tighter over my chest, shaking the smile from my face, needing to see his disappear. 'So what, anyway? Some song no one will hear?'

His face changes when I say this; a jolt of hurt, but also a kind of understanding, like something's clicked into place for him. He's shaking his head. 'You don't have to do this, you know.'

'Do what?'

'Push me. Try to make me say something that'll hurt you. That'd make it easier, wouldn't it? Well, I'm not going to.' He raises his hands up, either in surrender or provocation, I can't tell. 'You can be peak bitch to me all you like. It won't work.'

I take a deep breath. 'Will you just go?'

'Is that what you want?'

I look at him, his face slightly flushed, jaw tense. I want to rewind, that's what I want. I want kissing in his car, dancing in his room, beers on a bathroom floor. When love was something unspoken, something warming the space between us, instead of a promise neither of us will be able to keep.

'This is too complicated,' I say.

'Is it?' He takes a step towards me. 'Listen. Just listen, OK? I love you. I know you don't want to hear it, and fuck knows I never thought I'd want to say it, but it's true. You're like . . . *fire*, Suze. Being around you, it's just . . .' He shakes his head again. 'I don't know what love can possibly be if it's not this. If it's not how I feel right now, with you, even though you're looking at me like that. It can't just be a one-sided thing. I think you feel it, too.'

'Well, I don't.' There's a coldness in my voice I don't even recognize, and even as I speak I'm thinking, *What the fuck are you doing*? 'I don't even care about you.'

'I know that's not true.'

'Then you're kidding yourself.'

He looks so hurt. And sad. I suddenly hate myself so much I want to crawl out of my own skin, sink into the floor, disappear forever. So much of me wants to say, *Stop, no, I take it back*, but the rest of me is fighting, fighting, fighting. And all that battle inside me is exploding out in these horrible words to this boy who's been nothing but good to me. I am the worst person. I am cruel and empty and cold.

It's either cry or fight, and I won't cry. If I cry, he'll comfort me, and I'll be lost. So I try to fight, but he won't fight back. He's just looking at me like he's looking at me, and it's more than I can bear.

'Hey,' I say, letting my voice loosen and warm, relaxing my arms from their tight, shield-like grip across my chest. His eyebrows furrow at the sudden change in tone. I let my shoulders fall a little so I'm looking up at him, tilting my chin, trying a smile. 'Can't we just . . .' I take a step towards him and his eyes flicker over my face. 'Forget this? Please? We're good together, aren't we? Just as we are? No labels, no bullshit.'

'Suze,' he says, so soft. I can feel the heat of him, his mouth so close to mine.

'If you want me, you can have me,' I say, taking another tiny step forward so my body is almost touching his, a breath away. I'm so close to getting this back, to having solid ground beneath my feet. 'You know that.'

When I kiss him, there's a moment when he doesn't respond but then I feel it, the moment he gives in, his mouth opening against mine, his hand sliding around my waist. I unfold against him, the two of us fitting together so, so perfectly. Oh God, it's so right. *He's* so right. He shouldn't be, but he is. Him and me, this unexpected us. His hand falls on the small of my back and pulls me in tighter. I'm thinking, *This is perfect.* I'm thinking, *This is all this needs to be.* I don't need him to love me, I just—

And then he stops. It's not a sudden movement, it's more like he stills, his mouth breaking from mine. There's a second when we're breathing together, his fingers under my T-shirt, firm on my bare skin. He says, 'No.' He moves back so I can see that he's shaking his head. 'I don't want you like this.' His eyes on mine. 'I don't want you.'

My breathing is uneven. I say, 'Get out, then.'

And he does.

33

'The Night We Met'
Lord Huron

None of this has gone how it was supposed to go.

I'm lying on my back, staring up at the ceiling from the floor of my bedsit. The bed would be more comfortable, but I don't want to be comfortable. I want to lie on the floor, to feel the unrelenting hardness against the ridges of my shoulder blades. I want to indulge my self-pity, to think things like, *This is where I belong*.

Caddy has ignored all of my attempts to call or message her. I have a friend request from Tess on Facebook. Rosie has been absent from WhatsApp all day; no blue ticks, no nothing. I can't blame her. After Matt left, I messaged Kel: **Don't hate me.** He hasn't replied, either. It's too late to go and see Dilys, and I can't face the idea of trying to explain any of this to Sarah.

So I stay lying on the floor, staring up at the ceiling. My phone is balanced on my chest and I'm wearing the Beats headphones Brian got me for Christmas. Radical Face is filling my head like my own personal soundtrack. It's a good choice for my mood; sombre, mellow, but oddly uplifting. I know how easily I could spin myself into a spiral of depression right now; how much I deserve to go into a depressive spiral right now. The music is keeping me afloat.

My phone beeps through my headphones and I jolt upright, reaching for it. I'm not sure who I'm expecting – or who I want it to be, even – but it's Rosie, saying, simply, **Dinner?**

I reply, **Yes please.**

We arrange to meet at a burger place in the city centre at eight, but I get there fifteen minutes early. I'm jittery and wired, leaning against a bollard while I wait for her and Jade, smoking two roll-ups in a row. When they arrive, it's all I can do not to launch myself at Rosie and cling to her, wailing, *Do you still like me?*

'Hey,' I say.

'Hey, smokey,' she replies. She's smiling but holding herself slightly back from me, hands in her jacket pockets. 'Thought you'd quit?'

I shrug, smiling back, trying not to show how anxious I am. I want to say something cool and ironic about being an unsocial smoker, but I can't think of the right thing.

She tilts her head a little, eyes scanning my face. 'You OK?'

'Bit of a day,' I say. 'I've kind of lost all my friends.'

'Clearly not,' Rosie says flatly. 'As demonstrated by my presence. Anything else you want to be dramatic about?'

'Yes,' I say. 'But let's get food first. Hi, Jade. Sorry.'

Jade is hanging back, waiting. When I say this, she smiles. 'No worries.'

I wait until we've found a table, ordered our food and got our drinks before I say, 'Matt told me he loves me.'

Rosie chokes on her Coke. Her eyes fly to my face as she reaches for a napkin, spluttering.

'And that he wants to be my boyfriend,' I add.

Her whole face scrunches into an anticipatory wince.

'Yeah,' I say.

'Make my day,' she says. 'Tell me you told him you love him too and now you're a couple.'

'Not quite.'

'Oh God. Were you at least gentle with him?'

'No,' I say.

Rosie looks at me for one long moment, then drops her head on to the table with a *clunk*. Just lets it fall to the table; an actual head-desk.

'God,' she groans, voice muffled. 'You are so fucked up, I don't know how you even function.'

Jade raises her eyebrows at this, which makes me wonder if Rosie's different at university than she is at home. Less blunt, maybe. But this is what I love most about Rosie; how straight she is with me. It means I can trust her completely, because I know she'll tell me the truth, even if other people would worry that I wouldn't want to hear it. Plus, it means when she says something nice, it's worth double.

'We both knew what it was about going into it,' I say. 'That's the thing. We agreed. He's the one who blindsided me.'

Rosie lifts her head. 'Life doesn't work that way, Suze. *Love* doesn't work that way.' She sighs. 'Poor Matt. I liked him.'

'So did I,' I say. 'And this all means I'll probably lose Kel, too. But that might have happened anyway, what with Caddy and everything.'

Rosie rolls her eyes. 'Oh yay, this part of the conversation.'

'You knew it was coming.'

'This is all you and her,' she says. 'Can't I just not be involved?'

'You don't have to be involved. But can you just tell me if she's going to be mad at me forever?'

'One, that *is* being involved. I'm not your go-between. And two, obviously not. Don't be stupid. Just let her be mad for a while, that's all you need to do.' She glances up as the waitress arrives with our food. 'Gross, I haven't washed my hands. Be right back.'

When she and the waitress are gone, it's just me and Jade, sitting across the table from each other. 'I'm sorry about all this,' I say.

She looks up at me from where she's carefully separating her burger into parts. 'All this?'

'All the drama,' I say.

Jade smiles a little, more to herself than to me. 'Listen,' she says, reaching for the ketchup and knocking a splodge of red sauce on to one of the buns. 'This is the first time I've ever been to Brighton. I've come here with my girlfriend, who's pretty great, you already know, and I'm meeting her mum, and her best friends, and I'm seeing where she grew up. This is all kind of a big deal, you know? So, I mean this in a nice way, but I really don't care about whatever drama is going on between you and Caddy and whoever that guy was. Like, I literally don't care. Why would I?' She's looking at me like she's expecting me to tell her, and I can feel my face starting to turn red. 'Don't you think it's kind of self-centred to think I would?'

I open my mouth, but I've got no idea what to say.

'I'm not trying to make you feel bad,' Jade says, shrugging. 'Really. And I'm not trying to be a bitch. But sometimes people just don't realize things, you know? So, it might be a big drama to you, but to me, it's just a fight between my girlfriend's friends that has nothing to do with me. Hey, do you like onion rings? You want mine?'

'Sure,' I say, trying to regain my footing. 'Thanks. You're right. It is self-centred.'

She glances up. '*Kind* of self-centred,' she corrects, and I think she's teasing but I can't be sure.

'Kind of crap,' I say, hoping to self-deprecate myself into someone she could like. 'Sorry.'

'Don't be sorry,' she says, so easily I know she means it. 'Really.' She smiles over my shoulder and I glance back to see Rosie, beaming back, easing between the tables to return to us.

I watch them both as Rosie sits down, her hand sliding across Jade's back on the way past. I hadn't thought I'd had any preconceptions of what Jade would be like, but I clearly did, because I realize as I sit there that I'd been expecting Rosie to choose a girlfriend who was like Caddy; conciliatory, a bit quiet, happy to let Rosie lead. What a stupid thing to think. Why would her girlfriend be anything like her best friend, just because they're both girls? Jade is nothing like Caddy, and nothing like me, either, for whatever that's worth.

'So tell me about what you guys did today,' I say, moving the conversation to where it belongs. 'Be detailed. I want to know everything.'

By the time I get home, I feel better. I still have Rosie, and I trust her when she says it'll all blow over eventually with Caddy. 'Best friends fight,' she says, and Jade nods. 'They just do.' I'm trying not to think about Matt, because there's a deep pain somewhere in my chest when I think about how I spoke to him, and I don't want to poke it. So I push thoughts of him down and away, where I don't have to deal with them. I already miss him. And, weirdly, I miss all the potential of him that I've taken from my life; all the fun we could have had together, all the ways we could have been great.

Now I'm back alone in my flat, I can't stop thinking about how the night could have gone. How it *should* have gone, from his point of view. If I'd said yes, if I'd said, *I love you, too*. We'd both have been so happy. Isn't that the normal response to an 'I love you'? From someone whole and good and sane, maybe.

I message Caddy again, and get no response. I try Rosie.

Me:

Thanks for tonight. And can you say thanks to Jade, too?

Rosie:

Any time. Jade says no worries. We're going to get the train up the coast tomorrow. Want to come?

Me:

I'm working! But thanks ☺ Have a good time. I love you xx

Rosie:

Course you do, I'm great. Love you too.
Don't worry about Cads, OK? Just give it time.

I will xx

I spend the next couple of days at work, losing myself in the monotony of coffee cups and loyalty cards and wiping the same stretch of counter over and over. I end up telling Farrah, my workmate, about Caddy and Owen and Kel and Matt, and she's fascinated, demanding to see pictures of everyone so she can 'visualize it all properly'. We go to the beach together after our shift and talk on the pebbles for a while, and it's nice to spend some time in an ordinary friendship, where the stakes don't feel so high.

I don't hear from Matt or Caddy, but Kel invites me over the next evening and we watch *The Grand Budapest Hotel* in his conservatory with a couple of his housemates, sharing buttered popcorn and chocolate fingers. Neither of us talks about his best friend or mine. It crosses my mind that if mine and Kel's friendship is the only thing that survives romantic love going wrong, that wouldn't be so bad.

On Thursday I carry my guitar on my back and get the bus to the care home to see Dilys. I've got a small pot of daffodils in my hand, yellow and bright. I've decided that I'm not going to bring any of it up with her, I'm just going to play the Joni Mitchell song I've been practising – 'River' – and read the last chapter of *The Little Prince*. I'm hoping she might let me keep the book when we're finished, because I like it a lot more than I thought I would, and I kind of want to read it again. There's a bit about a fox that makes me think of Caddy and me, and I want to show it to her when we're friends again.

This is what I'm thinking about when I wave at Ines on reception on my way into the building and head down the hall towards Dilys's room. The fox and the wheat fields.

And then I see the empty room and everything goes out of my head, because I know.

And when I hear my name, and turn to see Marcus, I know all over again.

And when he says, 'I'm so sorry no one told you,' I know a third time.

And then, finally, I hear the actual words. 'Dilys died on Monday.'

I can hear my own breath, somehow still steady, in and out of me, and it's comforting in a weird kind of way. I focus on it, each breath, each heartbeat.

I've never known anyone who died before. My grandparents either died before I was born or when I was too young to know. The closest I've ever come to death is when it was me, thinking I was choosing it willingly. I'd thought of it as an exit, then. An escape route. I was used to it, I thought. But I'd always been thinking of death in terms of how it affected me. For all my obsessing – and I had obsessed a lot when I was really ill – I'd never thought beyond it being a choice I could make. My own death hadn't seemed scary to me. But the death of other people, people I love, people who are bright and kind and loving . . . Impossible.

I'd known Dilys was old. I'd known she was ill. But she wasn't *that* old, and she wasn't *that* ill. I'd thought there'd be years of daffodils and talking and music. She was going to get strong enough to have Clarence back. She was going to teach me to play the piano. But she didn't even get better enough to say my name.

'I'm very sorry,' Marcus says.

'What happened?'

'She had a heart attack,' he says.

'A heart attack?'

He nods gently, like he doesn't want to scare me.

'Not a stroke?'

'No. But sometimes, after a stroke, the muscles around the heart can be affected. That's how it was for Dilys.'

No one told me that. None of the pamphlets I read told me about that. I'd thought I'd been prepared, I really did. I researched. I tried, didn't I?

I feel like I should ask more questions, but I don't know what they are. I feel so young, all of a sudden. 'Was she alone?'

Marcus shakes his head. 'I was here.'

'OK,' I say, trying to smile. 'That's good. You'd be a good person to be here.' I don't even know what I'm saying.

'I'm sorry that no one let you know,' he says.

'Why would they?' I reply, more bitterly than I intended. 'I'm not anyone.' *God, don't be pathetic. Don't make this about you being pathetic.* I press the ridges of my knuckles to my eyes and take a breath in. When I open them again, Marcus is watching me, sympathy all over his face. I ask, 'Do you know anything about the funeral?'

He nods. 'Her nephew left his number and details in case anyone wanted to go along.' He reaches out a gentle hand to me and I step back in confusion. 'Do you want me to take those?' he asks.

I'm still holding the daffodils. I look down at them, incongruously yellow, and I think how Dilys will never see flowers again. 'No,' I say. I know it's rude to be so abrupt but if I have to speak any more I'll cry.

I walk slowly down the hall towards the exit. Kelly, the care manager, walks past me with a distracted smile. I don't know if she's forgotten who I am, or who Dilys is, or the fact that we're connected, but it hurts all the same. I detour on my way out and stop by the common area. An old man and a younger woman are playing backgammon. An old woman is asleep on a chair by the window. I go over to her and carefully, quietly, put the daffodils on the windowsill so they'll be the first thing she sees when she opens her eyes.

And then I go home.

34

'Song For You'
Alexi Murdoch

When I get back to my building, I can't quite face going inside it. I sink down on to the steps looking out at the street, thinking about Dilys. The last time I saw her, when she'd held my hands between hers, a contented smile on her face, while I talked about . . . What had I talked about? I don't even remember.

I pull out my phone and twirl it in my fingers for a while. I want to message Matt, but I know I can't. Not after the way he left, the things I said. Let him be free of me, that's the fairest thing.

But I still want to, so badly. I open WhatsApp and stare at his name. I type, **Dilys died.** And, **I miss you.** And, **Do you play at funerals?** I delete them all.

I press the call icon. The screen transforms, the rings sound in the air, his face in a little circle.

'Hello?' His cautious, confused voice. And it's the weirdest thing, because I feel how much he knows me in that one word. He's angry, he hadn't expected to hear from me again, and he doesn't want to talk to me. But he also knows that there must be something wrong for me to call, that I wouldn't even think about doing it unless I needed him. And he's answered, despite it all, because he cares.

Maybe I know him, too.

'Hi,' I say.

There's a long silence. 'What do you want, Suze?'

I look out across my tiny part of Brighton. The rows of Victorian houses stretching down a hill. There's a woman pushing a pram.

A man talking into his mobile. 'Dilys died.' My voice breaks, but I don't cry. 'I'm sorry. I'm really sorry. I just . . .'

He's saying, 'Shit.' He's saying, 'It's OK.'

'You're the only one who really knows about her, and . . . no one else would understand why I . . .' I try to swallow. 'I'm sorry, I know you can't do anything, I shouldn't call you.'

'Are you at home?'

'Yeah.'

'OK, I'm going to come over. Is that OK? Is that what you want?'

I wipe at my dry eyes. 'From London?'

'I'm in Brighton.'

'You're back in Brighton?'

'I never left. I'm staying at Mum's.'

I say, 'Why?'

He says, 'Suze.'

And I say, 'OK. Yes. Please. Come over.'

I'm still sitting there when he pulls up outside half an hour later. He gets out of the car and walks slowly towards me, pausing by the steps.

'Hey,' he says.

'Hey,' I say.

He sits down beside me, cautiously, like he's waiting for me to say no. We both sit there for a while, staring out at the street. At some point he puts his arm around me and I let my head rest on his shoulder. I think about what people would say if they could see us like this, how weird they'd think it was after everything. But they're not here. They're not us.

When we finally go up to my flat, I still haven't cried but my head is heavy with the denial of it. I unlock my door and let us in, feeling him hesitate behind me before coming inside.

'Are you OK?' he asks me.

I shake my head.

'I'm sorry,' he says. 'I don't really know what to say.'

'Me neither,' I say. 'It's like . . .' I swallow, trying to think of the right words. 'I feel *so* sad. But it's like I'm not allowed? No one even told me. And why would they? I'm not family. I don't even know how to explain who she was to me. It's not like I can say she was my gran or something. She was just . . . just this random old woman.' Tears are stinging my eyes. My throat is tight. 'And she . . .' I don't have words for this. 'She *liked* me.'

He tries to take my hands. 'Lots of people like you.'

I take my hands back, sliding them under my arms, holding myself in. 'No. No, you don't get it.' Maybe people do like me, when I'm in Suze mode, charming them with some stupid performance, but that's not real. Dilys never saw any of that, and she liked me anyway.

'Hey,' he says, so soft. 'Hey.' He touches my arms and I let my hands fall loose to my side. I let him hug me, and that's when the tears finally come, hot on my cheeks. Dilys, adjusting my elbow when I held her violin. Calling me 'my dear'. Smiling wonkily at me from a hospital bed, like she couldn't want anyone there but me. Dilys, never looking at me like so many people do, even people who love me, like they're waiting for my next mistake.

The knowledge hits me hard, a punch to the chest: I never told her. Never, not once. I never said, 'I'm really glad I got to know you. Thank you for giving me your washing machine and your time. Thanks for caring.' Would that have been so hard?

Matt kisses the top of my head, and a fresh jolt of guilt and pain sears through me. I take a step back. 'I'm sorry for all the things I said to you. I didn't mean them.'

'It's OK, Suze. We don't have to talk about that now.'

'We do. You're so . . .' So what? Kind? Patient? 'You deserve so much better than—'

'Stop,' he says, but gently. 'We really don't have to talk about that now. Let me make tea, OK? Tell me more about Dilys. How far did you get with your classical education? You never told me.'

Oh God. It hurts that he's so nice. It actually physically hurts.

I press my fingers together so hard the tips turn white. I watch him go to the kitchen and take a hold of the kettle. 'Did I tell you she was in the Hallé Orchestra?'

He shakes his head. 'I don't really know what that is, sorry.'

'It's a really prestigious orchestra in Manchester,' I say. 'Like, you have to be really good to play in it. The best. So that means she was this *incredible* violin player. Not just good, you know? I never got to see her play, because of how bad her joints were, but I saw a YouTube clip.' I take a deep breath. 'Her life was classical music, and she got to, like, the top level of it. That's pretty cool, isn't it?'

'Very cool,' he agrees.

'She was going to teach me how to play . . .' My voice breaks. I clench my teeth. 'The piano. She did that too, played the piano. And she taught it for years. I bet loads of people in Brighton can play because of her.'

'My sister's piano teacher was a woman in Brighton,' he says. 'I'll ask what her name was. Wouldn't it be cool if it was Dilys?'

'Why are you being so nice to me?' I ask. The kettle lets out a squeal as it comes to the boil. 'I was so horrible to you.'

Matt lifts the kettle and pours it into two cups. 'I care about you,' he says. 'And you're hurting. So I'm here. That's the only equation that matters right now.'

'That's a good line,' I say. 'Put it in a song.'

He looks up at me. 'Those were all good lines, weren't they? That's a whole verse, right there.' He pulls out his phone. 'One sec, writing it down.'

We sit for a while on my bed, drinking tea and talking about Dilys. Every now and then the tears come again, then fade.

'When's the funeral?' Matt asks. 'Do you know?'

'No. I'm going to ring her nephew tonight and find out.'

'Do you have anyone to go with you?' he asks. 'That seems like a lot to do on your own.'

I shake my head. 'I don't know anyone else who knew her. Maybe someone from the care home will be there? I'm not sure how it works.'

'I can come with you, if you want,' he says. 'If that would help.'

I look at him. His sweet face, crinkled slightly with the effort of saying the right thing. Way back when Matt and I first met, Caddy and Kel had been so full of warnings, but they hadn't warned me about his goodness. How nice he is. The thing I have no defence against.

I should say no. I should stop inflicting myself on him. He deserves so much better than me and my cold heart, how I take and take and give nothing back.

'Yes, please,' I say.

Graham sounds tired when he answers the phone. He tells me that the funeral is tomorrow at a church on the outskirts of Brighton. I think that maybe he'll say something nice about Dilys and me, like maybe that Dilys had mentioned me and he was glad I'd been there over the last few months. But he doesn't, and it occurs to me that he probably doesn't even remember who I am.

'Is Clarence OK?' I ask. 'Did you take him with you on the last visit?'

There's a moment of silence. 'I'm sure he's fine,' he says, in that patient, slightly sarcastic tone of someone who doesn't really like or understand dogs. 'And yes, we did, luckily.'

'If you ever need anyone to walk him . . .' I start to say, then stop. What a stupid thing to say. Graham and his family don't even live in Brighton.

'That's very kind,' Graham says. 'But actually, Clarence isn't going to be with us any more. We only ever intended to look after him while Dilys was unable.'

My voice comes out shrill. 'You're going to abandon him?'

'No,' he says, with more strained politeness this time. 'We're taking him to a rescue centre. He'll be well looked after, and I'm sure it won't be long until someone adopts him. Now, it was nice to speak to you—'

'You can't put him in a kennel,' I interrupt. 'He hates kennels. He gets traumatized. Didn't Dilys tell you that?'

'"Traumatized" is a very dramatic word,' Graham says. I can tell he regrets telling me about this plan. 'He'll be fine.'

He may as well say, *He's just a dog.*

'I'll take him,' I say.

'I'm sorry?'

'I'll take him. I love him. I'll look after him.' There's a long silence, so I add, 'I used to walk him for Dilys. He knows me. And, look, if you put him in a rescue centre I'm just going to go there to get him. So you may as well cut that bit out and give him straight to me.'

'I'm really not sure—'

'It's what Dilys would want.' I feel completely confident about this. 'She trusted me.'

'How old are you?'

'Why does that matter?'

'Don't you want to check with your parents first?'

My breath catches in my throat, but when I speak my voice is steady. 'They aren't involved.'

'In what?'

'In my life.'

'Oh.' He finally gets it, way too late for it not to be weird. He's probably thinking, *Oh yes, the bedsit girl.* I hope he feels awkward.

I hope he's cringing, wondering how to get off the phone without making it worse. 'Well. If this is what you want, then fine.'

'Great. If you bring him tomorrow I'll take him home with me.' I glance around my bedsit. It's small, but so is Clarence. This is the perfect solution; I should have thought of it so much earlier. Why should either of us be alone if we can have each other?

'fragile' (feat. WRENN)
gnash

On the day of Dilys's funeral, it rains. Big, heavy sheets of it. I realize the night before that I don't own any of what you might call traditional funeral clothes, but it's too late to go shopping, so I end up wearing black tights under a little-on-the-short-side black dress and hope for the best.

Matt arrives dressed all in black, and it reminds me of the time I saw him play in Hastings. He looks sombre, clearly worried he might get the tone wrong, so I make a joke about umbrellas to lighten the mood.

He smiles, relaxing. 'Nice dress.'

'Is it too short?'

'What *is* short?' he replies ponderously, tapping his finger to his forehead. 'Does it even exist, when not in relation to something else?'

I give his arm a gentle shove. 'Just lie next time.'

He grins. 'I'll bear that in mind.'

It's such a relief to feel easy with him again.

I'd been worried, for some reason, that there wouldn't be many people, but the church is full. I spot Graham immediately, sitting on the front pew with what must be the rest of his family. There are lots of old people, mostly women, but also lots of middle-aged people and even some younger. I wonder who they are, how they knew Dilys. I wish people wore name badges at funerals. Name badges with something like RELATIONSHIP TO THE DECEASED underneath. What would mine be? SUZANNE

WATTS. USED HER WASHING MACHINE.

Even though I've spent the last few months getting to know Dilys, it feels like I do it all over again at her funeral. Three people give eulogies: Graham; a childhood friend called Dennis, who starts weeping; and a woman who'd been her friend since the early orchestra days. I listen to stories of young Dilys, professional Dilys, family Dilys.

All of these people loved Dilys. She mattered to all these people. To me. The version I knew was just one tiny part of her, one colour in the kaleidoscope. That could make me feel distant from her, but it doesn't. I'm glad I got the piece I did, and I hope she was glad, too, to know this version of me, the one that only really existed for her.

After the funeral, we all end up gathered outside the crematorium. A small group of the old women I'd noticed earlier come over to me, all smiles.

'You're the laundry girl!' one of them exclaims.

'How do you know about . . . I mean, hi.' I hold out my hand awkwardly and the woman who'd spoken grabs it, squeezing enthusiastically.

'Dilys told us all about you. Very beautiful, she said. Blonde. Of course it's you. It is you?'

I nod.

'Of course it is. Didn't I say it was? And who are you?' She turns to Matt, eyeing him over her glasses. 'Dilys didn't mention a boy.'

'I'm Matt,' Matt says. He smiles his charming friend-to-old-ladies smile and I swear they practically coo at him. 'I'm here for support.'

One of the other women gives my arm a soft pat and I look at her. 'Dilys would be so pleased that you're here,' she says, quiet and simple.

'Thank you,' I say.

We end up staying until most people have gone, which is how long it takes for Graham to find a moment to get Clarence for me. I haven't actually told Matt this bit, so he looks completely baffled when Graham approaches with Clarence on a lead.

'Why's there a dog?' Matt asks.

I don't reply, because Clarence has spotted me and he's gone *beserk*. His whole body is wriggling, bouncing on the end of the lead. As soon as he's close enough he leaps for me, paws scrabbling all over my coat.

'Hi!' I say, feeling ridiculous tears building. He's just *so* happy to see me, and I'd thought he wouldn't even remember me. 'Hey, bud.' I lean down to pick him up.

'Oh, he's quite muddy—' Graham begins. 'Oh, OK, you're just going to . . . OK.'

I hug Clarence close to me, standing to my full height. 'Thanks for bringing him,' I say. The little dog is trying to burrow into my armpit. Beside Graham, two girls a few years younger than me, who I assume are his daughters, are watching with undisguised devastation.

'Let me just go and grab his bed and food and things,' Graham says. 'Back in a tick.'

'Bed and food and things?' Matt repeats.

'I'll put lots of pictures of him on Instagram,' I say to the girls. 'Sorry that you can't keep him. But, lots of pictures. I promise. Hashtag, Clarence Fairweather.' One of them smiles, then tries to hide it. 'Want to say goodbye to him?' I shift him in my arms and move closer.

'Goodbye to him?' Matt's voice has got a little louder.

It's not until we're back in his car, Clarence on my lap, and all of his things on the back seat, that I finally answer him. 'So, yeah. I have a dog now. Isn't he adorable?'

Matt looks at him, unconvinced. 'He's got a really grumpy face.'

'Don't be harsh!' I cuddle Clarence to me. 'Don't listen to him, Clarence. He likes *cats*. What does he know?'

'Don't take this the wrong way,' Matt says. 'But do you know what you're doing? Have you had a dog before?'

'Not since I was a kid, but yeah, I do know what I'm doing. They were going to put him in kennels, and he has a phobia of kennels.'

'A phobia of kennels?'

'Yeah.'

Matt glances from me to Clarence. 'Isn't it hard work, looking after a dog?'

'Yes, sometimes. But it's worth it. Anyway, I love him. And look, he loves me, see?' Right on cue, Clarence licks my face. 'You'll learn to love him too. I know it.'

I realize too late that I shouldn't have used the word 'love'. For a moment, Matt looks pained, and he turns away from me to look out his window.

We're both quiet for a while, listening to the rain on the roof. Clarence settles his little paws against my knees, watching it with us.

'Thanks for coming today,' I say. I want to tell Matt how much it means to me, but the words sound stilted even in my own head. So does *I really appreciate it*. And *I'm very grateful*. Adult words I haven't grown into yet. 'You're kind of great.'

He smiles then, but it's small. 'Thanks.'

Sitting there in the car with him, the rain beating down on the roof, I realize two things. One, I *am* in love with him. And two, it's not enough.

I watch his face as he glances at me to smile before sliding the key into the ignition and starting the car. This surprising, gentle, kind boy – more of a man, really – who is patient with me, who'd look after me. Who would love me. None of this was supposed to happen. We were meant to be safe with each other.

I want to be able to say, *Yes! Let's give it a go. Let's take a chance on love.* Because this is it, isn't it? This is the point when I'm meant to change my mind. I'm meant to let love in, or something. Open up, let down my walls.

But I can't. Part of me wants to – a *big* part of me wants to – but I know that I'm not ready. It's not a line, or an excuse, or a defence mechanism. It's knowing myself and trusting myself. I'm not ready. All of this time with Matt, who is so perfect for me, has been proof. Tiny acts of self-sabotage, the way I've held myself back.

Maybe he really is ready, I don't know. I *can't* know. But I do know that we'll hurt each other. I'll hurt him or he'll hurt me, and I honestly don't know which would be worse. Either way, I wouldn't be able to take it. Not now, while I'm as fragile as I am. Maybe one day I'll be strong enough to take it, or at least the risk of it, like so many other people seem to be able to do. But not now. Just . . . not now.

'Straight home?' Matt asks me.

'Yeah,' I say. 'But maybe we can go for a walk or something? With Clarence?'

He glances at me again, like he can see inside my head. 'Sure,' he says.

When we get back to Ventrella Road, Clarence stops at Dilys's old front door and looks at me expectantly.

'Oh God,' I say. 'My heart can't take this.'

'Didn't you explain it to him?' Matt asks.

'Clearly not well enough,' I reply, sticking out my tongue.

Matt squats. 'Mate,' he says to Clarence, very seriously. 'Dilys has died. That means she's not around right now to take care of you. But you'll see her again one day. In the meantime, Suze is going to take care of you. Isn't that great?' He points at me, and Clarence turns his head to look at me, as if he understands. 'You can look after each other.'

OK, yeah. I definitely do love him.

'Come on, bud,' I say, picking up Clarence. 'It's this way. Brand new home for you.'

It takes me a while to get sorted enough to leave the bedsit, because I take my time looking through the box of Clarence's stuff, carrying him around so he can sniff everything. Matt is patient and quiet, leaning against the wall by the door, watching us.

'Ready?' is all he says, when I'm finally clipping the lead on to Clarence's collar.

'Ready,' I say.

The rain has stopped and the air feels fresh when we walk outside and head towards Preston Park together, Clarence's little paws light against the concrete. Every now and then he looks up at me, like he's checking I'm still there.

'So, why dogs?' Matt asks when we reach the park.

'Why *not* dogs?' I reply.

'Cats are independent,' he says. 'I respect that.'

I shake my head. 'Dogs love you unconditionally,' I say. 'They give so much and expect so little back. They're like the opposite of people. How can you not love that? Doesn't it make you want to make the entire world better for them? Dogs are too good for us. We don't deserve them.'

Matt smiles a little, and I expect him to disagree with me. But all he says is, 'That's fair.'

'Dogs are proven to help things like anxiety and depression, too,' I say.

'Cats also do that,' Matt says.

'I'm not actually *anti*-cats,' I say, laughing. 'I'm just very pro-dog, that's all. Oh, damn, I should've brought a ball or something.'

'Hey,' Matt says, soft, and I turn to him. 'What did you actually want to talk about?'

I try to smile, but it falters on my face. 'Hard stuff.'

'Ah,' he says. He looks down and scuffs the concrete with his foot, like a little boy. 'I thought so.'

I take a deep breath. This is going to hurt. 'I'm really sorry about how I reacted when you said . . . what you said. After Kel's, I mean.'

His mouth quirks up. 'Yeah, I remember what I said.'

'Yeah. That. It wasn't OK, the things I said. It was so not OK. I'm not going to try and make excuses for it. But that's part of the problem, you know? It's part of why I can't say yes to you.'

He frowns a little. 'What is?'

'Me. Not being able to handle things very well. Being the kind of fragile that goes off sometimes and hurts other people.'

'Being in pain isn't a reason to not—'

'I know,' I interrupt. 'I do know that. But for me, right now, it is. I'm still recovering from a lot of bad shit. I'm still learning who I am and what I want. I don't have the space in my head to be . . .' I try and think of the right word. 'Unselfish? Does that make sense? I think I've got to put myself first for a while, for good and bad. I'm still getting myself together. I'm just not . . . I'm just not *ready* yet. And that's nothing to do with you. If I was going to want someone, it would be you, of course it would be you, every time.' The words are starting to tumble out too fast, my breath quickening, trying to make sense out of the confusion in my head and my heart. 'You know that, right?'

He hesitates, then nods. 'I want to make you happy,' he says. 'I want to be the one who makes it right.'

'You can't,' I say. 'And that's a terrible foundation for a relationship, anyway.'

'I know,' he says. 'But I want it anyway.'

I can't help smiling. 'You're soft.'

'For you,' he says. 'Only for you. You know, before we met, Kel said that I'd love you. That's what he said.'

'He didn't mean actually *love*.'

'So what? What's the difference, really? He was right either way.' He takes a deep breath in and looks away. 'It kind of hurts a bit.'

'I'm sorry.' I really am. 'I'd say yes if I could.'

He smiles, still looking slightly away from me.

'Are you going to all-or-nothing me?' I ask. I mean it to be light-hearted, but I know it's not. The idea of losing him from my life is painful; actually painful.

He shakes his head, turning back to me. Simply, he says, 'No.'

I hold out my hand and he takes it slowly, eyes on mine. 'I'm not . . . I'm not saying no.' I look at him, scanning his face for understanding. 'It's just not a yes.' I hesitate, then add, cautiously, 'Yet.'

A smile blooms on his face, soft and warm.

'Not that I'm asking you to wait,' I add quickly. 'Don't think you're waiting or anything. That would be crap.'

'It's OK,' he says. 'I get it. Friends. Right?'

Relief settles in my chest and I let out a breath. 'Definitely friends.'

He nods. 'Just friends.'

'There's no *just* about that,' I say. 'My friends are everything. They're my whole life.' I give his hand a squeeze, and he squeezes back.

'OK,' he says.

'OK?' I ask. 'We're all good?'

Matt lets go of my hand and puts an arm around me, pulling me in. He drops a kiss on top of my hair, rests his head against mine for just a second. 'We're all good,' he says.

36

'Always Gold'
Radical Face

On our first night together, Clarence ignores his bed and sits patiently beside mine instead, eyes fixed on me in the dark, waiting until I give in and let him jump up. I tell myself that it's just for tonight, a one-off before he gets settled in, but it happens again the next night. And the night after that.

I'm not sorry, though. Having Clarence in my life is even more joyful than I'd hoped, especially considering there's precious little joy to be found elsewhere. I'm still sad about Dilys – I keep feeling like I'm forgetting something, then remembering that I've got no reason to go the care home any more. Matt and I are back to sharing messages back and forth every day, but we haven't found a rhythm yet in our post-I-love-you, let's-be-friends space. I'm nervous to say the wrong thing, and I can tell he is, too. I know we just have to wait this awkward stage out, and that it'll be worth it in the end, but still. I haven't spoken properly to Brian for almost a month, which is by far the longest we've ever gone without a real conversation, including the times I've been hospitalized. I've stopped trying to pester Caddy into talking to me again, leaving her with a final **I can wait. Just message me when you're ready xx**, that she ignored, as she'd ignored all my other messages. I still feel sick with worry that Rosie's wrong, that this won't blow over and she won't ever forgive me. I hate that all I can do is wait.

And in the midst of all this human-related emotional confusion there's Clarence, licking my face in the mornings, skittering around the floor in excited little bounces when I'm getting ready to take him for a walk, wagging his tail at me when I say his name. He loves me, this dog. He doesn't care about my past screw-ups or the likelihood that I will screw up again.

It's not easy, though. I don't regret it for a second, but taking on Clarence has been harder than I'd expected. For one thing, the cost of his pet insurance is a shock, but even thinking about cancelling it makes me feel sick with guilt. The main thing, though, is work. I'd assumed – stupidly, it turns out – that I'd be able to take Clarence to Madeline's with me, because it's a dog-friendly coffee shop. But apparently that only applies to customers.

'I'm sure he's lovely,' Tracey said, looking like she's not sure about this at all. 'But what were you thinking, that he'd just sit in the staff room for eight hours?'

'Minus the half an hour during my break,' I said.

'I admire your hustle, Suze,' Tracey said drily. 'But no. He can stay here today, but that's it. You're going to have to find a dog-sitter.'

Dog-sitters cost money, though. Doesn't everything? I find a short-term solution in the form of Kel, who offers to look after him for my next couple of shifts while I figure it out, but I'm starting to feel the pressure. I put a note on the noticeboard in the lobby of my building, asking if anyone would be interested in looking after a dog a few hours a week, but the days pass and no one responds.

I've had Clarence for just a week when the buzzer jolts me awake on the only morning I'd planned to sleep in. I sit straight up, blinking, confused. I consider ignoring it, but it's a good thing I don't because it turns out to be Karl from the letting agents.

'Aren't you supposed to let me know when you're going to visit?' I ask when I let him in. I haven't even brushed my hair.

'Yes,' Karl says, in the kind of patient voice professionals use when they want you to know you're annoying them. 'Which is why we did. We sent you a letter last week reminding you that we'd be visiting. It's not an inspection per se, but we do like to check in after six months or so – this is quite overdue – to make sure everything's going fine.'

'Well, it is,' I say. 'Thanks.'

I expect him to start asking me questions or something, but he's gone quiet, his eyes on me. He's looking at me like I've just started tap dancing in the middle of the room. I look back, confused, waiting for him to say whatever it is that he's thinking.

'Is that *your* dog?' he asks eventually.

'Yeah,' I say. 'He's new. His name is Clarence.'

'And he lives here? With you?'

I nod. 'He doesn't take up much space.'

Karl puts his fingers to his forehead, closing his eyes for a moment. 'Right. Do you remember that contract you signed?'

'Yeah?'

'The tenancy agreement?' He drops his hand and looks at me. 'The one that stipulated . . . no pets?'

'Oh, that,' I say, trying to smile even as my heart sinks. 'I sort of forgot about that.' I lean over and scoop up Clarence into my arms, holding him close. 'He's just a little dog. He's really good, honest.'

Karl lets out a sharp sigh. 'Having a dog in this flat is a breach of contract. A very serious breach of contract.'

'His owner died,' I say. 'And they were going to put him in the kennels. You're not going to make me get rid of him, are you?'

'Miss Watts,' he says. 'Do you understand what I'm saying when I tell you that this is a breach of contract? What the repercussions are?'

'Are you going to fine me?'

He blinks at me. 'It's grounds for eviction.'

All the breath leaves my body in one loud choke of shock. '*What?*'

'Contracts exist for a reason. Breaching them is very serious.'

Unbelievably, he looks impatient, like I'm wasting his time. Like he's not standing in my flat, telling me that he's about to make me homeless. 'With all due respect, I shouldn't have to explain this to you. This shouldn't be a surprise. You haven't even tried to hide the evidence.'

'You can't throw me out for one tiny thing. And not trying to hide evidence is good, right?'

'The *contract* –' he emphasizes the word as patronizingly as possible – 'is there to protect not just you as the tenant, but your landlord as well. As letting agent, we act on behalf of each of you. I have to report this, and if your landlord chooses to evict you, he'll be within his rights to do so.'

'You don't have to report anything,' I say. 'Not really. The landlord literally never visits. I've never met him. And Clarence doesn't make any mess. He doesn't bark too much or scratch up the carpet. What's the problem?'

Karl has started pushing his notepad into his bag, clearly preparing to leave. *Oh God.*

'Please,' I say, switching gears, letting the panic that's been rising inside me spill into my voice. 'I'm sorry. I didn't realize. Please don't . . . tell on me, or whatever. Please? I'm nineteen, OK? I don't have anywhere to go. I don't have a home or anything. Can't you just let it go?'

Karl looks at me for a long moment. Me, still wearing the clothes I slept in, my rule-breaking dog in my arms. He's a person, isn't he? Maybe he has a little sister. Or a daughter. He says, 'Have you been smoking in here?'

And that's when I know that I've lost.

There was a time when I would have called Brian immediately, the first responder in my general wreck of a life. But that doesn't feel like an option any more, which is weird and painful. What role is there for him in my life if I can't trust him? *Oh God, don't think about that now. Think about the fact that you're going to be evicted.*

Evicted. Such a scary, unforgiving word. Being thrown out of my flat because I can't follow simple instructions. I glance down at Clarence and he shifts in my lap, letting out a gravelly sigh. I did it for him, not for me. Doesn't that count for anything?

Fix this. I need to fix this. I need to ask for help. Burrowing myself in my bedsit and hiding from the world won't solve this. OK, I can't talk to Brian, but he's not the only one who cares about me. I don't want to talk to Sarah yet, not while I'm still panicking, because I'll just worry her. Instead, I let out a long, slow, steadying breath and open the WhatsApp group I share with Rosie and Caddy, which has been completely silent since their disastrous trip.

I hesitate, looking at the screen, trying to swallow my usual instinct to shut down and keep everything from them. I type, **Listen, I know you're both still mad at me.** I send before I can talk myself out of it and begin typing the rest of whatever I'm trying to say, but before I can finish, a response arrives.

Rosie:

Excuse me.

I stop, my heart rate jacking up. Oh God, what's she going to say? Is she going to tell me to shut up?

Rosie:

I'm not mad at you. That's Caddy. Obvs.
Don't tar me with the grumpy brush.

I laugh, the sound loud and unexpected in my empty bedsit. Thank God for Rosie. Thank *God* for Rosie.

Me:

I'm in crisis.

Rosie:

Scale of 1–10?

10. Not joking. I need help.

I'm here. What do you need?

I'm getting thrown out of my flat. I have nowhere to live.

Holy fuck! Are you joking?

No.

Why???? They can't do that?!

So, kind of a long story, but I have a dog and apparently I'm not allowed to have a dog?

. . . why do you have a dog???

Long story. Later?

OK fine, priorities. They can't make you homeless!

They really can.

What are you going to do?

Me:

I have no clue. I'm seriously panicking.
Roz, what the fuck am I going to do?

Rosie:

Don't panic. This is fixable, OK? What are your options?

I don't have any!

You're being dramatic. Calm down. You obviously
do have options. Look, I've got a lecture in ten minutes.
It's about an hour. Go and get some tea or something
and play with that random dog you apparently now own.
I'll call you after, OK?

OK xxx

Chin up, chuck. X

I take her advice and drink a cup of tea sitting on my bed, Clarence curled up in my lap, his head on my knee. When I touch his head, he lets out a soft, contented, growly noise. I look around my bedsit, this place I've hated the whole time I've been in it, and try not to panic all over again.

For the next hour, I make phone call after phone call. I call a charity for care leavers, a housing charity, Citizens Advice. They all tell me pretty much the same thing, which is, yes, they're within their rights to evict you, but here are your likely options. I call the housing team at the council and hear the same thing again. Basically, I'll be put on a waiting list for another property that fits my needs, and in the meantime I'd be given some form of temporary accommodation.

'What about Clarence?' I ask every single one. 'Can I keep him?'

And they all say, 'No.'

I've just bitten down on to my nail so hard it's split halfway down, so surprisingly painful it made me yelp, when the letting agent rings. It's not Karl but a woman I've never spoken to before, confirming that I'm going to be served a notice for eviction, and that I have to be out of the property in two weeks. I cry down the phone because I'm too scared to pretend. I tell her I've got nowhere to go, that I was abused, that I'm on medication.

'Well,' she says. 'Everyone's got something.'

Finally, I call Miriam. She's calm, which calms me down, talking about contracts and contingencies. For once, it helps to think that this problem is part of her job. She's literally trained to deal with things like this, people like me, in tears on the other end of the line. She tells me to meet her tomorrow afternoon to talk it all through.

When I hang up, I look at my phone and see a stream of messages from Rosie and Caddy – *Caddy!* – and a voicemail each.

Rosie: Hey! Is your phone not connecting because you're talking to someone else? You haven't turned your phone off, have you? I will be VERY CROSS if you've done that. OK, so, anyway. I've spoken to my mum and she says that, yes, they can evict you for breach of contract, but you may be able to plead your case if you get rid of the dog. But you're not going to get rid of the dog, are you, Suze? I know you. Actually, what I was thinking is, you hate that flat, right? Maybe this will be a good thing in the long run? It's not good for you to be living on your own somewhere you hate. Do you know how much I worry about you? Shit, that sounds soppy. Forget that bit. I don't ever worry. Anyway. So, Mum said that there's plenty of room for you at our house. You can stay in my room while I'm at uni. Don't think it's an intrusion or anything. I actually think it'll make Mum really happy to have someone to make breakfast for again. I know it's not a long-term solution, but at least you won't be homeless, right? Call me back and let me know what you think. And the other thing is, what about Sarah? Have you thought about living with Sarah? Hasn't she always said there's a room for you? OK, sorry for rambling. Call me back. Love you.

Caddy: Suze! What the hell? They can't just chuck you out. They can't. I tried to call my dad, but he's bloody golfing, so I won't be able to talk to him until later. But he'll know what to do. Don't worry, OK? No way are we going to let you be homeless. Obviously. I've talked to Tarin and she says you can sleep on the sofa in her flat any time you want. She says you can go there, like, right now, if you want. And I spoke to Kel, and he said the same. About his sofa, I mean. And we . . . Oh God. Sorry. I'm fine. It was the first time I've spoken to him and . . . Sorry. I can't believe I managed a whole conversation with him without crying, and now one voicemail to you and I'm losing it. I'll call you back, OK? Sorry. And, God, I don't hate you, Suze. I love you. God, sorry. Bye.

I call Caddy back immediately and she picks up on the third ring. 'Suze!'

'I love you!' I burst out. 'I love you. Hi.'

'Have you got it sorted? Are you OK?'

'No, I'm totally being evicted. Officially. How are you?'

'Oh my God, what are you going to do?'

'I don't know yet. Cads! I've missed you so much.'

'OK.'

'I'm so glad you're not mad at me any more.'

Her laugh is short. 'I am still mad at you. I said that I don't hate you, which I don't. And I love you, which I do. But I'm proper mad at you.'

'Oh.'

'Suze, I don't want you to be homeless, OK? Priorities.'

Tears are starting to collect in my eyes again, heavy and hot. 'You're my priority.'

'Oh, Suze. Come on, this is important.'

'You're important.'

'Suze!' Three Suzes in a row. She must be mad. 'Stop it. I don't want to go into this now, OK? I don't want to fight with you. I just want to get this sorted out and go back to being mad for a while.'

'Can't we talk it over?' I ask. 'Please?'

'I'm seriously going to hang up on you if you don't let this go. You know I hate arguing. Why are you pushing this?'

'Because I don't want you to hate me.'

'Suze!' She practically shouts this down the phone. 'For fuck's actual sake.' OK, yeah. She really is mad. 'I don't hate you. You know I don't hate you. You did something that you knew would upset me and I got upset. And now you're playing your Suze card to guilt me into not being angry. That's not OK.'

'What's a Suze card?'

'Don't make me say it.'

'Say it.'

'Suze.'

'Say it.'

'Fine. *Fine*. You want me to say it? Fine. Sometimes, when you know you're in the wrong, you switch into victim mode. I'm sorry, but you do. *Oh, you hate me,* when you *know* I don't hate you, but that I'll feel bad because I know that you have an actual complex about people hating you. So it makes me feel like I can't feel actual legitimate emotions. It's like, however bad I feel, you'll always have felt worse at some point, so that trumps everything. Even when you've been a total bitch.' She's crying now. 'And now you've pushed me into saying all these horrible things to you, and Suze, you know what I'm thinking? I'm thinking, oh God, she's not going to be able to handle this, she's going to spiral, she's going to do something stupid, and it's going to be my fault. Do you know how impossible this is? I love you. But you make it so hard.'

My head says, *Oh, I'm so sorry my trauma occasionally makes your perfect life a little bit harder.* My head says, *I'm going to be homeless but I'm supposed to care about your hurt feelings?* My head says, *Grow up.* My head says, *It was just a kiss, for God's sake.* My head says, *Stop being such a baby. Why are you always such a baby?*

I say, 'I'm sorry.'

I hear the hitch of her breath down the phone, and I know she's crying again. 'Oh, Suze,' she says. I hear it all in those two words. The frustration and the love, all mixed in together. I'm hard work, I know I am. But somehow, she loves me anyway.

I let her cry for a while, the two of us quiet on each end of the phone. I'm thinking about those first few months of our friendship, how she used to look at me when I was shiny and exciting, before she saw the cracks. And then, later, when she saw through them. No one had ever looked at me like Caddy did, and it mattered in a way that I could never articulate, even in therapy, when I tried. Let me tell you, anyone who thinks romantic love is the pinnacle of human emotion has never had a friend who looked at them like she looked at me. Love might burn the brightest fires, but fires burn out. Friendship is warm and steady; constant. It keeps me alive.

After a while, she says, 'Suze?'

'Yeah?'

'I slept with Owen.'

I actually put my hand over my mouth to stop myself shrieking into the phone. This is not a shrieking moment. I know this instinctively anyway, but then she starts crying again, and my heart breaks for my sweet, naive friend. 'Oh, Cads,' I say. 'Don't cry. It's OK.'

'It's not,' she says. There's a sniffle, a pause, and then her voice again. 'It wasn't worth it. It completely wasn't worth it.'

'What wasn't?' I ask. Does she mean just the sex? Breaking up with Kel? Fighting with me?

'Losing Kel,' she says.

'Cads,' I say again. 'You didn't end the relationship because you had a crush on a guy. You ended it because you weren't happy.' It's both true and not true, but that's OK. Sometimes that's what being a friend is: choosing the truth they need to hear.

'I feel like I cheated on him,' she says.

'*Did* you?' I ask.

'No.' There's another pause. 'I wanted to, though. I know that's terrible. I know it makes me a bad person.'

'It doesn't,' I say. 'It really doesn't.' She lets out a quiet, high-pitched hiccup. 'Listen, I know about being a bad person, right? You're not a bad person.'

'Neither are you,' she says, her voice tearful again. 'Suze, I'm so sorry I yelled at you. And then ignored you. I just . . .'

'It's OK.'

'It's not. I miss you. I've missed you since you left. Even since you came back, I've still missed you. I know that sounds crazy. I can't even explain it.'

'You don't have to explain it,' I say. 'I've missed you too. Cads, I'm sorry I'm not always the friend you need me to be. I really am trying. I just . . . I find life really hard. A lot of the time, it's just really hard, and sometimes trying isn't enough, and I fuck up, or I know I'm going to fuck up, so I turn off my phone. Does that make sense? I know it doesn't, or at least it won't to you. But my life and yours are different, Cads. It's not just that you're at uni. It's everything.' I swallow hard, trying to keep my voice steady. 'We react to things differently. We need different things. And I think I always knew that, but maybe you didn't, and this year you've realized?'

'I've always known that, Suze,' she says. 'I think this year *you've* realized. I know you find life hard, but you have to let me in sometimes to help. Me *and* Roz. You have to let us help you.'

'I am,' I say. 'This is what this is. See? I'm trying.'

We're both quiet again for a while. Eventually, she says, 'Roz told me about Matt.'

'I guessed she would.'

'Are you OK?'

'Yeah. What about you? How are you feeling about Kel?'

'Sad. Lots of regret. I'm hoping we can be friends, but I don't know, maybe that's naive. We'll see.' She lets out a small laugh. 'God, there's so much I want to talk to you about. Matt stuff and Kel stuff, and why you have a dog, and . . . Oh, hey, Tess likes you now.'

I can't help the laugh that bursts out of me. 'Does she?'

'Yeah. The word she used is "baller". She says she's never seen anyone do anything so selflessly stupid. I was like, that's Suze.'

I laugh harder. 'That is me.'

'It is! She's been on at me to make up with you since Brighton. But I just . . . I don't know, I needed to be mad for a while. For a whole bunch of reasons.'

'It's OK. I get it. Really.'

She sighs. '*So* much to talk about. Want to come visit? I

promise I won't be weird this time.'

I smile at the wall, feeling my eyebrows lift even though there's no one to see. I want to ask her to elaborate, but there's no point. I know what she means. 'Let me sort out my living situation first, then I'll think about visiting.'

'Oh shit, sorry! I forgot! What are you going to do? Do you want to go stay with Tarin? She really wouldn't mind. You know she loves you.'

'I'm still figuring it out,' I say. 'I've got a couple of weeks. Honestly, though, Cads, I care way more about you and me than where I'm living.'

'I know,' she says drily. 'That's why I worry.'

37

'No Wrong Way Home'
Alexis Harte

I call in sick to work the next day, because there's too much going on in my head to shut out for eight hours. Instead, I spend what feels like hours online, scrolling through Gumtree and SpareRoom, going over and over my budget, trying to make the sums work. My eyes are starting to hurt when my phone rings, and it's Matt.

'Listen.' His voice is quick, breathless. 'One of my housemates is moving out.'

'What?'

'Lars. He's got offered a job in Bristol so he's leaving in about a week. His room is going up for rent. It's a double room, seven hundred pounds a month plus bills. I know it's pricey compared to where you are now, but you'd earn more living in London. I can get you a job at the bar if you needed something straight away. It pays well. What do you think?'

I'm clutching my phone to my ear. 'Matt, I can't just—'

'This is a friend helping out a friend,' he says. 'Honest. I'm not . . . asking for anything.' He groans. 'That makes it sound like I am. But I'm really not. It just seems like incredible timing. You'd love London, Suze. The city was basically made for you.'

'I . . .' I begin. 'Wow.'

'Think about it,' he says.

I *am* thinking about it. And I know exactly what would happen if Matt and I were living in the same house.

Would that be such a bad thing? a small voice asks.

Yes. I made a choice, didn't I? I'm not ready for a relationship.

And if I'm not ready for that, I'm definitely not ready for a probably-not-a-good-idea-but-let's-be-friends-with-benefits-anyway complicated living arrangement. I'd love to live with Matt, that's the truth. We could talk about music, and he could teach me to get better at the guitar, and we'd go to gigs together and just . . . hang out, like all the great times we have done over the last few months. But that doesn't mean it's a good idea. I'm not exactly known for my self-control, and it doesn't seem like he is, either.

'You know it's a bad idea,' I say.

'I know why it *sounds* like one,' he says. 'But I would never have suggested it if you hadn't just been made homeless. I'm trying to help.'

'I know,' I say. 'Thank you.'

It would be so, so easy to say yes. He could take care of me; there could be a whole new life waiting for me in London. Another new city to start again in, another new address, yet another version of myself, of my life. It could be really great. It could be everything I ever wanted.

'Suze?' he says.

'Yeah?'

'You're going to say no, aren't you?'

'Yeah.'

He sighs down the phone. 'Damn, are you going to make a habit of rejecting me?'

I feel the grin on my face. 'Looks like it, yeah. Listen, it's not that I don't want to. It's just really not a good idea.'

'But where are you going to live?'

'I'll figure it out,' I say. 'Don't worry about me.'

'Little bit late,' he says. 'Let me know what you decide, OK? And obviously just tell me if you change your mind.'

'Thanks,' I say. 'I better go.' I almost – *almost* – say 'Love you', like I would if it was Caddy or Rosie, but I catch myself just in time. 'See you,' I say instead.

I try to go back to my search online, but my brain is too frazzled. I look at the list I'd been writing of my options and I know – I just know, all of a sudden – that they're all the wrong ones.

I need to get out of this bedsit.

'Walk?' I say to Clarence, animating my voice, and he leaps up, tail wagging. 'Come on, then.'

It's a great excuse to go outside, having a dog. The two of us head to Preston Park first, walking the perimeter and then looping back through the middle. After, I'm still thinking, not quite ready to go home, so I take him through the city towards the seafront. Brighton is as busy and alive as it always is, almost buzzing with it. As I walk through the main city centre I scoop up Clarence into my arms so he doesn't get stepped on, pausing on the way to watch a street artist chalking patterns over the concrete.

I love this city. I love its vibrancy and colour. I love how I feel like I belong here, that it contains some of my best memories as well as my worst ones. Coming to Brighton when I was fifteen had changed everything about my life. It had given me the freedom I'd always needed, and the kind of people I'd always wanted. Maybe it had taken me a long time to realize all of that. Maybe I had to leave to know I could come back. But Brighton is home. I don't need another fresh start; I want to make it work *here*.

Muddles, the cafe Sarah owns, isn't that busy when I walk in. Sarah is ringing up a customer's order, nodding, smiling. Holding Clarence to my chest, I wait for her to see me.

'Hello,' Sarah says, beaming, when the customer takes her tray and goes to sit down. 'Was I expecting you?'

'Nope,' I say. 'Hi! I need to talk to you.'

'OK,' she says, glancing at the clock. 'Well, I'd say come around here and we can chat, but I can't have a dog behind the counter. Health and Safety.'

'Maybe I can come to yours later?'

She nods, curious. 'What's this about?'

'Stuff,' I say. I'm tempted to say 'I got evicted!' and then just leg it out of there, but the fall-out later probably wouldn't be worth it, however funny it would be for me. 'I'll come round at about seven?'

When I get back to Ventrella Road, I take a second to check my mailbox, even though there's never anything in it. I let Clarence off the lead but he just sits at my feet, looking up at me. Sure enough, my mailbox is empty, and I'm about to head up the stairs when the door to Dilys's flat opens and Clarence goes berserk. He bounds inside like it's the gates to dog heaven.

'Oh God,' I say, lunging after him. 'Sorry.'

The woman, who must be about Sarah's age, is standing in bewildered silence in her doorway, watching as I sink to my knees and pat my thighs, calling, 'Clarence! Here, boy,' like a dog owner from a children's TV show. I never say, 'Here, boy.' But he comes anyway, thank God.

'Sorry,' I say again, scooping him up as I stand. 'He used to live here, so he got confused.'

'I see,' the woman says. She doesn't seem very friendly. She squints at me. 'What's your name?'

'Suzanne,' I say, automatic but cautious.

'Oh!' Her face lights up and she points at me as if I should know why. 'I have something for you.'

'Excuse me?'

The woman heads over to her kitchen counter and picks up a parcel. 'This arrived the other day, but I didn't know who Suzanne was, so I didn't know what to do with it. I was going to return it. Here you go.' She hands it to me, her smile a little warmer now. The package is addressed to 'Suzanne, c/o Flat 1' in thick black marker pen. No Watts, just my first name.

'Thanks,' I say.

I don't open it until I get upstairs. Clarence has deflated since he was removed so unceremoniously from his former home, and he's just sitting in my lap, head on my knee. Every now and then, he sighs.

'Cheer up,' I murmur, stroking his ears between my fingers with one hand and peeling back the parcel flap with the other. I'm not sure exactly what I'm expecting, and I'm trying not to get my hopes up, but when the first item slips out on to my bed, my heart leaps.

The Little Prince. The same copy I'd taken to read to Dilys, my hospital-receipt bookmark still in place. I reach into the package and pull out the rest of the contents in one impatient sweep.

Photos of Clarence. 'Half tiger, half poet' on a Post-it note. The lyrics to 'Blackbird'. A pouch of dried lavender. A note:

> Suzanne,
> It seemed wrong to throw these things away, so I am returning them to you with thanks. Apologies for not passing them and the letter on to you at the funeral – I had so much to deal with at the time and I hadn't yet sorted through her trinkets from the home. Give me a call when you've made a decision about the piano. All the best to you and Clarence.
> Graham

Letter? Piano?!

I shove my hand back into the parcel bag, but it's empty. No letter. 'Find the letter, Clarence,' I say as he sniffs cautiously at the lavender.

I pick up *The Little Prince*, open the front cover and there it is, carefully folded, waiting for me. I'm expecting to see her handwriting when I open it, but the letter is typed, which I realize makes sense. Dilys couldn't handwrite anything after she was first taken to hospital. I wonder who helped her write a letter like this. Who printed it off. Marcus, I think. It had to have been Marcus. Does this mean she knew she was dying? Do people feel it coming? It doesn't matter. All that matters is that she has written a letter for me.

I'm stalling, because I know that this moment, the last time I will ever not know what Dilys's last message to me was, is precious. I squeeze the lavender pouch in my hand and let my eyes focus on the words.

To my dear Suzanne,

What a sincere pleasure it has been getting to know you these past few months. It has meant more to me than I think you realize.

It is my dearest wish for you that one day, when you are old and withered and cranky, you will meet a young woman with a good heart and fire in her soul who will sit with you and share stories. Perhaps she will play music for you. And then you will know what you have done for me.

My dear, you are a beautiful person with courage and strength. You are going to be a light in the world, and you are going to mean so much to the people you let into your heart. Keep it open for them. They need you.

I want you to understand that the people who have failed to love you simply do not know you. That is not your fault. And I want you to also understand that you owe these people nothing. Not your time, not your love, not your forgiveness. This is your only life, and it is short. Surround yourself with people who love you.

It has been an honour and a joy to share music with you. How I wish I could teach you the piano. Instead, please accept my old piano, which I am gifting to you. It is currently in storage, waiting for you. If you'd prefer to sell it rather than try to find somewhere to keep it, please do so with no anxiety or guilt. I ask only that if you do choose this route, you spend the money on something wonderful.

I wish I could have spoken more with you. I had so much I would have liked to say. My hope is that these words are the right ones, set down on paper for you that you may hold them in your hand and keep them forever.

With love,
Dilys

38

'Almost Home'
Keston Cobblers Club

When I go to Sarah's later that evening, I'm calm. It's probably a weird reaction to everything that's going on, but it's true. After an afternoon spent researching, making notes, making plans, I'd met with Miriam and we'd ended up having a kind of unscheduled pathway plan review. I'd thought things had fallen apart, but they haven't. I actually think they might have fallen together.

I have Clarence in my arms when Sarah answers the door and her smile — instantly wide at the sight of me — falters. 'Is that *your* dog? I thought you were just walking it earlier.'

'He,' I correct cheerfully. 'This is Clarence. I took him in after Dilys died.'

Sarah blinks at me, looking dubiously down at Clarence when I settle him down on the floor. 'Far be it from me to question you, Suzie,' she says. 'But can you look after a dog?'

'Yep,' I say. Henry Gale saunters down the hall, sees Clarence, and freezes. 'Uh, is Henry all right with dogs?'

'We'll see, shall we?' Sarah says.

Henry's tail twitches, his back arching. Clarence is just standing there, head slightly cocked, curious but unbothered. Henry lets out a low, grumpy yowl, turns on his heel and walks back towards the living room, tail flicking in haughty annoyance.

'Good boy,' I say, leaning to scratch Clarence's ears. 'OK, so. I've got some news, and it's not great, and you're not going to like it.'

'Oh, no,' Sarah says. She tries to smile, but I can see how worried she is. Which makes sense, considering how much bad news I've inflicted on her over the last four years. Detentions, suspensions, police visits . . . God only knows what she's imagining now.

'Yeah,' I say. 'We should probably sit down.'

We go into the kitchen and I slide on to one of the stools while she makes tea. I watch, chin on my hand, until she puts two cups on to the table in front of us both. 'OK,' she says. 'I'm ready.'

I decide to just say it. 'I'm getting evicted.'

Sarah closes her eyes, pressing her lips together.

'It's because of Clarence,' I add. 'I'm not allowed pets in the bedsit; I didn't realize.'

She takes a deep breath, then opens her eyes. 'OK,' she says again. 'Let's talk through your options. Have you spoken to the council?'

'It's fine,' I say. 'I've already done all that. That's not why I'm here.'

She frowns a little. 'It's not?'

'No. I've talked to a bunch of people, and I've thought about it. My friend offered me a room in his house, and basically everyone I know had a sofa I could sleep on.' I feel an unexpected smile on my face. 'Turns out people really care, you know?'

She smiles back, cautious. 'Of course they do.'

'So anyway, yeah. Eviction. That's the bad news. I would have told you earlier, but I didn't want to worry you before I'd figured out what I was going to do.'

I can tell I've surprised her, but she's trying to hide it. 'And what are you going to do?'

'Well,' I say. 'That's why I'm here.' I take a deep breath in. 'Is the offer still open to come and live here?'

Sarah's whole face changes when I say these words. It lights up, like I flipped a switch. 'Oh, Suzie—'

'Let me just make my offer first,' I say quickly. 'I don't want to just live here. I want to pay you rent and contribute to the bills.

It's not like a looking-after thing. And sometimes you have to let me cook.'

She laughs tearfully, wiping her eyes with the pads of her thumbs. 'That's fair,' she says, nodding.

'I'll pay you the same amount as I paid at Ventrella Road. I'll be like your tenant.'

'Counter-offer,' Sarah says, putting her hand up. She's smiling so wide. 'You'll be like my *flatmate*, not my tenant. You can pay *half* of the amount you pay at Ventrella Road. The rest can go into a savings account.'

'Counter-counter-offer,' I say. 'The rest can go towards studying costs.'

She blinks. 'Studying?'

I nod. 'I'm going to do an Access course. A nursing one. And then, if I pass, I'm going to apply to Brighton uni to study Nursing properly.' I can tell she's too surprised to know how to respond, so I add, 'I have a five-year plan now.'

'When did you decide all this?'

'I've been thinking about it for a while, but then Ma— a friend of mine suggested coming to live in London, and I realized everything I want is here in Brighton. Including the nursing thing. I can do the Access course in Lewes; I looked it up. It's one year, like an equivalent to A levels, to get me good enough to go to uni.'

She's crying now. The embarrassing, proud kind of crying you get from someone who really loves you. 'Nursing.'

'Yeah. The nurses who looked after Dilys were amazing. And it made me think about the nurses who looked after me. Not just in hospital, but at Gwillim, too. If I'm going to do something with my life, that's what I want to do. Be good for people. Help them, like I was helped. If I can.' I hesitate, worried that she's so surprised because she thinks it's a bad idea. 'Don't you think I'd be a good nurse?'

She grabs my hand spontaneously and squeezes, choking out a noise I can't quite interpret, but it sounds happy. 'I think you'd make a wonderful nurse.' She wipes her eyes again. 'Oh, Suzie, I'm so—'

'There's one more thing, before we get to that,' I say. 'One more serious thing.'

As if following a command, Sarah releases my hand and nods, straightening her shoulders and looking attentively at me. 'Go on.'

'I think I want to stop seeing Mum.' I swallow. 'And Dad, too, obviously. I don't want them to be a part of my life any more. I need to have actual distance. I don't want to see them at all, I don't want to talk to them on the phone, I don't want them to know what I'm doing. Do you know what I mean? There's a word for it? It begins with e?'

'Emancipation?'

'No, that's when you're underage. I don't mean legally. *Estranged*. That's the E-word. I want that to be what it is. Dad said it in an email once, but he was just being sarky. I want it to be real. I want to be estranged. I don't want him to be *able* to email me any more. No calls from Mum. Nothing.'

She nods slowly. 'OK. I understand.'

'And Brian as well.'

At this, her eyes widen, even as I see her try to cover herself. 'You want to separate yourself from your brother as well?'

'No, I don't *want* to, but I feel like I have to. If I can't trust him not to just tell them things, then he has to be part of it, too.' I bite down on my lip to stop it quivering. 'They just . . . They all just pull me down. That's what it feels like. Every time I start thinking I can be better, or do more, something happens with one of them that makes me feel worthless again. I shouldn't have to feel that way, should I?'

She shakes her head. 'No, you shouldn't.'

'So you think it's a good idea?'

'I think if that's a step you want to take, then I'll support it. Would you like me to do the same?'

I hadn't even thought of that. The suggestion lands directly into my heart. 'You'd do that?'

'If it's what you want, yes.'

'But Mum's your sister.'

'And you −' she takes a hold of both my hands − 'are my niece. And my priority.'

I look at Sarah's kind, earnest face, and start to cry. Because despite everything, even though we're talking about me becoming estranged from my parents and brother, even though I'm being evicted, I feel suddenly *lucky*. Lucky to have an aunt who loves me, who makes me her priority, after everything we've been through together. Lucky that she hugs me when I start to cry, quietly and with no fuss.

When I'm done crying, we both laugh at nothing and then finish our tea. She boils the kettle for another and we decide that, no, she doesn't need to cut herself off from anyone. She can be the intermediary, talking to my parents on my behalf as necessary, sorting out any problems, making sure they're respecting my decision.

'What about the money?' she asks.

I take a breath in. 'I'm going to take it, if they agree with all of this. That they have to stay away from me, I mean. And I won't sue, obviously. It'll be, like, an exchange. Would you mind talking to them about it?' It seems like a lot to put on Sarah. 'Is that OK?'

She nods. 'Don't worry about that side of things.'

I will anyway. How could anyone not? But at the same time, I trust Sarah, so it's like a different kind of worry. The safe kind. I know she'll protect me from it, from them, as best as anyone can. I've never wanted anything more than that.

'How do you feel?' Sarah asks. She's watching me over the top of her mug, her smile warm and hopeful.

I think about it, searching myself for the honest answer. I think about Caddy crying down the phone, Rosie offering her own bedroom to me, Matt inviting me to London, the picture Kel sent of his sofa with the message 'All yours!'. Dilys. *Surround yourself with people who love you.*

I look around Sarah's kitchen and I think, *home.*

'I feel good,' I say.

Summer

'Here Comes the Sun'
The Beatles

The party was Sarah's idea. She'd called it a house-warming.

'One,' I said, 'you've lived here for over a decade. And two, I've lived here before. The house is already warm.'

'Fine, we'll have it later,' she said. 'A house-warming slash summer party. A barbecue!'

And now here we are. It's the last Saturday in June and the flat is full of people. Sarah's in the garden in charge of the barbecue, holding a pair of tongs like a weapon. She's made way too much food, but no one's complaining. She promised, when we started planning the party together, that she'd let me help with the food. Now the party's actually happening, and she still hasn't let me help with a single food-related thing except ice.

'Control freak,' I tease.

'Menace,' she replies. She drops a burger on to the plate I'm holding. 'Off with you.' She's beaming.

It's been good, living with Sarah again. I don't know if it's because I'm paying rent or just because I'm an adult now, but everything is different from when I lived here before. I don't have to sneak out when I want to leave, for one thing. I go out the front door, not the window. I spend a lot of my time outside the flat, either at work, the care home where I volunteer once a week, or with my friends, but when our time at home overlaps we usually sit in the living room together, making our way through the box set of this old American hospital show *ER*, which she bought when I submitted my application to the Access course for Nursing a couple of months ago.

'You can see what the nurses do. It's research!' she said.

'Fictional American nurses in the nineties,' I said. 'Useful!'

I sort of love it, though.

I take my plate of food over to one of the blankets, where Caddy and Rosie are playing with Clarence. When I sit down, he rolls on to his back beside me, paws kicking in the air. 'All right, you,' I say. 'Don't beg. It's below you.' Rosie hands over the glass she'd been holding for me and I take it, pausing to lift it into a toast. 'To us! Happy summer.'

'Yay summer,' Caddy says, smiling. They've only been back from university for a week, and summer feels like it's going to be endless, stretching out ahead of us. Next month the three of us are going on holiday together for the first time; nothing fancy, just a package holiday in Greece. I'd paid for my share with some of the money I'd got after selling Dilys's baby grand piano. The rest went on a digital piano small enough to fit in the living room, and a tattoo. Three different but wonderful things. I think Dilys would be pleased.

'Hey,' Matt says, kneeling down on to the blanket beside me. 'I found Henry Gale. He's hiding under the piano, and he won't come out.'

I lift up my sunglasses so he can get the full effect of the look I give him. 'You tried to drag him out, didn't you?'

'I just wanted to say hi!' he says. 'Is that so wrong?'

'You can say hi later, when it's quieter,' I say. 'He'll come out when there's less people around.'

'Fewer,' Matt says.

I flick his shoulder. 'Shut up.'

I don't know what was the biggest surprise to everyone else: the fact that Matt and I really are friends, or the fact that that's *all* we are. There have been no slip-ups, no mistakes. No benefits. Just him and me, spending as much time together as we can. I go up to London or he comes down to Brighton and we drive around for a while, listening to music. Last week we went to a gig together, just the two of us, with alcohol and everything. Of course we teased and flirted and held eye contact for longer than you might call strictly platonic – that's just how we are together – but we didn't kiss and we didn't end up in the same bed. How's that for self-control? I'm pretty proud of myself. I'm pretty proud of us both.

It was actually Matt who helped me pick out my tattoo and sat with me when I had it done. It hurt, but not as badly as everyone said it would.

'Are you sure you want to get your first one on your spine?' Kel had asked, face scrunched with second-hand anxicty. 'Don't you want to start somewhere . . . less bony?'

'Needs must,' I said. 'That's where I want it.'

The arrow, about the size of my index finger, points up near the top of my spine. I spent so long staring at the design that I know it by heart, even though it's on a piece of my body I can't see. Sometimes, when I have my low moments – God, I still get my low moments – I think of that arrow, pointing constantly, solidly up. Whatever is going on in my life, however close I get to rock bottom, whatever the situation, there's a part of me that will always bc looking up. It helps, somehow.

I got the tattoo three years to the day since my last suicide attempt. I didn't tell anyone the significance of the date, and if anyone figured it out, they didn't say so. As the needle seared against my skin, I closed my eyes and thought of all the days I'd had since then, the days I'd thought I hadn't wanted or deserved. Southampton and Christie and Don. Ventrella Road and Dilys. Clarence. Kel and his open house. Sarah. Seeing Caddy wearing a University of Warwick hoodie, her bright, coppery hair. Watching Rosie hold hands with Jade, her smile wide. Matt.

There have been so many times in my life that I'd thought I was starting again, whether I wanted to or not. I thought that was what I had to do to finally get a chance to make things right. But that's not how it works, I get that now. Recovering isn't about fresh starts, or new beginnings. It's about the constant as well as the change. You build a foundation in layers, and that's what makes it strong. Maybe sometimes it means taking a step back, but that doesn't have to be a bad thing. Sometimes you have to take a step back to get a better view of where you're going.

I will never be better, because better is not a thing. I will always just be me, and maybe that's OK. Maybe that's even great. I am sitting in my garden with my dog on my lap, an arrow on my back that will always point up, and I am surrounded by people who love me.

Yeah. I'm doing just fine.

Acknowledgements

My first thanks, as always, to my agent, Claire Wilson, for once again guiding me through with patience, wisdom and enthusiasm. (Sorry for all the panicky emails – you were right. Obvs.)

Thank you to Rachel Petty, for championing this book from my first tentative pitch and through the early wobbles, and Sarah Hughes, who took up the editing reins with such insight and warmth.

Thank you as always to the team at Macmillan, without whom I would be just a writer with a Word document and a dream. I am indebted. (Especially to you, Rachel Vale. Pure art.) Special thanks to Kat McKenna, for being Kat McKenna. And former team members Bea Cross and George Lester – thank you for everything.

Thank you to everyone who read, loved and talked about *Beautiful Broken Things*. It means the world to be able to bring you Suzanne's story in her own words. I hope you love her as much as I do.

To all those who helped me with my research along the way, from the big questions to the small, the long emails to the shortest tweets, particularly Eileen Flavin, Alex Scott, Charlie Wilson and Ceri May – thank you. Special thanks, as always, to Tracy King – I feel so lucky to call you a friend.

No author would survive authoring were it not for their author friends, and I have the greatest ones. Melinda Salisbury, the most excellent dinobro of all the dinobros. Holly Bourne, sharer of tea and pancakes. Katie Webber, pure sunshine. Thank you.

Thank you to my family, particularly my wonderful dad, who gave me a love of music and words without boundaries or limitations, who read every word I ever wrote and always flips straight to the acknowledgements when I have a new book. Hi, Dad! I love you.

Thank you, Lora, who is still my very best; Anna, who I love beyond words; and Tom, my co-pilot in all things. I would be wordless without you.

And finally. Two weeks after I finished this book, I lost a friend. A friend who, when I was eighteen, was my light in the dark. Thank you, Nick Lloyd, for that, and for so much else. I will miss you.

Read on for an exclusive extract of

Destination Anywhere

SARA BARNARD

OUT
NOW!

The Plane

'Boarding complete.'

This is it. I'm out of time. I stare at the send icon on my phone screen, willing myself to press it. My heartbeat – already way faster than usual – thunders harder in anticipation of that one tiny moment, the final step in setting this all in motion.

Despite myself, my thumb swishes downwards, my eyes flicking to the start of the email I've been drafting since I walked out of my house, got on a bus, went through departures, boarded, found my seat and buckled up.

Mum and Dad,

Don't freak out. I know you will anyway, but don't.

(There's no point. By the time you read this, I'll be in the air. You always say how safe flying is, Dad. So you don't need to worry, because when you read this, I'll be the safest I've ever been.)

I'm doing this because I have to go. I just have to go. I tried to tell you about how I have nothing left and I HAVE

TO GO, but you weren't listening. Now I think you'll have to, because right now I'm on a plane.

I'm on flight BA037 from Gatwick to Vancouver. You'll be able to look it up, see? I'm not trying to lie or hide anything. You know exactly where I am. I just had to go, so I'm going. If you've been paying any attention, you know why.

I'll call you when I land.

I love you.

P x

P.S. I'm sorry about using your credit card, Dad.
P.P.S. I'll pay you back.

The captain is cheerfully talking about our estimated flight time, how sunny it is in Vancouver, how he expects there may be 'a few small bumps' over Greenland. He asks for all electronic equipment to be put into flight mode.

I swallow. I add a second kiss after 'P'.

Send.

There. It's done. I put my phone into flight mode and settle back against my seat, watching the terminal slide slowly by as we taxi to the runway. In a few minutes, I'll be airborne. England will drop away underneath me, getting smaller and smaller and further away, and all my problems and heartaches and regrets and mistakes will shrink along with it. The next time I set foot on this soil – who knows when that will be – I'll be someone different; someone changed. Not someone new, exactly, but maybe the person I was always meant to be.

We're on the runway. The engines roar, the plane pushes forward. Beside me, a woman in a green jumpsuit whispers, 'Off we go.'

I close my eyes. I finally smile.

Off I go.

About the Author

Sara Barnard lives in Brighton and does all her best writing on trains. She loves books, book people and book things. She has been writing ever since she was too small to reach the 'on' switch on the family's Amstrad computer. She gets her love of words from her dad, who made sure she always had books to read and introduced her to the wonders of second-hand bookshops at a young age.

Sara is trying to visit every country in Europe, and has managed to reach thirteen with her best friend. She has also lived in Canada and worked in India.

Best
Friends
Don't
Tell

Goodbye,
Perfect

SARA BARNARD

OUT
NOW!

A Quiet Kind of Thunder

SARA BARNARD

OUT NOW!